THE

DREAM

OF A

LIFE.

A ROMANCE.

BY THE AUTHOR OF "THE ORDEAL BY TOUCH,"
"GENTLEMAN JACK," &c. &c.

———

LONDON:
PRINTED AND PUBLISHED BY E. LLOYD, SALISBURY-SQUARE, FLEET-STREET.

THE
DREAM OF A LIFE.

In a solitary and gloomy cell, strongly barred and bound with iron, is one of the most beautiful of God's creatures. A woman, scarcely past the probation of girlhood, with clasped hands she is appealing to Heaven for protection, and for mercy to her destroyer.

A ROMANCE.

BY THE AUTHOR OF "VILEROY; OR, THE HORRORS OF ZINDORF CASTLE."

INTRODUCTION.

THE night clouds had loured, and one solitary man stood upon London bridge, looking with a melancholy aspect upon the giant city that lay stretched far and wide before him. So still and so wrapped up in his own meditations was he, that he might have been taken for some statue, or for some impalpable being of a past age, who had returned to note the spots he had known well in another state, and so mark the many changes which Time and Fashion had made upon the home of his mortality.

His eyes are fixed upon that gigantic dome which rises above all the palaces and the temples of London, and we may suppose that his thoughts wandered with many a painful aspiration after the good and the beautiful, from earth to earth's Master.

Suddenly a form appears beside him.— Whence it came could not be told, for it seemed as if it grew out of the night, and at once became observable to mortal eyes on that precise spot which it occupied.

This new figure had a strange and mysterious aspect,—it was tall and graceful in its movements, and the fashion of its garments appeared to be those of an age gone by, when greater amplitude of vestment was the fashion than at present. But yet it was very strange that although the cool night air that swept across the bridge blew aside the more scanty apparel of the first person whom we have mentioned, it had no effect upon the more flowing garments of the latter.

And now this new-comer, if either he could be called, who thus appeared so strangely to grow out of the very elements, stooped and whispered to the man who was thus so wrapped-up in meditation, and who started as the soft, low, thoughtful tones met his ear.

"You are musing upon London," said the voice; "and to the eye of thought you are conjuring up many visions of what may be some of its stupendous doings. You are thinking of the vice, the degradation, the misery—"

"Yes," said the musing man, "and of the virtue and the joy."

"But you found that they were but as drops in the great ocean of iniquity?"

"It was so; and such was the comparison that at the moment arose to my mind."

"I know it—I saw it written on the tablets of your brain; but know of me that you may take a wider and a healthier view of human nature and that condition which you consider so much that with a high you would regret, because but of the furnace of affliction forth whence comes the highest virtue, and such as any earthly part of the soul, obscuring its brightest lustre. Such circumstances are not evils, but processes of nature, by which the most glorious attributes of humanity are made manifest, and without which those qualities which, in their exercise, say

so much for your divine origin, would for ages slumber in the caverns of the heart."

"There is abundant truth," said the man, "in those words—they sink into my soul; but still is it not sad that through tears and through sufferings alone are the highest flights of virtue to be reached?"

"Not so—not sad, because natural and necessary; and were you to examine closely the results of human life, you would discover a nobler truth than any vain reflections you utter with a sigh, and clothe in language of regret."

"But is it not sad that the young, the good, and the beautiful should suffer life's severest pangs, and from their very sensibilities and high mental attributes, endure so much?"

"No; it is their proper road to happiness. Look about you : do you see no one on the bridge but yourself?"

"You are with me, and I hear words of wisdom from your lips."

"I mean, do you see no mortal forms? I am of those who have been, but who are now mingled with the past."

The man who came to that lone spot at such an hour, to muse upon human nature, shrunk a little from his companion, but after a moment's pause, he said,

"I see no one on the bridge."

"Look down into the stream then," said the stranger, "and tell me what you see."

"There is a small boat, rowed by two men, and in it are a woman and an infant."

"'Tis well! would it please you to have a lesson on the subject of our argument?"

"It would, much; but the hour is late.— Hark! twelve o'clock commences to strike from St. Paul's."

"The lesson will be short. Will it suit you if it cease before those sounds that herald the progress of time have passed away?—if so, look still upon that mighty dome, and utter the words, Let me have the lesson of life!"

"And the result?"

"The result will be, that painted to your mental eyes, will appear the better portion of the life of that young child, which you have seen in that boat that even now glided beneath the arch on which we stand."

"St. Paul's strikes seven—eight—nine— ten. Be it so!"

CHAPTER I.

THE LONELY MANIAC IN HER CELL.

IT is night, and the loud thunder, rushing in tumultuous and unchecked vehemence, awakens in the breast of the conscience-stricken sensations of awe—in the breast of the philosopher, ideas of the sublimity of Heaven, and an acknowledgment of the wonders of creation. But to one, the battling of the Heavens is as nothing; the lightning may blast, and combat with, and destroy all that is good and beautiful—but no sympathy or interest is awakened in the breast of the lonely one.

In a solitary and gloomy cell, strongly barred and bound with iron, is one of the most beautiful of God's creatures A woman, scarcely emerged from the probation of girl-hood, is kneeling on the earthen floor of that loathsome cell, with upraised hands appealing to Heaven for protection, and for mercy to her destroyers. Traces of many tears hav-ing bedewed her cheeks are visible, and as she lifts up her eyes to Him who has our destinies in his hands, a slight indication of that appearance of madness was about them which there is no mistaking. Occasionally in her prayers a little incoherency would be detected ; but, except to a close observer, it would escape unnoticed. Ever and anon her prayers are interrupted by the growling of the thunder, which finds its way even to the depths of her underground place of con-finement.

"Oh, God! oh, God!" she cried, " me, me, why have you abandoned? And yet ought I to declaim against the decrees of Him by whose favour I exist? Oh, heavenly Father, forgive me ! my wrongs have almost made me mad! Mad—mad—I am not mad ! —oh, no, not mad ! I hear—I see—I have all the faculties of my mind in play—my memory fails not. Oh, no, I am not mad.— My child! God protect my child! Abandon me, but not my little one Hark! answers He me in his thunder! Again! oh, God, speak to me! say that I am heard and heeded. Hush! again comes that joyful sound—thanks—thanks !—hush, again !—ah, who's there ?—you shall not rob me of my only love, my only hope—my angel boy !—back, back, I say !" And the poor maniac crept up to the corner of her cell, awaiting the en-trance of the keeper, whose preparations for opening the strongly-barred door had thus disturbed her.

"Come, come," he said, "we can't have this noise here nohow, marm, and the sooner you leaves off this here sort o' nonsense the better. You're always a bawling out about your young 'un, you is, and I can't get not no manner of peace at all whatsomdever, blow me, marm !"

"Oh, spare me, spare ! Do not put on those dreadful implements of torture again. I will be patient—oh, do not!"

"Well, you needn't make such a fuss about it," replied the man ; " there's many a patient here what's blessed glad, I can tell you, to have the straight vaistcoat a' covering his precious body, cos it saves him the fatigue of twisting his arms about like a porcupispi-cubuscos, which is all the same as Latin for the fish with long arms as catches his prey with 'em, and sucks or insinuates their livosity in his carcase. But what's the use of lightening, or rather attempting to lighten such as you on the sublime truths of nat'ral history ? A institution established for the purpose of repressing reason aint the sort of place exactly for 'livering mechanic institu-tion lectures in any how—acos why ?—why acos for this here simple reason—that those poor unfortunate varmint as hasn't got, or has lost their reasoning powers, or in other words, who is mad—"

"I am not mad! Oh, God, I am not mad —say that I am not mad, and I shall wor-ship you!" shrieked the unfortunate crea-ture. "Mad! who says that Maud Selby and her child are mad, eh? Ha, ha! Maud the Mad—oh, that sounds well—wondrous well—mad!"

"Come," said the fellow, " I can't stand this. You seems to me to be getting up a scene. D'ye see this blessed little instru-ment—the wonder-worker? Two inches of this between your teeth will stop your gag, my worthy, and if I don't pretty soon do it, I shall have all the other ungracious waga-bonds blustering and bawling, as if Bedlam itself had broke loose."

"Oh, God, have mercy and prevent this outrage !"

"Ay, ay," roared the fellow, "call on whom you please, but no one, not even he who you now calls on, shall step atween me and my dooty ; so—"

Many people would—perhaps supersti-tiously, as to which we will leave our readers themselves to settle—we repeat, many peo-ple would say that that electric stream, which at that moment had pierced its way into the solitary habitation of the wretched maniac and struck down the man, was the special act of Him whom he had so outrageously defied ; but, be it as it may, the ruffian, while in the very act of advancing to carry his threat into execution, fell a lifeless corpse on the floor, and, falling with his face downwards, the gag which he carried in his hand intro-duced itself with such force into his own sacrilegious mouth as to completely knock out his front teeth, and penetrating through his neck came out from under his ear. Al-together the spectacle was a ghastly one : the charred appearance of the face over which the blood trickled in copious streams, pro-ducing an effect perfectly horrible to behold.

The first thought of the maniac was to take advantage of the circumstance, and effect an escape from her horrible position ; but the man had fallen across the door of the cell, and the utmost exertion of strength of poor Maud Selby was as nothing against the dead weight of the obstruction.

"Grant me strength, Heaven," she said, " to remove this corpse ; or, if I do not quickly rid myself of the horrible presence of this body, I shall indeed go mad. My ! child ! my child! I live for thee, and liberty shall be mine."

As these words were pronounced, she again exerted what strength her long confinement and scant and miserable sustenance had left her ; and in one grand effort she partially succeeded in lifting the upper part of the body in an upright position ; but that grand effort produced a contrary effect to that which was intended, for her feet slipping in the poo of blood which surrounded her, she fell with the horrible mass of corruption upon her, and the small hand-lamp which the keeper had brought in with him was upset in the fall, and the light extinguished.

This, indeed, was a situation for the poor maniac of the most terrible and appalling nature. Not the remotest glimpse of light shone into that wretched cell, except occasionally the faint flash of the now departing storm, and which only served to make the scene more startling.

The last attempt to raise the body of the ruffian had so exhausted her, that it was a considerable time ere she could find sufficient strength to free herself of the horrible burden she was bound to; but, when she did succeed, a reaction took place, and before she could crawl into her accustomed corner, she fell senseless on the body of the keeper, and in that position remained until a clap of thunder, more startlingly terrific than any that had preceded it, again awakened her to a consciousness of her awful situation. She started to her feet, and a dim, shadowy outline of all that had passed since the entrance into her cell of the keeper, came gradually across her memory.

"Ah! 'tis a dream," she exclaimed, "a terrible dream. Oh, God! I have had many dreams here, but never such a one as this before. Surely it is—it is not reality—it cannot be—and yet it seems too vivid to be a dream. I am not mad! no, no, not mad! They placed me here to make me so! but God knows I—oh, my child, how came you hither? They parted us, my love. Let me come to you, my pretty babe—my soul. What! wet upon your face, my child! Horrible! horrible! my thoughts rush back upon me— it is the body of the keeper! Help me, Heaven! oh, help! Lights! lights! for Mad Maud. Ha! ha! They think to make me mad; but God temper the wind to the shorn lamb—and Maud Selby is not mad!"

The latter words were occasioned by the lovely maniac stumbling against the dead body of the keeper, whom in the confusion of her intellect she fondly imagined to be her child; but the fearful truth suddenly flashed across her intellect, and all the dreadful circumstances came fresh upon her.

The storm that had apparently slackened in its fury now came on again with twofold force. The white, forked flashes of the electric fluid came hissing in continued streams, and Heavens artillery followed in almost one incessant roar. It was a night, indeed, to make wise men think, and bad men tremble.

The full knowledge that the maniac now had of her terrible situation added fresh strength to her—once more she endeavoured to remove the livid corpse which obstructed her way to liberty.

"Ha!" she said, "Mad Maud is a Goliah in strength! The lightning is the breath of God's nostrils, and it enters the soul of Maud —adds strenth to her arm, and she will succeed in evading the pursuit of her enemies.

Ha, ha! another inch less between Mad Maud and liberty! and—and another!— Flash on, flash on!—more strength, more strength! Ha, ha!—another! Once again, once again, and I shall be free! Oh, God! one more blast from your nostrils, one more! It is here—I have it! Thanks! Now 'tis done—'tis done! I am free! Ha, ha, ha! I am free!"

Poor Maud had, indeed, by most persevering efforts, succeeded in removing the corpse of the keeper sufficiently from the door to allow her to open it wide enough for her passage through it; and heedless of consequences, and probably unconscious of any further impediment to her progress to liberty, she at once stepped out from that dreadful cell.

CHAPTER II.

THE INTRICACIES OF THE PRISON HOUSE.— THE IDIOT.—THE ESCAPE.

THE aid hitherto afforded to poor Maud by the incessant flashes of lightning, was now entirely withdrawn, for the passages leading to the underground cells of that establishment were without the means by which any extraneous light could be admitted.

After proceeding some little distance, feeling her way by the course of the wall, Maud determined to return to her cell and await the first streak of morning to accomplish her enterprise; but on her attempting to retrace her steps, she became confused as to which route to pursue, and at last, utterly bewildered, she lost herself in the intricacies of the passages. Many anxious prayers were uttered for one flash of light to enable her to see her path, but in vain: no light ever entered there, except the feeble and sickly ray of the lamp carried by the keepers in their daily visits to the miserable occupants of the cells which thickly lined each side of that subterraneous labyrinth.

Passage after passage, doubling and redoubling her track, did the unfortunate explore, but no outlet presented itself to her touch—no sign of life came gratefully upon her ear, to cheer her in that desolate spot— no sound, but of the low rumbling of the thunder, was to be heard, though occasionally she fancied that the low and melancholy moan of some confined wretch might be heard, wailing his complaint, between the short intermissions of that almost continuous roar.

Exhausted by her efforts, she sunk on to the earth which formed the flooring of the passages, and which, from the continual dripping of the roof. and the damp exuding from the walls, was completely saturated, exclaiming,—

"God! God! why do I live? Better far that I had remained in my cell, and suffered all the agony of torture that it has so often been my fate to suffer, than to remain here till I am found and punished more severely for this attempt to recover liberty. Stay—

murder! I didn't murder the keeper—no, no! I had no weapons. God knows I did not do it. Ha! ha! 'tis false! I loved the man—I loved him because he preserved my child. Who accuses me of murder? Help—help! I did not do it! God knows I did not do it. Appeal to him, he will reply that I did not. If all be liars, the truth will come from him. Do not—do not—I cannot, will not be again confined. Release me—help, help! The keeper, eh?—dead—dead—no, he sleeps—sleeps merely. Touch him, he will awake. Why do you not touch him? See you not the gag in his hand?—he only sleeps. Release me—call him by name—he'll answer. Hark ye now—listen—listen—again he answers. God! are you all deaf? Release me—I am not mad! Maud Selby is not mad, nor ever was—and murderess she scorns the name of. Maud Selby, the maniac, murderess! Ha! ha! Oh God, preserve to me my senses—arouse me from this dreadful dream! I still am in my wretched, loathsome cell, and a frightful vision surely has oppressed me. Oh, great God! on my knees I humbly, fervently return thanks that this is but a vision of the brain—that I am not mad, and no murderess! Heavenly Father, vouchsafe to pour the balm of forgetfulness on my eyelids—I will seek my wretched pallet, and with thy aid will seek an hour of repose."

Poor Maud really thought all that had happened was but a disturbed dream, and rising from the ground, she made the ineffectual endeavour to find her wretched pallet of straw—to seek forgetfulness of her injuries in the heavenly boon of sleep; but, alas! no sleep darkened the eyes of Maud that night, and fearfully was she awakened to a sense of her startling situation by a violent concussion with the wall of the passage in which she was. She knew, by long acquaintance, the locality of every individual nook and cranny of her cell, and, with perfect confidence, was making what she thought her way to her resting-place, when she came into such violent collision with the wall.

She was silent for a minute, till the full knowledge of her awful situation came like a thunderbolt upon her senses, and she uttered a long, loud, and terrific shriek—such a shriek, if once heard would never be forgotten—a shriek that might be heard above the battling of the tempest.

"God!—God!" she cried, "then it is no dream, and I am a murderess!"

Another shriek, and yet another, echoed through the vaulted roof of that dismal place.

"Hark!" she said, "a noise! listen—it comes! a footstep and a light! I am betrayed. Oh, God! I shall be scourged—scourged to death! Well, be it so. Why should the poor maniac live to enjoy the glorious gifts of God—the sweet flowers—the forest tress, and the green sward of the rich earth?—a maniac—oh no, these joys are not for me, or such as I. Hark! nearer it comes! the light, the light—a voice! I will cringe down, that they may not see me. Ha! ha! I will elude them. I am not so mad as not to have some cunning—oh! I am cunning, very cunning, but not mad. Listen—they come, they come—down, down—hush!"

The poor maniac huddled herself up into as small a space as possible, and as it happened, a buttress, against which she crouched, effectually hid her from the view of the person who was advancing.

The man was muttering curses both loud and deep, as he approached towards the humbled Maud's place of concealment.

"D—n the vagabonds!" he said, "screeching and howling like hungry tigers. One would think that hell itself had broke loose, and that all the devils were pulling each other's tails, there's such a gallus row! And there's that 'ere Bill Gag, too, with his d—d yarns about feelisoppical subjects, and macranical lectures and penny magazines, and all that 'ere sort of rubbish, he,—d—n him,—has been away these three hours or more, the humbug. He went away with the lubberly excuse of attending to those wild animals, but I s'pose left 'em to take care of themselves, and has gone skulking about, follering some itinerant lecturer, sucking in a parcel of gammon about man living upon bread and meat and drink, that his disgusting organs is all formed to live upon insects, and that he is not a carnivorous animal, but partly a granuous, partly a carnivorous, and partly a habituous animal. Dang it, I think the man's nothing more nor less nor a fool. Whoever heerd of a animal being a man or a man a animal? And then he comes with his gab, and tries to poke fun at me, but he gets nothing by his motion, egad. D—n my rags, the next time he calls me a animal, I'll slip into him, and no mistake. What! does he think a man what has been a keeper for the matter of five-and-thirty years, man and boy, is to be gammoned in that sort of manner? I should think not, my hearty, oh no, we doesn't do it, we doesn't. No, no, try back; my young fellow, you don't ketch old Andrew Stumps."

By the time this soliloquy was brought to an end, old Andrew Stumps had brought himself up to the first door in that loathsome passage, and, giving it a violent kick, which made the place ring again, he shouted,—

"All right in here? No answer! well, the row didn't come from you, I s'pose.—You're a gallus sight too old for that 'ere sort of thing. Why, let me see—ah! for the last fifteen years, to my sartain knowledge, you've never been out of this here habitation of yours, and that, added to fifty-five, make you, according to Cocker, seventy years old. Ah! you are a rum'un—there's no mistake about you. You're about as much mad as my grandmother, and she, poor old soul! is only in her dotage. No, no! I believe you, my boy. It all comes along of your having such lots of property, and grudging some of the shiners to the young un—

that's it! Why, you old jackass, you should have given him a little more length of rope, and p'raps you wouldn't have been here, and he might have hung himself."

So saying, the veritable Stumps proceeded to two or three doors in succession, soliloquising, contemplating, and animadverting in a similar strain, until his thoughts again reverted to the ruffian Bill Gag.

"Ah!" said he, "that d—d Bill Gag—I'll be bound, he's not given some poor wretch his dole, and that's the reason that the poor devil set up such a shout of hungry defiance. D—n that fellow, I've a d—d good mind to go mad in downright real earnest, that when I am locked up, and he attends upon me, I may have the satisfaction of pitching into him; it'll be a good excuse, at all events; and I long to pay off some of my old scores against him for his eternal lecturing me with his second-hand sermons. I've often promised him a sound drubbing, but never have had an opportunity. But what do I want a opportunity for—can't I drub him first, and wait for a opportunity to come afterwards? To be sure, I can. Why, what a jackass I must be, never to have thought of that before; nothing can be clearer, and if I were to meet him just now, I feel as if I could just so slip into him, that his own blessed mother shouldn't know him from a black pudding in a sweat. Hilloa! what's this? Why, Bill Gag, my covey, if this isn't an additional reason why I should slip into you, poker and tongs, I should like to know what it is. D—n me! if he hasn't gone out and left one of the blessed doors open, and his bunch of keys in the lock. Well, that's pretty tidy, I don't think. Hilloa, there! anybody at home—anybody at home? Come — Maud—Maud—come, open the door. What—arn't you!—well, I'll soon see who's the strongest—here goes."

Old Andrew Stumps put the lamp down at his feet, and after three or four vigorous efforts, at the fifth he succeeded in pushing the door in; but, in his early attempts, having removed the body sufficiently from the door, to prevent it being much obstruction to its easy opening, Andrew Stumps, instead of going in, as any man in his ordinary senses would have gone, most insanely went in head first, and heels high up in the air.

Poor Maud had not been an inattentive observer of what was passing, and seizing the opportunity, she like lightning sprang from her place of concealment, and before the astonished Andrew Stumps could recover from his inverted position or surprise, the door was closed upon him with a loud bang, and the key quickly turned in the lock; and the beligerent Andrew Stumps, with the dead body of his fellow keeper, was, like the father of the bride of Lochiel's chief, left lamenting.

"Ha! ha! ha!" shrieked Maud. "Who now is mad? Not Maud—not Maud Selby—no — no — no. The gaoler is insane—poor fellow—poor fellow. Shall mad Maud gag the gaoler?—oh, yes, she will bring the gag for the madman. Will he have on the straight-waistcoat? Ha! ha!—it will be a luxury to him to restrain his arms—ha! ha! I will bring you food in the morning: wholesome, black bread, and cool water from the spring—you shall enjoy your repast, or if not, the whip shall titivate your appetite. What, ho! shall I bring the wrist irons, or the mustard plaster?—you have a choice of pleasures. Ha! ha!—farewell, till I come again—ha! ha!"

Maud seized the lamp, and, with wild and hurried, though cautious, steps, again began exploring the tortuosities of that cavernous place. All was profoundly still, for the violence of the storm was finally quelled. On, on, she paced, now turning down some dark entrance to a long line of cells, in the hope of meeting with some symptom of egress; and then, when she had reached the end, returning and pursuing the same process with another winding of the labyrinth, but without any prospect of a successful termination to her labours. Wearied and terrified with her unceasing endeavours to find some means of escape, and at the extreme quietude of the place, she had well nigh given up her task, and determined to remain where she was until some one of the establishment should come the usual morning round, when, leaning against one of the doors for support, she thought it gave way slightly to her weight. She turned, and with the slightest effort the door turned upon its hinges, and she at once stepped into the cell to which it led.

On one of the usual pallets of straw, lay extended, in deep sleep, a man, of apparently about the age of twenty-two, or younger. In his ears were two straws, after the fashion that merchants' clerks wear their pens while they are discussing their sandwiches and soda-water in the hours of business. He was not undressed, but had thrown himself carelessly across his wretched bed, and seemed to enjoy the profoundest repose. No trace of restraint was upon him, and, by his door being open, Maud conjectured that he was not confined there against his will, but that he probably was a servant engaged in the establishment.

Hesitating what to do, Maud held the lamp close to his face, and narrowly observed his countenance. Forming a conclusion, from the character of his lineaments, that he was of a peaceful disposition, she hesitated not to awaken him. Acting upon this resolution, she laid her hand gently upon his shoulder, and a slight shake brought him back from the realms of wild and fanciful imagination to the practical reality of life.

The young man, after rubbing his eyes for a few moments, sat upright on his bed; and, with a stupid look of half amazement and indifference, with lack lustre eyes, gazed at the intruder to his cell.

After gazing at her some time without a word having passed on either side, he mechanically, and as if he had been used to it from his cradle, placed the thumb and two forefingers of his left hand on his chin, and with the thumb and finger of the right squeezing the tip of his nose, opened his mouth and thrust out his tongue simultaneously; then removing his hands, and letting his tongue remain lolling out, he caught hold of both ears, and giving them a sudden jerk, and making an indescribable sort of cluck in his throat, he suddenly drew his tongue in again, making the two acts of protruding and withdrawing his tongue seem to depend upon the respective preliminary operations he had so cleverly performed.

"There," said he, "what think you of that, eh? Was it done well? Stumps taught me that. You know old Stumps, eh?"

"No," said Maud, "I do not know Stumps. Is he a madman, confined here?"

"Madman?" observed the idiot, for so he was, "madman? Oh, no, he's a keeper. What's a madman? Old Stumps is a friend of mine. You must know Stumps, cockalorum tilly-ta-la. Stokes gave me these two straws, and told me that they were sugar-candy sticks, and that if I stuck them behind my ears, they would grow into hogsheads of sugar; but lor! here they've been for six weeks, and they are nothing but straws still. You don't know Stokes?"

"No"

"Oh, he's a fine old fellow, is Stokes. Lawks-a-daisy me! I do all manner of things for old Stokes—clean out his room—feed his birds—all sorts of things, and he never whips me more than six times a day, and gives me a bellyful of bread once a week. I love Stokes—nobody else cares for me—and I love nobody else, though I could love anybody who was kind to me."

"Will you love me," said Maude, "if I am kind to you?"

"Cockalorum, yes—ah me!—are you a keeper?"

"No."

"You don't keep a whip?"

"No."

"Nor ropes to tie poor Jacky's hands when he steals a crust from old Stump's cupboard?"

"No."

"And when Jacky feels empty, will you give him food, and let him sleep?"

"Yes, yes; poor fellow, I will do all this."

"Then," said the idiot, "I will love you, and do anything for you. You and I will be always together. Oh, God-a-mercy! what fun we shall have together. We will play at straws, and counting the bricks here. I have counted these bricks dozens of times—I know how many bricks there are in this place to a single brick. Look at me."

The poor idiot repeated the performance, with which he had amused, or rather attempted to amuse, Maud at the opening of the interview, and would have gone on so, *ad infinitum*, had not Maude suddenly interrupted him, by asking—

"Do you ever leave this cell?"

"Oh! yes, they leave my door open o' nights and all day long, and I ramble any where I please amongst these corridors, I think old Stump calls them. Oh, I have a pleasant time on't, a pleasant time; old Stump takes me with him sometimes to his room, and I see from his window the green trees, and smell the fresh air. Oh, I'm very happy, very happy; I forget the whip then, and fall down on my knees, and I think that I have sometimes, a long while ago, walked amongst the trees; and I pray, I think it's called praying, that I may walk there again. Hush! I've got a secret, jig, jig, jackety jo; heigh-ho! a secret."

"Will you tell it me?"

"Will you tell it again? Ha, ha, you'll tell it again, and poor Jacky Jingle will be shut up close, and will never more walk in the quiet lanes amongst the dark shady trees, and smell at the golden flowers on the green grass. No, I must not tell you that I walk about o' nights when the keepers are all in bed; no, no, because you'll know my secret; Jacky Jingle knows better than that. Did you ever see a dead frog jump upon a rat's back and swim across a stream, eh? I have. Ha, ha, ha! Jacky's a good boy, and knows how to keep a secret. Ha, ha, ha! Jacky Jingle, Jingle Jacky—Jack, Jack, Jack!"

"And how do you get out to walk in the green fields and smell the golden flowers, my poor Jacky?"

"Ha! who told you my secret—who told you? Have you found the hole? Oh, I have been careful to conceal the hole. Months, months have I been making the hole, and nobody knows where it is. Old Stumps thinks he keeps me pretty close, but he's not so cunning as Jacky Jingle."

"But where," said Maud, "is the place you wish to keep so secret? Will Jacky tell poor Maud?"

"What! for Stumps to tie Jacky to his ring, and never let him see the bonny green trees again? Why should I tell my secret?'

"Because," said Maud, "we can ramble together, and Jacky will have some one to cheer him in his strolls, and enjoy the same scenes with him, and converse with him, and we can come back again as you do now, and old Stumps will never be the wiser. Come, come, shall we go?"

"Will you keep the secret?" asked the idiot.

"Most assuredly. For why should I tell? I should be deprived of the same privilege that you enjoy if I betrayed it."

The idiot rose from his wretched pallet, and dragging it away from the wall against which it was placed, the means of escape presented themselves to Maud in unmistakable colours.

"There," said the idiot, "there has been the work of many months. Ha! ha! months did I say?—days, days—nay, minutes. Every moment that old Stumps would give me liberty, these nails have been dig, dig, digging into that massive wall, and piece by piece I have got it out. Ha! ha! ha! Jacky's no fool—no fool—old Stumps is the idiot. Shall we go?"

"Instantly," said Maud; "not a moment is to be lost. Oh, God! I thank Thee for this happiness. My child! I come, I come."

"But we must be back before old Stumps comes his rounds—mind that! Ha! ha! ha! if old Stumps were to know this, he would pinch and kick me, and keep my food from me. What precious fun it would be! but Jacky is not such a fool as they think him. Well, here goes to hear the cockey-biddies sing, and the trees whistle, and the waters murmur their prayers. Come, Maud."

The idiot crept through the hole, dashing through the thick and rank herbage that grew outside the wall, hiding from the view of any casual observer the no inconsiderable orifice made by poor Jacky, as he called himself. Maud followed in his steps; and the idiot, thrusting his arm through the opening, restored the pallet to its original resting-place, and once more the poor maniac enjoyed the pure breath of Heaven.

CHAPTER III.

THE DISCOVERY, AND THE PURSUIT.

THE keeper, old Andrew Stumps, when he had recovered from the unexpected *denouement* to his visit to the cell, was in a perfect bewilderment as to the occurrences which had produced such a a disagreeable result. He heard the door shut and locked upon him, and the hysteric laugh and taunts of Maud; but he was utterly at a loss to comprehend how she should be without instead of within, and what obstructed his entrance in the first instance.

Not the smallest particle of light yet struggled into that dreary cell, and Stumps knew that, whether he would or no, he must there continue until some of the establishment should come to ascertain the reason of his long absence; and as this was not at all likely to take place before the morning, he thought he might, with more ease to himself, quietly remain at rest, than pace up and down the small and circumscribed space of his confinement, grumbling and growling like an excited bruin.

"Well, I suppose I must wait here, and be d—d to it! until that vagabond Bill Gag comes his round in the morning. But how the devil did that mad wench get out?—surely he warn't fool enough to leave her door open? No, no; I give him credit for being a ass, but not such a ass as that. Bill Gag knows his business well enough—can tickle a foot, apply a plaster, slip on a waist-coat, and gag a blab as well as e'er a blessed keeper I knows on; and if he'd only stick to his perfession arout following in the wake of these here penny-showmen sort of blessed lecturers upon subjects as they knows nothink

whatever about, and what they do knows is altogether wrong—why, d—n me, I should be proud of him, instead of feeling, as I do, a strong wish to give him a blessed licking. I owes it all to his confounded perpensity, that I'm in this pretty pickle, and d—n me, if I don't pitch into him the very first time I comes across him. A man what is appointed to watch over the creatures placed under his care, should stick to it like a blessed brick. What business, I should like to know, has he to want to understand anything else nor his trade—besides, in our perfession, we don't require no feelings; and they says that hearing these lecturers gives a man entirely new feelings, thoughts, and ideas—we doesn't want 'em—we ought to be satisfied with our old ones, as our fathers were afore us—d—n me if I don't lick him! What has such men as Gag and I to do or care for, 'cept to get the place already for the visiting commissioners; to clean out the cells, and get the wagabonds into a state of fury—o'course that's the ticket. For if a man isn't zackly mad, but only a little stupid like, why it's the business of a proper, downright, well-trained keeper to get him out of that 'ere insensibility sort of 'pearance, and make him as lively on certain 'casions as any man need wish to be, not only for the credit of the establishment, but for its profits too—for why? it's to our interest to have as many wild beast in our establishment as it'll hold; now what asses we should be to wish to get rid of 'em; besides we should hurt the feelings of their friends to send them back again as well as ever, and we should lose our custom—no, no—it may be all very well in thery, but I don't like the practice. But, however, as there aint no sort of chance of my being released from this here place, I may as well sit as stand—it costs no more."

Andrew Stumps began feeling about for the pallet whereon to stretch his limbs, and his hand rested on the cold face of his brother keeper.

"Ods bodikins, what in the devil's name is this? Maud, Maud are you asleep? No, no; she is outside; ah, 'tis a rough face! Hilloa, hilloa, here—come awake! who the devil are you?—up, up. What, no reply? Why, d—n me if it isn't the foller of learning, Bill Gag. I know him by his scent, I'm sure it's he. Why, man, what do you here? Bill Gag, Bill Gag—get up, and be d—d to you for a sleepy, stupid hound—get up I say. There, take that; I promised myself I'd lick you the first time I'd a opportunity; and now I'll give it yer—take that, and that!"

These words were accompanied with sundry hard knocks on the head and shoulders of the insensible Gag, who, indifferent alike to censure or blows, lay motionless as a stone.

Andrew Stumps now began to think that there was something more in the matter than he had originally thought, and placing his ear upon the breast of the defunct Gag, he was convinced that he might have knocked at the empty tenement for an unlimited period of time without meeting with a response.

" Ah," said he, " he's a stiff 'un, and no manner of mistake. This comes of his cursed lecturing to the poor devils instead of minding his own business : so it sarves him right. If he'd not come down here, as he'd no business to do at the time he did come, he would not have been here, and not being here, he'd a been somewhere else ; but not being somewhere else he's here, and being here, here he is, that's sartin, and a well as-certained fact, as he would have said. Now I should like to know how Mad Maud got the better of this ere fellow—he's not a sort of chap to be trifled with, and that she had something to do with it there can't be the smallest matter of doubt. D—n it, she'd more cunning than caution, for she'll be catched, of course, afore she gets out of this house, or else the locksmith's a humbug. The fast-enings of this house are not boiled carrots, and I locked the door leading to the passages after I came through : by-the-by, I left the key outside, like a jackass as I was; but no matter, the governor's got them as belongs to the outer doors, so she's safe anyhow. What could she have done it with ? There's nothing as I knows in this place of a very deadly character to settle such a man as Bill Gag ; perhaps he talked himself to death, as I've often told him he would, for he had a devil of a tongue—clack, clack, clack ! from morning to night—like it, or not like it, all the same to him—and now he's got a settler, and I hopes he likes it."

Andrew Stumps continued this sort of con-versation with himself until the first streak of light straggling into the cell displayed to his astonished eyes the horrible and terrific remains of Gag. The face was one mass of livid corruption,—the coagulated blood, hanging in thick ropy strings, standing out in striking contrast, adding greatly to the horrible appearance of the corpse. The head rested on the earthen floor, and around it was a pool of congealed liver-complexioned blood, in which the head had the appearance of being placed, like a floating substance, fixed and imbedded in ice.

The usual hour for the commencement of business in that house of questionable charac-ter now came on apace, and Andrew Stumps had no alternative but to wait till he was relieved from his imprisonment by the pro-prietor of the place, who was not long in observing and remarking on the quietude around him, and the absence of all prepara-tion for the routine business of the day.

Stumps was not only principal keeper, but was also employed in the capacity of cook ; for it was a great principal of the master to get as much work out of his men for as little remuneration as he could conscientiously give ; and the only female servant in the place was an old crone, who made herself generally useful, as advertisers say, meaning that they do no more than they can help doing, and do that to the best of their ability,

that is, with about one-half the ability of any one else, who would say nothing about their qualifications.

Mr. Ironsides, which, we beg to observe, was the patronymic of the amiable proprietor, happened on that morning to be particularly affected with an inclination to patronise his six-and-thirty yards of bowels with more than the ordinary amount of food he was in the habit of bestowing on them ; and, as hunger, at the best of times, is far from a pleasant companion, and not at all calculated to preserve the usual equanimity of a man's temper, and as the worthy Mr. Ironsides was unusually hungry on that morning, his irri-tability rose higher and higher in beautiful gradations, with every additional tug he gave the unoffending bell, to whose tongue no other tongue deigned to utter a response.

" Confound the blackguards,"he exclaimed ; " as sure as my name is Ironsides, I'll give it the rogues for this. Times have come, in-deed, to a pretty pass, when a man can't get the ordinary attentions of his domestics. I'll soon see what's the meaning of this—you'll soon see, my boys, that Ironsides is not to be played with ; playing with edged tools is silly practice, and requires some amount of assu-rance to do it skilfully—look out, my fine fellows."

The latter part of this sentence was mut-tered as he hastened down stairs towards the culinary department, but on looking up, and seeing that the doors of the apartments in which the two sleepers slept were still shut, which was against the rules of the house, because for his convenience he should be able to know whether the sleepers were about, then calling, he hastily re-ascended the stairs, and proceeding to the respective rooms, found that they were unoccupied, and con-cluded that either their late occupants had slunk out on some drunken frolic, and had overstayed the time, or that they purposely abstained from answering his repeated sum-mons.

Wending his way down the long spiral staircase, and through the passage leading to the kitchen, muttering and cursing, and vow-ing vengeance against his men, Ironsides found himself at length at the goal of his journey, but not at his desires ; for no Bill Gag nor Andrew Stumps was there ; nor were there any preparations for his own meal, nor for those of his unfortunate patients.

For a time uncertain what to do, he at length resolved that the alternative he should take, should be that of making a diligent search throughout the house for the men.

As it generally happens when a thing is mislaid, that every place is thoroughly searched except the right one, so it was in the case of Mr. Ironsides ; and had he gone down into the subterranean passage in the first instance, he would have saved himself a deal of trouble, and his ears would not have been shocked with the backslidings of his tongue, as verily they were.

As soon as his master-key entered into the

lock of the outer-door of the passages, the sharp and practised ear of the keeper was quickly alive to the fact, and with a voice that resounded from wall to wall and from roof to floor, he roared—

"Hilloa, hilloa! hoi, hoi! stop her, stop her—d—n her, stop her! Death and fury! if she escapes, the place won't hold old Ironsides—not so fast, not so fast," said he, as the thought struck him that it might even be old Ironsides himself, who was coming to ascertain the cause of the unusual absence of his two men. "I'll wait a bit—d—n it, there goes the door: that has either let somebody out or somebody in, at all events. In either case I can't help it, so I may as well remain quiet. Oh, curse your soul, you blessed Bill Gag, what a pretty hobble you have got us in. I've a towering great mind to lick you—come now."

By the time this humane and feeling expression was uttered, Ironsides had reached the door, from which he was convinced the sound of Stump's voice had come, and giving it a violent push and a hearty damn, he, finding it did not yield to his pressure, exclaimed in a loud and angry voice—

"Stumps, you scoundrel, what infernal scheme have you here? How dare you, sir, lock yourself in with any patient of mine? Undo the door, instantly—instantly—do you hear, you vagabond?"

"Lord, sir," said Stumps, "you must think that I, who have been a keeper a matter of——."

"D—n your matter, sir—unlock the door!"

"But I can't," exclaimed Stumps, "the door's locked upon me, and I must trouble you to unlock it, and instantly too, or I shall be stunk to death."

"What do you mean, villain, by bandying words with me?"

"The blessed keys must be about the passage," continued Stumps, "and if you'll take the trouble to find 'em, and let me out of this beastly den, I shall be very much obliged to you I think you'll find them somewhere about the end of the passage, near Jacky Jingle's cell, for it was there I'm sure I heard 'em drop."

"Why, d—n the fellow, he's drunk or mad. Where's Gag?"

"You be so good as just go and look for my keys as I told you, and I'll answer all your questions, and show you a sight as 'll make you rather astonished a little, I don't think—do you hear?"

"Well," exclaimed Ironsides, "it seems as I must submit to your demands, without question; but whether justified or not, in assuming this style of language to me, you shall remember this day as as a black letter, one in the catalogue of your reminiscences—mark me!"

So saying, Ironsides carefully searched for the lost keys, and having found them just outside the idiot's cell, as the keeper anticipated they would be found, he returned;

and without one single word, he introduced the key into the lock, opened the door quickly, and before Andrew Stumps, who had as quickly thrust out his head to catch a breath of somewhat purer air, before he could withdraw it again, he received such a tremendous, crushing blow on the tip of his probosis, as made the blood gush out in a brilliant spouting stream, and his eyes to emit much light, that he afterwards declared, that if the flashes had been collected and bottled up, they would have saved the governor something a week in the shape of oil.

"There," said Ironsides, "I never break a promise; put that in your memoranda. It is my maxim, and the great principle on which I act, never to look over the disobedience or want of proper respect in any one connected with me, when I am the stronger—put that down."

"And put this down," retorted Stumps—"I never forgive a blow, and, one day or another, you will recollect that I said so—mark that. And now for business."

Andrew Stumps flung the door wide open, and pointing down to the dead body of Bill Gag with the finger of one hand, he with the other directed Ironsides' attention to the empty pallet of Maud.

Ironsides stepped back a pace or two, and, with his hands uplifted, exclaimed with an alarmed and terrified glance—

"In the name of all the devils that are, what is the meaning of this?"

"Put this down in your collection of memorandas," coolly observed Stumps.

"Nay, nay; this is no time for idle retort. The meaning of this, I say?"

"Mark that," said Stumps.

"D——n!" roared Ironsides.

"Rather an unpleasant thing that at all times, sir."

Ironsides looked at the keeper for a moment or two. His face changed almost to the colour of the corpse with passion; and, his fury getting the better of his cooler judgment, he, with all his strength wound up to one powerful focus, aimed, with the keys in his hand, a deadly blow at the head of the collected Stumps, which, if it had succeeded in its aim, Stumps could never have recorded it in his collection of memoranda; but happily, Ironsides tripped at the moment, and the blow which he intended for Stumps came with fearfully increased momentum on to the skull of the already defunct Gag, into which the largest one in the bunch penetrated and buried itself up to the very handle.

"That's what I call uncommonly well done," remarked Stumps, with the same coolness he had hitherto displayed,—"uncommonly well done; but now as I sees you mean mischief, why you can't blame me for looking arter myself; now mind your eye."

Before Ironsides could recover his position, Stumps fell upon him with the full intent, if not of doing something very outrageous, at least of giving him a sound drubbing, but from either of these alternatives Ironsides saved himself, by saying—

"Come, Stumps, I confess I was wrong in being so hasty, and regret what has taken place. I am quite cool now, and you may rest satisfied that I mean no mischief, and the best thing we can do is to be friends again."

"I don't know how it is," replied Stumps, "I know you well enough to feel satisfied with what you say, and as you always perform what you promise, why, if you promise a licking or not a licking, it's the same thing, you will or you will not do it. And I have that amiable little peculiarity of never forgetting to perform what I may have promised, and so long as this precious nose continues a ornament on my face, so long shall I bear in remembrance the insult it received from your hands. So get up, and behave yourself like a gentleman."

Ironsides was not long in recovering his footing, and throwing off the appearance of strong passion he had hitherto displayed, what he had failed to extort from the keeper hitherto, he got from him by cajolery.

Andrew Stumps entered into a long narration of all that had taken place before, at, and since, his entrance into the passages leading to the cells, and when he had arrived at the completion of his tale, he said,—

"And now, governor, what is your opinion of things in general, and this in particular ?"

"In the first place," said Ironsides, "what think you of Maud ?"

"Oh," replied Stumps, "she must be about these 'ere passages. She can't have got through the outer one, for this reason : I locked it after I came into this, and I heard you unlock it ; therefore, it's clear the critter hasn't gone that way."

"Why, you idiot, couldn't she bring the keys, unlock it herself, and again lock it after she had passed through."

"True, sir, but inasmuch as she would have had to unlock it again, to return the keys to where you found them, I don't see as how that that's quite possible."

"Ay, ay, you're right ! But stir yourself, man, and let us carefully examine every nook and corner of the place. I would not that she should have got outside these walls, for all that I am worth."

"Ay, to be sure, sir, she was a good one to pay, wasn't she ? Her friends were——"

"Come, come, we've no time to talk, let us begin the work."

Ironsides and Stumps now left the cell, and beginning in a systematic manner, they commenced the search from the entrance to the termination of the passages, thoroughly examining every cell on either side, but without of course the desired result. The idiot's cell was the last one to be examined, and the amazement of the governor and his man on perceiving that that was empty was intense.

"Hell and the devil," roared Ironsides,

"has he gone too ? I shall be hung, I shall be hung ! How could he have got out ?— Stumps, this is a planned thing—some conspiracy to ruin me. Villain ! tell me all the particulars. Where's Maud, the idiot—where, where—how did they escape ? You must have let 'em out."

"There you go again," said Stumps. "nothing but abuse. Haven't I already told you all that I know about the matter ? Wasn't I a involuntary prisoner ? Was it not a trial to be locked up in the dark with a dead putrid body, Mr. Ironsides ? Very likely I should take upon myself such a pleasant part in the conspiracy. Now, if Gag wasn't dead, I dare say he'd be able to 'lighten you, as he would ha' said ; but as he is, why o' course he can't, and there's an end of it. It's very clear to me, that the two critters has escaped, and if they has, I know who'll suffer for one on 'em."

"Ah !"

"Yes, the idiot."

"What of him ?"

"Oh, nothing much. He sometimes was not altogether a fool. I have seen him and spoke to him, when he has had some slight recollection of times gone by."

"What did he say ?" asked Ironsides, anxiously.

"What he told me," said old Stumps, with a sneer.

"Did he disclose anything of moment ?"

"May be he did, and may be he didn't.— But that's not the question, and no part of my perfession to enter into. The question now is, where are they, and how did they get out ?"

"Tell me, Andrew, what passed between you and the idiot—come. Although I sometimes treat you rather roughly, I in my heart really do feel and acknowledge that you are the best man I ever had. Come, tell me what passed."

"Why, if you come to that, and acknowledge my superiority, and are penitent for what you have done to me in the shape of hard work and harder blows, I don't mind."

"A trump of a fellow," exclaimed Ironsides—"go on."

"Why, then," said Stumps, "you know there are some things that are important, and some that are not important ; the important things are not the unimportant things, nor are the unimportant things the important things—that I believe there can be no dispute about. Well, then, this being so, it becomes necessary to know what things are important and what are *not* important, so as to keep them distinct and separate. Admitting this fact, and having separated the important and the unimportant, the next question is whether it would be of any importance to you to relate the unimportant things, and to keep to myself the important things, or to relate to you the important things, and to keep to myself the unimportant things. And as this is a question requiring some deliberation, I have come to the conclusion to keep both the important things and the unimportant things entirely to myself, until I have maturely considered the point."

"Fool and knave!" exclaimed the governor, "how dare you play with me in this unheard-of manner? As God is my judge, I will pay you for this!"

"Thanks, master of mine! the receipt shall be quite ready."

"What do you mean?" roared the governor.

"Why, this is what I mean," answered the keeper: "at any time I feel the slightest wish, I can make you crawl upon your knees before me; but I am a tender-hearted individual, and it's against my feelings of proper respect and all that 'ere sort of thing, to see a master humbled to his servant—quite entirely against my nature; as a proof, I need only let you know that I have been in possession of the fact that gives me this 'ere power a long, long time, and you've never heerd me utter a syllable to you about it.—That I believe's a sufficient and satisfactory proof, aint it? But when you comes with your hard words and your blows, why, for your own sake as well as for your own protection, I think's it's time to let you know that I'm up to snuff, and can see through a millstone as far as anybody else."

"Tell me what you do know," said Ironsides.

"No," said Stumps, "I should be a spooney to do that. Oh, no, I keeps what I knows to myself. When the proper time comes, it'll come out, and no mistake; and mark me, that if I don't meet with that proper respect, as you so much talks about, between master and servant, you'll find that some sunshiny morning, that it's come out a little afore I intended it. I means to keep it over your head, Mr. Ironsides, in territory I thinks Gag used to call it; and mind ye, from this time, if you don't behave yourself towards me as I think you ought, but it 'll come; and Master Maurice Ironsides will be an unkimmon way off from the land of his fathers. Will you be good enough, Mr. Ironsides, to put that down in your small collection of curious memoranda, and let it be in *italic*, as my friend Compo says."

Ironsides buried his face in his hands, and a sharp spasm crept through his frame, as he said,—

"Stumps, I feel convinced that your acquaintance with some part of my life, which I would wish to conceal, is too true—that you have my liberty in your hands I feel is true likewise—henceforth, then, I promise——"

"Nay, I want no promises," said Stumps; "you only behave to me as I believe you ought to do, and you'll find me what I have always been, a useful, zealous servant, ready at all times to do what you require, in the shape of any business, one you can always depend on, and no mistake I believe——"

"That'll do Stumps—now to business. These people must be found, there's no doubt about that, but more particularly the idiot, Jingle."

"Not quite an idiot, master—not all a fool always."

"Be it so, as you please. But I suppose you admit that they having escaped, it is part of your business to endeavour to recover them."

"Undoubtedly."

"Then I may depend upon your best exertions to assist me in tracing them?" asked Ironsides.

"Of course you may."

"Then at once prepare—not a moment is to be lost. If that idiot be picked up before he is caught, I dare not think of the consequences. It is clear that they have both escaped, but how, to me, is a great mystery. We have searched every place."

"Yes, not a nook but what has been looked into, and they must have got a pretty tidy way by this time, considering that I had been locked up in Mad Maud's cell four hours, and we've been here another hour. If we find 'em, I think we shall be clever fellows. However, if the thing is to be done, the sooner we set about it the better."

"True, true. But, Stumps, what makes your jacket fly and flap about as if exposed to the wind? No wind can come into this place, we well know. Do you see?"

"Yes," said Andrew; "I have felt a cutting cold against my ankles ever since I have been here, which I am quite unable to account for."

"Observe," said Ironsides; "it seems to come in the direction from the pallet. Remove it, and see if there be a break there."

Stumps did as he was bid, and the grand secret was at once discovered.

"Done, done!" shouted Ironsides.

"Done brown as a baked tater!" ejaculated Andrew: "they've slipped the leach, sir, and are off like a couple of greyhounds. What do you mean to do, sir?"

"Do? We must find them again. We must scour the country—move Heaven and earth to recover them, or I am a lost man. And that old jackanapes, Gag, to lecture himself into a fit just when we most wanted him."

"By-the-by, sir," asked Stumps, "what are we to do with poor Bill Gag, the varmint? I suppose we must have a crowner's inquest?"

"Inquest? His death must be hushed up. Bury him in the cell in which he is. No one would be the wiser—or, at least, the better for knowing that he died before they had sufficient warning of it. An inquest won't suit me. The very facts I wish to conceal would at once come out. Oh, no—no inquest. We must bury him here, and say nothing about it. It saves time, trouble, and expense, you know, Andrew. But we'll see about him when we return from our hunt."

"But, in the meantime, sir, what are we to do with the other critters?"

"Oh, give them a double quantity of provisions, and if they get through that, why they must chew the cud till we come back—eh, Andrew Stumps—eh? It'll save expense, eh?"

"True, sir," said Andrew; "and so long as we give 'em sufficient to keep soul and body together, that's as much as their friends need care about; for the longer they live the better for us; and, as I used to say to Bill Gag, just keep 'em alive, and tickle 'em up now and then: don't let 'em die, and don't let 'em get into their senses agen, just for the good of the house. I believe, sir, that's the correct thing, sir—eh?"

"Yes, Andrew; I see you know your business; but we must now proceed to make our inquiries. I shall just get a snack at once while you're supplying the patients, and then we will begin. Take care to lock up those cells and passages before we leave, for I would not have any one intrude upon any account. You understand, Andrew?"

"Ay, ay, sir," replied Stumps.

Ironsides left Stumps to dole out the double allowance of provisions, in case of a prolonged absense, which having done, and carefully locked and barred all approaches to the cells, he retired into the kitchen to fortify himself for the expedition, by devouring enough to supply three ordinary appetites with a breakfast.

"Ay, ay, Master Ironsides," he muttered to himself, during his masticating occupation, "you and I are upon different terms with each other since that blow. From that moment I became your master as well as your enemy; and if I don't retaliate one day or another, may I never ticle another patient into madness. A blow! no, Andrew Stumps never forgets nor forgives a blow—it isn't in his natur; and not being in his natur, it is not natural that he should; and if it is not natural, it is unnatural; and if unnatural, it is immoral and wrong; and being so, it would be a most immoral and wrong thing for Andrew Stumps to forgive a blow; and so I've got reason and gospel on my side, and Master Ironsides shall have the benefit of it, and no kind of mistake."

Andrew Stumps might have continued to reason with himself upon his system of logic, as to the justification of any act he might think proper to perform, Heaven knows how long, had not the voice of Ironsides called his attention to the matter in hand; and grasping his stick, and thrusting on his hat, as if he intended never more to remove it, he issued from the kitchen, and joined his master on the stairs.

"Now, Andrew, we must be cautious in our inquiries," he observed. "If any one has observed them, they cannot easily be forgotten; and if we are lucky enough to hit upon the right track, I have little doubt that we shall come upon the trail before any mischief is done. Call up the deaf old fool, Goody Godstone, and let me endeavour to make her understand that we shall probably be away for the remainder of the day, and that she is to let no one in on any account."

Old Stumps went at once into the scullery, for he knew he might as well call to the scullery itself to come up, as to Goody Godstone, and with as much chance of success; and poking his stick into the old crone's ribs, he beckoned her to follow him, which the old lady, with more alacrity and activity than one could expect, proceeded to do.

"Now, Goody," bawled Ironsides. "we shall be absent the greater part of the day."

"Eh, eh?" jerked out the old woman.

"We shall be absent the greater part of the day."

"Slay who?"

"Psha!" bellowed Ironsides; "why th dence don't you open your ears? I say tha', very likely, we shall not be at home for some time. Do you hear?"

The old lady nodded assent.

"And if anybody wants to come in——."

"At what time did you say it was to be cooked?"

"Cooked! what cooked?"

"Very good—it shall be done to a turn.'

"You stupid fool!" roared the governor, "I said nothing of cooking, nor doing to a turn!"

"Oh, no—I'll take care—you may depend upon me—it shan't burn."

"Idiot, idiot! I can make nothing of you: get down—get down!"

"Yes, yes; and it shall be done brown—very brown. Shall I save you a sop in the pan?"

This was rather too much for the patience of Mr. Ironsides; and placing a hand upon each shoulder of poor Goody, he—not with the most gentle roughness—thrust her down the few steps leading to the scullery, and pushed her in, evidently much to her surprise and bewilderment.

"The best way, after all, will be," said he, "to lock up the place entirely, and leave it to chance. Chance has befriended me before, and I dare say it will again. If anybody comes, they must go away again; and to prevent any disturbance, Andrew, just take off the bell, and the visitors may pull till they're black in the face before they hear its clapper. Off with it; and now for business.

They opened the massive and iron-bound door of that hell upon earth, and passed through; and carefully locking it, walked down the tortuous gravel path leading to the entrance gate, which, having passed through, they also locked; and feeling satisfied that everything was safe and secure as if they had been on the premises, they issued forth on their pursuit.

CHAPTER IV.
THE PURSUIT CONTINUED.

THE house in which took place the scenes we have described, was situated in a retired part of Hampstead, the exact locality of which we refrain from pointing out, as it still is used for the same purposes that it was at the time we are writing of, though we have reason to believe that a more humane system is pursued towards the unfortunate wretches who are consigned there.

We have many times walked down the lane in which the house stands, without the remotest idea of there being such a place there, or, indeed, of any habitation ; and had we not been specially directed to it by one of the principal actors in our tale, we should have still been in ignorance of the fact.

The lane we speak of is near the extreme verge of that beautiful suburban village, Hampstead. On each side the chesnut and beach, with a large proportion ot oak, grace the walk, the interstices of which are filled up with the usual vegetation of English hedge rows in wild luxuriance. Through the occasional openings of the hedge may be caught a glimpse of thickly clustering trees, venerable from age, yet none the less vigorous. A few yards behind this ample screen stands the asylum we speak of. Sombre and heavy in its construction, the windows guarded with massive bars of iron, and the general aspect of the place would be conclusive at once of its application.

About eight o'clock in the morning of the 16th of June, 1806, might be seen two men making their way through that ancient clump of trees, peering about them carefully and cautiously, as if they expected an attack from some hidden intruder.

They were Maurice Ironsides and Andrew Stumps, in pursuit of the fugitives, Maud Selby and the idiot Jacky Jingle. They were in close conversation, and in the face of Ironsides might be observed the most intense anxiety.

"Stumps," said he, "we have lost too much time already in searching about the grounds for the runaways. It is not likely that when their object was to escape from the house, that they should remain in such close proximity to it, not at all."

"I don't know what you mean by próxmy, but if you means that they would have cut a long way off, why, that may be or it may not be ; but I have known many cases when I was in a different line of business, where men who have been obliged to keep out of the way, instead of cutting off, as we would think they would do, a long way out of the reach of the officers, they have gone into their very haunts, and thereby completely put the blood-hounds off the scent; acos who'd think of looking for a fox in a dog's kennel, when the dog was only the length of his chain from it ?"

"That may be true ; but here the motive is different. You see by staying in this locality they would get no good, but by proceeding at once to London they would ; there can be no good in arguing the point—they must be found, and found they shall be, dead or alive."

"Well, I know you are a man of your word," said Stumps ; "but something strikes me that we shall have more difficulty in laying hold on 'em than what you imagines ; and if so be as they haven't taken the road to London, as you thinks they have, why it's clear that they must have taken some other road to somewhere else ; and as there are a great many roads to a great many places, it strikes me that if we doesn't come into their track, we shall get nothing for our pains."

By this time the worthy couple had advanced to the hedge-row ; and opening a little gate, which was merely on the latch, they stepped forth into the open lane. Looking for some time anxiously along that part of it that led into the country, they turned, and bending their steps towards London, they proceeded onwards at a rapid pace.

At every wayside house they made inquiries, hoping to gain some clue to the fugitives, but were entirely unsuccessful until they came to the 'Load of Hay,' where, after ordering a glass of hot brandy-and-water at the bar, Ironsides opened the conversation with the landlord with the agreed-upon caution, leading the way to obtain the information he required.

"A boisterous night we've had, sir," observed he.

"Yea, truly," snuffled out mine host, who was, besides a publican and sinner, an evangelical saint. "Yea, truly, was it. The Lord showeth his might in the storm, and the wicked are slewed down with the might of his vengeance."

"A hard night for the houseless wanderer," continued Ironsides.

"Yes, and one calculated to recal him from his wanderings. Ah me ! if the wicked would but open their eyes and soften their hearts, such a scene as last night might have converted many sinners."

"It may be all very true," chimed in Andrew Stumps, "but perhaps you will inform me what you really consider to be a sinner, and what's the real difference between a sinner and somebody what isn't a sinner? According to my notions on these 'ere matters, there's little difference between them. I have sucked in this much, that all things which are considered sins meet with exactly the same punishment ; that is—hell-fire for ever. The warrior and the murderer meet with the same reward, and makes it out all are sinners, and all men will share the same fate ; for as all men, according to the scriptures, are liars, so all men are sinners ; and being all sinners, and all sinners being to be damned for ever, why, it's a sound conclusion, I apprehends, that we're all sold, and no kind or manner of mistake whatsomdever."

"Ah, man, man," replied the landlord, "pray that you may be put into the right path. You are badly informed as to that which it should be the mainspring of your precious life to arrive at a knowledge of ; but if you will come to our chapel to-morrow evening, and hear the inspirations of our pious Jonas

Jellybelly, oh, if you would—if his holy conversation wouldn't put a little charitable feeling into you, I don't know what would. Now, what do you want?"

This question was addressed to a poor starving wretch with scarcely a rag to cover him, who at that moment stepped on to the threshold of the door, and with his hand raised to his brimless hat, in the most humble and meek manner possible, intimated his desire to be relieved from his pressing emergencies, one of which evidently was, from his sunken cheeks and haggard appearance, a crust to keep him from dying of actual starvation.

" Be off, be off," said mine host; " I have nothing for you—work, work—I work; and why shouldn't you ?"

The man, without saying a word, but with a respectful bow, was about retiring, when old Andrew Stumps, stepping up to him, slipped a coin into his hand, and wished him Godspeed.

" There," said he to the landlord, " that's what I call a practical illustration of a saintly man, and a moral man, who is not a saintly one."

" Verily, you know not what you do," returned the landlord. " You saw that the Lord had deserted him ; and is it for the poor worm, man, to hold out his hand to succour him whom the Lord has forsaken ? Truly, truly—nay, it's a flying in the face of the Lord."

" You are a man of peculiar ideas," remarked Ironsides, " and permit me to remark, that if every one was of your way of thinking, the hand of charity would be always closed ; for the more unfortunate the object, the less entitled to sympathy. Do you always turn away the famishing man from your door as you have done this poor, ill-clad, shivering miserable man ?"

" Yea, verily and truly I say unto you I would, and consider that I had done good service to the cause—I take glory in it. It was but this very morning that I sent from this place two wretched sinners, who had taken shelter under the shed from the raging of the storm, with a flea in their unrighteous ears and head. Hem! hem!—merciful to them—and yea great was their tribulation of spirit."

" Indeed ?" said Ironsides; " and what sort of persons may they have been, Mr. Landlord ?"

" Yea, of a verity, they were old stagers, and well practised in their art: one was a woman, and the other a sort of half man, half boy, who endeavoured to affect the idiot."

" I think I must have seen the pair," said Stumps. " What sort of appearance had the man ? Had he anything particular striking about him ?"

" Yea, brother, the first moment our eyes caught each other, he began to put out his tongue, squeezing his nose and chin at the same time, and then laying hold of his two

ass's ears, and giving them a pull, he drew it in again. That was a peculiarity which struck me as being very ridiculous, and a making game of the likeness which we are taught man resembles the original. He wore an old white hat trimmed up with green, with the stump of a cabbage tied upright in the front, and two pieces of straw stuck behind his ears."

" How long ago might it have been since these poor devils were here ?" inquired Ironsides.

" Two hours ago at the least," drawled out the saint.

" Which way did they take ?"

" Townwards."

" Thanks," said Ironsides, and the two men hurried on.

CHAPTER V.

THE RETREAT OF THE PURSUED.—THE PURSUIT CONTINUED.—THE CHRISTIAN.—AND THE DISAPPOINTMENT.

As soon as the idiot and Maud had effected an egress from the place of their confinement, and the rank herbage had been restored by the idiot to its pristine appearance, in order to better conceal the means of their escape from any outward observer, the two forlorn creatures started to where chance might lead.

Jacky Jingle had no intention of doing more than he had done on former occasions, that is of returning to his wretched den, for he had no place but that to hide his miserable head, and no hopes or thoughts of better days—he never knew them, or if he had, time had withdrawn them from his memory ; and so long as he could steal a ramble in the fresh fields, his happiness was at the full.

Not so with Maud. The remembrance of happy scenes which she had passed through from her cradle upwards almost to the opening of our tale, was fresh upon her memory. Once released from the confinement of her prison-house, nothing but necessity could force her back again.

The storm, though it had some time ceased, left a drizzling, soaking rain ; and from the appearance of the sky no prospect of a break in its monotony gave promise.

Thinly clad, and ill-provided to resist the weather, she yet determined to proceed in her resolution of reaching London. Hesitating, as if which way to turn, she caught a glimpse of the steeple of Highgate old church, and directing her course by it, she made her way into the lane, of which we have spoken in a preceding chapter, followed by the idiot. Keeping her back to the church, she proceeded onwards, till at length, reaching the high-road, she felt perfectly safe as to the route being the right one, and offering up a thanksgiving to Him who watches over the unfortunate, and a prayer for the successful termination of her enterprise, she put her arm into that of the idiot, and on they strolled. They had reached about half way between the asylum and the entrance into the High-street, when Jacky began to feel some inclination to return. He had not intended to run away from, to him, his home; but merely to do as he had many a day done before, just taking a quiet ramble in the surrounding fields, and sneaking in again before any of the people were about. The fear began to come upon him that he had already proceeded too far, and should not be able to regain his cell before his absence would be noticed, and in that case, not only would a stop be put to his attempting anything of the same nature again, but, in addition, he anticipated the whip of Andrew Stumps, who, upon all occasions when he thought it was called for in the slightest degree, never omitted to bestow it with a hearty good-will, not only to keep his hand in, but as a principal feature of his calling and an imperative duty to do.

"Jacky's very cold," said the idiot; "la, la, my fingers are stiff and as straight as a brick; Jacky will go back now and get into his bed; he's very hungry and wants his gruel. Come, Maud, let us turn home again. Brother Stumps will stop up the hole close, and we shan't be able to get it again. I'm very wet, cold and hungry, and I can't get my lips to make a hole to whistle—whew! no, I can't do it. Come, let's get home, the cockabiddies won't sing this morning, and if we go on, we shall get nothing to eat."

Maud, whose malady had ever been but trifling, had, with her liberty, so far recovered her reason as to be convinced that had the idiot returned to the house the probability would be that she herself would, in consequence of the information he might give, be quickly pursued, overtaken, and again placed in the horrible asylum; and therefore to her it was of the first importance that the idiot should remain her companion until her resolves had been executed; and if they should succeed, she intended to provide for him in a way wherein the tender mercies of Andrew Stumps could be dispensed with. She earnestly begged of the idiot to accompany her to her journey's end, undertaking to keep him from the wrath of Stumps.

Very little persuasion was necessary to induce poor Jacky Jingle to do as she required him; and having indulged in two or three repetitions of his favourite little peculiarity of thrusting out his tongue and withdrawing it again in the manner we have described, he stuck a cabbage stalk, that he had picked up in the road, in the front of his tattered hat, and valiantly declared that he would follow her all over the world, ay, or even to London, if that was all.

It will be recollected that the occurrences we have related, which took place at that solitary house at Hampstead, happened on the preceding night, and as it is well known when the unfortunate inmates of these establishments are left for the night, the last meal is delivered to them about seven o'clock in the evening, consequently it can easily be supposed that both Maud and Jacky Jingle were hard pressed with hunger, for the fresh air to which they had now been exposed for some time had induced an appetite which they never felt in the close confinement of their prison-house.

Exhausted with hunger and fatigue, drenched to the skin with the pelting rain, and almost maddened with the taunts and insults of the few stragglers whom they met in the High-street at that early hour of the morning, they hastened with the best speed they could to get through the inhospitable town, and having got as far on the road as the public-house called the Load of Hay, Jacky Jingle could not proceed further, and pulling Maud by her garments, he threw himself under the shelter of a friendly projection against that house, and bringing up his knees, he dropped his head between them, and in a few minutes fell into a deep and quiet slumber.

Poor Maud, we can no longer call her the maniac, who felt as strongly as the unfortunate at her feet the necessity of repose, yet forbore to close an eye—thoughtful of her safety, yet determined not to desert the poor fellow by whose means she had so far succeeded in her escape—resolved to remain by him; and if in a reasonable time he was not awake, then she would disturb him, and together proceed on their journey.

Having thus made up her mind, Maud crouched up into the other corner of the door-way as far from the pelting drift as she could, and folding her arms across her breast, wept over the remembrances of the past, and calling upon God with a fervour that came from her heart of hearts, He bestowed upon her the most beneficent of all His gifts; and despite her resolution, her eyelids closed, and she was alike insensible to the happiness or misery of the world around her.

Heaven knows how long they might have slept had they not been awakened by the pious landlord of the Load of Hay, upon the opening of his house for the business of the day; for though subject to the observance of the stragglers and the labouring men who were proceeding to their work, and who, in small groups, had their say concerning the unfortunate objects of their attention, yet none of them presumed to disturb Maud and her companion in their slumbers, but passed on, some with an inward chuckle that they were not as those in the true spirit of the divine Watts; and others, with a more christian feeling, pitying their misfortunes, at the same time earnestly wishing that their means would allow of giving them relief.

Ebenezer Bung—the pious and so-called evangelical publican, and occasional preacher at the methodist chapel in the neighbourhood, and whose services were often called into requisition when Mr. Jonas Jellybelly, the dear man, had been over-indulging in the mortification of the bottle—was in the cellar, in the midst of qualifying his malt to the tastes of his customers, when he was interrupted by the entrance of his potboy, who, with his mouth wide open, and his hands in his breeches pocket, exclaimed—

"Master, there's a couple of rum 'uns outside, what is collecting quite a mob round 'em; they're a rummy lot—precious."

"Verily, then, Samuel, I will speedily send them adrift," snuffled Ebenezer; "this is no place for the idle and dissolute—yea, verily, no."

"No," said Sam, "nor for the desolate neither; is it, master, eh?"

"Do you mean to bandy words with me, you son of a—saintly mother?" exclaimed the landlord in a passion, just checking himself of a most unorthodox expression. "Do you mean to bandy words with me? dissolute or desolate is the same to me; for they whom the Lord hath deserted, I desert, and those whom the Lord hath exalted and fattened up with the good things of this wicked world, I exalt myself, by submitting to. He whom the Lord despiseth, let no man succour, for I say unto him, yea, Ebenezer saith unto him, verily he sinneth much. Here, Samuel, fill these cans with Adam's ale, and just drop a little of the extract of colocynth into them, while I go and rout these vagabonds that flee before the vengeance of the Lord."

So saying, the good, pious honest-dealing Ebenezer Bung departed on his errand of mercy and having reached the portal of his own door, deliberately, with the stick he had in his hand, with which he had been stirring up the beer in the casks, well intermixing and incorporating the ingredients therewith, which he had found so palatable to the tastes of his customers, he, without saying a word, or giving the least intention of his design, gave poor Jacky Jingle such a tap on his almost unprotected head, as most effectually awakened the idiot to the realities of life.

So sudden and little dreamed of was this uncharitable blow to poor Jacky that it was some time ere he could collect his scattered senses—at all times scattered in the true sense of the term—and when he had arrived at a sufficient reflection of his real situation, the fancy took possession of him that it was old Stumps who was inflicting the customary castigation for any lapse of discipline he might have been guilty of.

His first idea was to pray forgiveness, and dropping on his knees for that purpose, he looked up into the face of his supposed tormentor, and finding that it was not that of the man he suspected, he immediately commenced the insane attack upon his nose, ears, and chin, which the saintly landlord had related to Ironsides and Stumps.

"Come—troop, troop, you vagabond," said Bung; "and you, you baggage; we don't want any ungodly exhibitions here—come, troop, I say; do you hear? or, by the Lord's assistance, I'll break every bone in your ungracious skins."

Down came the stick again thwack upon Jingle's shoulders this time, by way of a change, and the poor idiot passively received

the gratuitous benevolences of the sanctified Bung; there is no knowing how long that individual would have continued those gracious acts, had not Maud suddenly started up and interfered for the idiot's protection.

"Ruffian!" she exclaimed, "would you murder the poor innocent? Do you not see that he is not like other men? Forbear, forbear—hold, I say, and strike no more, or may the terrible vengeance of your offended God strike thee."

The landlord stood transfixed for a moment, for he did not expect such a spirited resistance on the part of poor Maud, whose appearance of animation was sufficiently against her to warrant him in his assumption; but feeling irritated by the sort of language Maud had used, and also that his peculiar province was invaded by any allusion to the Power she had invoked, his passion got the better of his discretion, and leaving the idiot, he rushed up to Maud, and with his stick upraised, he exclaimed—

"May the Lord confound thee—I mean enlighten—thou strolling baggage. Is it not enough that he has cast thee off in his infinite mercy, but you must needs prowl about to seek man's contumely? Pack off with your cheating knave—your innocent companion. I have no spoons within your reach! confound you both for a pair of precious thieves! Nay, verily, answer not me, or, by the Lord's grace, I will make every bone in your beggarly skin crack again."

"If you do, I'll be dom'd, Mr. Landlord," said a country carrier, who had just heard and seen sufficient to authorise him to put in his veto; "no, no, Mr. Fatguts, if thee dost, may I be dom'd. Let moi zee thee raise a finger agin that poor ooman, and I'll loi this whip across thee accursed shou'ders, that I'll warrant me ye'll think all the jockeys o' Newmarket were cracking joikes on thee. No, no, doan't 'ee touch her—doan't 'ee touch her."

The deputy shepherd of the Hampstead flock of dissenting lambs dropped his crook at this dicisive declaration, and casting a keen glance around at the tolerable good scattering of idlers, to see how their inclinations went, whether for or against his proceedings, his doubts were speedily solved in a much more unsatisfactory way than a pleasant one; for first came upon his astonished nose the most unfriendly greeting of the butt-end of a tolerably sized cabbage stalk, which, while in the act of feeling whether his nasal disfigurement remained in all its ancient rubicund integrity, was speedily followed by the cabbage itself in *propria persona*.

"Ha, ha, ha!" laughed one of the mob; "a cabbage is all very well in its way and in its proper place, and I suppose, Mr. Godlyguts, you'd rather have had that 'ere vegetable in your in'ards, than on the top o' your bladder o' lard."

"Well thrown," said another. "Old Boniface, why doesn't you put it by for a wig?"

" Let dear Brother Bung alone," screamed an old withered hag. "Did you never hear the dear lamb bleat in the Tabernacle? Oh, he's a dear man, is Brother Bung! If ever there was a blessed saint, he's one. Oh, you're a parcel of heretics, and will be all d—d to eternity, and ever so long after! Isn't there anybody else who's going to have a shy at the martyr? Is Hampstead without it's saint? Are there no rotten eggs in this blessed place to make a martyr with? Oh, I'm ashamed of you! What! can't you stand by, and let a man bully and beat a poor wretch of a woman without illusing him for it? And you call yourselves men, do you? Let the poor, persecuted Ebenezer Bung alone. Don't — pray don't anoy Brother Bung—don't, don't

The mob were at first rather doubtful of the old woman's meaning; but, during her harangue, they caught the cue, and mud, garbage, and filth, flew fast and thick on the devoted Bung.

There can be no doubt that the wisest course for him to have pursued would have been to have retreated into his house for shelter; but he was so completely astonished —so utterly and entirely bewildered at this most outrageous attack upon him, that, like one oppressed with that devil of the brain, nightmare, he had all the will, but none of the ability to move one step.

Fast and thicker came the incongruous mass of missiles on to the devoted person of the self-elect: the mob became more dense, and fresh comers—without the trouble of inquiring into the particulars, like all English mobs, right or wrong—followed the example set them.

Ebenezer at last recovered from his astonishment, and like a prudent man, considering that discretion was the better part of valour, turned his face towards his own door, with the full intent of taking advantage of the protection his house should afford him; but, alas! for human designs, in this he was disappointed; for, during the state of the confusion, some of the mob, more cunning, or, perhaps, less scrupulous than the rest, had made their way into the sanctorum of the bar, and, with the most liberal and patriotic ideas, had helped themselves, and retired to the door to keep guard while the rest of their confederates were doing as they had done.

The pious Ebenezer Bung tried to shoulder his way in; but in this he was not successful, inasmuch as the few vagabonds who were guarding the door signalised to the rest who were within that it was time for them to leave the enticements of the bottle; and closing round, ejected him with considerable force into the midst of the mob. Bung, personally, had hitherto not been very seriously injured by the proceedings of the mob, as nothing harder than cabbage stalks, or more offensive than rotten eggs, had been used as weapons of offence; but now that some of that motley group had given the remainder a start—for mobs always require some one to do the initiative—he got bandied about from one to

another, and there could be no foreseeing the consequences of the rough treatment he was experiencing; and had not a few strong old rams—part of the flock over which Ebenezer occasionally presided—taken up the cudgels in his defence, probably Ebenezer and the Load of Hay would have for ever cut their mutual acquaintance.

These staunch friends and brothers vigorously applying their shoulders to the wheel —or, rather, to the Bung—succeeded in forcing him through the mob and into his own house; and closing the door, Bung and his friends uttered defiance to their enemies.

Ebenezer certainly had got the worst of the rencontre; and feeling that, for his own satisfaction, he must take vengeance upon somebody for the outrage that had been committed upon his sanctified and moral person, he rushed up to the unfortunate potboy, and catching hold of his attenuated ears from behind, he, with his foot and knee alternately, and with the regularity and precision of a falling hammer, operated upon the latter end of that interesting specimen of his class.

 * * * *

Long before the sun had reached its climax, Maud and the idiot in the confusion had left, and were a considerable distance on their journey.

The day was now hastening into the bustle and activity of life, and the nearer they advanced towards the metropolis, more numerous became the people.

The appearance of Maud and the unfortunate companion of her flight, was too remarkable to avoid observation. Maud, without bonnet or any other outward habiliments of dress adapted to the inclemency of the weather—her hair streaming down her back, and her miserable attire drenched through with the soaking rain, presented an object to a well regulated mind of commiseration, but to an uncultivated, rough, and brutal one, an object of derision. And Jacky Jingle, too, poor fellow, in no better plight than Maud, of the two, excited most observation. A tall, thin, sunken-cheeked, black lustre-eyed youth, neither man nor boy, whose dress was neither adapted to one state nor to the other— for his jacket came up almost to his armpits, and his trowsers to his knees—a cabbage-stalk stuck bolt upright in the rim of his dilapidated hat, and the two straws sticking out from his ears, was not an object to excite, in the ill-trained minds of a mob, any other feelings than those of derision and contempt.

Maud, with one hand resting on the shoulder of Jingle for support, the miserable pair entered into the High-street of Camden-town.

One or two of the idlers, boys, who had witnessed the scene at the Load of Hay, when Maud and Jacky retired from the scene, followed their steps; and by the time they had reached Camden-town, the train was very considerably augmented; and ever and anon one of the mob, more callous to all right feeling than the others, would utter some piece of impertinence, which is considered by the vulgar in general to be wit, and which is understood and known to them by the term "chaff."

One young urchin, with more impudence than breeches, very coolly faced Jingle, and looking up into his face with the utmost *sang froid*, asked—

"Excuse me, sir, but does your mother know you're out?"

"Mother!" said Jacky, "mother! what mother?"

"Why, the old lady in the workhouse; I owe her a small washing bill," continued the young vagabond; "and as I've a few surplus coins, I wish to inquire whether she knows you're out."

"I don't know any mother," said Jacky.

"My good boy, can you tell me where this poor man's parent is to be found?" inquired Maud.

"Blow me tight! why, ain't you his aunt that was murdered? and as such you must know your sister better I. There's a pretty couple, ha! ha! Hurrah for the fool! I say, old fellow, what 'll you take for your cabbage-stump? are you going to take your vegetables to Common Garden, or your straw to the Haymarket? ha! ha! ha! What a silly looking ass you would look, to suck sherry-cobler through a reed. Why, you'd beat all the other fools to immortal smash, ha! ha!"

"I say, Jack," chimed in another, "what's them 'ere straws stuck behind his ears for?"

"Blessed if I know," said Jack.

"What, don't you know?" said another; "why, you boobies! ain't it to give him an air of importance? why of course it is. What 'd he be without his straws and his cabbage-stumps? Why, all the world like ourselves, ordinary individuals, and men of straw."

"I'll be blowed, if I don't think he wears 'em to to insult my perfession," said a cabman; "I've a great mind to give him a bonneter, and no mistake. Want a cab, your honour?"

"What's a cab?" inquired Jingle.

"Why, that's a cab, your honour," said the cabman, and down went poor Jacky's hat, completely burying into it the whole of his face.

Poor Jingle was not at any time viciously inclined, but human nature could endure no more; while he, with both his hands, was trying to free his head from the confinement of his hat, he made free use of his legs, and indiscriminately kicked out, right and left, and backwards and forwards, which course of proceeding, instead of checking the mischievous inclinations of the mob, only added fuel to the flame.

"Inhuman monsters!" exclaimed Maud. "Do you not see that he is bereft of the same reason that God has given to you, and that you, instead of tormenting and cruelly treating him, should protect and sympathise with him? Shame on you! shame!"

"Bravo!" said a stout fellow, "bravo! all attention for a sermon. We can listen patiently to the sermon while your pal is getting the lining of his tile over the tip of his nose."

"True," said another; "true, old Fatguts."

"Who the devil are you?" said the stout one. "There, take that (and he felled him with a blow on the chest), Guts, in your teeth. Well, I'm blessed!"

"Yes," said a friend of his fallen hero, as he gave the stout one a tremendous tap on the nose. "Yes, I'm blowed if you ain't. All's fair in fair time; and what one does, all should do, and not mind a little joking and chaffing. Now, I've given you one for my friend, and if so be you'll stand up, I feel inclined to give you another for myself, for your interrupting diversion"

"I decline the honour," said the fellow; "but howsomdever, I begs to observe that I don't like personalities; and I've a particular objection to being called Fatguts, and that's what I say."

"Well," said the other, "every man's entitled to say his say, and you having said yours, and your conk having stopped bleeding, and the yokel there having got his shell off, why 'up, boys, and at 'em.'"

But "up, boys, and at 'em," was rather disappointed in his expectation of taking part again in the cruel entertainment the mob were making for themselves: for Mr. Fatguts, watching his opportunity when "up boys, and at 'em" was off his guard, like a coward, as he was, gave him such a violent kick in the lower region of his stomach, that laid him sprawling senseless at his feet.

This diversion of the mob's attention was favourable to poor Jacky Jingle and Maud, who was terrified nearly to fainting, and, unobserved, they cautiously left the spot, seeking refuge at the first house of accommodation. Maude prayed the kind services of the landlady to protect them from further injury and outrage.

"Ay, sure! ay, sure!" said the good, kind-looking old lady—"come in, my child, come in; the Eel and Frying-pan never shuts its door on the unfortunate. Why, bless me, how ill you both look—cold and hungry, I suppose; come along, come along. We'll soon make you right again. Betsy Clutterbuck's always got a sop in the pan for the unfortunate."

The kind Mrs. Clutterbuck led the way into the spacious kitchen of the Eel and Frying-pan, and pushing them both down with a friendly violence into the seat of the ample settle, entreated of them to make themselves comfortable until she came again.

"Heaven reward you for your kindness to the friendless and, to you, unknown," said Maud, and she covered her face with both hands and wept. "Oh! it is a long time since a word of kindness has fallen upon my ear—a very long time. May God bless you, and forgive my persecutors."

"Come, child, I don't want any thanks, for I consider it my duty to assist any one who requires assistance; and so far as I am able to render it, I will."

"Can you give poor Jacky Jingle any

food?' said the idiot; "Jacky's had no food, but the rain and the mud, for many a day. See, can you balance a straw on the tip of your nose while you're blowing it? I can't. Old Stumps can, and Maud can't; but Jacky's very hnngry and very wet; but the fire loves the wet and the cold, and will soon eat it all away from Jacky. A straw for a crust—a straw for a crust!"

The landlady looked at Maud, and from the peculiar expression of her countenance, in answer to the silent inquiry, her suspicions were confirmed as to the state of the poor idiot's mind.

"Poor dear lad," said Mrs. Clutterbuck; "God have mercy on him! You shall have some food presently, Jacky—my poor fellow, you shall have some food."

"Ha, ha, ha! food; ho, ho, ho! do you hear that, Maud, do you hear that? A straw for some food—a straw for some food, heigh-ho, Jacky Jingle! Jacky Jingle! Listen—nearer, nearer. Can you jump over a black cat without cutting your throat? La! how you stare; ah, Jacky's cold, cold," and Jacky huddled himself up in a corner of the settle, and remained motionless.

"Pray," said Maud to the landlady, "let no one know that we have found shelter here, or we shall be lost—lost; oh, do not breathe a syllable."

"Why, God a' mercy!" said Mrs. Clutterbuck, "what has the poor child to fear? No one here shall harm you, don't fear, don't fear, my dear."

"Oh, if they come and find us here, we shall be locked up again, and lost for ever."

"Who come—who come? Nay, child, you're mind's disturbed. No one shall harm you."

"Do not, do not let them know."

"Well, well, poor child, be easy; no one shall know that you are here."

"Thanks, thanks, good madam; if we elude their pursuit until the light of day is gone, we shall be safe, safe."

"My dear child, what can you mean? Safe—pursuers—lost? really you speak in mysteries; but you may depend upon my secrecy with the most perfect security."

"I will—I will," said Maud; "I see it in your face; you will not betray me? no, no, you will not—you will let me bide here till to-night—you will—you will, say you will let me till the night, only till the night."

"Yes, my child, longer if you please."

"And you will not betray me?"

"Nay, nay, child, surely not."

"Then I will be calm and happy; happy, did I say? ah, me! no, Maud, no happiness for thee! But why, why should I spurn all hope? I am innocent, quite innocent, but the proof—ah, the proof—the proof!"

Some fearful mystery seemed to hang over the devoted head of the unfortunate Maud, the remembrance of which agonised her very soul, and caused her pallid cheek to glow with injured innocence.

While this paroxysm lasted, the good Mrs. Clutterbuck busied herself in preparing a hasty though substantial breakfast for her two poor customers, and which, when prepared, she herself took into that comfortable kitchen; and, drawing up the table opposite the fire within the settle, she invited them to partake, and while they were satisfying the natural craving of their appetite, or rather while Jacky Jingle is doing so, we will return to Maurice Ironsides and Andrew Stumps.

"What say you now, Andrew; shall we have them, think you, now?"

"That's a question," replied Andrew, "that may be answered in three ways—first, it may be answered positively in the negation; secondly, it may be answered positively in the affirmation; and thirdly and lastly, it may be answered in the doubtivation, which last is capable of being again divided into two heads; that is, the positive-affirmo-doubtative, or the positive-negato-doubtative, which may be again further amplified, divided, and split into many more ramifications."

"I tell you what, Andrew, if you go on with your ramifications and denifications, I shall be obliged to take insult at the English language and learn Cherokee. Why, man, what in the name of all the devils in the Roman Calendar, has possessed you to join in this kind of tomahawk business? You seem to have no sort of compunction at slaughtering your mother-tongue; in fact, it seems to me that you take a particular pleasure in it."

"That's entirely a matter of taste; there's no conventional rules or standard by which to measure a language, and that perhaps your edication may have taught you; but whether it has or not, or not or has, which is about the same thing, I believe, and I belive being the same, there can be no dispute about it; but I speak from actual practical knowledge—for when I was a young 'un, I used to be in a bookseller's shop—and I've seen an ancient book in which I could only read a word here and there, and then another, not so old, in which I could read a few more words; and so on, the newer the book, the more words I could read, until we comes upwards to this here present blessed minute; and I think that's a pretty conclusive argumentation that there ain't not no conventional standard by which a language can be measured."

"Well, well," said Ironsides, "I find you are a very learned man, and I must no longer argue with you; but now if you have quite done with your lucid explanation and defence of your murderous attack, I beg pardon; but will you favour me with your opinion as to the chance of success we have to find Maud and Jingle?"

"Why, let me see," replied Stumps, "it is now a matter of nearly two hours since the landlord of the Load of Hay sent them away; now, two hours would take them very comfortably to London, and if they've got into that 'ere den of sharpers, we shall find it a hard job, I'm thinking, to find 'em—that all."

" That's all ? What'else ! Come, come, step out, man, and I'll venture to say that we shall be successful yet. *Nil desperandum* is my motto, and I've never disgraced it by showing a faint heart."

" Ay ! I believe you, my boy."

" Eh ?"

" Did you speak, sir ?"

" No."

" Oh, I axes your parden."

Ironsides and his man pursued the search with unremitting ardour ; every house that was at all likely to conceal the fugitives was entered, and the usual inquiries made ; and as they had something at each place they stopped at to warrant these inquiries, Andrew felt himself to be getting a little muddled; and as his spirits were becoming gradually elevated, so also was his importance, and he considered himself quite on an equality with his master, and behaved accordingly.

" We shall have tight work of it now," exclaimed Stumps ; " you may depend on't, the vagabonds have got to London by this time. What think you, Ironsides ?"

" Eh, eh ! Stumps, do you know who you are talking to ?"

" O' course I do—Maurice Ironsides, the lunatic keeper of insane mad people. I'm not so drunk as you think I am, Mr. Maurice ; no, no, I believe you, my boy."

" Well, said Ironsides, " I think a little more respect in your mode of address is desirable ; and while I continue to be your master, I will have it."

" That's all as may be. If I don't choose to show you respect, why, no respect you would have from me, that's clear ; and it's a matter of calkilation, whether or no I gets anything by it; and as I have reckoned it up and can't come to any satisfactory conclusion, whether it would be best to be submissive and quiet, and all that sort of thing, but find that the odds are in favour of a little more independence : and I tell you what it is, old fellow, I'm blessed if I ain't been a gallous sight too submissive, and if I don't make up for it, my name's not Andrew Stumps. Hillos, look a-head, governor, there's a tarnation row, and we shall have some sport mayhap."

A bright gleam shot across the face of Maurice, as the thought entered into his brain that it might be Maud and the idiot who were being mobbed—a very natural thought too.

" Ah, ah !" he said, " Stumps, come on, we shall have them now !"

They made their way for the crowd which was about a quarter of a mile distant, and having reached the scene of the affray, Ironsides anxiously peered about him, in hopes of discovering his victims in the hands of some of the motley group. If he had been there ten minutes before, he would most assuredly have found whom he sought; as it was, he was in the midst of a furious col-

lection of ruffians, who were indiscriminately attacking each other with sticks and stones and fisty cuffs, which much puzzled Ironsides an Stumps to account for ; but which, in fact, originated entirely with the quarrel between the gentlemen so politely designated Fatguts by one of the mob, and " up, boys, and at 'em," whom Fatguts had assailed in so cowardly a manner, and who was then in a neighbouring house, still in a state of insensibility. The partizans of each of these heroes had taken up cudgels in the defence of their respective chiefs, until at length, in their blind fury, friends and foes were alike indiscriminately attacked.

Ironsides seeing that their views were not at all likely to be assisted by staying among the rioters, with some difficulty retired from the presence of the crowd ; though, by-the-by, not without a hard crack or two on their respective skulls, as a sort of affectionate farewell memento ; and getting quite clear from all danger, notwithstanding the urgency of the matter he had in hand, he inquired of a youth the reason of the row.

" Oh," said the youth, " they were having a lark with a couple of queer-looking coves, and they quarrelled about something, I'm sure I don't know what, and pitched into one another."

" Indeed ! Did you say two coves ?"

" Yes, two coves."

" Two men, I suppose you mean ?"

" Why, there's a blessed idiot," said the youth : " thinks as two men must be two coves, and that two women musn't be two coves—well, I am blowed."

" Then they were two women ?" asked Ironsides.

" Who said they were two women ?" said the lad. " I did n't ; I said they were two coves ; and yet they were neither two men, nor two women, nor two boys, nor two girls, nor a woman and a girl, nor a man and boy, and so, Mr. What's-your-name, riddle me, riddle me, ree."

" Why, don't you see," said Stumps, " that if it ain't one or other of these 'ere couplets, that it must be a man and a woman !"

" Bravo, Mr. Chops," said the boy, " you deserve a medal."

" I tell you what it is, young 'un," said Stumps, " if you 're imperent, I'll give you a topper, for luck,"

" Top away," said the boy, and he began signifying to old Stumps that he might take a sight, " top away, old fellow, and when you 've done, just let me know, will yer ?"

Stumps made a rush at the boy, but was prevented bestowing his promised topper by Ironsides, who whispered him to remain quiet, while he got more information from the lad.

" Come here, my boy," said he, " come here ; I wish to speak further with you.'

" Do you see anything particularly green in my eye ?" said the boy, at the same time pulling it a litttle open with his fingers, and showing a most comical expression of phiz.

"Why don't you go and teach your dear old granny to suck eggs—eh?"

"Why, my boy," said Ironsides, thinking to humour the lad, "I've taught her long ago to do that, and she's a perfect wiseacre now, and requires no more teaching; but will you earn a shilling?"

"Why," said the lad, "if there isn't much to do for it, I doesn't mind; but hands off, you know."

"Oh, to be sure. Come here."

"Chuck me the shilling first, then," said the boy. "I don't like to come to close quarters upon a promise. No, I should rather believe not. Come, chuck us the bob."

"There it is," said the governor, as he threw the young rascal the coin, "there it is; and now pehaps you'll be kind enough to come and earn it."

"Now suppose I cuts," said the boy, "wouldn't you call yourself jolly green, old boy, eh?"

"I should call you a cunning young scoundrel," said Ironsides.

"And it would just sarve me right, too," said the boy; "and as I never does unto others what I wouldn't like others to do unto me, here I is, and now what's to do?"

"Tell me, as accurately as you can,' said Ironsides, "what sort of people were the two coves that you were just now telling us about."

"Ay, to be sure," said the boy; "one was a woman, a beautiful one too, by the-by, although unkimmonly plastered with dirt, and altogether in a queer sort of trim; she'd no bonnet nor shawl, and a white handkerchief was tied round her head, I suppose to keep her long hair from flowing into her eyes. As for t'other, he was a lanky, lamp-post sort of feller, deficient in brains, with a white hat, turned up with green, and a cabbage stalk."

"That'll do—that'll do," said Ironsides. "Which way went they?"

"Nay," said the boy, "I've earned my shilling, and every labourer is worthy of his hire; and if you want any further information, you must come down again. We doesn't work for nothing in this here part of the town."

"So it seems, my boy. Here's another shilling—now answer my question."

"Why," said the boy, "I consider that my conscience is quite satisfied in taking this here shilling for answering the question, whether I says yes or no; and as I was a good deal occupied in the general skrimmage which took place, I really can't inform you positively, for they took the opportunity of cutting away like bricks; and when I looked round, they were clean gone; but I can say that they did not go this way towards Hampstead; and if they're not still among the crowd, they must be on their road to London; and, if so, they can't have got far, and you'll catch 'em if you come up with 'em. Ha, ha! Do you see anything green about me?" and off went the boy into the midst of the dense crowd, who were still battling with undiminished vigour.

"They can't be far off," said Stumps, "anyhow, and as the boy says they didn't go towards Hampstead—which, I think we may very well believe, as if so be they had, we should have met 'em—why, I thinks we shan't be doing wrong in going straight on, not, however, forgetting to look in at the houses on the road; and this opinion of mine is strengthened by not observing them in this here mob. What say you, sir?"

"Why, Andrew, I'm your way of thinking, and I am more than almost certain—I feel sure we shall have them in their domicile before the day's out."

"Very good," observed Stumps, "very good; I wishes we may get 'em, that's all."

The first house they came up to was the respectable one yclept the Eel and Frying-pan, in which, at that very time, Maud and the idiot were ensconsed, and were quietly partaking of the refreshment the landlady, the good and Christian-like Mrs. Clutterbuck, had so charitably, so seasonably provided for them.

"Hilloa, here, hilloa! Bar, bar! Why, the devil—are the people of Camden-town so honest that you keep no better look out than this?" exclaimed the half drunken Stumps. "Come, draw me a glass of something short, and while you're doing it, tell us if you are much infested with beggars hereabouts."

Mrs. Clutterbuck had stepped from the little bar-parlour into the kitchen, to see how her unfortunate guests were getting on, when this rude appeal met her ear. She was not the only one who heard the voice. Maud and Jacky Jingle immediately recognised to whom it belonged; and the latter, dropping his cup of tea on to the floor with extreme terror upon his countenance, threw himself with amazing activity behind an ample screen, which stood in the corner of the apartment. Maud sprang to her feet, and grasping the hand of Mrs. Clutterbuck, gave her such an imploring and significant gesture that she immediately understood the meaning of it, and returning the look, she bustled out, and confronted Ironsides and Stumps.

"Well, my masters," she exclaimed, "you need not make so much noise. This is a quiet house, and I am not used to any disturbance. What is it you require?"

"My good dame," said Ironsides, "you must excuse my man here, who has made rather too free this morning, and is a little boisterous."

"Too free indeed!" said Stumps; "your man, too? pooh, pooh! Come, old ladybird, let's have a glass of old Tom, with a lump of sugar in it, and if you don't look alive, blow me if I don't come round and be my own barman."

"I don't know, sir, whether you be this man's master," said Mrs. Clutterbuck, addressing Ironsides, "but if you are, I must beg of you to insist upon his behaving himself in a proper manner."

"My good woman, I am his master, as I said before; but you see what with his exertion this morning, and late hours last night, and excitement, and, may be, a little too much in the way of strong drinks, he has forgotten the relative situations between us, and is now doing what he'll regret to-morrow."

"Regret? ha! ha! ha! Well, I'm pretty considerably bundled well-nigh all up in a heap," said the half drunken man; "regret? —why regret, if I understand the word right —and I believe I am not half so muddled as not to do so—implies that I should be sorry for what I've done. But, mark me, Ironsides, you're most confoundedly mistaken if so be as you suppose that 'ere sort of thing; for didn't I tell you a piece of my mind this very blessed morning, when you hit me the un-called-for blow on my precious nose? Didn't I say then that I should never forgive, but that one day, let it be ever so long first, I'd out with the secret about the——"

"Hold, hold, Andrew Stumps; I thought that was settled," said Ironsides.

"Ah, well, be it so," said Stumps: "but don't let's have any more of your bouncing, acos I won't stand it; and now you knows my mind upon that interesting subject. Let's have that 'ere glass of gin, and while you're drawing it, old girl, just let's know if you can give us any information about a fool and a mad woman who have been in this neighbour-hood this morning."

"What, in God's name, have you got into your hend now, you idiot?" said Ironsides.

"I aint no more an idiot than you, although you are a governor of an asylum, and I am your keeper; no more a fool than you; and I insist upon being answered afore I leaves this blessed place. Now, old dame, tell us all you know about this worthy couple."

"I shall be very ready to anwer all ques-tions you may ask," said the old lady, "pro-vided they are proper and decent ones for a woman to answer."

"Ah, never you fear," said Stumps; "my questions will be all proper and decent enough, and all that I shall require of you is, that your answers may be of that modest descrip-tion as that they will not offend my ears. Now, marm, first and foremost, do you know the nature of an oath? But, however, as that's no part of our present business, I'll forego the answer to question the first.— Secondly, would you as soon speak the truth, without calling God to witness it, as if you didn't? Answer—never mind, upon second thoughts that's akin to the first, and I'll dis-pense with the answer to question No. 2."

"For Heaven's sake!" said Ironsides, losing all patience, "if you don't put your questions in a buisness, straightforward way, I think I know what you require to ascertain, and I'll put the questions for you. You jack-ass, don't you see how much time we are wasting?"

"I tell you what it is," said Stumps; "if you don't let me do this thing in my own way, I'll have nothing more to do with it, and

I'll leave you to find it all out yourself; if I don't, I'll be blowed."

"In God's name, then," said Ironsides, "go on, and be quick about it."

"Now then, marm, we're coming to busi-ness. Do you know the difference between a man and a—no, that's not what I mean. Have you seen a man and a woman this mor-ning, of a peculiar appearance, in this neigh-bourhood?"

"Is that all ye have to ask, man?" said Mrs. Clutterbuck. "Methinks you're made a great fuss about nothing. Why, if you had put the question to me at once, I should have got rid of my answer and your company to-gether. I have seen a man and a woman of peculiar appearance this morning. The man was one that I should say might be considered a witless one—he wore a white hat turned up with green, two straws in his ears, and a cab-bage stump in his hat. The woman was miserably ill-clad and quite unprotected from the weather; and they both looked as if they had escaped some terrible ill-usage, and a long confinement."

"And what became of them?" said Iron-sides.

"They were not in my keeping," said Mrs. Clutterbuck.

"You saw them?" said Ironsides; "where —when did you see them?"

"In that dreadful crowd."

"And after?—they are not there now."

"When some sort of fresh commotion took place in the mob, they both took the oppotunity of slipping from it, and bent their footsteps towards London," answered Mrs. Clutterbuck.

"How long ago might that have been?" said Ironsides.

"About half an hour," replied she.

"We shall have them yet," said Ironsides; "we shall have them yet. Come on, come —no time is to be lost."

"Not so fast, Mr. Master of mine. I thinks we may as well be more particular in our inquiries. Now, madam, as you have promised to speak the truth, the whole truth, and nothing but the truth—just let me ask you if so be as they didn't look in here?"

"And let me ask you in return," said Mrs. Clutterbuck, "what if they did?"

"Why then all I've got to say upon tha 'ere pint, is this here:—If so be as they didt why, for all we know, they may be here, now."

"Indeed," said the landlady; "and so you in your wisdom have come to the con-clusion that this is a harbour and place of refuge for the insane? Why, my good man, if you step outside and look up at the sign, you'll see that this is a public-house, and not a lunatic asylum."

"Never you mind that, my old gal. I'll see what you've got here besides eatables and drinkables, or my name's not Andrew Stumps. Now, clear the way."

"Now, Andrew Stumps, listen to me in my turn. You see that public parlour, this tap-room, and the open bar—those you are perfectly welcome to walk in, to talk in, and to stay in as long as the rules and regulations of the house will permit you to do; but if you dare to put one foot forth in any direction that is not free for the public, I shall not scruple to have you thrown out into the kennel neck and crop; mind that, Mr. Andrew Stumps."

"These are plucky, plucky words, Mrs. Landlord, uncommonly plucky words," said old Stumps; "but I'm too old in the tooth to be talked into a fit by a female woman; oh, no, I should like to see the man that would turn Andrew Stumps out of this here house anyhow."

"Ready at your service, always ready to do anybody a service of a reasonable capacity. Now, my boy, how would you like it —a cross buttocker, or a summerset, or a cut and thrust? Eh, I'm the lad to teach the exit exercise—come, which way will you have it? Come, quick's the word, and sharp's the action; come, look alive, right about face. Tramp, tramp, or look out for your hind quarters."

This harangue was uttered by a brawny fellow some six feet two without his stockings, who had been a life guardsman, but now honoured the Eel and Frying-pan, in the capacity of potboy, waiter, and occasional barman.

"And who the devil are you?" said Stumps.

"Your servant to command at all times, my lad; come, are you ready? I shan't wait much longer; and you, Mr. Thingummy, I suppose, are of this same kidney? Come, bundle both of you. What, you won't—there—what Mr. Stumps, you will make your way to the private parts of this establishment? very well, very well; here goes then; look out for squalls."

Old Andrew Stumps was no mean antagonist, for he was a strong-boned, sinewy man; but the valiant potman laying hold of the collar of his jacket behind with one hand, disdaining to use the other in the encounter, completely lifted the pot-valiant Stumps off his feet; and, giving him a sort of swing, brought up his foot, which at the return of the vibration came with such effectual force on the largest part of his person, that it sent him clear out of the house. The force of with which he came must have been of serious consequence to him had he fallen on the stones, but luckily for him his fall was broken by his coming in contact with one of those lazy Italian mendicants, who was at that moment striking up "See the conquering hero comes," on a snorting worn-out organ, the tune of which was completely lost by the overpowering mass of bass it bellowed forth.

"God for, what dam," roared the Italian

"Hold your row," growled Stumps, "and think yourself well off you 're whole, you mongrel-looking son of an Italian."

"Come on," said Ironsides, who at that moment came against Stumps, most unequivocally showing that he had been ejected in a similar manner. "On, on; this delay is all owing to your stupid drunken obstinacy; on, we shall catch them yet, we shall catch them yet," and grasping hold of Stumps's arm, he hurried on towards the metropolis.

It would be impossible to portray, so as to carry any adequate idea to the minds of our readers, the state of terror into which the visit of Ironsides and Stumps had thrown the unfortunate Maud. Hers indeed was an agony of fear, harrowing and intense. Jacky Jingle was alarmed, but his dull senses only calculated on a few additional stripes from Stumps, and the being debarred from his night wanderings in the green-fields and quiet sequestered lanes around the establishment; otherwise he would as soon be there as anywhere: it was all the same to Jingle.

As soon as the intruders had been so summarily ejected from the Eel and Frying-pan, Mrs. Clutterbuck bustled into the kitchen, exclaiming—

"There, my dears, you see that I told you truth when I said no harm should come to you; you see I've kept my word."

Maud threw herself upon her knees, and grasping the hand of Mrs. Clutterbuck, she passionately and with huge drops of gratitude swelling in her eyelids, exclaimed—

"Kind and noble protectress, Heaven will reward you a hundred fold for your assistance to the unfortunate. I am safe, safe now; no more shall that dreadful place enclose me, no more shall the cruel whip cut into my flesh. Oh, you will let me stay until the night sends forth its friendly shadows."

"Poor thing," said the kind-hearted old lady, "poor thing, you shall remain here as long as you please, for I know human nature sufficiently well to be satisfied that your case is genuine, and that you are speaking the truth; in fact, my opinion has been confirmed by those two rough men who have just left the house in pursuit of you. Stay, my poor lady, for I see you are not what you seem: stay till it please you to leave, and anything I can do to forward your plans, depend upon me for doing."

"Good creature, I am sure you will. It is my business to reach the metropolis tonight, and therefore I will take advantage of its darkness to leave this spot, and by its aid I hope to elude pursuit."

"Well," said Mrs. Clutterbuck, "as you please; but you really must not go out of here in that thin and scanty dress; you must have something to protect you from the cold, and also that will assist in making you less conspicuous."

"And what's poor Jacky Jingle to do?" said that demented individual. "If old Stumps sees Jacky's hat, he's sure to recollect it, and he gave me these straws, and he'll be sure to know them again."

"Why, Jacky," said Mrs. Clutterbuck, "I am sure Corporal Tim, as I call him, will make an exchange with you in respect to the first article, and as to the second, you know, why you put them into the fire at once."

"Anon, anon."

"And I dare say," continued she, "we shall be able to reclothe you from head to foot, so that you won't even know yourself or each other. And now, while I go and attend to the business, you make yourselves as comfortable as you can, and don't fear any interruption; and if, my dear child, you should please to make me your confidant, so that I may give you the benefit of my experience in the course you wish to adopt, you can do so in the course of the day; but if you have reasons for witholding your melancholy tale from the ears of strangers, far be it from me to wish to know any of the circumstances; but whether or no, you may depend upon me at at all times to render you all the assistance in my power, both in advice and otherwise; so make yourselves quite comfortable on that score; and for the next hour or so, I should advise you to snatch a slumber, for you may be some time before you get another opportunity, though God forbid."

Saying which, the old lady departed into the bustle and activity of the public business, and left her miserable, though comparatively happy, visitors to snatch an hour of sleep, which they so much required.

We will now return to Ironsides and Stumps, who, after a wearisome search, arrived at length in the vast metropolis—Stumps much improved by copious draughts of spring water, which he had taken in to counteract the effects of strong drinks he had previously indulged in.

If the search from Hampstead to the metropolis had been fatiguing, they anticipated that the continuation of it through that long labyrinth of streets would be an Herculean task; and divers were the reasonings, *pro* and *con*, as to the manner of their search. Suffice it to say that they at length agreed to take a portion of the work between each, making it a point to call in at every police station on their route, leaving an accurate description of the fugitives, with a request that, if they should be met with, information should be immediately forwarded to a public-house kept by a friend of Stumps.

High-road and by-road, street, lane, passage, and court, were diligently searched that day by the indefatigable Ironsides and his assistant; but no trace of poor Maud and the idiot could they discover. Hour after hour passed away, and still with unabated resolution, but with far less vigour, did they, each in his own locality, trace and retrace, ramble and wind in, about and through the intricacies of London, till thoroughly done up, and giving up the job as utterly hopeless —at least, for that time—they went to the house according to previous arrangement, where any news was to be forwarded in case the police authorities should have anything to communicate.

Dispirited and chagrined, Ironsides threw himself into a chair, and remained sullenly silent, while Stumps, carelessly bringing himself to an anchor on one of the tables, with one leg resting on Ironside's chair, and his chin buried in his brawny hand as a support for his head, coolly remarked—

"Well, old Stick-in-the-mud, I thinks we've had a pretty decentish wild goose-chase, in which, something strikes me, we've been the geese. How do you feel after your delightful excursion—eh?"

This query was only answered wit a scowl of malice, and old Stumps continued—

"Never mind, my old boy, you needn't be cross with me. I can assure you I am not angry with you—not at all: oh dear, no—not at all."

"This is no time for foolery, Andrew," said Ironsides. "If the worst comes to the worst, I shall be a ruined man without hope of redemption; and if it does not, it might as well, for to be in a state of uncertainty as to what has become of them is as bad, if not worse."

"Oh, bother," replied Stumps: "what's the use of reckoning your chickens afore they are hatched?—none whatsomdever. My father always made himself miserable with thinking on how he should be obliged to go into the workhouse in his old age. Now, he need n't ha' done that ere, for the old fool did n't go into the workhouse at all, but finished his career at the government lodgings in Cold Bath-fields, and all because his key fitted the lock of somebody else's house, which he at the time thought was his own, and where he was grabbed afore he discovered his error. Now you see the folly of reckoning upon anything in this 'ere mortal world of ours, where everything is uncertain, except the times as they come round for paying of your rent and taxes. Now, stop a bit —I'll give you another instance. Dang it all, don't be impatient, else you sha'n't hear it all. Well, as I was saying, I needn't go very far for an instance. There was my brother—a finer, bolder, stronger man never stepped. Well, what he was always miserable about was just this 'ere. Some old gipsy-woman had told him that he would be drowned, and this harped upon his feelings so, that everybody he knew was almost pestered to death with his unceasing inquiries for a child's caul to preserve him from a watery grave; but he needn't have given himself any trouble about the matter, for one night, while he was just stopping a gentleman's horse on Hounslow-heath, as he thought was going too rapidly for the gentleman's safety, the ungrateful owner sent a bullet clean through poor Jem's skull. Now, you see how wrong it is to worry one's self about things as may never happen."

"Well, Stumps," said Ironsides, "you have partly convinced me that I am wrong, and that I had better wait patiently the result; and if the worst comes to the worst, why let it, and there's an end of it."

"Now, that's speaking like a Briton," said Stumps; "and after that, I think I am justified in calling for something to drink at your expense."

"Call for what you like," hastily replied Ironsides, "and let's be gone."

"Ay, to be sure. I don't care how soon, for, to speak the blessed truth, I'm most rascally knocked up, and I suppose we shan't be able to get a conveyance; well, never mind, I'll have a long rest to-morrow, at all events." So saying, and Andrew having emptied his grog which he had ordered, they started on their return to the Lunatic Asylum.

As they passed the Eel and Frying-pan, where Stumps had been so unceremoniously ejected, Corporal Tim was closing the house; and, catching sight of the worthy couple, he could not refrain from hallooing after them.

"Stumps, I beg pardon—all right—have you caught 'em, eh?"

"Caught who?" roared Stumps.

"Why, Maud Selby and Jacky Jingle, to be sure; who did you think that I meant?"

"Hilloa!" observed Ironsides, "he's got their names pat enough; what in the name——"

"Stop," said Stumps. "No; I haven't caught 'em," said he, in reply to the corporal; "but how did you know their names?"

"Lord bless your green age!" said the corporal; "odd if I didn't know 'em; why, they've been here all day."

"Umph!" said Ironsides, "were they here when we called this morning?"

"I believe you, my boy," said the corporal.

"And how long have they been gone?"

"Why, as you can't catch them to-night, and as they'll be pretty safe after to-night is over, I don't mind letting you know that they left here as soon as it was dark enough to make it a difficult matter to distinguish their features."

"Umph! and did they go as they come?"

"No; they went the other way," said the corporal.

"I mean," said Ironsides, "was there any alteration made in their dress?"

"Why, you old jackass, you don't think we'd turn them out, as they turned themselves out of your den, do you? You must be jolly green, Mr. Gaoler, to think that."

"Confound you, your house, and your lying mistress, too," said Ironsides. "Stumps, we have been betrayed—made fools of, and we are ruined—ruined—ruined!"

Ironsides bit his lips till the blood spurted out, and stamped and raved like any madman. But the intelligence seemed to have very little, if any, effect upon the keeper, who, putting his hands into the pockets of his jacket, cooly observed—

"Ay, ay, Ironsides, we shall catch 'em yet—we shall catch 'em yet; oh yes, we shall be sure to catch 'em. My motto is, ' *Nil Desperandum!*' we shall catch 'em yet—ha, ha!—put that down in your memorandum-book, Mr. Ironsides, and you'd better do it in red ink, as it will catch your eye better."

"Hang you!" said Ironsides.

"The same to you, sir—remember my vow—I never forget! Put that down; come on, come on—mark that."

CHAPTER VI.

THE HOUSE OF REVELRY AND THE RIVER.

As the corporal had said, Maud Selby and Jacky Jingle, as soon as the darkness of the night had come on, had left the kindly shelter of the Eel and Frying-pan, where they had been so humanely treated by the good landlady, Mrs. Clutterbuck.

The Maud of the morning was in outward appearance very different to the Maud of the evening; for by the assistance of Mrs. Clutterbuck, she had been completely metamorphosed, and no one who had seen her in the deplorable condition in which she had escaped from the madhouse, would have recognised her in her present condition.

Jacky Jingle, too, doffed his white hat, so elegantly turned up with green, and in lieu thereof had substituted one belonging to the corporal—his short trousers and equally short jacket, had given place to a pair of black trousers and a coat, also belonging to the same individual, and altogether the appearance of the poor fellow was much improved.

When they were quite equipped and ready for starting on their nocturnal ramble, Maud felt her heart too full to speak a word to the good woman who had so kindly and gratuitously given a helping hand to her and Jingle when they so much required it; but grasping the hand of Mrs. Clutterback in her two, she kissed her cheek and burst into a torrent of tears.

"Nay—nay, my child," said Mrs. Clutterbuck, "I know what you would say, but I have only done a Christian's duty; and, indeed, I am better pleased without thanks; it only oppresses me to have more than a simple acknowledgment. Come—come, you have looked enough without saying anything. Be of good cheer, and hope for better days."

"Excellent woman," said Maud, who had partially succeeded in repressing her intensity of feeling. "Oh, that I may have it one day in my power to requite you for this unheard-of kindness. Never, to the longest day that I live, will I forget your goodness. Deserted by all, abandoned by those who should prize me above all earthly things, one who has been scorned, cast into a prison, scoffed at, and ill-treated by a cruel, heartless mob—oh, where should I have been, what miserable fate would have been mine, if you had not held out your hand and saved me?"

Jacky Jingle, who had been watching Maud's proceedings with a sort of lackadaisical expression of curiosity, now suddenly threw himself upon Corporal Tim, and imitating Maud's actions, began to splutter and maul the poor corporal till he was obliged to shake him off in self-defence.

"Hilloa, my beauty!" said Tim, "your servant always to command; but I don't understand the merits of this case at all—why, what's there to do now?"

Jingle caught hold of Corporal Tim's hand in both of his, as he had seen Maud do with Mrs. Clutterbuck, and giving it a severe grip, which made the sufferer wince again, he began in a most lachrymose wine—

"Oh, that I may have it one day in my—eh, eh? ah, I see—Jacky Jingle's not in his right wits to-day—he's not so bright as the sun, nor so dull as an oyster-shell—what is next, eh? Cockolorum, I have it—deserted by all the earthly prizes above me, scoffed at by an ill-treated mob, and cast in a miserable fate—eh? I say, Mr. Corporal, where are my straws that old Stumps said would turn into sugar-candy, if I left 'em in my ass's ears long enough, eh?"

"Oh, you don't want any straws, now, Jingle; old Stumps was only playing with you when he said it," said the corporal.

"I can't get along without them," said Jingle; "I'm looking at 'em every half hour, to see whether they are ready to suck, and Jacky Jingle must have his straws."

"Ah!" said Maud; "poor fellow, I suppose he requires something to produce excitement; we must give him something to cherish and care for, or he will be dull indeed."

"Here," said the landlady, handing Jacky a short pipe; "if you put this into your pocket, and don't look at it, except when nobody's looking at you, at the end of fifty years, it 'll be a pipe still."

"Lor, will it, though?" said the idiot.

"Of course it will," observed the corporal. "Then Jacky Jingle's a made man. Jacky, Jacky, Jingle, Jingle, Jo. Come into my pocket, you little fellow, and we'll often get a peep at you in the dark; poor thing—poor thing; there, there, don't make any noise; nobody shall disturb you, and old Stumps shan't touch you; you needn't be afraid of old Stumps. Ha! ha! ha! I've got him in my pocket; he can't get out, can he? He won't want to steal out o' nights to smell the fresh air, and to stuff his pockets full of green leaves to smell at in the day, when he's locked up; poor little fellow, he's very quiet, he don't kick. Ah! perhaps he's gone—eh? No, there he is, fast asleep; well, well, lie quiet, I won't whip you. Ha, ha! Jacky's a happy boy;" and the poor fellow skipped about the room, much delighted with the treasure in his possession.

The night was sufficiently shadowed for Maud to proceed, and once more thanking Mrs. Clutterbuck, and promising to let her know the mystery connected with her unhappy fate, if her enterprise that night should succeed, she left the hospitable old lady, and went on her road with Jingle by her side.

They were quite safe now from attracting particular attention, as they were both dressed in the same manner as ordinary foot passengers; and feeling thoroughly refreshed and invigorated by the kind treatment and repose they had had at the Eel and Frying-pan, they pursued their route with much easier feelings than they had done in the early morning, when the dread of pursuit was strong upon them.

Maud knew her way perfectly well, and nothing interposed to prevent her reaching the first object of her destination.

The neighbouring church clocks had just struck the hour of ten, when she found herself opposite to a large house in the then fashionable, or rather more fashionable than it is now, Russell Square. The place was all bustle and activity; coaches came rumbling along the road, and link boys, with their torches, were skipping and flashing about like so many imps in a fairy scene. Such a swearing of coachmen, and rumbling and creaking of wheels, and neighing of horses, and bawling, and calling, and shouting, and joking, were seldom heard in that locality. Then the running commentary on the company as they alighted from their carriages, which was kept up by the mob who were curiously looking on, and which was by no means uttered in a *sotto voce* tone, added to the liveliness of the scene; and then the bawling out the names of the lacqueys in the hall, which were passed up through a retinue of that exalted class, till the announcement reached their final destination, undergoing a most wonderful degree of metamorphoses, in addition to the amusing incidents aforesaid, creating in the mind of the sensible, but personally uninterested, observer, a scene of rare amusements; but not so with Maud, who, making up to this house of revelry, and grasping the railings for support, became a most attentive observer of all that was passing around her. An intense expression of the most painful interest she was taking in the proceedings, she could not help exhibiting. No smile at the light raillery indulged in by that crowd that lined each side of the passage, from the road to the door, kept free by the domestics for the easy passage of the visitors, relaxed a muscle of that face. No; like a beautiful statue, she remained immovable; but like one still, she raised a feeling of interest in her beholders. No one could observe that beautiful face which bore an expression of sadness, lighted up with the most eager intensity of curiosity, without feeling surprise and sorrow that she should appear so interested and anxious concerning the proceedings that were going on around her. She could have no feelings in common with them, that could induce her to display so much anxiety. Why should she remain so stoical, so transfixed, so immovable, when all about her, within and without, were full of life and frivolity? Yet there she stood, a living proof that she *was* more interested in that revely than the idlers who were remarking upon her conduct; but how or wherefore remained a mystery.

"The Marquis of Brindleback," exclaimed a lacquey's voice.

"Make way there for the Marquis of Biddlebat," echoed another at the door; and as the noble marquis entered the hall, the name might be heard gradually changing it's character, until the marquis descended into a Tittlebat."

"I say, Jem," said a link boy to another of his tribe.

"Well, old fellow, what do you say, when you say nothing?"

"Why, that's neither here nor there, and aint to the purpose; but that fellow they calls marquis is a rum 'um."

"Indeed!"

"Yes, and I believes he's precious short of the stumpy, although he is a marquis; he owes my old woman a mint of money for washing, and he won't come down with the tin."

"Lor' you don't say so? Well, I lighted his honour from Pall Mall one foggy night to his own house, in Grosvenor Square, and how do you think he paid me?"

"How should I know, you Sam, eh?"

"Why, you ought to know. He gave me a bill for it."

"Yes, you vagabond, and I cashed it for you; and as I could'nt get the money for it, I had it framed and glazed; and there it is stuck up in my drawing-room. And it's my great amusement when I'm at home enjoying my *otium cum dig*, as we used to say at the University—to lollop o' top of the sofa, and contemplate this 'ere piece of precious waste paper."

"Why didn't you sue him for it?" said a third.

"So I did, spooney, and I got a blessed judgment against him."

"Gammon," said another.

"Gammon! why you ignoramus, you just go and put down the blessed fee, and you'll see it registered; and my lawyer says, he must soon think of reviving it, or it 'll run out."

"Hear him, hear him, run out? Why, what's the use of registering it, if it runs out; why doesn't they keep it in; they're paid for it, I suppose?"

"Oh, what do you know about the law," ejaculated the holder of the bill. "I suppose you think a judgment is sum'at alive, and can cut away if it isn't chained up. What a blessed ignoramus you is, as I said afore; but, hilloa, here comes an ancient dame—who the devil's she?"

"Who's an ass now," exclaimed the ignoramus; "just as if everybody didn't know that that's the wife of the noble marquis."

"That, that 'ere piece of antiquity?"

"Why o' course it is."

"Well, some people take strange fits sometimes, but what could induce my noble marquis to marry his grandmother?"

"Why, just this here; he wanted tin, and she wanted a husband; and so apparently there was a mutual benefit. But all isn't as fair as meets the eye, and they were both disappointed; he didn't get the tin, and she in a manner of speaking didn't get a husband; for why?"

"Perhaps you'll favour the company with an answer to your question."

"Of course I means to do that; well then this was why. The old lady gammoned him that she had plenty of the stuff that 'makes the mare to go;' well, he being very deficient, I mean in that respect, flat proposed himself as a husband, which she being very anxious for, of course closed the bargain; and one of the stipulations on his side was, and to show the world it was pure love between 'em, and not a matter of business, that she should not require him to make any settlement of her property on herself; and as he had nothing of his own to settle on her, except his title, why, no settlement would be required at all; besides, the satisfaction they would have in dishing the lawyers, who, I know from experience, stick it in nicely in these matters, as they did into me when I married my virtuous blessed old gal."

"Well, go on, old fellow, we've swallowed that 'ere last one; go on."

"Well, as I was saying," continued the speaker, "the old lady gave in at once to this 'ere stipulation, and when a decent time had passed, they got tied together like a couple of asses, as they are; though God forgive me for speaking disrespectful of the nobility, our reditory rulers. Well, o' course the husband was very anxious to know what tin the old woman really had, expecting to make a precious grasp at the whole of it in consequence of their being no settlement, when it came out that she was only an incumbrancer, I think it's called, on a large estate, and used to receive her annuity half yearly; and I understand by some arrangement between her lawyer and the trusts of the deed under which she is entitled to receive this 'ere annuity, it is payable to her on her own receipt alone, and o' course the old woman takes care to receive it herself."

"Come, Joe, cut it short."

"Well, I'm coming to a climax, if you'll only just wait till I pick my teeth. Well, the noble marquis was very much surprised and annoyed, as you may well suppose, and he felt so disgusted at being so taken in, that I understand the tying of the insoluble knot 'atween 'em was the only ceremony that he could even bring his mind to perform; and so, as I said afore, he didn't get what he expected, nor did she get what she expected, a quiet kind-hearted, loving, stay-at-home, domesticated, hen-pecked husband. But, arter all, she's pretty liberal to him, for I hears, on good authority, that she allows him a matter of three bob and a kick a week."

"Well done, Joe," said one of the link-boy crew; "well done, my man: I gives you more credit for invention than I thought you possessed."

"God bless your unhappy soul," said Joe, "I'm so blessed full of it, that I means to set up a patent office, and register nothing at all more than my own inventions."

"Oh," said another, "and if they're all similar to the last, you'll get lots of patronage, and 'll be setting up your carriage, by-and-by."

"Why, I means to do that; and, by-the-by, you may as well give me your card while I thinks of it; and if I don't forget, I'll give you a turn now and then, in the way of your perfession, eh?"

"Very good," said the other; "I'm always ready to oblige my friends. Ah, here comes Mr. Schwabcauzt and his lady."

"Who?"

"You know well enough what I said; but I suppose you have an inclination to spoil my masticatory process; but if you really don't know, I'll chance it by giving his name again—it is Schwabcauzt."

"Well, I'll be hanged if I wouldn't rather be called Smith than that 'ere jaw-breaking name, at all events, though that's a very wulgar name. Have you anything to enlighten us with regard to this 'ere Swabgots?"

"Only that he's one of these 'ere beggarly German humbugs, who can't live in his own country upon fourpence a day, and consekwently has come over here to join some of his royal relations, and fatten upon the taxes that we poor injured link-boys is robbed out on, that's all."

"And enough too," said another.

"Yes, I believe you, my precious creature," said a previous speaker. "And you may chrondole this 'ere up in your treasury of knowledge, that so long as our blessed monarchs are foreigners, or are obliged, according to a stupid etiquette, to marry foreigners, so long will this 'ere state of things exist. Native talons are swallow'd up by German mendiocrity. English vocalists may sing like blessed angels; but a big-bellied German, with a voice rivalling a town bull roars 'em down, and they must shut up their 'tater traps. English painters may paint and daub till they're black in the face, their bootiful imitations of nature—but the palace patronises nothing but German art, where art is not natur; but a sort of something I don't know how well to describe—it puts me in mind of pieces of sculptor squeezed into canvas and varnished over—and the warst of it is, that our own artists, like jackasses, as they are, I daresay, will one day or another be obliged to imitate 'em to get a living at all. Oh, it's a blessed scheme, and all I can say is, that if by any miracle all native talons could be combined in one, blow me if I wouldn't emigrate to the very back of all the backwoods of America, and get a living among the savages."

"Ah, you is a specimen of true patriotism —you is," said another; "and you've come to wear some order of merit at your buttonhole. It would be a great loss if you were to leave us, even as you are, without any native talents; and it's my opinion, that we ought to make a special affidavy, that we thinks you are about to leave this blessed country, and that you owes us lots of tin, merely for the sake of keeping such a prodigy amongst us."

"Come, none of your gammon, Mr. Timothy Spindleshanks, for, although you do profess to honour your superiors, you know well enough it's only to humour Old Plush, one of the royal flunkies, who sometimes gives you a sixpenny job. I've often heard you at the Opera hoot the sentimental 'Talian screaming; and you well know that it acted on your inwards in a most unbecoming and disrespectful manner; and yet, when your employer, the aforesaid Old Plush, condescended to converse with you on the judicious patronage of the royal family, and of course the nobility, and hangers on, who are led by the nose like puppets are moved by them wires, you've been in raptures. No, no, Mr. Timothy, you're not the man for my money. Ah, fresh company."

"Hilloa!" said another, "that's Sir Giles Tunbelly, and a queer old fellow he is."

"What of him?" asked one.

"Why, a very curious history is Sir Giles's, very curious, indeed."

"Now, I dare say," said Joe, "you pretend to be very intimate with that 'ere knight's tale; but, howsomdever, go on, and I won't interrupt you whilst you stick to the truth."

"Well, among gentlemen," said the other, "no offence should be taken when one gentleman corrects another; and you and I being gentlemen, barring all the necessary elements of one, I shan't take no manner of offence at being set right when I was wrong."

"Very good," said Joe. "Now, perhaps, you'll go on."

"O' course I will. Let me see—where was I?"

"You were about to commence," said Joe.

"Ah, true. Well, you must know that this 'ere Sir Giles Tunbelly, who's just gone in, wasn't always a knight——"

"And consequently didn't always want a link-boy," interrupted Joe.

"Consekently not—but, as I said afore, he wasn't always a knight. His family was of a very ancient sort, the original stock of which it is said is so very ancient, that no records exist of its birth, parentage and education."

"Very good," said Joe; "so far, so correct. Go on, my lad, and sharpen your tongue a bit."

"I'm blowed if I go on at all, if you interrupts me," said the other; "you keep on putting the thread of my history quite out of twist."

"Beg pardon, my fine fellow. I forgives you—go on."

"Well, as I was saying, the history of

his stock is completely lost in the dark ages of time."

"Poet Laureate next death," said Joe, winking one eye at the rest of his companions.

"What, you will then—never mind. But," continued the narrator, "what written history was deficient in, tradition in some measure supplied; but as that tradition never reached me in all its beautiful simplicity, I'm only able to say that the belief of people in the part of the country from which Sir Giles came, is strongly in favour of its having been something most unkimmon. All that I actually knows upon the subject, from my own knowledge, is that the father of Sir Giles was a very small farmer in Sussex, and having a very large family, he was rather obfluxtigated to know what to do with them, some'at like the little old woman as you will recollect disposed of the superfluities of her matrimonial existence by stuffing them into her shoe."

"When I advised you," said Joe, "to sharpen your tongue, I meant you to deliver your history in a quick, sharp, narrative kind of way. I said nothing at all about oiling it, acos, if you lapses out in this here manner, interlacing a bit of nursery tales with your discourse, why we shall have this blessed history spring out into a regular three volume novel, which we can't by no means allow, not having the necessary time to hear it in to spare. But go on—go on."

"You're an interfering coxcomb," said the narrator, "and I should have been in the very pith of my matter if you'd only a' kept quiet. Well, this state of things sorely puzzled old Clodpole Tunbelly; so, after making his calculations very shrewdly, and to the merest fraction of a farthing, he came to the result that he couldn't keep young Giles much longer on his hands; and so, thinking he might as well start him at once on his road for his own account, he called him into his private room one day, and giving him a very tender and fatherly lecture, popped a crown piece into the palm of his hand, and affectionately bid him begone, and do the best he could for himself."

"Well, that was a kind old brick," said Joe: "I should have liked a dozen such fathers every day in the week."

"Don't regret it," said the other; "probably, for what you know, you are well provided in that 'ere respect. No offence, I hope. Gentleman, you know—gentlemanly remarks, eh?"

"Yes, yes—go on."

"Well, young Giles didn't much care, or take it to heart, but, like a wise lad, resolved to make the best of his fortune."

"A crown?" said Joe.

"Yes, his earthly crown. He spat upon it for luck, put it into his pocket, shook the old boy by the hand, turned his back upon the ancestral halls——"

"Draw it mild," interrupted Joe.

"I will, by your leave. Giles determined to try London: he was a wary bird, and tramped the distance from his home to London—cadging where he could, and fasting where he couldn't."

"Couldn't cadge, you mean?"

"Yes: and having arrived in this here metropolis, he pulled out the identical crown, and spit upon it again for further luck. Now, it strikes me, gem'men, that the man who could travel from a distant part of Sussex to London with only a crown to start with, and bring it to London whole, is just that sort of fellow who's likely to have so many on 'em, that he'll hardly know what to do with 'em."

"Give us your history," said Joe, "and keep your commentaries to yourself."

"As you please," said the other; "ornament, I dare say, is thrown away upon you."

"Not at all," observed Joe: "your whole history is ornament, and you know it is very foolish to gild gold."

"True; and I feel flattered by your purlite compliment. And," continued the narrator, "as Giles stood for the first time in London, he felt sore puzzled what course to pursue, or what line to take."

"Excuse me, brother Jerry," said Joe, "but it strikes me that what course to pursue, and what line to take, are tantamount and the same thing."

"Let those who live in glass houses be careful how they throw stones," quietly observed the other. "Well, as I was saying, Giles stood in a bewilderment as to what he was to do. He knew that nobody in London knew him, and he knew nobody in London; and he knew also that a crown wasn't a fortune, and that no investment he could think of would give him a dividend that he could live comfortably upon; and it struck him that if he went into every shop as he came to, and inquired if there were a vacancy, he might be lucky enough to hit upon something. No sooner resolved upon than done; for, let me observe, he was not one of those 'ere sort of fellows what puts his whole trust in Providence, and thinks no exertion of his own is required to get him on through the dangers and the difficulties of this life. No; he was quite a different chap entirely—quite entirely."

"Well, well, we'll take your word for less than that," said Joe. "Do get on, you warmint, or we shall never get through this 'ere blessed Tunbelly."

"All in good time my tulip. Well, he goes into shop after shop till at last he hears of a sort of office-boy being wanted at a certain large brewer's, and as he never let the grass grow beneath his hoofs, off he trudged like a sparrow after a hawk."

"Although I don't see that wery clearly," said Joe, "you've got my permission to go on, if it's only for the sake of getting to an end."

"If you interrupt me many more times, my jewel, I shall finish before I've ended, and then you'll be very sorry; you'll never sleep quiet o'nights for the memory of what you've lost. Am I to go on?"

"By all means," said Joe; "and the quicker the faster."

"True—well, then, when he was ushered into the presence of the great guns, cap in hand, he very respectfully made known his case, and the long and the short of it was, he was engaged as a sort of useful lad in the counting-house. In this situation he behaved with ever so much propriety that he became a sort of favourite; the clerks took pains to instruct him in all things necessary to qualify him for a higher situation; but as the rules of the house was, no one was put above another, but every one advanced in gradual procession."

"Progression, I should surmise?" said Joe.

"Be it progression then, if you please, though I don't see the difference, as the senior hands dropped off by death or other cassities."

"Casualities, would be better," observed Joe.

"Come, come, I can't stand this, Joe," said Mr. Jerry; "perhaps you'll finish the story yourself?"

"Oh no, pray go on, pray go on, it can't be in better hands; though I should like to see a little more attention paid to the king's English."

"Well, I'm blowed, you 're what I calls nasty particular; just as if you didn't know what I means by cassities, as well as if I'd said casselties. But no matter, here goes again. Well, as the old 'uns dropped off, the next hopped up into his perch, and a wery good rule too, and Giles was a very long while indeed in his first seat, afore he got a kick on the behind upwards, acos the old 'uns seemed to stick with very great pernacity."

"With what?" said Joe.

"Ah! my boy, there I've got the better of you, have I? What, you don't know the meaning of pernacity? then I'll just tell you, it's all the same as if a bird had got stuck to a twig covered with bird-lime, and couldn't get away, with this here difference, however, that they could have got away if they'd liked, but as they didn't like—why they stopped there. Well, Giles was a very clever hand at figures; rather a progedy."

"Prodigy's the correct word," said Joe.

"And," continued Jerry, "they found him very useful, indeed; and, at last, being quite aggravated at not having it in their power to advance him without breaking through the rules of the establishment, which had been observed for upwards of a century, they had a conversation together—that is, the governors—and determined that, upon the very first vacancy, they'd slip him in. Well, it happened as one of their travellers, who was rather addicted to the bottle, but a very honest chap for all that, was driving on his way homeward, wery fresh, wery fresh, indeed, with the swag that he had been collecting the few previous days—they've a better system now—he was stopped by a highwayman, and not being able to resist,

he lost all that 'ere swag; and when he became conscious of his folly, and considered over the matter, he hadn't got the face to see his old governors again; so he blew out his brains. That's how the story goes, though the fellow who robbed him was afterwards traced, and hung for his murder."

"Come—come," said Joe, "cut it short—cut it short; don't you see how many visitors are tumbling in, and we're losing all about them?"

"Oh, never mind them," continued Jerry, "we shall come at their lives some of these days; and in the meantime, I'll finish my story; there's not much more to come. Well, here was a blessed opportunity for shoving in Giles, and with a sort of desperation, they did it all at once, and all the other chaps, who were delayed rising a step in the ladder of promotion, had a cheque each, to the tune of £50, accompanied with a wery handsome apology. Well, sirs, time slipped on, and Giles walked into his governor's favour with prodigious strides, for he did a wonderful stroke of business; he had the knack of getting into the good graces of all he came across. Well, sirs, he was in the high road to fortune, and everything seemed to favour him; one blessed fine morning, the head of the firm was found dead in his bath, supposed to have been seized with a fit of plexy."

"A fit of what?" inquiried Joe.

"Why, I said plexy for short, but I meant appleplexy."

"Oh, very good—well?"

"Well, here was a chance for Giles anyhow; and so the remaining governors whipped him in at once as a junior partner, with a very liberal share in the profits, at the same time repeating the joke of the fifty pound cheque to the poor devils below. Well, gemmen, Giles was the youngest man among 'em by about thirty years, and in the natural course of events the elder partners dropped off one arter the other, until Giles was the oldest and only partner, and very rich he was—very rich! and you see what may be done with ability, economy, prudence, and all that 'ere sort of thing. He came up to London with a solitary crown in his pocket, and that 'ere very blessed crown as he never spent, is the medal most prized in all his collection."

"Ah," said Joe, "very well told for a young sort of a fellow like you: but you commenced your tale by stating that he wasn't always a knight, and left out at the last how he did become a knight.

"Very true," said Jerry; "that's done in no time. One day in conversation with a friend of his, who was the friend of somebody else, who knew a great man who was intimate with the nephew of a noble who was in the habit of occasionally dining at royal table, it came out that the king spoke in high terms of the malt he was smacking his precious lips over, and inquired whose it was. Now, Giles was not a man to let a hint drop, but he brewed a lot of special stuff, fit for a emperor, and sent it to the royal cellars gratis. Now we all knows that our blessed sovereign pays partickler attention to his bowels."

"True," said Joe; "I believe you, my tulip; he's a precious sight more bowels than brains."

"No blasphemy against the state," said Jerry. "Well, this tickled the royal fancy, and he sent one day to the blessed brewhouse for Giles to come and receive the royal thanks in person, and then and there he dubbed him a knight."

"Well," said Joe, "I doesn't think that Master Giles deserved such a honour for such a trifling act."

"Different men have diff-rent notions," continued Jerry, "and it's my opinion that to be a knight is no honour at all. After all, what is a knight?"

"Why, it's my particular opinion," joined in one of the crew, "that if all the knights are no better nor this one, we shan't become rich, for dang my buttons if I've picked up my crumbs yet."

"Wait a bit—wait a bit," said Joe; "our turn 'll come by and by. We shall do an alarming stroke of business when the party are sick of it—wait a bit."

During the whole of the joking and inventions of the light-hearted link-boys and idle crowd, Maud continued still in the same immovable attitude—the same expression of intense curiosity; as if she wished to have the power of seeing through the walls all that was passing within them; she maintained her place. Not a muscle of her face relaxed from its fixedness—not the shadow of a smile illumined her blanched cheek—though occasionally the dry remarks of the speakers succeeded in provoking the risible faculties of the other listeners. We say other, because, by what will appear after, she must have listened attentively to all the conversation that took place around her, though seeming not to do so. And poor Jacky Jingle, too, was an interested listener among the throng, and laughed when others laughed, and was grave when others were; not that he saw the point of anything that was said, but because he felt a sort of inward satisfaction at seeing so many happy faces about him, and laughed from mere sympathy.

"Room for Mr. Smith—room for Mr. Smith."

"Ay, ay—room for Mr. Smith;" and Mr. Smith capered up the steps with an alacrity that implied he was not the most favourably impressed with the pronunciation of his name, and wished at once to escape from the observation of the people.

"It's my turn now," said Spindleshanks, "to tell about half-a-dozen anecdotes, to make up for lost time, and to commence at once with this Mr. Smith. The name of Smith, you know, my boys, is as old as the hills, for the name originated from the trade to which the first ancestor gave his time to. Now, the more ancient a thing is, the more honourable it's generally considered to be."

"I don't exactly see that," said another.

"Give me a reason," said Spindleshanks, 'and I shall be content."

"Here's one just to the purpose:—I've got a grandmother, who, bless her old soul, is upwards of a hundred and four. Now, it doesn't follow acause she's ancient she's honourable—in this particular case more t'other, because I know from her earliest years up to the present time, she's been one of the most uncommon devils what's been allowed to take up room in this planet of ours.—Now, you see the more ancient the less honourable, as I feels convinced I have proved in the most logical manner as is; because being more ancient than most people, and being a wery bad old voman, why, she's the less honourable than if she hadn't been so ancient."

"Well," said Spindleshanks, "there are exceptions to every rule, and that's one on 'em; but be it as it may, this Smith dropped into something very smart, and then it occurred to him that S—m—i—t—h, Smith, was altogether too vulgar for him; and he conned it over with hisself day after day, until he badgered hisself into a belief that he had heard from some connection of the family that his name was spelt and pronounced differently in by-gone days; and the result of his cogitations was, that he most unmercifully slaughtered his original patronymic—and softened it into the more oily, smooth-going sound of Smythe, S—m—y—t—h—e, pronounced as I have spelt it, long, about the longest pronunciation of a short word that I know of."

"Well," said Joe, "I sees nothing wery pertickerly interesting in that anecdote, if it be an anecdote."

"I can't help that, my boy—it isn't in my power to furnish you with brains," replied Spindleshanks; "and I take leave to say, you must be very pagnatious not to see what I intended to illustrate."

"Pugnacious!" sneered Joe; "well, if that arnt a good 'un. Blow me, I shouldn't wonder, gentlemen, if he doesn't mean ascute, that is, dull, heavy, not able to comprehend the proposition; but as to pugnacious, that's quite out of the question, and I means to say that no man ought to dabble in hard words what he don't know the meaning of. Pugnacious is a term used, and much employed among Churchmen gemmen, and signifies a sort of pacificator in their quarrels; and I don't see how it applies at all to a man not being able to comprehend something stated —ascute is the word—ascute."

"Ha, ha, ha!" joined in one of the crowd, "you're a pretty corrector of an error. I'll undertake to say that there's no such a word in the English language, and the word you really mean is, after all, astute."

"It matters not two straws," said Spindleshanks, "whether I said pugnacious, ascute, or astute: you all knows what I meant; and I only brought this 'ere anecdote forward to show the absurdity of some people about

THE QUARREL BETWEEN IRONSIDES AND ANDREW STUMPS.

trifles. Now, who cares whether the man's called Smith, or Smythe? The man's the same, and no spelling nor pronouncing his name in a different manner will make him a jot different; and yet I've known him to be so anxious upon the subject, that he's actually feed the postmen of his district to alter all letters that may be directed to him in his old name of Smith afore they delivers 'em at his house, acause the blessed servants shan't see 'em; and don't he think of giving a lecture to the unconscious varmint who so directs 'em? Ah, I believe you, my boys, he just does."

"Well, I think," said Joe, "after that 'ere specimen of the quality of your anecdotes, we'll give you credit for the other five, and I, for one, haven't the slightest wish to take up your valuable time; and as I see a fresh character a coming to be dissected, why I proposes that Dicky Dishclout cuts him up."

"Bravo! bravo!" cried several voices. "Let Dicky Dishclout be the man."

"Gentlemen all," said that respectable individual, "I am a cove not much used to public speaking, as you are all well aware, if you knows it; but in as much as I am called upon by the voice of the people, in whom I acknowledge to be the sovereign power, I feels compelled to clear my throat, and do myself the honour to address this very select and permiscous audience. Gemmen—ahem! I must crave your indulgence for any defects of recoric, and can only assure you that defect in eloquence will be made up by quality. Well, to cut the matter short, as I see you are all anxious for me to commence, here goes."

No sooner said than done, for Dicky Dishclout took to his heels, and was out of sight in the twinkling of an eye, leaving his companions completely staggered at so sudden a disappearance.

"Hilloa!" said Joe, something must be in the wind to make Dicky leave such good company in such a violent hurry."

"Why, didn't you see the man arter him?" said Spindleshanks; "that man owes Dick some tin, which he was ordered to pay by the Court of Requests, in weekly instalments, and Dick was afraid that he wanted to pay him some weeks that were due, and so, to prevent the unpleasant necessity of incumbering himself with the blunt, he took to his heels."

"Ay—ay, I see," said Joe, "a queer chap that Dick, and one of the right sort. Well, genmen, as we've lost the benefit of Dick's eloquence, I'll endeavour to do the amiable. The lady and gemman who've just been ushered in under the name of Lawrence are very much to be pitied, particularly Mrs. Lawrence; there's something very melancholy in their story, and I never think on it without viping away a tear. Mrs. Lawrence's father was a decayed merchant; he he had once been at the very top of his profession, and he and his family had enjoyed all the luxuries of life, and never expected a turn downwards in the spoke of fortune's wheel."

"Did you speak of spokes?" interrupted Spindleshanks, who himself had been so much interrupted in his conversation; "because, if you did, I'll just thank you to speak of matter of fact, and don't launch out into metaphysics."

"Very good," said Joe, "I must adapt myself to the caparisons of my audience. Well; dropping fortune's wheel, suffice it to say, that when he did drop down through a misfortunate speculation, the old man couldn't hold up his head anyhow, and took it so much to heart that one fine morning he was found dead in his bed, and it is supposed in consequence of loss of blood, occasioned by a desperate slash he'd made in his throat, which the doctor said had severed the vertigo. And notwithstanding they sewed up the wound with a very fine needle and thread he never spoke again as I ever heard of, at least."

"Very surprising," said one.

"Very so, indeed," returned Joe, "but there are more things in Heaven and earth than are dreamt of in our physionom."

"The same remark has been made before," observed the other, by our national poet, Shakspere, with a slight difference."

"Not at all unlikely," said Joe, "the same idea will occur to different ind'viduals who've never thought at all about it. Well, after the old man was decently laid by the side of his forefathers, a desperate struggle was made by the friends of the family to secure from the wreck of his fortunes enough to put his wife in some sort of way of maintaining herself and her only daughter; and after a deal of trouble and difficulty, enough was scraped together to get her into a comfortable house, and stock it with furniture; and when this was done, they thought she might contrive to get her head above water, by letting furnished lodgings to them as hadn't got any furniture of their own, or as didn't want to be troubled with it. This scheme succeeded, and they were getting a very comfortable living, and might have put by money if they had been regular lodging-house-keepers, bred and born to the business; but as they'd never been used to it, why they hadn't got any of the dodges belonging to that maternity. Well, what are you tittering at now? I suppose I have made some blunder, but you're so precious critical, that I'm blessed if a man mustn't spell his words afore he speaks 'em in this here learned society."

"You merely said maternity, instead of faternity; go on, go on," said Spindleshanks.

"Is that all?" remarked Joe; "well, if that's all, I don't mind that; it's only a little wrong. Well, they hadn't been very long in this line of life, when a young man of the name of Lawrence, that same gent as has just gone in, and who was studying for the medical profession, takes up his abode with 'em, and boarded at their table as well as lodged with 'em. Somehow or another an intimacy sprang up atween him and the young lady, which was very natural considering that they were human creatures, and that she was a very nice young creature and very amiable, and all that sort of thing—and he a handsome, plausible sort of a fellow, and a clever fellow too. Well, the old mother never saw anything that was going on between these happy pair, as was not till it was too late.

"And how did she find it out," asked Spindleshanks.

"Ah," said Joe, "you're just one of those sort of chaps as wants to get at the marrow of a thing before you've broken the bone; and as I doesn't choose to begin at the ending and leave off in the middle, why, you must be content to get it as I chooses to give it you."

"I'm in no hurry for the matter of that," said Spindleshanks, "only if you don't bring your story to a close soon, we shall have to put off the interesting affair until a fitter opportunity, for the time's coming on when our professional abilities will be called into requisition, that's all"

"Never you fear, my hearty, all in good time and I shall cut it uncommonly short when I begin to see a movement in the house, but it strikes me the company haven't all come yet; and they keeps wery bad hours here, wery bad hours, indeed. Well, to go on again, the old woman at length found out what couldn't be very well much longer concealed—and you may guess her constipation at the discovery. An explanation was demanded and given, and it turned out that the young man had acted honourably, though injudically, which, for the benefit of that part of you which is without a liberal edication, I translate as doing the thing without sufficient forethought; he had married the girl unknown to her or his friends, in a devil-may-care sort of way, not thinking at at all of the consequences, thinking that he might have all the comforts of a home without any of the responsibilities, and acting as he had always acted—that is, as a single man. Well, this was all very well for him, but it didn't suit the temper of the old woman, and she insisted upon his making not only his father and friends acquainted with the affair, but the public in general by means of public papers, for her daughter's own credit. This stuck in his throat, and feeling himself a very ill-used man, he took other apartments for his wife, and they both left the old woman to do as she pleased. Well, sirs, the old lady published the announcement in all the principal paperss making some excusable apology for the lateness of its appearance, which you'll admit was highly necessary, considering that an announcement of a different character would so shortly have to make its appearance by means of the same vehicle."

"You means a carriage, o' course," said one.

"No, I mean a noospaper," said Joe.

"Why, then, didn't you call it a noospaper at once?" asked a querest.

"Acos I hadn't properly estimated my audience," retorted Joe, " or I should."

"Well, cut away, old brick" said the other. " I forgives you this once; but don't do it again, that's all."

"Well, sirs," continued Joe, "the old gentleman, the governor, who was a very religious old fellow, being one of the clergy, and a good Christian, as a matter of course, and, without his knowing all that, a very charitable man, and full of the milk of human kindness, was in a towering passion at the news; for he was very high in his notions, and fancied his son had lowered the dignity of his house, in marrying the daughter of a mere lodging-house-keeper, without name, rank, station, or fortune; and he wrote a very severe and cutting letter to the old lady, accusing her of planning all that had happend, for the sake of her blessed daughter, and a great many more unkind reflections which so preyed upon her mind, that she took ill, and died of an asthma in consequence; and, as the old man had discarded his son, and stopped his allowance, for very the impudent step he had taken, why the young 'un dropped down upon the furniture, and put it up to the hammer, and, in course, got through the produce in no time. Well, sirs, he ruminated and ruminated, over and over again, upon the hastiness of the step he had taken, and having finished his calkilations, and summed up the total, came to the conclusion that he had been a very great ass; and accordingly very much neglected his wife, as if she were the aggressor, instead of the victim. From neglect he came to blows, and many a time has he left the poor creature and her young 'un on the very brim of starvation."

"Brim?" asked Spindleshanks.

"Ay, brim. Won't that 'ere suit you?"

"No. not by no means. I want an explanation."

"Well, if you don't know what a brim is, I declines informing you, acos you ought to know."

"You'd make a precious good schoolmaster," said Spindleshanks, " I don't think. You would turn out some wise scholars, you would. A pupil who knew a thing, o' course, wouldn't want to be told, and that that he didn't know, you would't tell him because he ought to know."

"I stands corrected," said Joe. " I didn't see it in that light. I shall do myself the pleasure then of informing you, that a brim is—is when a person is on the very werge—that is—about to do—do—"

"That'll do," said the other; "I quite comprehend, and am much obliged, to you. But how long are you going to spin this out? Besides, I don't see anything very melancholy in the affair."

"Ah, we haven't come to that yet, although I have murdered two of the actors; and as to the length of it, why, if it don't agree with your feelings, do as I does when I am reading a interesting thing, skip what I think's just as well without it. Well, sirs, as I was saying, the continued implacatibility of his precious paternal parent rankling in his breast is the cause of his dissipating himself into a swine, and of avenging himself on his innocent wife and unoffending child ; and many's the time when he's been swizzling his bowels at the alehouse, there's not been a crust of bread for either of the poor devils at home, and they've been obliged to creep into bed, to sleep of the knawing pangs of hunger. I knows what hunger is, and, therefore, I pity 'em. And all this too, recollect, while the unfeeling husband has been drunk for a week, taking all the happiness to himself. Now, Mrs. Lawrence is a women, that, while she's got health and strength to do it, never refuses getting a miserable pittance by needlework, or any other light employment suited to her ; and, what I considers the worst part of the story is, that when he comes home after a week's rioting, he storms down the house until he gets her little savings, and goes out and spends it on himself. He's a confirmed scoundrel, and I hope he'll die of a *delirium tremens*."

" And what's that, pray ?"

" Why, it means," said Joe, " and, in fact, is short for a most tremendous delirium."

" Very good ; and now having brought this cock-and-a-bull story to an end, how is it that, they are here to-night, and look as if nothing were wrong behind the scenes ?"

" Simply for this reason, because the people here are friends of hers, and as Mr. Lawrence is in hopes of getting something out on 'em one of these days, he's hypocrite enough to appear as if he were the best and kindest of husbands in their presence, and she, poor creature, like all womankind, has never said a word to 'em about his goings on ; she never complains, never. She's a angel, if ever there were a angel, and if she doesn't deserve a pair of wings, why, I'm rather mistaken, rather I think."

" Well, to cut the matter short, as I said afore—"

" Here goes," said a voice behind, and the voice was discovered to belong to Dicky Dishclout, who had that moment again joined the throng, and was about to commence his narrative as if nothing had happened to prevent the delivery of it before.

" Much obliged, my beauty," said Joe ; " but we've taken that 'ere trouble off your shoulders, while you've been taking a turn round the corner. Why, what's up, man, anything the matter ?"

" A mere trifle," said Dicky ; " one of them things that we're all subject to, and makes us run round corners occasionally more or less."

" Oh, an infirmity of nature, in coorse," said Spindleshanks.

" I rayther think," said Dick, " it must be an infirmity of the blessed law."

" An infirmity of the law ?"

" No, a blessed warrant I takes it."

" You were prepared for something then, at all events," said Joe.

" Why, o' course I'm never asleep.— While I was preparing to make myself ready for this tale of the Lawrences, I caught sight of a couple of little, twinkling, sharp, grey eyes, looking rather suspiciously at me. ' Hilloa,' thinks I, ' I ought to know them 'ere eyes, for I've seed them afore ; and they've seed me, and as he seems to have brought 'em to a fix, I'd better be off, for I'm sure he wants me for that last little job ;' so off I cuts and doubles him ; and he'll never think of coming back here to-night to look for me, the ass ; and as I'm pretty safe, I am at your service, gentlemen.'

" What little job is that you were speaking of ?" asked Spindleshanks.

" If you think you'd be any the better for knowing," replied Dick, " why, I'll be your medical practitioness ; it was this here—a neighbour of mine, who's a large householder, had a tenant of his'n that gave him notice to quit, because the rain found its way through the roof ; and as the landlord, my friend, didn't believe him, but thought he was grumbling merely for the sake of grumbling, as is an amiable peculiarity of a good many people, why, o' course he didn't do nothing to the roof ; and, in course, his tenant did quit. Well, knowing my friend, the house, holder, to be a very obstinate man, and I, being desirous of doing him a good turn, determined to see if there were really any ground for complaint ; and, accordingly, one fine dark night, when all the neighbours had gone to bed—for I didn't like to excite their curiosity, which I should have done, if I had commenced my operations in the daytime— I mounted on the top of that 'ere house, and began a very careful scrutinisation of its roof. Well, for the life of me, I couldn't see no place where the wet could come through, and was wery much inclined to believe that the complaint of the tenant was tenantless ; but suddenly thinking that water will find its way through the merest pinhole, and as I couldn't get into the room below to find out where the damage was done, I had nothing left but to strip off the lead, to see if any traces of the mischief could be detected. Well, gemmen, I did the job in a masterly manner, until the very last moment, when I should have been most careful ; for in rolling it up, of course, to keep it out of the way of my examination, it somehow got too near the coping, and afore I could catch it, down it tippled into the back yard. Well, gemmen, in its fall, one end of it came against the parlour window, and not being a light weight, why, it played old gooseberry with sash, frame, and everything else, tearing away the stone-cill, and making a most violent and outrageous row. Such a noise as this was likely to make some disturbance in the dead of the night, in a quiet neighbourhood, and soon the place was all in a blessed commotion ; and that man with the little grey eyes was soon on the spot, and being rather used to this sort of thing, he made some calkilations which seemed to satisfy him, as to how the lead came into the back-yard; and looking up, he caught sight of my confounded nose hanging over the coping. Well, gemmen, perhaps it had been better for me to have faced the matter out, but it struck me I should have much difficulty in making him believe my story; and more, perhaps, in getting my friend, the householder, to recognise me as one of his most intimates; and, therefore, I made the best of my way from that 'ere roof, and managed to elude the man with the little grey eyes until this blessed evening.— Now, you see, gemmen, that I'm as innocent as the babe unborn, and it's a practical lesson to me, and I hope to you all, never to meddle with business that in no way concerns you."

"Very good, very good, indeed," said Joe. "You are a blessed innocent, a poor suffering lamb; but it strikes me that you'll be nabbed afore long; that nose of yours 'll be sure to betray you. Why, Dick, I think it more ponderous than ever; you'll be obliged to have a prop fastened to your chin, by-and-by, to prevent its hiding your shirt front. How much do you think it weighs now—; pound and a half?"

"Now, I can't say exactly, but I certainly admit that you can't be far off the truth. I've a very great mind to have it operated upon, and pared down to the ordinary level of noses, for it's got me into many a blessed scrape, when, if it hadn't been for that, I should have got off scot free. But I proposes to get back again to business; and as you've heard of the story of Lawrences, and as there seems no fresh company stirring, mayhap it would not be out o' place to give you a short sketch of this here worthy gentleman what is the occasion of this rout to-night."

"Very good—go on, my man; but don't go off as you did afore, else we shall exclude you from our social throng altogether."

Maud, who had hitherto remained apparently a listless listener, now, for the first time since she had reached that house, seemed to give the whole of her attention to the man who was about to relate something appertaining to the owner, who, having cleared his throat with the usual ahem! proceeded as follows:—

"Gemmen," said he, "you will be good enough to take the introduction that I gave to the story, which I expected to have had the honour of favouring you with, with respect to the Lawrences, as the introduction to this."

"Oh, never mind any introduction," said Spindleshanks; "we can very well do without that."

"You may do so," observed the other, "if you please. Every man to his taste, I say, and no dictation. Now, for my part I'd as soon tell a story without an introduction, as I would eat bread and cheese without an ingun, for like the last named vegetable, it gives a zest to the principal commodity; and

let me ask if a comedy or a tragedy were brought upon the legitimate boards in less than five acts—the old established rules—let me ask, I say, whether it wouldn't be d—d, without hope of redemption? Of course it would: and, therefore, an introduction is necessary for a story."

"Oh, bother," said Joe, "that's all very well for crickets, as don't know any better; but we who does know a little more will overlook that defect, if it be a defect."

"Well, I maintain the justice of my observations, and having been brought up a scholar, I can't forget what is due to edication, and I insists upon that 'ere introduction being appended to what I'm going to tell all the same, as if it were meant for it; and, if so be as that don't please you, why, the long and short of it is, I must furnish up another for you."

"Well, well, as it'll suit one story as well as the other, there can't be much in it; and I, for one am quite content to submit, although, at the same time, under pretext," said Joe.

"And I, and I," said the others, "all under pretext."

"Your protest be jingoed," said Dick. "Well, gemmen, I can't say much of this here gemman afore he got married, or much after; and as I'm not given to invention, and say nothing more than I can pretty tolerably be bound for, what I have to say will not be very interesting; but as it's merely to fill up a blank until some one more gifted with the gab has a opportunity to exercise it, why, you shall have all I know. Well, as I said before, he got to France——"

"Stop, stop," cried several voices. "France! why, jiggered if you'd commenced at all."

"Oh, hadn't I," said Dick, "well, I'm very sorry—then I had better commence again, and take up the story where I left off, after he'd returned from the continent. Well, then——'.

"Hold hard," said Spindleshanks, "it seems to me you're poking fun at us, and if you doesn't come to the point at once in a roundabout sort of way, I'll just take your job off your shoulders, and astonish the natives myself."

"Oh, that's a very different matter," said Dick; "and rather than submit to such an infliction, I'll endeavour to scatter my collected thoughts, and tell my tale in such a straightfor'ard way as shall be perfectly exceptionable to everybody. Well, sirs, this here gentleman, it is rumoured, some time ago had a most beautiful, interesting, affectionate, and amiable wife."

"He's got her now, hasn't he?" asked Joe.

"Wait and see," said Dick. "Whom it was also rumoured he was very fond of— very fond of. In the course of time they had a child, it is also rumoured; which also it is rumoured——"

"Confound your rumours!" exclaimed Spindleshanks; "we shall have nothing but a tale of rumours."

"Probably so," said Dick; "the beginning of which will be rumour, the middle rumour, and the end rumour. I told you I didn't know the early part of the story of my own knowledge, and you must take what you can get. Well, it is rumoured that he loved the child as much as he did the mother—in fact, that he doated upon 'em, and what was the consequence? Why, when they went to the continent, as I was going on with when you interrupted me, the wife, as I said before, after a residence of a few weeks with her husband there, died."

"Died!" said Maud.

"Hilloa!" exclaimed Dick; "why, yes, died; is there anything very extraordinary in that?"

"Are you sure she died?" anxiously inquired Maud.

"Sure," said Dick; "ay, as sure as I've got a nose on my face."

"Then there's no mistake about that," said Joe.

"None whatever," continued Dick, "for I saw it myself in a list of births, in the *Times*, and you know that that being a paper which never inserts anything as isn't true, particularly when they isn't paid for it, why, I means to say that there isn't much doubt upon it. Well, sirs, the husband didn't wait the usual period as such an event required, particularly as he was so very fond of his deceased wife when she was alive, for afore he'd been a widow six months, he brings home another, a fine strapping crummy French woman, and left his kid behind him to be edicated."

"'Tis false," cried Maud, "he could not have brought home another wife."

"Well, marm, you seems to know all about it—perhaps you'll finish what I've got to say?"

"Monster!" exclaimed Maud

"Did you apply that 'ere to me, marm?"

"No, no—forgive me, forgive me—I meant not you. Go on, go on—for pity's sake go on."

"Well, I hav'nt much more to say, but as you seem so very anxious about it, I'll give it to you in no time. "Now," continued he, "I didn't say that he brought home a wife as you interpretated, although he's given out such to be the fact, but I doesn't believe it not a bit the more for that, not I. No wife would go galivanting about as she does, and somehow or another she doesn't look like a wife, but all the precious idiots believe she is his wife."

"I'm a idiot," joined in Jacky Jingle; "I'm a idiot, Bill Stumps says I am—ha, ha!"

"Quiet, Jacky, quiet," said Maud, "they'll find us out."

"I'm a idiot—I'm a idiot," reiterated Jacky; "oh, I'm a rare idiot! But I look like one, Stumps says; I do—don't I?"

"Here's a lark in the wind," said Joe; "we'll have him out for a scot."

"What's a scot?" asked Jacky. "Is it anything to eat? Jacky Jingle's getting very hungry again; give us a scot—give us a scot."

"Can you play upon the fiddle Jacky?—Eh?"

"Oh, I can play a rare game upon my chin," said Jacky, "hear me;" and with that Jacky gratified the mob with a very scientific display of chin-chopping, equal to anything of a similar nature exhibited at our national establishments.

"Bravo, bravo," cried several voices, "bravo Jacky, can you do anything else?"

"Do you think Jacky's a fool?" said Jingle, "look at me;" and he immediately repeated his favourite amusement, which we have before mentioned he was so proficient a performer in. "There," said he, "old Stumps taught the idiot that."

"And a very pretty accomplishment too," said Spindleshanks, "and you do your master much credit."

"Shall I do it again?" said Jacky, and without waiting for a reply, he commenced, and repeating the operation in rapid succession, there is no knowing how long he would have continued, had not some one from behind very unceremoniously put an end to it, by giving him a sharp chuck under the chin, which had the effect of nearly severing the poor fellow's instrument of amusement into two.

"Coward!" exclaimed Maud, "would you strike one whom God has deprived of his intellect, one who is incapable of protecting himself? Would you strike the child, or the defenceless woman? Yes, yes—for you dare not attack a man! I am ashamed of you, mean, spiritless, and dastardly coward!"

"You're quite right," said Spindleshanks, "and the fellow who did it deserves a licking, and I swear he shall have it too, let him be who he may." Saying which, Spindleshanks turned up the cuffs of his coat, and putting himself into a sparring attitude, hit a tremendous blow at the cowardly scoundrel who had been guilty of so unworthy an act, who, just before the blow came home, ducked his head, and it took effect upon the *chapeau de France* of an exquisite, who had just popped his head in to see what was going on, while the individual for whom it was intended made his escape in the confusion that ensued.

When things had settled down again into their former state, Maud implored Dicky Dishclout to proceed with his story, which he did in the following manner:—

"Well, sirs, my opinion is that the woman he is living with is no more his wife than I am his wife, which of course I am not; and I feel satisfied of this for a good many reasons—one of 'em is, that he doesn't much mind what society he introduces her to; another is, that he lavishes a mint of money upon her, which husbands are not in the habit of doing on their wives; one more is, that when he's out o' town, which he is occasionally, madam's at the Opera, where she goes alone, but seldom returns so; another grand one is, that she is intimate with a French milliner in this city, where she spends a good deal of her time, which is very suspicious; another is, that she doesn't behave to him like a wife; and the last and best is, that I don't believe her to be his wife, and there's the long and the short of it.

"Crikey, Dick," said Joe, "catch hold of the young woman. Don't you see she's going?"

"Going where?" said Dick.

"Go to the devil," replied Joe, as he sprang forward and caught the fainting Maud in his arms. "Don't you see that she's dying? Here, Jacky, where does your sister live?"

"La, la! Jacky hasn't got a sister," said the idiot; "and we don't live anywhere."

"Haven't you any home?" asked Joe.

"La, home! What's a home?"

"Where do you sleep?" continued Joe.

"Sometimes in one place, and sometimes in another. La! isn't it pleasant?"

"Poor fellow, we shall never get anything out of you," said Joe. "What's to be done, comrades? We can't let the woman die in the streets."

"It strikes me," said Dicky, "that the interest she felt in what I was saying about the proprietor of this house, bespeaks a nearer connection with him than we suppose. Perhaps she's a cast off piece of his'n, and 's precious jealous at his keeping another. And if it be so, why, there can't be any harm in letting him know what state she's in—so here goes," and advancing up the steps of the mansion, Dicky rang a tremendous peal upon the area bell. "That 'll bring 'em," said he.

A spruce flunkey with a powdered head immediately answered the door, and Dicky imparted to him the intelligence that a particular friend of his master's had fallen down at the door-step, and he believed she was in a dying state, and requested that she might be brought into the hall and properly attended to."

"Let's have a squint," said the flunkey. "What! she a friend? Why, dash you imperence, do you want to make a fool of me?"

"Not by no manner of means," said Dick, "for that's impossible, old Powder-plush, quite impossible. You go and acquaint your master that a friend of his who can't come in, is anxiously waiting to see him at the door. Do you hear?"

"I'll see you pretty well blowed first, you common fellow. Well, I never."

"Then I tell you what it is," said Dick; "if you doesn't do it, and directly too, blow me if I don't act the flunkey myself for once, and tell him myself."

"La! Ha, ha, ha! I should like to see you, indeed."

"You would?"

"Yes. Ha, ha, ha. I should indeed."

"Then I'm blessed if you shan't. So here goes."

No sooner said than done. To put his leg between the two bandy ones of the footman was the work of the hundredth part of a second, and giving it a sharp jerk, Powder-plush, as he lay on his back in the hall, was an apt illustration of the power of leverage. Dicky made his way without hesitation into the ball-room, and bawled out in his professional way—

"That a lady visitor was below anxiously waiting to see the gentleman of the house; that she was taken so suddenly ill she could not possibly get further than the door, or she would."

The suddenness of Dick's entrance into the room, and his announcement produced a consternation amongst the company to no little amount; and the gentleman to whom Dick's message was destined, evidently much annoyed by the manner in which the news had reached him, exclaimed—

"Where are my servants, sir, that you—how am I to account for your pæsence here?"

"Why, your honour," said Dick, "old Powder-plush I think has been drinking a little, for I left him in the hall, on his back, studying the graining of the ceiling; and finding I could get no one to communicate my message, I was necessitated to be the bearer of the news, and that, your honour, accounts for my presence here. Is you a-coming?"

"Go," replied he: "I shall be there presently."

"Your honour had better look sharp, as the cloth said to the needle, or your honour 'll be too late, and no mistake. Come, are you a-coming? I'm waiting for your honour"

"Go, instantly, sir, and say what I have told you."

"Oh, very good," said Dick, "very good, if your honour pleases, as they says in the Vice-Chancellor's Court, when they commences making a motion. Then I am to say you're a-coming, am I?"

"Curse the fellow. I suppose I must go with you, or I shall never get you out of the place."

"Of course, you wouldn't. Come—come along, or we shall have the lady die; and as she was very particular in requesting me to let you know she wished you to see her afore that 'ere sad event happened, I was too tender-hearted to deny her, and too much a man of honour not to do what I promised. Come—come along."

This last speech took place as the couple were coming down the staircase, and at the end of it they had reached the street-door. Dick made way through the crowd for the free passage of his companion, who, following in his wake, looked around him for his visitor, who was so ill, and was so anxiously waiting to see him, fully expecting to find the sick visitant to be some fashionable lady whom he had invited to the ball; and he was not a little dismayed to see before him a woman in anything but visiting array resting in the arms of Joe; but having proceeded thus far in the adventure, he determined to see the end of it, if only to gratify the curiosity which had been raised in his mind by the occurrence. Stepping close up, therefore, to the object of his scrutiny, with a lantern he had borrowed from one of the men, he stooped down to look at the face of Maud, and no sooner had he done so than, dropping the lantern, a strong spasm shot across his face for a moment, and, with violent excitement, he exclaimed, in loud and rapid tones—

"How came she here? Who brought her? I know her not. Curse her—trample upon her—drown her—do anything with her, but take her from here."

"Well, but she's dying," said Joe, "and she says she knows you. You wouldn't let her die like a dog, would you?"

"Let her die," said he: "what is she to me, rascal? I know nothing of her, I say, and want to know nothing of her. Let her die—let her die!" and having delivered himself of this humane speech, he hastily withdrew into the house.

"Well," said Dick, "he's a nice one, and no mistake."

"You're just about right," said Joe; "and it strikes me he knows more about the poor woman than he wishes us to know—that's my opinion."

"And mine, too," said Spindleshanks; "and I felt very much inclined to give him a wipe on the side of his nob, if it were only just for his barbarity. She might well call him a monster."

"It's no use talking over the matter any more," said Joe; "something must be done for the poor creature; and the sooner the better. Come, Spindleshanks, will you take charge of her?"

"Well," said that individual, "I don't mind if I do, for a short time; but if she's going to be ill, or to die, why, you know, I can't afford to keep her for long, and I must, in course, sign her over to the workhouse; and there's that poor chap with her, too—what's to be done with him?"

"Oh, take him with you; you can keep him till the morning, and then you know you can see better in the daylight what's to be done with 'em."

"True—true," said Spindleshanks; "my old woman's a true hearted one all up her back, and she'll take care of the critters, I dare say, till we sees what's to be done. Now, Joe, she's in very good hands, I supposes you'll bear a hand in getting her to my crib."

"Oh, certainly, my boy, come along. Here, you Jacky Jingle, follow behind, and mind we doesn't step on your heels."

"La!" said Jacky, "how funny; who's to carry me?"

"Come on," said Joe; "we'll carry you when we come back."

"La! will you? poor Jacky's a lucky idiot. Old Stumps always said I was born to good luck, he did—always said so—upon my life,

he did. What, won't you believe me? La! how funny."

"Come—come along, Jacky, put your best leg foremost, and keep the other in front; come, step along."

The two men proceeded slowly to convey the wretched Maud to the dwelling-place of Spindleshanks, which was situated in a place called the Colonnade, in the immediate neighbourhood of the scene which we have just described. Poor Jacky Jingle walked listlessly by their side, sometimes earnestly gazing at the pale face of his unfortunate fellow traveller, sometimes repeating his favourite amusement, notwithstanding the pain it must have given him, in consequence of the rough play with which his tongue had met; and at others whistling and humming a few wild notes, tuneless and meaningless as his own wandering thoughts. They soon reached the home of the benevolent link-boy, and having explained to his better half the particulars which led to the visit, every care and attention that was possible, and within the means of Mrs. Spindleshanks to bestow, was bestowed with a hearty good-will, that did her infinite credit; but it was long after the two men had left Maud in the hands of Mrs. Spindleshanks, and returned to their avocation, before she was restored to the consciousness of all that had passed, and of her situation. She recollected all that had happened up to the time of her having fainted, and Mrs. Spindleshanks told her the scene which had afterwards ensued between her husband and the gentlemen.

"Lost, lost!" said Maud, "for ever lost! cruel and unkind man, may the great God in his mercy yet open your eyes, that you may see the enormity of your sins. My child, too—my dear little one, whose pretty prattle once so charmed me, never shall I see you more—never again will those little arms twine themselves round my neck. O God! O God! soften his heart, that he may protect and love my little one. What did he tell them to kill me—to trample me to death—to drown me? And did he, when he thought I was dying, curse me?"

"So said my husband, ma'am," said Mrs. Spindleshanks; "and I have no doubt he did."

"La! I heard him," said Jacky Jingle, who was employed at a little table, examining the anatomy of a Dutch doll that belonged to some one in the house. "He said, let her die and be d—d. La! how this child moves its legs and arms—la! how funny."

"Inhuman, unfeeling man!" exclaimed Maud; "but I will not reproach you—I will not return evil for evil. No more happiness in this world for me. It is my destiny—it is my destiny. Trample her to death—drown her; unkind, heart-breaking words! And I love him so, even now, after all his persecution of me—above all things I love him!" and she sobbed convulsively. "Drown, drown," she continued; "ay, 'tis well, 'tis well—but, oh God! oh God! upon

THE LANDLADY OF THE EEL AND FRYING PAN GIVING REFRESHMENTS TO MAUD AND THE IDIOT.

my head be the blame, not upon his—oh no! not upon his."

A boy whom Mrs. Spindleshanks had sent out a few minutes before for some writing materials, at the request of Maud, now returned with the same, and Maud wrote a letter, which, having sealed and addressed, she placed carefully in her bosom, and rising from the table, she hastily put on her bonnet and shawl, preparatory to her issuing forth once more.

"Ma'am, ma'am, what are you going to do?" said the good woman; "surely, you'll not leave to-night."

"I must," said Maud; "I have an errand to perform, and I must go."

"Surely it may be done by a messenger," said Mrs. Spindleshanks. "Is it to deliver that letter?"

"It can only be done by myself," said Maud. "I must return to that house of revelry, and watch, and watch, till it is deserted."

"Well, well, if you're only going there, why I don't much mind, only it is very late for you to go out again: but, however, excuse me; of course, you know your own affairs better than I can, and therefore can best judge what is fit and what is unfit. Can I see you to the place?"

"No, no," said Maud, "I can find my way; and now let me thank you for the kindness which you and your husband have shown to me and this poor youth. Although I cannot reward you, God never forgets those who have been charitable to the unfortunate."

Maud and Jacky retraced their steps to Russell-square, but they did not stay an instant before the house which had been the object of so much contemplation by Maud; and, walking on the opposite side, they hurried on in the direction of Holborn, and continued their route in the direction of the Strand, uninterrupted by the few stragglers that were about the streets at that time of the night, or rather morning.

Some fixed determination had evidently taken possession of Maud, for she continued on her route, not like one who has no object to arrive at, and who is indifferent which way his steps might lead. Not wavering for an instant as to the track she should pursue, she walked steadily onwards until she arrived in the Strand, down one of the little alleys of which, leading to the river, she proceeded, followed by Jacky Jingle.

The night was bleak, windy, and obscure; the rain beat in the face of Maud in squally gusts; and the sharp easterly wind penetrated her very bones with its coldness. To about half way across the river might be seen a few lazy barges, heavily laden, creeping up or down the river, as the case might be, but beyond that all was obscurity, except the twinkle of a few lights, which might be seen on the opposite shore, looming out through the darkness. All was still as death, except the elements themselves; not a human crea-

ture was to be seen, nor a human voice to be heard. Like a city of the dead, the great Babylon slept. It seemed to Maud as if she and the poor idiot, her companion, were the only two inhabitants of the vast metropolis, and the sensation of melancholy produced by the thought of her loneliness was intense. Maud stood at the very edge of the water, contemplating the scene for some moments; and with the big tears coursing down her pale cheeks, she sank upon her knees, and was soon absorbed in a long, fervent, and silent prayer to her Maker.

And let us hope that He will forgive her the deadly sin which she evidently is contemplating.

Poor Jacky Jingle fell upon his knees too, but why or wherefore he knew not; and as Maud rose, so rose he; and looking in the face of Maud, he said—

"Maud, what did you bring Jacky here for? La! this is not so pleasant as the green fields that I used to steal out to look upon. Come—come away, and let us go back to our old home. Come, cock-a-biddy, come, let's get back; come, it's so cold here."

"Poor fellow," said Maud. "Maud will never go back with you again. She will leave you here, and may God in his infinite mercy pity you, and protect you. The time is come, Jacky, when you and I must take a long farewell, and may He also forgive me the sin of leading you from, to you, a happy home, to further my purposes, though innocently done, and without a thought as to the result. Jacky, do you think you could find your way back to that house we stood so long opposite to?"

"La, what all alone?"

"Yes, my poor fellow, for I cannot be with you to show you the way. Will you try?"

"Yes," said the idiot; "and if I lose myself, old Stumps will find me, and he can show me the way,"

"No, no," said Maud, "wait not till Stumps finds you, but take this letter. Can you read?"

"I could at one time," said Jacky, "but I haven't tried so long, that I don't know whether I can or not. La!"

"It's of little consequence," said Maud; "take this letter, and if you have any difficulty in finding your way back, show it to any passenger."

"What's a passenger?" asked Jacky.

"Any one you may meet with on your road; and ask him to direct you to the place described on it; but, Jacky, be sure you don't let it get out of your possession—no, not for all the world, but deliver it to the person to whom it is addressed yourself. Jacky, do you understand?"

"How funny!" said Jacky; why, of course I do. Do you think I'm a fool?"

"Will you promise to do that, Jacky? It is the last request that ever I shall make to you, and, I am sure, for my sake, you will religiously observe what I require of you."

"I will do all that I can do for you," said Jacky; "but you must tell me again what I am to do, because I may make some mistake."

"First find your way back to the house I speak of."

"Yes."

"If you lose your way, show any one you meet that letter, and ask him to direct you."

"Yes."

"When you get to the house, deliver it yourself to the person to whom it is addressed."

"Yes."

"And do not, on any account, let it go out of your hand till you have delivered it to him."

"Yes—no, I mean—I will do so; that is, I will do what you say. La, how funny this is; but why can't you come back with me, Maud?"

"I am going to meet my God face to face, for good or evil. Farewell, Jacky, poor fellow, farewell. Drown her—trample upon her—let her die—I knew her not—drown her: those were his words. Lost, lost for ever, my child, my child! may Heaven protect thee."

For one moment the dark waters divided, and then closed over the unhappy Maud Selby and her troubles.

The idiot stood transfixed to the spot; and, although he had all the inclination to rush in after Maud, to endeavour to draw her back, he felt that he could not move one step from the place; but during that short space of time between the act of Maud, and the knowledge of his inability to rescue her, a miracle had been performed, which will be related in its proper place.

CHAPTER VII.

THE OLD HOUSE OF THE MENZIES.—ITS PEARL AND ITS ADMIRER.

SOME three or four years previously to the opening of this narrative, there stood in the immediate neighbourhood of what is now the Regent's-park, one of those old family mansions that brings to the mind's eye, scenes of long by-gone ages; but which has long been swept away by the improvements in that locality. It was one of those glorious old buildings of red brick, dressed with stone of the Tudor and Elizabethan styles, and had been for many ages in the family of the Menzies—a family at one time of considerable standing.

At the time of which we are now writing, its possessor was old Ralph Menzies, a very worthy and eccentric old gentleman, who had all his life been in the legal profession, which, when he found that his energies were too much used up to allow him to exercise them with that skill and ability so necessary for his own credit's sake, and for the good of his clients, he very hesitatingly gave up. Old

Ralph did not retire from the busy and exciting profession of the law without a severe struggle; but three slips following in rapid succession had at once the effect of bringing the argument to a conclusion with one who never had made a slip before. He very truly thought that a reputation well earned had better be well preserved; and, accordingly, with a good grace, he gave up his business to an old and faithful clerk, and used all his interest to secure it to him.

Ralph never could forget the regularity of habits long cherished and continually practised by him when actively moving in his profession, and what he had been used to do for forty or fifty years previously, every day if he had lived to a hundred, he would have been found doing precisely the same thing at precisely the same hour, that is, those things which continued necessary to be done. He was a man strictly of his word; what he said he would do might be looked upon as done; and calculations might be made with perfect safety upon his slightest promise. Punctuality, too, was another great trait in his character; and if he should happen to be a minute before his time at an appointment, he would wait until that minute had elapsed ere he made his presence known; a minute after he never was; and the same rule he made hold equally with those who had to keep an appointment with him; if they were a minute too soon, he made them wait; if a minute too late, he would not see them at all. He was not only the spirit of punctuality, but the very letter also.

Another peculiarity of of Ralph's was, that having been so completely absorbed in the love and the study of the law from his very childhood, he could not get rid of using legal phraseology in common and ordinary conversation; and this, in many instances, was excessively awkward to those with whom he was conversing, whose station in life precluded them from having attained that general knowledge which will enable a well-educated man to understand what is said to him, notwithstanding the speaker may use the technical terms of the legal or any other profession.

Ralph Menzies was the last male of his branch of the family. He was never married, for, as he said, he had never had time to court, even if he had had any one to court, and as no lady had even come to him for the purpose of being courted, he had never had the opportunity, and therefore he did not deserve to be censured. It certainly could not be from any selfish motive that he remained single, for he was the most open-handed man in the world, and was liberal to a fault; nor could it be from scanty means, for, besides the profits of his profession, he was rich by inheritance; but the truth is, his whole soul was absorbed and buried in the law, a sort of mind, idiosyncracy—law, nothing but law. Even the time bestowed for his meals was given with an ill grace, though, by-the-by, even then, when he could do so without a positive breach of good manners, he would indulge in what he called the amusements of the law—that is, the reading of a treatise on some difficult and abstruse point that had arisen, but which might never again arise. He was a very great authority, was Ralph Menzies, and was much looked up to by his professional brethren. It is said that more than once he had been consulted by the highest legal fudctionary of the day, when he had been at a loss for a precedent; and that, by-the-by, recals to our recollection that the memory of Ralph was of a most marvellous character. He was a perfect legal encyclopedia of dates, cases, volumes, pages, and sections; and, as an instance of this most precious gift, we need only instance a case in point. It was this :—It happened that a link in the title to an estate he had sold was required by a certain limited time—it was a will—and as the time before the required copy could be obtained from Doctors' Commons would exceed the time limited for an abstract of it to be delivered, Ralph, not doubting his powers undertook to furnish the required abstract within the time ; he, accordingly, went to Doctors' Commons, read through the will, which was very long and awfully complicated, and returning to his office, dictated to one of his clerks a full and perfect abstract, which was found, upon examination, to be all that could be required

It happened that Ralph had a sister, a few years younger than himself, who was also wedded to a library, his only sister, and whom, notwithstanding, a natural acidity of temper, which was a little heightened by a supposed disappointment in love, he was particularly fond of. This maiden lady now, since the death of their parents, had kept house for Ralph, and Ralph had surrendered into her hands the entire management of all the domestic affairs ; and as she made it her study to humour all his peculiarities, everything passed to their mutual satisfaction. He never interfered with what he had surrendered to her generalship, and, of course, his pursuits were of that character that left him likewise free from the interference of his sister. But as human perfectibility is a thing yet to be seen, Grace cannot be blamed for a little peculiarity. common to the tender sex : she was a little given to contradiction, which, if she had been gifted with that faculty which is not common to her sex. that is, the ability to reason, she might not have lain herself open to the accusation of. And as Ralph used to tell her, that ladies were incapable of doing four things, that is, understanding Latin, Greek, Hebrew, and reason, he never quarrelled with her for flatly contradicting anything which he stated to her, and which might be proved with a very little amount of argument to be perfectly true and above dispute.

Such were the worthy pair who occupied Menzies' house ; but there was another whom we have not yet named—this was Maud Menzies, familiarly called in the neighbourhood the Menzies' Pearl. She was the daughter of a deceased younger brother of Ralph's, and her mother had departed this life soon after the death of her husband, leaving Maud an orphan.

Immediately upon the death of her mother, Ralph, who was much attached to Maud, insisted upon her taking up her abode with him and his sister, merely, as he said, that she might throw a little more light into the gloominess of the scene at home ; but in fact Maud had been but very indifferently provided for, and this was the kindliness of the way in which he let her know that he intended to take care of her, making the obligation on his part, not on hers.

If ever there were an amiable and humble creature, Maud was that one ; she was the general favourite of the neighbourhood, and there was quite a rivalry among her friends and acquaintances as to which should have the pleasure of sacrificing to her wishes.

Of course a young female of this description could not expect to remain unsolicited for any lengthened period, nor did she ; and there was one young gentleman at the house of whose father the family of the ;Menzies frequently visited, who was really much interested in Maud, and who, notwithstanding that gentle creature's indifference to him, which was apparent enough, continued with wonderful pertinacity to urge his suit both by oral and written communications ; but which alike were ineffectual.

Rowland Symes, notwithstanding the most positive denial of his addresses by Maud, enlisted his father, who was a highly respectable man, a partner in a large banking establishment in Lombard-street, in his cause, who certainly did his best both with Maud and her uncle in pleading his son's suit, but Ralph soon cut the matter short, so far as he was concerned, by declining to interfere in a matter in which the affections of his niece were alone concerned. He succeeded no better with Maud, who candidly and without reservation explained her feelings upon the subject, and the old gentleman at once withdrew from the contest, leaving the matter entirely in the hands of Rowland either to succeed or fail as might chance.

One would have thought that this would have been quite sufficient to put an end to the affair, but it certainly did anything but succeed. From importunity Rowland descended into right down persecution, so much so indeed, that it succeeded in putting a stop to Maud visiting at the house of his father, as she had been in the habit of doing, and upon every occasion when she found one of the party visiting Ralph, she took special care to be out of the way. Rowland being thus intercepted for his personal communications with Maud, had recource to his pen, and letter after letter came pouring in until at length they became a perfect annoyance to all parties concerned or not concerned.

The last letter that was ever read by Maud, written by her importunate and headstrong lover, was received one morning while the small family were at breakfast: it was the last that was read, but by no means the last that was written.

Ralph, his sister, and Maud, as we have said, were at breakfast, when a female servant entered the room, bringing with her the letter.

"A letter, sir, if you please."

"For me?" said Ralph.

"No, sir, for Miss Maud."

"Then serve it upon the right party, Mary," said Ralph; "another letter, I presume, from Master Rowland. Eh, Maud, he certainly intends to get possession of you."

"It is from him, uncle, certainly, but I think I may answer in the negative to the second part of the sentence.'

"May be so, Maud, may be so; but I'd have you be careful, or he may catch you off your guard, and take forcible possession."

"No, no, uncle, I must give him credit for a better feeling than that. But really, uncle, I wish he would cease to annoy me so with these epistles; I never answer them, and I should have thought that my silence must have been a sufficient hint to him that his conduct was unpleasant to me."

"Oh, by no means, my child — by no means. I suppose he understands that silence gives consent, and he'll never stop till he gets an answer put in of some sort or another. You certainly must enter an appearance."

"I tell you what I will do," said Maud: "I will return him his letters, and surely that will be answer enough for him, or he must be wilfully dull."

"Oh, my dear, you are not sufficiently versed in the ways of the world," said Ralph: "you may depend upon it that such an answer as that would be exceptionable, and he'd move to have it taken off the file for impertinence. No, my child, I think we must send him a threatening letter."

"No, no, uncle; I will not write to him —I will not write, for I am quite sure that that would be a sufficient excuse for a reply. No, I must not write. I will return him his letter, for I am tired of being so importuned."

"Now, really," said Grace Menzies—"really, niece, I think you are much too scrupulous. Open the letter, and let us hear what he has to say for himself."

"Ah, sister!" remarked Ralph, "woman's curiosity, woman's curiosity! Now, I dare say, you would be very unhappy if you didn't know the contents of the letter."

"Oh dear, no!" bridled up Grace: "I've not the slightest wish to know, only I think Maud stands too much upon niceties. It may be that he's sorry for having annoyed her so long; and it may be that he's apologizing for it, and don't mean to do so any more."

"Well, well, Maud, break the seal, and let's see what it's all about."

"Well, uncle, if aunt wishes——"

"Oh dear, no!" said Grace: "not I, I assure you. Don't you hear it's your uncle who wishes you to break the seal? I said nothing about breaking the seal. Send it back, if you like—send it back; but mind, don't lay it to me, that's all, if you should be sorry afterwards."

"Break the seal, Maud—break the seal, and put your aunt out of her fidget."

"There, uncle," said Maud, handing the letter to him; "you read it, and let us have the benefit of your advice upon the subject matter of it, and read it aloud for the benefit of all of us."

"Very well," said Ralph, as he broke the seal. "At all events, it commences familiarly enough."

"Now don't read it to yourself," exclaimed Grace. Now, pray go on."

"Well, here it is ;" and he read aloud as follows :—

"MY DEAREST MAUD—This is the sixth letter I have addressed to you, to none of which have I received even an acknowledgment. This leads me to conclude that they have never reached you; and, to be certain of the fact, I have caused this to be delivered to you personally, and do hope that my suspicions are well grounded; for I cannot believe that you, who are above all other women in opinion and candour, would so allow me, to whom you have shown some esteem, to remain in a state of doubt in a matter, to me, of so much importance. I really do not understand why an interruption should be allowed to exist to the continuance of those little familiarities with which we were wont to beguile a tedious hour——"

"Uncle, uncle," interrupted Maud, "this is cruel, very cruel. I can assure you——"

"Stay a bit, my girl, and let us see how he proceeds."

"I am quite certain that no conduct of mine has occasioned the interruption, and am satisfied there must be enemies in the camp, who have watched our endearments, and most maliciously interfered to prevent a repetion of them."

"I cannot hear it out," said Maud. "I will not hear more of it. Uncle, pray proceed no further."

"Nay, Maud, pray do not interrupt your uncle. I really must hear it to the end—I must, indeed. Go on, Ralph—go on."

"I do suspect," continued Ralph, reading from the letter, "that your worthy aunt has had a hand in it——"

"The monster!" exclaimed Grace.

"Nay, nay," said Ralph, "do not interrupt me : pray let me go on, and see what sort of a case he makes out against you."

"Case against me!" said Grace; "I'll case him, the impudent rascal—I'll case him. Case, indeed—me—no case——"

"Well, aunt, we might as well hear the remainder of it now. Pray go on uncle, go on."

"For," continued Ralph, still reading from

the letter, " I have often observed her watching our movements very closely, and if, as I hope is not the fact, she is the actual cause of the difference of behaviour in you towards me, I must call her to a severe account."

" Now did you ever hear the like of that—did you ever? Why, the impudent rascal—call me to a severe account—an account! Why, brother, you sit there, as if nothing wa the matter—account, indeed!"

" If this be so," read Ralph, " I can only account for it in this way, that she feels chagrined at my paying my addresses to you, instead of a relation of yours, not very far removed from her in consanguinity."

" Very good, indeed," said Ralph, stopping short in his reading. " Why, sister, he means you again; but, I suppose, he didn't like to say so boldly, and at once. Surely, you have not been pulling your cap at him?"

" There's many a better man than he that would have been delighted to see it," said Grace; " but let's hear what further the impudent fellow has to say."

" Oh, I've no objection to go on with it," said Ralph; " he continues :—And now, dear Maud, hoping that my suspicions are well founded in respect to the non-receipt by you of my letters, and that they are groundless in respect of your aunt interfering in the matter, let me entreat of you, as you once loved me, to restore me to that enviable position. Maud, dear Maud, I love thee beyond all that I can imagine. I am miserable out of your devine presence; I cannot exist without the heavenly beams of your love surrounding me. Send an answer to this letter, my Maud, without delay, as until then, I shall be in a state of anxiety, which will amount to little less than madness.

" I am, my dearest Maud,
" For ever yours,
" ROWLAND SYMES."

" There," said Ralph, " what do you think of that declaration, Maud? Have you any cause to show against it?"

" I shall not reply to it, uncle," answered Maud. " Such a letter to me is perfectly unjustifiable; and he must have written it for the purpose of insulting me. I am determined not to answer it."

" Well, my dear, do as you please," chimed in Grace, " do as you please. It appears to me very plain that the young man loves you."

" I do not see that, aunt, for, if you observe, the terms of the letter are couched in such a way that to a stranger it would appear he was justified in writing to me in such a style, which, you know, he is not. No man who really loves would allow any letter of his to be capable of a double interpretation, so much to the prejudice of the supposed object of his affection."

" What is your objection to him?" asked Grace.

" I have no other objection," said Maud, " than that I do not like him otherwise than as a friend."

" Ay, ay," said Grace, " there must be some other reason than that—there must be somebody else in the background."

" What do you mean, aunt?" inquired Maud.

" Why, there's somebody else you like better."

" No, indeed, aunt."

" Oh, nonsense—don't tell me. I ought to know—aint I older than you, and consequently don't I know more than you do? Of course, I do."

" Far be it from me, aunt." replied Maud, " to dispute your superior knowledge. And if you affirm that there is somebody else in the character of a lover that I like better than this Richard Symes, I must candidly admit that you do know more than me, for I am totally ignorant upon the subject."

" There now, brother," said Grace, " isn't that right down contradiction now—isn't it?"

" Not at all, Grace, not at all, as the man said, on the contrary, quite the reverse, for I take it to be a very strong admission of your assertion."

" Why, brother, I asserted that she liked somebody better than Rowland Symes, and she denies it—isn't that a contradiction?"

" Ah, Grace, Grace, I never shall make anything of you, I see. Your assertion was that you being older than Maud, you knew more than she, which she assented to, and gave an illustration in proof."

" Ah, well, there's no getting anything out of you, at all events; but there must be something to account for Maud's dislike to this Rowland."

" Well, Grace, with all due submission to your superior knowledge, that is a matter entirely resting with Maud, and which we have no right to inquire into. If Maud have somebody else in view, which I do not believe she has, as she asserts the contrary, well and good, be it so—she is wise enough not to require the interference of either of us in the affair."

" Oh, I don't wish to interfere—of course not," said Grace, " only I think youth should be tempered with age."

" No, no, Grace, take my word for it, you are mistaken—let age be tempered with age, and youth with youth; it's much more pleasant, never doubt me, particularly as regards youth."

" You are not competent to talk upon these affairs, brother, these little affections of the heart——"

" Hold, Grace, hold—there we are at issue, and will at once go to trial, and our niece Maud shall be our evidence."

" Excuse me, uncle; I really must decline to appear without a subpœna and the regular fee."

" Very good," said Ralph, " then as I shall be nonsuited, I must withdraw; but your aunt, there, talks about the little affections of the heart, as if she had ever experienced any. Now, I should like to be informed who could be the temerarious man who ventured upon trying Grace's little affections of the heart?"

"Really, brother, this language is very unkind, and you seem to think the thing an impossibility."

"Not by any means," said Ralph. "Oh, no, do not mistake me, pray; for there are men who are guilty of many foolish things; but still I should like to know, Grace, just for the sake of knowing, not that I am at all anxious to know, as you would say, who he was. Come, let us know, Grace, let us know."

"Brother, I don't see what this has to do with the question," said Grace. "What is to be done with respect to this letter?"

"Either one of two things, Grace; answer it, or return it. What say you, Maud?"

"As I said before, uncle, I certainly shan't answer it, and having broken the seal, I cannot return it: but I do wish I had sent it back without reading it. It has made me very unhappy."

"Oh, stuff," said Ralph, "it is evident that the youth is a little touched in his mind, and is a subject for a writ *de lunatico inquirendo*; he must be taken care of by his friends, till he comes to his senses again, that's plain; and I promise you, if he continues this system of annoyance, Maud, I will take the matter in hand, and rid you of him."

"Thanks, dear uncle; but don't use any harsh measures with him."

"There," said Grace, "as I thought, you see she relents, and there's something more in it than she'd have us to know."

"Nay, aunt, that's very unkind of you; I really am quite innocent of having given him the slightest encouragement to address me in the familiar manner in which he has done so; but yet I do not like that my uncle should adopt any extraordinarily harsh measures to prevent a recurrence of it."

"Well, Maud, never mind what Grace says about it. If you receive any more of these epistles, return them immediately without opening them, and then we shall be able to advise further; and until we see that after a few trials he still continues to follow the same course, we had better remain in *statu quo*. And now, having settled this knotty point, take care of that letter, and wish me safe to the old office in the inn."

"Bother the old office in the inn," said Grace; "I thought you'd given that up altogether; but you can't rest at home long, like any reasonable being, but must go fidgeting about at your old practices; and I daresay Edwards would be much better satisfied if you were to stay away, and leave him to follow his own course."

"That's one of my little affections of the heart, Grace, and which you are quite incapable of appreciating, and therefore are not in a situation to reason about, even if you had the faculty of reasoning, which, as I have said before, you have not, for that is one of the few things unattainable by woman; but if a woman should be found capable of putting these ideas together, which are necessary to form a proposition, she is a blue-stocking, and as somebody has said, cultivates a dirty thumb. She is not only an exception to the rule, but a positive disgrace to it; and so, Grace, I wish you a very good morning. Good morning, Maud, and get me some merry story to amuse me with after dinner." And, so saying, old Ralph left the two ladies together, during his usual visit to the old office in the inn.

CHAPTER VIII.

THE AMBUSH. — THE DECLARATION.—THE DENIAL, AND THE RESCUE.

"I CAN'T understand," said Grace, "why your uncle should take so much pleasure in going to that miserable den, day after day, as he does. One would imagine that he would only be too glad to have got clean out of it."

"Why, aunt, it has become a habit with him. I daresay he would be very miserable were he not to do so. One gets attached to that which one has been intimate with for many years; and it is a positive pleasure to him, no doubt."

"Oh, pleasure, nonsense; what pleasure can there be in pulling a parcel of old musty deeds about? Why the very smell of a lawyer's office is enough to create nausea in any one of sensitive nerves and feelings. I have no idea of such rubbish—pleasure, indeed!"

"It must be so to him, aunt, or he would not go so repeatedly; besides, it might be prejudicial to his health if he were to be interrupted in that which he says is so necessary for him; for, aunt, you must recollect that if a man who for many years had indulged in the pleasures of the bottle—if pleasures they may be called—were to be suddenly checked or restrained altogether from his usual indulgencies, the probability is, that he would not be able to exist, and that is the opinion of all medical men; for I have heard, and I believe it to be true, that a certain tradesman who was in the constant habit of tippling throughout the day, at length happened to be taken exceedingly ill, and all his friends attributed it to the excessive indulgence in dram drinking, and very improperly, as it turned out, refused him the slightest thing in the shape of spirits. The man became accordingly worse, and when the doctor was consulted and was told the course the man's friends had pursued, he denounced it at once, and on inquiring of his patient how many glasses of spirits he was in the daily habit of taking, forty-five was the answer. 'Then let him have at least, two-thirds of that quantity; and instead of cutting off the quantity at once, reduce it two or three glasses a day.' This plan was adopted, and the patient gradually improved—a pretty good proof, aunt, that it is not at all advisable to resign suddenly those habits to which, all our life, we have been accustomed."

Though hardly convinced, Grace did not say anything more upon the subject, and for the time it was dropped, only to be renewed when Mr. Menzies should afford a similar opportunity.

Several days passed away, and with each day came a letter from the indefatigable Rowland Symes, all of which were thrown aside unopened; and though Maud felt some slight irritation at his obstinacy, which now almost amounted to persecution, still she endeavoured to let it dwell upon her mind as little as possible.

One evening, while passing through the city in company with her uncle, they had encountered Rowland Symes, and with an effrontery almost unparalleled, he obtruded himself upon them, urging his suit even in the public street. Maud repulsed him with the greatest indignation; and when he would have still persevered, the old gentleman himself interfered with some spirit, and the young man himself was obliged to quit them overwhelmed with mortification.

*   *   *   *   *

Rowland Symes had in his service a young man who gloried in the name of Tony Thong, and whose peculiar talent chiefly found a vent for its display in the classic air of the stable. He was well versed in the details of his profession; and it was his boast amongst his fellows, that though not one of the largest of the male creation, he wore as neat a pair of white unmentionables, and could ride as well as any groom in London. As these assertions were undisputed, we have a right to suppose there must have been some truth in them.

By some strange coincidence, Tony had scraped an acquaintance with the parlour-maid, who honoured the establishment of Mr. Menzies with her services; and that young lady, who was ignorant of his being groom to Rowland, had conceived an affection for him, which, though highly flattering to the personal vanity of Tony, was most inexplicable. However, as it brought frequent treats in the shape of cold meat, pastry, and other savory things (at the expense of old Menzies, be it understood), Tony did not find any fault with it; but, on the contrary, cultivated the acquaintance with the tact he possessed.

Now, it so happened that on the particular evening on which Maud and Ralph Menzies' had encountered Rowland Symes, Tony had promised Susan Snipes (the musical name in which the young lady rejoiced) to pay her a visit; the young lady in question being perfectly aware that on that evening she should have the place entirely to herself.

Punctual to the time appointed, Tony reached Menzies House, and calling into exercise a preconcerted signal, he was soon admitted to the soft embrace of Susan, the parlour-maid.

"Well, Sukey, here I am, you see, as true as a dial—a matchless piece of clockwork. I'm a regular chronometrical piece of machinery; my wheels go round and round, and one tooth fits into the other so uncommonly exact that I always keeps my time. You may always go by me, Sukey, without any fear of going wrong."

"Then you're just the very thing, as my missus says, as I must look arter—one that won't do me any wrong; and master often talks about wheels within wheels—I wonder whether he means you."

"Of course he does, Sukey, there's no manner of doubt about that; your master and I are most outrageous friends. La, Sukey, I've often had a long talk with the governor; he's a wery good kind of a critter, and keeps a wery unkimmon good table."

"La! you don't say so, Tony?"

"Yes, I do," replied Tony, "a wery good table."

"La, how funny! I don't mean that, Tony, I mean, what a go that you should be acquainted with my master, and I not know it. Well, that is funny, ain't it?"

"Ay, funny, I believe it is, above a bit; but I've got something funnier than that for you, after I've just taken the edge off my appetite."

"You have! No, you haven't now; come, none of your confabulations, Mr. Tony, you're a joking, I know. What have you got more funny than that, eh?"

"Ha! ha! my little Tippitiwichet, wait a little; bring out what's in the precious larder, and we'll talk over t'other when the enemy's satisfied. It's a most singular thing, Sukey, but I do assure you I never can get on with an outraged stomach, never. You might just as soon expect to get out a tune from an organ without any in'ards, as to get anything good from Tony when his dear stomach is disgusted with unkind treatment. No, no, it's all very well people talking about food for the mind, but the body must be looked arter first. Now, I know a blessed old gentleman, who is so preciously ill-informed on this 'ere subject, that it is quite lamentable to see him go on in his ridiculous ways.— I'm wery much grived, wery much to see it."

"What is it, Tony?"

"What is it, Sukey? this is it:—He belongs to some religious society, I believe, the members of which are all angels on earth, at least, so I've been misinformed; but whether ﬁﬀ true or not is not a matter for me to decide. I believe they thinks so themselves, and o' course they knows best; but, however, this old gentleman is one of the members—man or angel. Now, whenever a poor critter stops him in the streets and begs a bit o' bread to stop him from starving, what do you think he does?"

"Gives him a penny, Tony, I suppose, to get him some——"

"On the contrary, quite the reverse:—no, he fumbles in his coat-tails, and brings out a bundle——"

THE SERVANT KICKS ANDREW STUMPS OUT OF THE " EEL AND FRYING PAN."

"What does he carry the bread about with him?"

"Stop a bit, Sukey, you'll never go to heaven if you're so fast. No, he pulls out a bundle of tracts, and makes the poor varmint a present of four pages of print, entitled 'Crumbs of Comfort for the Soul,' 'A Handful of Dates for the Famishing,' or some other equally comforting and satisfying production. Now, this isn't the sort of thing.—Sukey, you know, the man wants bread, he don't want crumbs for his soul. If these 'ere generous critters were to give a penny wrapped up in one o' them 'ere papers, why while the poor wretch was driving his fangs into his crust, he might at the same time amuse himself by reading the tract; and if there is any good in reading them 'ere things, which I very much doubt, why his soul might be comforted as well as his bowels; but as it is, depend upon it, Sukey, it only brings religion into contempt, and not one on 'em out of a thousand is ever put to the purposes for which it was intended; and if it's read at all, it is only for the purpose of ridiculing it."

"That's just what I heard master say," said Susan; "he says it's very apt to get religion into a reticule.' "

"Your master's a sagacious individual, and knows as well as anybody how many one and one make," said Tony; "and now, Sukey, my gal, let us have something savoury from the larder, but let it not be a tract."

"Track me, if I shall," said Sukey, "you remain here, and don't leave on no account, because why, Tony? nobody doesn't know you are here—d'ye see—d'ye see, Tony."

"You're an artful dodge, Sukey. See! ay, I think I does, indeed—when did you ever catch Tony napping, when there was ever anything that required him to keep his peepers from blinking? Go, let's have summut, and let it be summut good; come, be off, or I shall go and fetch it myself."

"Oh, Tony, don't move a single step, or I shall be a ruined gal. I wouldn't have not none of 'em know of my integrity, no, not for all the very Hingies of molten gold—no, that I wouldn't."

"Ha, ha, ha!" laughed Tony, as Susan left the room, "I'm in for a blessed good thing, I guess, and no kind of mistake; only think now of these 'ere precious pair of kicksies bringing me this 'ere spice of luck—why, they're worth their weight in gold. I'm blowed if I don't get a common pair, and wear these only for special occasions. Curse it, I see nothing very uncommon in 'em, and I'm puzzled above a bit to know what the gal could see in my Bond-street breeches to make her so smitten with the wearer; it must be the kicksies, I'm sure, for I saw her twigging them all the time. Well, there are more things in heaven and earth than are dreamt of in my limited philosophy, as Ben, the coachman, very truly observed to his lady, when he couldn't account for the alarming deficiency in the stock of oats. Well, it's no use thinking upon it—too much thinking, I've larnt by personal observations, softens the brain. I suppose my master has, by this time, laid his proposals before Miss Maud. She don't seem to care a fig's end for him anyhow, and yet he's a jolly good fellow—he's good to a fault—he throws his money about like tin, while I, who knows the true valley of it, picks it up like gold—ha, ha! He'd make a good husband, I'd venture to say, because he's never guilty of any recesses, and is temporary in the highest degree. I don't think I ever seed him the worse for liquor—no, no, I'm sure I haven't—he's as mild as a sucking baby, when the milk isn't sour, though; but let that pass, his irritability sets off his sincerity, and shows his general softness and calmness more to advantage. Come, Sukey, you're a precious long time gone for the wittles; I shall talk myself off my legs afore you come back. I can't help thinking about these waluable whites. It's wery odd—wery odd. I suppose there's somethin' wery particular in the cut, for they're not over clean, so that couldn't ha' done it. Blow me, if I don't ask her when she comes back. Well, I'm getting rather fidgety—I don't like this at all. Ah! ha! perhaps, she's just grilling a kidney, or something o' that sort of thing, while something more substantial is getting ready—oh, I shouldn't wonder—she's a nice gal—a wery nice girl, and I think I'm getting wery fond of her. Well, this won't do—now really—why, does she suppose that I'm going to be bound up here, like a sheep in Smithfield? No, damme! Ah, ah! hilloa! what's this—something little Sukey's been getting ready for her Tony after dinner? Thank ye, my girl. No, of course, you haven't. I don't particularly want her back just now, until I've the bottle cleared away again. Now, my covey, come to my arms, and let me squeeze you."

Saying which, he reached from a shelf in the room, a green glass bottle, half full of liquid, and seizing a cup, he hastily emptied into it some of the contents of the suspicious-looking bottle, and, with equal haste, returned it to its repository.

"Now, Sukey, my gal, here's to your undoubted good health, and may every hair of your head turn a deaf ear to the insinivations of Time—here goes."

No sooner said than done; with one gulp he swallowed that which was ejected in about just as quick a time, for as ill fortune would have it, it was anything but what he expected it to be, inasmuch as it was the savings of lamp oil which Susan had put away for the purpose of settling, and making useful another time.

"By the Lord Harry! heugh! heugh! s-s-spa—s-s-spa! What the devil! heugh! heugh! Damme, here's a pretty—heugh! I shall bring my very heart up—go! What the devil shall—heugh! heugh!—whew!—I do? Look at my—oh, here it comes again!—heugh! heugh!—here's a nice treat! I shall disturb everybody in the house! I shall be seized with a fit of delirious trepans! I am sure I shall—oh! oh! here it is again! There—there's a pretty mess for Sukey!"

"Tony, Tony! what are you making so much noise about?" asked Susan, as she entered the room. "Why, goodness gracious me, Tony! what have you been doing?"

"Doing?" said Tony, "for God's sake, get a mop and pail!"

"Tony, my dear, how come you so? Tony, pray tell me."

"The oil, the oil!" said Tony.

"What of it, Tony? What of it?"

"There, there," said Tony, pointing to the cup.

"Where?"

"Why, there! Don't you see that 'ere cup?"

"Of course I do."

"Well then," said Tony, "imagine that full of rank lamp oil."

"Yes, Tony."

"Yes, yes; well then, imagine it in your hand—at your lips—in your stomach; and having imagined all this, don't ask me how I came so. I am so, you see, and very so so too."

"Goodness, gracious me! come defend us, you doesn't mean to say that you've been drinking the lamp oil?"

"I do mean to say so though," said Tony.

"What! and do you mean to say you like it, Tony?"

"Like it be blowed, Mrs. Sukey; come—come—none of your gammon, you know I doesn't like it."

"Why, then, goodness gracious, Lor' a mercy upon me, why, in Heaven's name did you drink it for, then?" said Susan.

"Why, you hussy," said Tony, "do you suppose I drunk it from choice? No, I should think not a little, I believe yer, no, I thought it was summit fit for a human critter to drink, and as I was beginning to lose my spirits acause you was so long absent, why, I thought I'd make free and steal a march upon time, by having some afore dinner; and accordingly I poured it out, and seeing as how it was all right to the eye, it being wery much like my favourite liquor, whiskey, I never inquired further into the matter, but put it out of its misery at once, and you see what a pretty pickle it's made."

"Goodness gracious, lawks a daisy!" said Susan, "why my grandmother used to tell me to look before I leaped; now, Tony, if you'd only have smelt before you tasted, you wouldn't have made such a mess."

"True, and if you hadn't placed the bottle there, I shouldn't ha' seen it, and consequently shouldn't ha' tasted it, and more consequently you wouldn't ha' had to reproach me with it."

"And pursuing the same line of argument," said Susan, "if master hadn't burnt oil instead of tallow, I shouldn't have saved the dippings, and consequently——"

"Yes—yes," interrupted Tony, "and cetterer and cetterer and cetterer. But the question is now, what's to be done? There's the rub."

"Why, how do you feel now?" said Susan.

"A little more comfortable," said Tony, "but the confounded oil's hanging about my gums, and I stink worse than a tallow-chandler's shop in the very midst of a melt."

"Then, look here, Tony—if you'd just used your eyes with a little more crimination, you'd have seen this cupboard in which there is a bottle of whiskey—real whiskey—now, Tony, what will you give me for a drop?"

"Why, I'll give you a toast and sentiment," said Tony.

"What's a toast and centrepiece?" inquired Susan.

"Oh, let's have the stuff, Susan, and I'll give you a practical illustration of what it is."

Susan advanced to the cupboard, and taking out a bottle of mountain dew, helped Tony to a bumper, whose eyes glistened with delight, as the small bubbles of air rose from the bottom of the glass, and settled round the rim in thick, bead-like clusters.

"Now, Susan, my gal, here's a toast and sentiment—'May the wick of wickedness never be fed with the oil of humanity.' Devilish good stuff that."

"Thank'ee, Tony! that's a toast and centrepiece, is it?"

"Yes, it is, and one of the right sort too."

"Well, I can't say as I understand the meaning of it."

"You can't?"

"No, that I can't."

"Well, I'm rather surprised at that, because it's very plain, and very much to the purpose."

"Lawk! I must be very stupid, then, not to see it: perhaps you'll just edification me by complaining the mystery."

"It means just this 'ere: the wick of wickedness—that is, you know, a candle's got a wick?"

"Yes, of course."

"Well, then, and that the candle wouldn't burn without a wick?"

"Yes."

"Nor the wick without the candle?"

"No, you're wrong there, Tony."

"I say that it wouldn't burn long without the tallow."

"True."

"Well, then, that makes out my point. Now, you see, I looks upon mankind as the wick, and wickedness the flame—and wickedness the flame—the flame."

"Yes, yes—I see—I see."

"Well then, and again the evil passions of mankind is the fat what keeps wickedness, that is, the flame, a going—do you see? Well, there you now have the explanation of that 'ere toast and sentiment in all its beautiful plicity and stinctness, and there's an end of it."

" Good gracious me! why didn't I think of that afore? Well, that is the neatest explanation I ever heard. I now understand what's a centrepiece. But, lawks a' me! Tony, what a mess your breeches are in; why, what in Heaven's name have you been about?"

" Breeches, breeches?" exclaimed Tony. " Ah! there it is as I thought ; that's the—my eyes, here's a pretty go!" and Tony lifted his hands and eyes in astonishment and dismay. " Here's a lamentable piece o' misfortune. Blow my bags if they aint all covered with oil."

" Well, Tony, that comes of prying into matters that don't concern you."

" Sukey, Sukey, don't reproach me—don't. I'm a ruined, unhappy individual ; and the cherished object of all my blessed affections is snatched away from me for ever."

" Never mind, Tony—never mind," said Susan ; " they'll wash."

" Wash! wash be damned! Excuse my excited feelings, Sukey. Man places his affections upon a rotten foundation, and builds up his hopes on sand. I was srong in my faith as to these 'ere blessed breeches, once so beautiful and bright ; but the hand of adversity has fallen upon 'em, and never more will they call up a beam of satisfaction into the hazel eyes of Tony Thong. Oh, Tony Thong, Tony Thong, thou art fallen—ho, how art thou fallen!"

" Don't, pray. Oh, Tony Thong, you'll break the tender heart of your Susan Snipes, if you go on in that'ere romantic way. Tony, forbear, for the love of Heaven! and, gracious goodness, stop these larningtations."

" Well, well, Sukey, the thing's done, and there's no help for it ; and as I thinks we're both getting a litttte too romantic over what, after all, are only a pair of leather breeches, we'd better cut it, and try something else. Now, to come to the point at once, what's to pay ?"

" To pay, Tony ?"

" Yes, what's to eat? That's the question."

" What do you say, Tony, to a nice pigeon-pie and oyster sauce—or cold roast pork and capers ?"

" Why, I'll pay my respects to the oysters without the sauce first, and then walk into the pigeon-pie. Sukey—anything to accommodate you."

" Walk into the pigeon-pie ?"

" Yes, like a brick, Sukey. Come, out with 'em. Let's have the oysters first, and bring us a knife to open them with. I always opens my own oysters, and eats one afore I prepares another, for it's my opinion that they ought to be popped into the mouth immediately they're unloosed, and afore they knows it, for they're precious artful dodgers are them oysters ; for if you opens 'em before you're ready to stick your teeth into their jackets, I'm blessed if I don't think they smell a rat, and part with all their delicious

briskness, on purpose to disappoint you—that's my opinion ; and there's another great fact in the art of eating oysters—never soak their tails in vinegar, because you destroy the flavour of the sacred juice ; and always use cayenne pepper, if you can get it. Have you got any, by-the-by ?"

" Oh, yes ; plenty, plenty."

" That's right, my little dear."

" Now don't, Tony. I shall certainly faint away if you call me that again."

" Come none 'o that nonsense, at all events, until the oysters are disposed of. Now, look alive, Sukey, a bit. Five or six dozen, just to give me an appetite for the pie, previous to looking under the crackling of the pork, will just be about the thing. Come, I long to be sticking my knife into 'em."

" Ha, ha! Tony, you'll not stick your knife into any oysters of mine."

" None ?"

" No."

" Why ?"

" Because I haven't got any."

" What, Sukey, do you mean to say you've been badgering me all this while ?"

" Oh dear, no, Tony," said Susan ; " you've been badgering yourself, as you call it. I only asked you what you said to oysters. I didn't say I had any."

" Well, I'm blowed! So, arter all my eloquent disquisition on the subject of oysters, it is a take in, is it? Well, never mind—we'll be content with the pigeon-pie, eh? What, is that fudge too? Well, I can stand a good deal of nonsense, but this is going a little beyond a joke. What have you got, that's all about it ?"

" I'll tell you—I haven't got goose and apple sauce, mutton and currant jelly, curried veal, haricot mutton, fried eels, fricasseed frogs, rumpsteaks and mushroom ketchup, nor beefsteaks and inguns."

" You're ever such a nice 'un, Sukey, for tantalising one of the superior sex. But, after all the rigmarole of the haven't gots, let me hear something of the have gots, because my in'ards are really preying upon themselves."

" Well, then, Tony, to be candid witb you, and as I know you haven't come here merely for what you can get, I don't mind saying that I've got a fine sirloin."

" Why didn't you say so afore ?" said Tony : " there's nothing better than a sirloin——"

" Of bread and cheese," interrupted Susan.

" No : you doesn't mean it though, Sukey, do you? Is it a fact, without any gammon? It is. Well, there's many a better cove nor me as has been obliged to put up with worse fare than that, so I'll bear my disappointment like a flossifer, and walk into that."

" Wait a bit," said Susan, " and I'll bring it to you. In the meantime, Tony, don't be walking into the oil bottle again. Ha! ha!"

" Be off with you, you young warmint, do, and don't keep me so long a waiting as you did afore."

Susan left Master Tony Thong once more in solitude, while she went to perform her promise; and no sooner had she got clean out of sight, than Tony, with some confidence, at once seized the real bottle this time, and as fast as he could pour out one glass after the other, and swallow the contents, he did so, and disposed of two glasses very completely before Susan made her appearance again with a tray before her, covered over with a clean white cloth.

"There," said she, as she set down the tray upon the table, "there, Tony, draw up, and make yourself quite at home. I don't eat 'em myself, I'll wait until something else comes."

"Eat 'em, eat what?" said Tony.

"There," said Susan, at the same time lifting off the cloth, and exposing to the admiring eyes of Tony a large brown earthenware vessel filled to the brim with the real natives.

"Oysters, oysters, Sukey, why, gal of my bosom, let me clutch thee. Don't! be done—don't, be done. Oh, well, I will have a smack, though—there."

"You might as well have waited until after the oysters," said Susan.

"That'll come afterwards, o' course," said Tony, "that was grace before meat. Now, you'll see a real oyster eater, and no mistake. You see, I know the very exact place where to introduce the knife; and observe, a clean twist of the wrist exposes my gentleman to view; now a dexterous turn head over heels, and I save all the juice, you see, in the hollow shell. Never spill your juice, Sukey. Now, a little cayenne and no vinegar, and in he goes. There, he's just found out, as my teeth go through, that he's got another habitation; and a gentle squeeze against the roof of my mouth to get all his juices out on him, thoroughly convinces him that it's all up with him—and—good-by, Mr. Oyster."

Tony continued his comments on the art of opening, and the luxury of eating oysters, until he had finished the pile before him, very much to the satisfaction and edification of Sukey; immediately after which the pigeon-pie made its appearance, and was despatched with equal facility, and the meal was finished with a cut or two from the roast pork.

Tolerably satisfied, and in very good humour with himself, with Susan, and everything else, even with his soiled breeches, Tony now had time to do the amiable with the fair parlour-maid; and she having cleared the table and produced the materials for compounding Tony's favourite tipple—whisky-toddy—they became very fond of each others—very fond indeed, and which fondness became increased in exact proportion to the decreasing depth of the liquor in the bottle. There is no knowing to what lengths the happy couple might have proceeded, even to that of a proposal on the part of unfortunate Tony, only that, in consequence of the liquor

overpowering his usually cautious habits, and occasioning him to forget where he was and what had brought him there, and to make as much uproar as if he had been in his master's stable; the probability of hi arriving at the aforesaid climax was speedily put an end to by the entrance into the apartment of Ralph Menzies himself, who had just returned with Maud from his encounter with young Rowland Symes, and who, hearing the loud talk and laughter of Tony, occasionally relieved by the simpering titters of Susan, felt extremely anxious to ascertain what could be the reason of such an unwonted hilarity, in that quiet and retired place.

As Ralph put his foot on the threshold of the door, Tony looked at him with a sort of half idiotic stare of recognition and surprice, while Susan, having lost all sense of the degree of relationship between herself and her master, undoubtedly occasioned by her imbibing rather too much of the bottle, quietly lifted the glass to her mouth and handed the remainder to Ralph, who stood with mouth and eyes extended to their utmost limits for some time.

"Come, old cock," said Tony, "just dip your beak into that, old boy—and—and let's have your opinion—o—o—pinion of it. Come don't be bashful, never m—m—ind me. Come."

"And who are you, pray, sir? Where do you come from? I don't recollect having had the pleasure of seeing you before," said Ralph.

"Probably not—probably not, old fellow," hiccuped Tony, in a tone of the most ineffable independence. "But—but, I dare say, old cock—we shall be excellent friends."

Mr. Menzies gazed at the drunken Tony for a few moments, and then closing the kitchen-door, he adopted the wisest plan available upon the occasion, and that was to seek assistance in expelling Tony from the house.

In a very short time Tony found himself comfortably seated by the roadside, and bewailing the humanity of mankind in general, and of Mr. Menzies in particular, who had thus unceremoniously torn him from the arms ot Sukey Snipes, and from the enjoyment of so many comforts.

As for Sukey herself, she was in a state of excitement from the whiskey imbibed, that raised her far above any reproaches her master might bestow upon her, so she was suffered to remain, her future disposal being a matter of consideration for the morrow.

CHAPTER IX.

THE JEW'S HARP.—THE GANG.—THE ROBBERY.—THE PRESERVATION.

At the time of the opening of this narrative there stood within half a mile of the residence of Mr. Menzies, a place of accommodation for man and beast, well known, in those days, by the sign of the "Jew's Harp," but which has been long swept away by the modern improvements in that neighbourhood. No doubt the house may be in the recollection of many of our readers, who in their strolls, in school-boy-days, to the great cockney rendezvous, Primrose Hill, most frequently have observed the large concourse of idlers generally congregated within its precincts.

The Jew's Harp was not always known by the name it then bore, but at a much more remote period might be seen, rather clumsily executed, to be sure, the representation of a scarf, painted by an artist of some obscurity, and whose name has not been handed down to posterity, swinging on the post opposite to the door of the (at that time) road-side inn, underneath which was written, "The New Scarf," the origin of which was a gift by a gentleman, who accidentally sought shelter within the walls of the inn, to the landlord's pretty daughter, with whom he was much pleased, of a very handsome silk scarf. The landlord, who had been for some time beating about for a new sign, and whose ideas were something like the settlings of his beer, rather inclined to be of the description called muddy, seized at once the happy incident, and got most gloriously happy the day on which he stood beneath the new and flaming sign. Time, which has no more respect for sign-posts than it has for anything else, suffered this pride of the ancient landlord's heart, in the course of years, to become exceedingly obscure, so that, in fact, although tradition still continued to that house the name of the New Scarf, its customers much doubted whether or not, in the course of time, that sign had not been corrupted from something which must have been of a more intelligible nature; they could make nothing of the New Scarf. From a simple doubt it became a question of considerable interest to the customers of the place, and various were the discussions, *pro* and *con*, on the mysterious production of the obscure artist whose name has perished, until at length an old gentleman who had the credit of being about as good an antiquary as here and there are, to the great delight of the assembly before which he made the discovery, announced it to be a corruption from the Jew's Harp, and proceeded to point out to the company the various parts of that instrument, as displayed on the sign-board. It was the fashion then, as it is now, for credence to be given to a dogma uttered by one presumed to have authority in any particular science, and consequently the New Scarf became the Jew's Harp, and, for anything unknown to the company, did just as good a business under one sign as it did under the other.

It was on the evening of the day when the scene described in the last chapter took place, that in the parlour of the Jew's Harp were collected a company whose general and individual appearance was sufficient to create in the mind of an observer a dubious feeling as to the nature of the pursuits in life carried on by them. That they were not gentlemen, was satisfactorily proved at one glance; that they were not tradesmen, their appearance at once bespoke; and that they were not mechanics, their could not be the remotest plea for presuming. But to put an end to any doubt that may be engendered in the reader's mind on this matter, we will take the privilege of introducing him to the company.

At the upper end of the low-roofed room, elevated above the rest of his companions, who were arranged on each side of a long deal table supported on trussels, sat a tall, powerful man, whose countenance was chiselled with such a careful regard to the qualities of the owner, that no one could have mistaken him for other than a leader or head of a class. His features displayed a character of decision and command, and inflexibility of purpose, of which to doubt would have been considered a heresy. His hair clustered about his face and neck in thick crisp curls; a line of distinction between that of his head and face, there was none. His eyes were overshadowed by brows as black as night, and met over the nose with a slight undulation, just sufficient to escape forming one continuous arch; his beard he suffered to grow, and kept it in proper limits by the aid of the scissors; the only part of his face which ever felt the razor being the upper lip, which he kept particularly clean. His nose was an extraordinary feature of his face, being an aquiline one of most unusual size. In fact, he was never to be forgotten, after being once seen. Such a peculiar nose, standing prominently out of such a mass of hair, produced an impression on an observer's mind, that he who could see without feeling must have been as extraordinary in his way as was the gallant captain of whom we are telling. The rest of the company do not call for a distinct description, being of the ordinary character, except that there was in all of them something which might be taken exception to, and stand in the way of their getting any encouragement in honourable pursuits.

"I'll swear by our noble captain there," said one of the company, "that what I have said is quite true, ay, as true as the gospel, and I believe that's pretty correct."

"You may swear by what you please, Skinny Walliam," said another, "but I wouldn't give a fig for your word, and as for your oath, pho! 'tis not worth a solitary d—n off a common."

"Civil words, Mr. Ugly," said Skinny William, "or you and I shall fall out. My oath's as good as yours, and is to be believed as much."

"That may be," observed the captain, "and yet not the more to be believed by honest men, nor dishonest ones either; but let the matter rest, my men. I have no doubt in the world of the grievances of your story, and don't understand what difficulty Ugly has in believing it too. But every man may enjoy his own opinion."

" True, captain, but he should keep it to himself. If Ugly Dick didn't believe it, he shouldn't have said so, but have made it appear that he most devoutly admitted it! That's what I call gentlemanly behaviour, and what all of us ought to expect from each other.

" I tell you what it is, my boy," said Ugly, " before I'll submit to play the hypocrite to satisfy any man, I'll cut off my precious head, and once more, to speak in plainer language, I say that my opinion is, and, mind, my opinion will neither make it more nor less, false nor true, that it's a gross lie."

" Then so much for your opinion," said Skinny William, at the same time aiming at the precious head of Ugly Dick, as that gentleman had designated it, a thick, heavy glass which he had in hand at the time, and was about to convey to his mouth with its spirited contents. Happily the intent was defeated, for Ugly Dick dropping his head as he saw the missile about to be whirled on its message, the unoffending wall beyond him received the blow, and at the same time a dreadful wound in its plaster. As quick as thought, Ugly Dick sprung across the table, and grasping the throat of his opponent, a most determined conflict ensued, which must have terminated tragically to one of the belligerents, had not the captain interfered for the restoration of peace.

" Hold, hold," he said ; " who dares in my presence to set my authority at defiance ?—Will you not cease, there? Then I will make you." Saying which, he sprung upon the combatants, and grasping one in each hand, with the strength of a Hercules, he parted them by main force, and continued to shake them with such violence, that they had scarcely sufficient breath left in them to acknowledge in words their submission to his dictation.

" Now," said the captain, " shake hands, and, mark me, if either of you express any ill-feeling towards each other, that moment will I put a ball into you, and you well know that I keep my word ; and, my men, I give you all authority, in my absence, if anything passes between these vagabonds, similar to what you have just seen, to do what I have threatened to do ; and he who hesitates, when it comes to my knowledge, I will serve him the same ; and now depart into your seats once more, and resume the harmony which has been so ungraciously interrupted. Stockings, ring the bell ;" which Stockings having done, the landlord made his appearance.

" Ho ! bring !—bring glasses for the company, a bumper a piece, and see that you put not too much water into it, and be a little less careful of your sugar. D'ye hear ?"

" Ay, ay, captain—most noble captain ! I've not been in my trade so long without knowing how to treat such honourable gentle-

men—such right honourable and downright gentlemen."

" Attend to your business, landlord, and when I ask for your familiarity, let me have it, and not before."

" No offence, your honour, I hope," said Mr. Bungo, " none was meant, and really—'

" Skull," roared the captain, " kick the prater out."

Skull was bound to obey his captain's orders, but he felt inclined to exceed them a little, and very graciously laid hold of the landlord's ears, and with much grace and elegance of action repeatedly brought his patella in connection with the most obese part of that gentleman's person, until he had got him entirely clear of the door.

" Well done, Skull," said the captain, approvingly ; " you rather exceeded my commission, which you know with me is as bad as not fulfilling it. However, I shall over-look that to-night, but mind to keep within bounds for the future. Now, gentlemen, here is the grog ; let each man take his glass and drink success to the trade ! All ready? Ugly Dick, you glass is before you. Do you drink the toast?"

" Why, the fact is," commenced Ugly Dick, " I don't feel satisfied with the——"

A loud report interrupted the termination of Dick's speech ; he gave a convulsive start, and in another second his tongue was still for ever ; his brains were scattered amongst the company.

" Now, gentlemen," coolly continued the captain, as if nothing had happened, "drink to the toast, but not a bumber ; reserve the rest for another. Success to the trade !"

Every man lifted his glass to his mouth in turns, and repeated the words.

" Now, my men, another, and in silence. ' In memory of the dead !' and of your charity pray for the soul of your comrade. ' In memory of the dead !' "

This was also responded to, and a tear moistened the eyes of many of the gang as they thought of the companionable qualities of their deceased comrade and the suddenness of his death.

When their glasses were empty, and the men had resumed their seats, they looked at each other in a sort of stupid amazement engendered by the scene which had just taken place ; not a whisper was heard, not a muscle was observable in any of them.

" I don't know," said the captain, " whether I am expected to say anything upon this occasion, but for my own satisfaction, probably it will be as well. You all know, my men, how necessary it is in a society such as ours, that unqualified submission should be given to its head, be he whom he may—our safety requires it. Your dear comrade joined us with a full knowledge of the rules by which we are bound—he broke through them, and incurred the penalty which has been meted out to him. If he had been suffered to continue in his obstinacy, no one can tell what mischief might have ensued.

He was contumacious, and is dead. No one respects him more than I, but I respected all of you equally. For your sakes, and for mine, I carried out the rule which was sanctioned by yourselves, and which applies to his case. I regret his death, but it was inevitable. His death has saved some of our lives, probably, and it is better that one should suffer than all."

" True, true," exclaimed many voices.

" I am glad," continued the captain, "that some of you view the matter in its proper light. I regret that all of you do not. Let him who has anything to say to the contrary, speak freely—I give him full permission. What, has no one anything to say in favour of breaking the laws that were made for our security? No one? Then I presume all agree that the act was necessary. Am I right ?"

" Yes, all, all," said several voices.

" I rises," said one of the gang, a strong, burly, thick-headed looking fellow—" I rises —I——"

" Go on," said the captain, " I crave attention for the observations of Brutus, which I have invited ; pray proceed."

" Well, most noble Captain Cutt," continued the speaker, "I rises, since I have gotten your permission, to say a few words in accountation of some of us here coves ; I speaks not only for myself, but I believes for others, and what I have got to say is this much, that our unfortunate comrade was one of the best hands at cutting a purse, or letting the wind out of a corpulent gemman as there is amongst us, and one of the best born companions that we had ; he could sing a good song, and tell a merry tale ; and what bangs all, he could walk away with three bottles of the best port under his belt without being the worse, and he was a devil of a fellow among the girls ; now, captain, its nat'ral that we, who so much admired his excellent qualifications, should feel for his untimely end, though it is better that he should have died so, than with the assistance of a cord."

" A fine, a fine !" cried one of the company, " a gallon of wine and a go in the mouth with a brimmer of brandy, to get our palates right, first."

" Quite correct," said the captain ; " you understand, Brutus, that any of the crew making such an unpalatable allusion as you have just made, renders himself liable to the fine mentioned."

" All right, my noble captain, and I willingly submits, and it serves me right too, and as soon as I have had my say, I will down with the dibs ; well as I was saying, we feels in an inkimmon degree the loss of such a pleasant fellow, and speaking for myself and, as I said afore, for others, I say that our silence is not caused by any ill feeling against your noble self, because we think you did your duty, and what we should each of ourselves have done if we had been in your sitivation ; at least, I for one would have done so, without a word about it, and I speaks for myself and others. Is it not so, comrades ?"

" That's the ticket, my boy," cried several, "go on, you're quite right."

" And therefore," continued Brutus, "our silence must not be put down to the wrong cause, because we applauds the decision of your action, as it confirms the confidence we has in you as our captain, one who will and can take care of our interests ; but it is entirely owing to our respect and love for our comrade what has taken his departure, that has laid hold on our feelings, and has made us melancholic-like. A better captain, nor a better man, never drew a trigger, nor slipped a knife into the bowels of an enemy. Three cheers for the captain, gentlemen."

The whole of the company heartily responded to the call, and if any suspicion had lurked in Cutt's mind, as to the opinion entertained by any of his men, on the act that had take place, he quickly dismissed it, or at least, appeared to do so.

" Thank ye, my men," said he, " for your good opinion ; your interest is mine, and you may always depend upon my best exertions to keep us unassailable and intact. Now remove the body, you know where, and then we'll have in the fine incurred by Brutus ; and as I believe the state of his exchequer is not in the most flourishing condition, I will be responsible for the costs, and will add a similar dose."

" Bravo, bravo !" broke from the throats of the company, who now exerted themselves to the utmost in disposing of the defunct Dick, which having accomplished, they resumed their seats as if nothing of any importance had happened, and entered into the conviviality of the evening with the most joyous hilarity.

" Now, my men," said the captain, "previous to a song from Lanky Bill, charge your glasses, and drink a bumper ' To the road, and its collectors.' "

" Please, you, noble captain, I'll do my best, though bad is the best."

" That's all we require of you—begin."

Lanky Bill cleared his throat, and after driving down, with a libation, any remnant of huskiness that might remain, he broke forth into a professional song, in praise of the Romans, whom the song declared to be regular old bricks in the art of war making, and wherein the present company, and all others of the same profession, were designated as the toll collectors. Lanky Bill did himself much credit in the performance, and elicited the uproarious approbation of his companions.

" Well done—well done," said the captain. " Where did you pick up that good song ? It seems as though it were made on the toast that I have just given."

" You're quite right, captain, so it was."

" Indeed, you rather surprise me, for the toast was quite original, on my honour, and it is, to say the least of it, a very singular circumstance."

MAUD WATCHING THE VISITORS TO THE HOUSE IN RUSSELL SQUARE.

No. 8.

"Not at all, captain; with all due submission," said Lanky Bill, "you've got more talent in your company than you thought, I dare say; but that was also an original song—perfectly original, for it had never been seen, never been written, never been said or sung."

"You speak in riddles," said the captain, "explain."

"I begs pardon," said another; "but doesn't the captain know that Lanky Bill's an improvisitationary."

"A what?" asked the captain.

"Why, a man who can soliloquise upon any subject temporarily—a sort o' somnambuler."

"Oh, I see—I see; and I'm glad to find that I've got another clever fellow in the troop—why, Snodsdam, you have a wonderful command of the English language; you are a complete walking lexicographer."

"I scorn the assumption," replied Snodsdam. "I have always been that a lexicog was a harmless drudge, that busies himself in tracing the originals, and retailing the significations of words. Now, I'm not one of that 'ere sort, for the thing comes naturally to me, and I've always got a perfect responsibility of words at command; most of them original, and what I've never seen before; but, however, be that as it may, I knock under to the superior debility of Lanky William, and give praise where praise is most due. And now I calls upon that gentleman to make a call upon some other gent. for another song; and let it be sentimental, for of all songs, a sentimental one best suits me, as it calls up the more tenderer feelings of my constitution, and puts me in mind of old times when I was courting."

"Well, gentlemen, I believe I am entitled to a call, and therefore as I know our noble captain doesn't sing, I shall make bold to call upon his lieutenant, as a substitute."

"Bravo—bravo," cried several voices, and the glasses jumped upon the table in a perfect frenzy at the thumps bestowed upon it by the company. "Bravo for the lieutenant—silence for the lieutenant."

"Now, really this is very provoking, gentlemen," said the lieutenant; "you see I am rather the worse for this wine, and somehow or another, when I have had a little too much, all memory vanishes, and I fail in the attempt, and I think I may on this occasion say with Dryden—

What greater curse could envious fortune give,' than to be asked to sing when I am almost drunk?"

"What!" exclaimed the captain, "have we another clever man among us? Why, Plympton, I didn't know that you were a man much read in the poets."

"So I suppose," replied Plympton, "for as Shakspere says—

'Men's evil manners live in brass, their virtues We write in water.'

It is not my fault that I have been suffered to lay dormant so long; but as to the matter in dispute, most noble captain, may I be excused the call?"

"I must refer you to Lanky Bill," replied the captain; "he, perhaps, may let you off."

"Most certainly not," said that individual. "I know that the lieutenant can sing, and sing he shall, or make the usual forfeit."

"Well, be it so; but marke me, when I once commence,

'I'll never pause again
Till either death has closed these eyes of mine,
Or fortune given me measure of revenge.'

Will you let me off now?"

"Why, certainly, that's a terrible threat; but still I don't mind risking it."

"So be it, Lanky William, as you insist upon it, you must take the consequences. My memory is sure to fail, and when I break down you assist me—and, comrades, I must have a chorus, and take heed to

'Move
In perfect phalanx to the Dorian mood
Of flutes and soft recorders.'"

The lieutenant at once struck into a labryinth of verses, which, as he threatened, would certainly have lasted out the remainder of the evening, had he not been suddenly brought to a stand still in a way little expected by himself or the company. The attention of the party was first called to the presence of an intruder, in the shape of an ugly, wiry, half-bred sheep dog, belonging to the house, by his joining most heartily in the chorus which the lieutenant had called for This tickled their fancy not a little, and none more than that of the lieutenant. As regularly as the chorus came round, so did the deep yell of the animal strike in with something more of harmony in it than in that of his more enlightened companions; but, alas! what was mistaken for a mark of pleasure was, on the contrary, a sure sign of disapprobation; the loudness of the yell, and the growing ferocity of the dog's appearance, plainly bespeaking that fact. As verse after verse came pouring out in quick succession, the more excited became the creature, until, at length worked up to a perfect pitch of frenzy, without even the courtesy of a friendly warning, he seized the calf of the unhappy lieutenant between his grinders till he made them meet again; nor could he be made to let go his hold until Lanky Bill thrust his knife up to the very hilt repeatedly into his bowels. This was a most effectual stoppage to the harmony of the lieutenant and the rest of the company, which the captain took advantage of, by calling on one side another of the crew, and entering into a short but earnest conversation with him.

Whatever might have been the purport of the conversation, on the captain resuming his place, he gave orders that his unhappy lieutenant should be provided with a bed in the house for the night, and well looked to as to his requirements, and gave full leave and licence for the remainder of the gang, except the one he had been speaking to, to continue their orgies to as lengthened a period as they pleased; and bidding them a farewell, he and his man left the house.

It was about eleven o'clock that night that a solitary traveller on foot might be seen approaching the Jew's Harp. He seemed particularly merry, if one may judge from the jocund tune he was whistling, as he proceeded. Now and then he would leave off his merry carol and talk to himself aloud, and, with our readers permission, we will take advantage of one of his conversational intervals, and see what was the tenour of his mind.

"Well, upon my word," said the stranger, "I begin to think I am acting a very foolish part at my age. It is time that I began to sober down, and lead what the old folks call a respectable life. Pshaw! their idea of respectability hinges upon matrimony. It may be a very blessed consummation to a single life, and I daresay is, in some instances; but I never yet knew an instance in real life of that connubial bliss so much talked of by novel writers, and men of their kidney. Now, there's Horace Splashdale, a better-hearted, better-tempered man there cannot be, and he, poor devil, expected all kinds of unheard-of happiness in the married state, but he tells a very different tale now, I guess. Poor fellow! he'd better have remained single after all.

'Needles and pins, needles and pins,
When a man's married his troubles begin.'

That's true enough, and, by-the-by, I think that was tolerably well chaunted. And look again at young Spikemore; why he was a poor devil, indeed, in a pecuniary point of view, and when he married the rich banker's daughter, he thought the change would be a perfect El Dorado; but he found out, in an uncommonly short space of time, that a suspicion lurked in his mind that his wife entertained some old-fashioned crotchet that she had raised him from poverty, and was entitled to hold the reins; and quite correct he was. Poor devil! I think I see him now, petitioning his heiress for a little pocket-money No, it won't do for me that same matrimony, I cannot at all matrimonially inclined-although my present mode runs away with more money than I can well afford. Confound it, I forgot to write to Emily that I was coming to-night. Why, she'll think all manner of things, suspicion—trap—caught—cast off, &c., &c. Oh, but she knows me better than that, though, I hope. Hilloa! What's that? I heard a footstep. Hilloa! hilloa! No answer? Imagination, I suppose."

The stranger quickened his pace, and commenced another lively tune upon the principle of the school-boy whistling to keep his courage up, for he had now entered a very lonely part of the road, on one side of which was a thick plantation. Several times he started as he thought he heard the sound of steps amidst the decayed leaves and the underwood of the plantation; but by reason of the darkness of the night, and the thickness of the wood, he was quite unable to see anything decisive; but once or twice he felt half inclined to fancy that he could just perceive some dark outline stealing cautiously between the trees.

"This must be fancy," said the traveller, "and yet this place doesn't bear the most reputable character, and it would be nothing very wonderful to be attacked. Some scores of times I've come this road, at all hours, but I must confess that I never before felt such a presentiment of mischief. There, again, I'm positive now there's some one dogging my steps. Yes, most distinctly; and they say to be forewarned is to be forearmed; and I think I am a match for one, ay, or even two upon a pinch. Hilloa, there."

This ejaculation was addressed to a man who suddenly sprung out of the wood right across the path of the stranger.

"Stand!"

"It don't suit me. My business requires expedition. Stand out of my way."

"Easy my young gentleman. I'm not in the humour to be played with; and it's not my habit to parley. Your money, if you please; and without delay."

"Well, of all comical fellows, you beat all I ever heard of. So you've got the absurd idea in your head that I should quietly empty my pocket into yours without a struggle. Ha! ha! ha! Stand back, I say, and let me pass."

"What if I don't?"

"I must force you."

"Force! It is my turn to laugh now, if it were my habit; but I'm a man of business, and cannot afford to laugh in the wrong place; so as you refuse to give me your money, I must even take it. Now, sir, your money or your life" And, as the robber ended his sentence, he presented a pistol at the head of the stranger.

It was but the work of a moment for the traveller to seize the arm of the ruffian, and in the struggle that ensued, the pistol was discharged into the air without committing any damage to either of the parties, and the chances were in favour of the stranger getting the best of the encounter had he not received a stunning blow with a bludgeon dealt him by some cowardly ruffian from behind, which levelled him to the ground.

At this juncture, the two ruffians fell upon him, and without much difficulty proceeded to rifle his pockets of their contents He was quite incapable of further resistance.

"Cowards," he said, "petty larceny dogs, bad as your calling is, you are a disgrace to it. You may triumph for a time, but rest assured it will last for a very short time, for I know you both well."

"An idle vaunt," observed his first assailant, "an idle vaunt."

"I know you well, I repeat, and you shall find it so to your cost" replied the traveller.

"Liar! you shall never speak any more. There—there—there; shall I find it to my cost now? There, and there again. Ha, ha! I'm sorry you knew me, you might have lived a long and honoured life."

As the ruffian spoke, at every "there" he plunged into the breast of the unfortunate man a long Spanish spring knife. The stranger uttered a moan and a wild shriek or two, and was silent.

"What shall we do with the body, captain?" asked the other ruffian.

"Throw it in the wood," replied the captain, who our readers will have already anticipated to be Captain Cutts; "but, as in these matters it is best to be cautious, and not to incur more responsibility than there is any occasion for, return the purse into his pocket with a guinea or two in it. And stay, it will be as well to let him have a watch, so I'll leave mine in his fob and take his; the difference between a gold and silver one will not be perceptible to him now, and throw this knife by the side of him, it will disarm suspicion, and the jury will have a good foundation for their verdict, when the time comes."

"Cuss me, captain, I don't like to leave anything about him! Come, let me take the purse and its contents, and the watch—I am sure the knife will be quite sufficient for the jury, as it has been for him."

"Silence, dog! don't you know me yet?"

"Begs pardon, captain, no harm meant—but not even one guinea, nor the watch?—"

"Not an article, scoundrel. Come, lift."

"Ay, ay, captain, it's hard lines—but of course, you know best. He's no light weight anyhow, and was pretty good in a struggle: and if it hadn't been for this good crab-tree, my noble captain might have been now where we are laying him."

"Yes, and a word or two about that, my man: mark me, that whenever I honour you above your comrades by selecting you to accompany me in any similar expedition, take care that your assistance be given in a manly way, face to face; for, as this fool rightly observed, you disgraced our profession, yourself, and me. I will not confirm what he said as to your cowardice, because I know to the contrary. I attribute it to inadvertence; but take heed for the future."

Captain Cutts and his comrade having disposed of the traveller in the plantation, and arranged everything to their satisfaction in the firm belief that, when the discovery of the body should take place, the death would be attributed to the suicidal act of the deceased, left the place in a comfortable state of mind, and retraced their steps towards the Jew's Harp.

The knife of Cpatain Cutts was a good, serviceable, matter-of-fact instrument, and had done some service, if not to the state, at least to its owner, but fortunately for the unlucky traveller, it failed in its deadly aim for once. Only two out of the five stabs were dangerous wounds, the others striking upon the ribs, without coming in contact with any vital part. No doubt if the temperature at the time had not been so intensely cold, the sufferer would have bled to death; but as it was, a very considerable quantity of the blood had been set free.

The stranger lay for some time in the position in which he had been placed, unconscious of all around him, till at length nature coming to his assistance, he opened his eyes, and memory slowly brought back in vivid colours the scene in which he had acted so prominent a part. He tried to raise himself upon his feet, but most lamentably failed in his attempt; and the utmost of his remaining strength was exerted to enable him to crawl out of the thickness of the plantation, so as to be within sight of any casual passenger whom business or pleasure might bring that way.

Perseverance often conquers what at first sight would appear an insurmountable difficulty, as in this instance. The unfortunate man one or twice gave up the attempt to drag his wounded body to the requisite distance, but a strong hope of timely assistance added fresh vigour to his exertions; and after excruciating agony, by reason of the stiffness and irritability of the wounds, he at length succeeded in reaching a place where he made certain of being discovered by the first person whom chance might bring near the spot.

Nor was he disappointed. It will be recollected that Tony Thong had incurred some disgrace at the hands of Mr. Menzies. Although Tony was not a youth of the most sensitive feelings, yet he felt mortified at the treatment he had received, and was too much ashamed to go to his young master's to change his habiliments, in case he should be seen, and an inquiry made as to the cause of his sorrowful plight. This he really could not encounter, so he determined—whether wisely or not we leave to the reader's judgment—to walk about until his clothes should become thoroughly dry, and then make some plausible excuse for his absence during the night. This resolution he carried into effect; but unfortunately for his theory, he might have walked about for a month, in the fond anticipation of so comfortable a consummation to his wishes, without being at all nearer to it; as after the first few hours, to his dismay, he discovered the delight of all the servant maids—those incomparable buckskins, those once immaculate whites, had a decided antipathy to evaporation, and stuck to his well-proportioned legs as closely as the skin sticks to the eel—ay, and quite as wet, too.

Tony had walked for several hours, till completely foot-sore, and seeing no sensible alteration in the appearance of his lower apparel, he determined to make haste and get through the business in the best way he could.

The first tinge of morning was just breaking on the horizon when he reached the commencement of the plantation, leaving the Jew's Harp behind him. There was not sufficient light yet to observe anything very clearly, except the tall trees that overshadowed the road; and therefore it was not to be wondered at that poor Tony, who was quite absorbed in his calamities, should stumble over the body of the traveller—and stumble over him he did, very much to his terror and amazement.

The sufferer had heard the approach of some one, but was too weak to raise his voice above a whisper, and what little breath he had left in him was nearly squeezed out by the concussion.

"God have mercy!" exclaimed Tony. "What in the name of all that's living is this here? Spare my life, and take my money, good gentleman: do—pray do! I will willingly part with it! I haven't got much, but take it all—all!"

The traveller stretched out his hand, and with much exertion grasped the collar of Tony, and gasped out, in a faint, husky voice, "Help me!" and at the same time, leaving hold of Tony's coat, caught hold of his hand, and pressed it on his bloody breast!

Tony forcibly withdrew his hand, and the fact, in all its appalling truthfulness, flashed across his almost besotted senses. He looked closely at his hand; and notwithstanding the darkness of the morning, he at once discovered it to be bathed in thickly coagulated gore.

"God!" he said, "here's been horrible doings in this blessed place! Poor gentleman! poor gentleman! How do you feel? Speak to me, and say what I shall do for you!"

"Help me—help—me—or—I—die!" uttered the wounded man, in a dejected strain.

"Keep alive," exclaimed Tony, "till I come back! Now, mind that. If you die I shall never forgive you. I'll bring assistance to you in a twinkling, or my name's not Tony Thong. Keep up your spirits, sir, and you shall be currycumbed in no time. I'm off! Now, mind what I say, and keep alive till I come back!"

CHAPTER X.

THE ALARM.—SUCCOUR.—LIFE YET.—AND THE NURSE.

TONY made the best use of his legs in hastening from the spot, intent upon providing assistance for the wounded man, but was suddenly brought to a stand still, as the thought occurred to him to whom he should apply, and particularly at that early hour of the morning.

"I have it!" he exclaimed, at the same time giving his hat a severe knock on the crown, which nearly brought it on to the bridge of his nose. "I have it! Why, who so likely in this wilderness of a place as Mr. Menzies? To be sure he's the man that can and will do it; and, besides, it'll make me all right again with him, as it'll show him in what respect we hold his feelings for the

distressed and unfortunate. I wonder I thought at all about it"

Having come to this conclusion, Tony started off again, as if all the robbers in and around London were at his heels; and, notwithstanding sundry tumbles, he arrived at the mansion from which he had been so unceremoniously expelled the previous day in an incredibly short space of time. He waited not for unbarring the gates, or announcing the majesty of his presence in the usual way, but leaping over the garden gate, made up to the door of the mansion, and laying hold of the knocker with one hand, and the bell with the other, hammering with one and pulling at the other alternately, with all the regularity of a pendulum, at the same time bawling, at the very top of his voice,—

"Fire, murder, and thieves!"

Such an infernal din as that never before occurred at the quiet retreat of Mr. Menzies.

Mr. Menzies was by no means a light sleeper, and not by any means subject to dreams; but on this occasion all manner of unaccountable visions of calamity, fire, murder, robbery, inability to escape, and divers chimera of the like nature, took possession of his mystified senses for the first minute or two of the dreadful attack Tony was making on the unresisting communicators; till, at length, believing in his dream that there was no other mode of escape from the burning mass than jumping from his window, and that he had taken the fatal leap, he suddenly awoke, and suspected that there was reality in his dream, from the alarming commotion in the house.

The screaming of the women, the clattering and battering of the knocker, and the ding-dinging of the bell, all considerably heightened by the loud and frantic shouts of the unconscious sinner without.

Hastily jumping out of bed, Ralph Menzies threw up the sash, and inquired the reason of the disturbance, but Tony was too much absorbed in his own thoughts, and the occupation he was employed in, to hear anything but his own clatter; and it was not till Mr. Menzies had emptied the contents of his pitcher on the unlucky Tony's head, that that individual's attention was aroused to the fact of his calls having been responded to.

"What, in God's name, is the meaning of this horrible din?" interrogated he.

"There's murder!" said Tony.

"Where, where? Who's murdered? What is it all about?"

"In this plantation. You must come directly."

"Aint you the young vagabond who was here yesterday?"

"I am that same gentleman," said Tony; "but what has that to do with it? I tell you here's a horrid murder been done, and you're wanted."

"I tell you what, young gentleman," said Ralph, "I see what all this is about. This is your mode of returning what you consider you owe me for yesterday. I'll punish you severely for this, my man, you may depend upon it."

"I speak the truth, upon my soul," said Tony. "I tell you that there is a man murdered in the plantation, and that if you don't give him help, before much longer he'll die, and, as the parson says, 'the blood will be upon your head!'"

"Are you really speaking the truth? Is this no practical joke, and is the man living?"

"Ay, as true as my name's Tony Thong; and there, you just hold that 'ere hat, and if I'm joking, you keep it, that's all."

And Tony, with a good aim, threw his hat in at the window from which Ralph was looking.

"Well," said Ralph, half to himself, "this seems like the truth, and I must give my best assistance to help the man. Here, Tony, take your hat again, and wait till I come down. You're a better fellow than I thought you were. Go to the out-offices, and call the men, and tell them I want them immediately upon urgent business, and then return here and wait; I shall not be long."

Tony did as he was desired, and had some trouble in making the servants believe the truth of his message, but he did succeed; and Ralph, in the meantime, having hastily thrown on his clothes, and quieted the alarm of the females, made his appearance at the door in time to meet Tony and two of his men.

No time was lost in proceeding to the spot where Tony had parted with the wounded man; and, under his pilotage, they soon reached the place, where, in the same position as he had left him, he still lay.

"True, by God!" said Ralph, as he neared him; and as Ralph was not a man at all given to the utterance of profane ejaculations, he may reasonably be considered to have been in a state of very considerable excitement.

The day had advanced sufficiently since Tony's discovery of the body, to enable them to see distinctly the state of affairs. The unfortunate gentleman was lying on his back, with one arm stretched across his breast, and the other resting by his side in a pool of coagulated gore that had trickled from his many wounds. The blood had ceased to flow and was congealed into large gouts upon his breast, over which a white hoar frost had accumulated. His face bore the pallor of death, and had it not been for a convulsive twitching of the mouth, though at distant intervals, one would have accounted him as with the dead. In fact, Mr. Menzies was satisfied that all aid was useless, he being, in his opinion, as dead as man could be. But having by mere chance observed the slight movement of the mouth—a mere tremulous motion, and then but for one instant—he suddenly sprang to his feet from his kneeling position, and with a franticness of gesticulation that, on any ordinary occasion, would have certainly entitled him, in the opinion of his nearest and dearest relatives, to a sojourn at one of the suburban retreats for incurables, exclaimed, with a rapidity perfectly confounding,

"There is life yet—there is life yet—there is life yet! Spread out your blanket—spread out your blanket—spread out your blanket! Tony, John, James! all of you, look alive! Life and death—life and death wait upon your exertions. Now gently lift him—there, there—a little more. Stretch the blanket under him, Tony, my good lad, that's it. Now, now, each take a corner and lift him gently, and away for the house. There is life yet—there is life yet!"

At an easy pace, so as not to incommode their burden more than they could avoid, the party proceeded in the direction of Menzies' house, the old gentleman repeating to himself occasionally, "There is life yet." The morning was yet too early for them to be interrupted by chance passengers, otherwise the strange sight of a gentleman and three assistants carrying such a suspicious load might have occasioned some vexatious inquiries, and caused delays very detrimental to the health of the wounded man, and assuredly, if there had been policemen in those days, he would have been shut up in one of the cells as a drunken and disorderly character, and would not have had the assistance of the doctor until they had found him dead when they opened the door at the usual time in the morning.

Immediately upon the arrival of Mr. Menzies at his house, the stranger was carried to bed, and every attendance paid to him until the assistance of a professional man, for whom Tony had been despatched, could be procured. The women were much terrified at first at the dreadful spectacle before them, but soon became reconciled to the sight; and like all the sex, when their services are required in a case of distress, showed the utmost alacrity in rendering their best exertions towards the comfort of their unfortunate visitor, who had never rallied from the state in which he had been found, but remained in a perfect state of syncope nearly approaching to death.

The doctor, for whom Tony had been despatched, and to whom he had explained the nature of the case requiring his attention, at length arrived, bringing with him an assistant and a formidable display of instruments, enough to make a strong nerved man shake again at the sight of them.

"Good morrow, Mr. Menzies," said he, as he met that gentleman in the passage; "a bad case here, I understand, eh?"

"I am much afraid it is of that nature, Mr. Tweedle," replied Ralph; "a very bad case, indeed, sir."

"Ha! hum, yes. Five wounds in the chest, eh? bad place, bad place—very.—Deep, deep, eh? Is he sensible, eh? What does he say for himself, eh? Trouble, I suppose, trouble. Suicide, *felo-de-se*—devil of a bad wife, eh? Drove him mad?"

" Really, Mr. Tweedle, I am not sufficiently informed to give you any advice upon the subject, but I should recommend your immediate attention to him, otherwise we shall have nothing left of him but his body."

" Ay, ay. I see, I see, bad case, bad case; show me to him, we'll see what's to be done. Come, Dobbins, bring up the things—any brandy in the house, Mr. Menzies?—can't do without brandy—white brandy if you have it; if you haven't brown—eh, Dobbins, eh? Dobbins can't see an operation unless he fortifies himself with a dram, eh? Chicken-hearted, very, eh? And warm water, Mr. Menzies—warm water."

" No water for me, sir," said Dobbins.

" True, Dobbins, true, you're a comical fellow. I didn't suppose you wanted it; the patient wants it, Dobbins, the patient."

By this time Mr. Menzies and the chattering surgeon had reached the apartment of the stranger who still lay in the same unconscious state. The doctor ordered the bed clothes to be lightly lifted off, and proceeded to remove every article of dress that impeded a full view of the injury, cutting away those parts which were difficult of removal otherwise with the scissors.

" Lucky dog, lucky dog—dreadful cuts these, murderous attacks—no suicide—not strength enough—couldn't have done it. Lucky dog—bled to death if the cold weather hadn't stopped it. Now, Dobbins, scrub the decks as we used to say on board, and let's see what's the matter."

Dobbins, as directed, by the aid of a sponge and warm water, soon made a bare breast of the sufferer, exposing to view five most ghastly wounds.

" Ha, hum," said Mr. Tweedle, " I don't like that. See, Dobbins, that's an ugly customer on the right nipple; if it's touched aorta it's all up, and pack up the tools is the word, Dobbins, eh? All above the diaphragm, you'll observe, Mr. Menzies; more chance, you know, if cuticle with the sternum and ribs, eh, Dobbins, eh?"

" He's still alive, my dear Mr. Tweedle," inquired Mr. Menzies, " still alive, I hope?"

" Oh, yes, and hope to keep him so; we'll plumb the depths directly, Mr. Menzies."

" Is the circulation still going on?"

" Going on—going on? why, of course it is—why, Mr. Menzies, I thought you more of a lawyer, than not to know that the whole body is an anastomosis of vessels, and that although the cavity of the aorta may be obliterated, the circulation will not be interrupted. I knew a man who had that disease; he was one of our crew, and the blood expelled from the heart was transmitted into the trunk of the sorts, below the constriction,—and how do you think it found its way there, Mr. Menzies, eh? how do you think?"

" Upon my word, I can't say."

" Why, this way, Mr. Menzies, this way—by passing through the subclavian, axillary,

and cervical arteries into the mammillary, intercostal, disphragmatic and epigastric arteries; and from there it went into the vessels of the thoracic and abdominal viscera, and others of course."

" I dare say," observed Mr. Menzies, " that is all very true and very singular; but it is entirely beyond my understanding; and I'm sure you will excuse me for suggesting that your patient really requires the benefit of your skill."

" Ay, to be sure—to be sure—I quite forgot him; now, Dobbins, the probe. Ah, as I hoped," continued the worthy doctor, as he successfully probed the wounds, " as I hoped; two glanced off on the sternum, and one cut a notch in the rib by way of *memento mori*. But I don't like these two cuts at all, particularly the one over the right nipple, eh, Dobbins, eh? It's a dangerous wound, but I've seen worse. I recollect a patient once who had received a wound exactly in the same place with a foil, which came out at the left loin, making a most serious wound in the aorta; and I should have got him round again, if he hadn't been a little too impatient. Hasty—ungrateful vagabond—died before I got him well. Reputation would have been up a hundred per cent —deal of pains—deal of pains. They all said sudden death—wound of the aorta. Pho, sudden fiddlesticks—lived a month, eh, Dobbins, eh?"

" Very likely, sir," said Dobbins, " but I wasn't with you then."

" True, true, Dobbins; you were in long clothes then—pap, sugarsticks, castor oil, and gripes—eh, Dobbins, eh?"

" No doubt, sir."

" Of course, Dobbins, of course. But now you know, Dobbins, you're a man—seen practice—know the fore arm from the tibia, eh, Dobbins?"

" Under your tuition, sir," said Dobbins, " I should be much to blame if I did not."

" Good lad—good lad, Dobbins; and now let's see what's to be done to the patient—what do you say, Dobbins, eh?"

" Certainly, sir, and with all the most profound respect for your superior abilities."

" And all that sort of thing," interrupted Mr. Tweedle.

" I should, had he been my patient," continued Dobbins, " have looked to him long before this."

" Oh, you would, eh, Dobbins, eh? Ah! a little more experience, I see, wanted. I shall put you in short clothes to-morrow, Dobbins, and then breeches, and so on, and when you've worn a man's coat as long as I have, you'll not be in such a wonderful hurry, Dobbins. What say you, Mr. Menzies, eh, eh?"

" I'm entirely in your hands," replied that gentleman, " and so is our unfortunate patient; but, to tell the candid truth, I really do feel much alarmed at the lengthened period the poor fellow remains in this unconscious state."

" Don't wonder—not at all; but we'll soon

bring him back again, won't we, Dobbins, eh?"

"I hope so, sir."

"Now, Mr. Menzies, here's an artery here requires to be tied. You see, as the temperature of the body increases, the blood begins to flow. Stop, Mr. Menzies, stop, eh?"

"I am very anxious to see something done for the stranger," said Mr. Menzies; "so, with your permission, I will stop and see the operation."

"Very good—very good. The axilla has received a wound from above, downwards, through the pectoral muscles; and if you look intently, you'll see my mode, Mr. Menzies. Make a surgeon of you—lawyer-surgeon, not barber-surgeon. Now, Dobbins, the knife and director. There, now you see the artery exposed. These that I am now tying are the thoracic arteries divided in the operation. Understand, understand? system, Mr. Menzies, system. Dobbins, remove the clots, and give me the sponge; that's it. There, Mr. Menzies, that's what we call cleansing the bottom of the wound."

"Cleansing the bottom of the wound, or cleansing the top," exclaimed Mr. Menzies, "I can't stand this any longer; so you may finish your job by yourself, and when you've done, perhaps you'll be good enough to call me in: I shall be in the picture gallery."

"Very good, Mr. Menzies, very good; we'll soon bring him to rights. So you won't stop, eh? ha, ha! Well, well, every one to his trade, eh, Dobbins, eh?"

"Ay, ay, sir. Mr. Menzies is not very strong in the nerves, although a lawyer."

"Although a lawyer, Dobbins! What d'ye mean by that?"

"Why, they say that a lawyer has no conscience, and having no conscience——"

"No conscience, Dobbins, eh? Mistake, mistake—all conscience, Dobbins, all conscience—stretches wonderfully!"

"In that sense, true, sir; but they do say that a lawyer, like a doctor, is made so callous to human suffering and woe through his profession, that he feels for nothing."

"Fools, fools, Dobbins. Jackass, for believing it."

"Excuse me, sir, I don't believe it. I'm an example to the contrary; I feel now as sick as a dog, and without you let me have a glass of brandy, I shall be obliged to leave him all to yourself."

"Well, Dobbins, it's an infirmity, and I really must look out for another assistant; disgraceful—very. You must conquer your infirmity. By-the-by, you may pour me out a little—now are you any better?"

"Yes, sir, I'm all right again now."

"Then let's proceed, Mr. Dobbins, eh?"

Mr. Tweedle, who was really a clever practical surgeon, though somewhat given to diffuse conversation, as the reader will have perceived, proceeded with great dexterity in tying the ligatures above and below the wound of the artery.

It would be tedious to follow Mr. Tweedle in the remainder of his operations; suffice it to say that he did his business in a scientific surgeon-like way, and succeeded in reviving the stranger to a consciousness of his situation.

When this was accomplished, he despatched his attendant to the gallery for Mr. Menzies to witness the result of his skill; and when that gentleman made his appearance in a state of feverish anxiety, Mr. Tweedle grasped him by the hand, and led him to the side of the bed.

"There, Mr. Menzies, there's your visitor all right again—here for a blue moon or so—keep him low; don't stuff him with solids, you know. Tie up his jaws with a handkerchief—and your own—and gag the women."

"God bless me, Mr. Tweedle! what's all that for?" interrupted Mr. Menzies.

"Quiet—quiet. Mr. Menzies, we must have no talk aboard—that's what it's for. Understand, if he attempts to speak until I permit him, give him a slight tap on the head, eh, Dobbins, eh? I've just done so—he was giving his tongue the rein, but I stopped. Get some quiet woman to attend upon him, Mr. Menzies—a wonder—any deaf and dumb wretch, eh? She'd be the thing."

"No," replied Mr. Menzies; "but I think I can find a substitute. I can depend upon my niece, Maud, she is very discreet, and I am sure can be trusted—depend upon her, doctor."

"Good, good—we'll see her before we go, and instruct her. Since all that can be done has been done, we'll leave him to himself for a bit, eh, Dobbins? Come, pack up the tools, and take a drop more brandy."

Dobbins was not a man to decline the invitation, and having helped himself pretty liberally, and packed up his tools, as Tweedle called them, the three worthies proceeded to the breakfast-room at Mr. Menzies' solicitation, to partake of something congenial to the cravings of the inward man.

The two ladies were already there busy in the preparation of a substantial repast, in anticipation of the company of the surgeon and his assistant, whose abilities in that line were equally well known as in that of their profession.

"I understand, young lady," said the doctor, addressing Maud, "that your uncle has assigned to you the duty of nursing the young gentleman up stairs?"

"I shall be very happy, sir," said Maud, "to do that which my uncle requires: but I am afraid I shall not be found a very competent nurse."

"Oh, the best in the world—the best in the world!" said Mr. Tweedle; "you've not been used to nursing, eh?"

"Not at all."

"So much the better: professed nurse, too much tongue—shouldn't have any tongue—conceited, too conceited—shouldn't have any conceit—counteracts doctor's orders. Doctor orders weak broth—nurse gives beef

THE SERVANT BEARING A LETTER FOR MISS MAUD.

No. 9,

tea; patient to be kept low—nurse thinks, he's weak enough, and should get strength so gives him a mutton chop and pickled walnuts. Inflammation—devil know's what all —doctor's draught turned into a publican—won't do. Clever man to find out automaton nurse; do what's wanted—nothing more; make fortune—string all the old nurses up. We want a fresh breed of nurses, eh, Dobbins, eh?"

"Yes, sir," said Dobbins, "I entirely agree with you there; in my opinion, it's highly essential for the welfare of the community, and particularly for the rising generation, that the old nurses, as you observe, should be strung up, and a fresh breed be introduced in their place."

"I'm inclined to be of the same opinion," said Mr. Menzies; "and though a conservative to the back-bone, and consequently an upholder of old institutions, old houses, old customs, and everything else ancient, the institution of old nurses, I think, requires reform. By-the-by, doctor, how is it that all nurses are on the wrong side of youth?"

"Various reasons, Mr. Menzies—various reasons, as almost all ordinary day school-mistresses are of the same class. Husbands die, children desert, workhouse, work or starve, open school; teach young ideas—a dead cheat, a dead cheat—can't write their own names; know their letters; child teaches itself. Same with nurses; come into it naturally—nothing to learn, so they think. Know better than the doctors, of course they do. Old women have seen some service. Haven't they been mothers? haven't they had sick fathers, and mothers, and children? of course they know all about it. I recollect being called in to a gentleman who had swallowed opium enough for the whole navy. Two nurses (old women) sent for; told them to walk him about; then stopped a short time; they thought he must be fatigued, so they laid him down on the bed—died of course. Clever women—asses!"

"They are a very strange class of beings," chimed in Grace, 'I admit, and very opiniated; and as we are upon the anecdotal theme, I will mention an incident that came across my own observation. A lady of my acquaintance, who had favoured her husband with a son and heir, had to attend upon her a remarkably ignorant woman in the capacity of nurse—so extremely ignorant, that she could not string together a sentence without committing the most flagrant abuses of the language in which she spoke. Indeed, so extraordinary was her proficiency in this science, that it was with the utmost difficulty we could comprehend her meaning. But still, as the doctor observes, with regard to the class generally, she was excessively opiniated, and knew as much—ay, more, than any doctor in the profession; for, as she used to say, she'd 'valked the spitals,' and 'resisted at many oppositions,' meaning, as we afterwards understood, assisted at many operations. Well, my friend was one who

placed every confidence in the dictum of the doctor, and most religiously persisted in following out his directions, notwithstanding the art the woman used in endeavouring to supplant the doctor in his proceedings, by substituting her pernicious and old-fashioned, I may say, superstitious practices. But much to her chagrin, the steadiness of the wife, and the watchfulness of the husband, succeeded in warding off her various attacks, and all things went on well. When the time came for the nurse to be dismissed, she, with much diffidence, suggested to the mother that, on her dismissal, she was in the habit of administering to the infants under her care a dose of castor oil, and begged that she might not be disappointed in her wish to follow the usual course in the present instance, as she was certain that things would not go well with mother, child, or nurse, if it were omitted to be done. Now, doctor, the child was in perfect health, and all its functions in good and active operation, and this insidious attack was very properly resisted. The nurse implored, and the mother refused, till nothing would satisfy her but my friend assenting to the proposition that, as she wouldn't let the child take it, she should take it herself. This satisfied the nurse, and she felt comparatively easy in her mind."

"True enough, I'll be bound," said Mr. Tweedle; "true enough. I could tell you many such anecdotes; but time flies—must talk of something more important. And now, Miss Maud, allow me to impress upon your attention the necessity of keeping perfect silence in your patient's presence. If he speaks, say nothing in answer. Now mind what I say, and let me depend upon you."

"If the whole of my duty depends upon my silence," said Maud, "I shall have little difficulty in becoming an excellent nurse."

"I don't want you, my dear," said Ralph, "to be an entire nurse, but only to superintend, and see that the proper silence and attention is observed by the professed nurse I mean to hire for the occasion."

"Professed nurse, Mr. Menzies? Get no professed nurse. Get a woman who doesn't write 'professed nurse' on her cards, or I shall have my patient on my hands longer than I expect—mind that."

"Is the gentleman very ill—dangerously ill?" inquired Maud.

"Ay, as ill as a man can be, I assure you."

"Do you think he'll recover?"

"That's asking more than I will take upon myself to answer. If he be of an irritable temperament, I have little hopes; if he be patient, and attends to my directions, I'll put him on his legs again—eh, Dobbins?"

"Undoubtedly," exclaimed Dobbins; "for after that memorable operation which I had the honour of assisting you to perform, I will believe anything."

"What, pray, was that, Mr. Dobbins?" asked Tweedle.

"When George Witherington shot himself in the abdomen."

"Ay, ay, to be sure, Dobbins. I ought not to forget that, for it was the first case I saw, and the first, of course, I had ever attempted—a very singular case, indeed."

"May I be honoured by the recital?" asked Mr. Menzies.

"Certainly, certainly. I suppose you feel interested, having known the gentleman?—You did know him, didn't you, Dobbins—eh? I beg pardon—beg pardon—Mr. Menzies, I mean—eh?"

"Oh, yes. His family were clients of mine for a very long period."

"Well, sir, when I was sent for, I found that the ball had divided the muscular parietes of the cavity on the right side, and a portion of the ilium. The two ends of the intestine were protruded, separated, and inflated—a queer case, Mr. Menzies—eh, Dobbins?—The upper end was everted, so that its contracted edge strangulated the intestinal tube, the same as the prepuce in a case of paraphymosis. The fecal matter was obstructed, and the contents of the stomach, of course, were accumulated above the constriction. This was the case, Mr. Dobbins—eh?"

"Precisely, sir."

"Well, through the constriction, with a pair of scissors, I cut four small holes, and put the bowel into its place again. Through the piece of the messentery I passed a ligature, corresponding to the two extremities of the bowel. These I reduced as far as the margin of the opening, which I had dilated, and applied the usual dressings. Well, Mr. Menzies, I must confess I was by no means confident of a fortunate result to the operation; but he's living now, as you know, Mr. Menzies—eh, Dobbins, eh? I hope I'm understood, Mr. Menzies—eh?"

"Why, I do think I've got a glimmering of the case, but to tell you the honest truth, I don't understand much of the phraseology used by the gentlemen of your profession."

"All a mistake—all a mistake. I thought I'd studied the most simple phraseology, so that no one could misunderstand. What do you think, Dobbins, eh?"

"Why, sir, it might have been made plainer to a non-professional man; and if I may speak my mind, some of the sentences had they been a little less involuted, would have been a little better; and if the company have no objection, I will repeat the cure in a more intelligible manner, so that the ladies may understand it."

But the ladies without much ceremony declined the extremely liberal offer of Mr. Dobbins, and that gentleman once more buried his head into a monstrous pigeon-pie, which he had been attacking with exceeding vigour ever since his entrance into the breakfast room.

"By-the-by," said Mr. Tweedle, "there's something out of the common way in the history of Mr. Witherington, is there not, eh?"

"Yes, but nothing very extraordinary."

"I should like to hear it, nevertheless," said Mr. Tweedle. "I'm rather interested in this case."

"Well, Mr. Tweedle, the tale is very short, and here it is. The father, you are aware, Mr. Tweedle, was an immensely rich man, and was the owner of very considerable estates."

"Oh yes, I remember—I remember."

"Well, sir, on the old gentleman's death, George stepped into his shoes, as the eldest and only son. He had been kept short in his young days, and as a matter of course, when he had the means, he failed not to use them; and in consequence he soon got through the ready money. The rents came in too slow for his necessities, and a portion of his acres were put in the market and sold. The abstract was sent to the purchaser's solicitor in the usual way; and among the requisitions, was one requiring a certificate of the birth of George. The vendor's solicitor, or rather his clerk, made the necessary search, or perhaps I should say, a little more than was necessary; for he not only found the required entry, but one of a preceding date, bearing the name of Edward, son of George and Sarah, the names of his parents. This rather staggered the clerk, who immediately upon his return, communicated the intelligence to his employer, who was equally surprised at the news, he having known the family many years, and being entirely ignorant of the fact; but it was beyond dispute; there was the book; there was the entry; there the names, and the same residence. Now many lawyers would have concealed the fact, and satisfied the requisition in all that he was asked for; but this stupid lawyer, as some people called him, felt bound in honour to make the fact known to the solicitor for the purchaser, who, of course, required that Edward should be killed before George could deal with the property."

"Killed!" interrupted Mr. Tweedle; "God bless me, you don't mean that he was to be murdered? Bloodthirsty, very outrageous, eh, Dobbins, eh?"

"I can't believe it," said Dobbins.

"Excuse me," continued Ralph, "it is merely a term used by our profession, meaning that satisfactory proof should be given of the death."

"Then why not speak in plain language so that a non-professional man may understand it, eh, Dobbins?"

"True, sir, true."

"I stand corrected," exclaimed Ralph, smiling. "You see, George Witherington had a mere naked title?"

"Naked title," asked Tweedle; "what's a naked title?"

"Well, I thought you were more of a lawyer not to know what a naked title meant; but, however, it is the lowest and most imperfect title there can be. It consists, you see, in the mere actual occupation of the estate, and you must understand that a man having a naked title has nothing to show that he has any right to continue the possession. I hope I make myself understood."

"Yes, yes—go on, pray; but in as plain language as you please. Eh, Dobbins, eh?"

"Well, sir, having discovered this unfortunate hitch in the title, and stopped the sale, I felt bound to ——"

"Oh, Mr. Menzies, you were the stupid lawyer, eh—eh? I see—modest—modest. D—n it, man, never repent for doing a good action. Confound me, I often cut off a fellow's leg, and never blush, never ashamed to own it; pho! sir, pho! Eh, Dobbins, eh?"

"Why, Mr. Tweedle, I didn't intend to praise myself; but as it slipt out—so let it be. Well, as I was saying, I felt bound to kill this James or bring him to life. I caused numerous inquiries to be made to come at the truth of the tale, and at length stumbled over an old domestic who was intimate with the whole affair. It appeared that this James was born some years previously to George, and, notwithstanding all his father's precepts and wise lessons, he turned out a heartless, obstinate young rascal, and broke his mother's heart nearly. Nothing could improve him; kindness or harshness were all the same to him. The old gentleman got heartily tired of him, and sent him abroad, consigned him to a friend in the East Indies, and supplied the means to keep him. Well, from the very day he parted for good from his father's house, that parent made it a rule never to mention his name to any living soul, and nobody, who knew anything of the family, made inquiries, and so the matter dropped; he might be dead or alive, for what they knew or cared. The old gentleman had banished him from the house some years before his final departure, and no one but the mother and this domestic, who was my informant, knew of the real circumstances of the case. The second boy, George, was entirely ignorant of having so near a relative, as it had been the peculiar care of his parents to keep him in ignorance of the matter. The mother shortly after died, and no doubt, if the old gentleman had not died so suddenly, he would have set everything to rights; but it was not to be. Now, you see, the *actual* possession was in George, but the *right* of possession was in Edward, if living; therefore, George's title was a naked one and bad. Edward's was an actual right of possession, and not an apparent one, and if he had been living, he could, of course, have entered upon the disseizor and ejected George."

"I wish to Heaven, Mr. Menzies, you'd speak in civilised language. I have to stretch my attention to a most fearful extent to catch what you mean."

"I'm very sorry," said Mr. Menzies, "but I beg you will interrupt me when I make use of a word not strictly in the ordinary phraseology of the common everyday language, and I'll endeavour to explain."

"Thank ye, thank ye; I'll take the liberty, eh, Dobbins, eh?"

"I shall be very glad if you do, sir," said Dobbins; "for dang me if I understand a syllable of it."

"Now," continued Mr. Menzies, "perhaps I had no right to make myself busy in the affair, and should have allowed the matter to rest, in the chance of thirty years expiring from the entry of the disseizor."

"What benefit would have accrued from that?"

"Why, this:—Edward having the right of possession and the right of property, as he unquestionably had, and not attempting to recover possession of the lands for thirty years, which the law calls acquiescing, George would have gained the entire right of possession, which he had not before."

"I see, I see, eh, Dobbins, eh?"

"I don't see, I confess," said Dobbins.

"Well, Mr. Menzies, and then, I suppose, Edward would have been shuffled out?"

"No, he would still have retained the mere right of property."

"Oh, indeed!"

"Yes; but if he still took no steps for another thirty years, he would nave lost that too."

"Ah, true, true; you understand, Dobbins, I suppose, eh?"

"I understand more about rolling up a bandage," said the worthy assistant; "but I suppose I shall soon hear the upshot of it."

"I shall not detain you much longer, Mr. Dobbins. Now whilst debating with myself what was the best course to pursue under the circumstances, I received a letter from the gentleman in the Indies, to whom the eldest lad had been engaged, and which letter confirmed, in every respect, the particulars I had obtained from the domestic, and it also contained the pleasant intelligence that the devil had been roasted out of the young scapegoat, and that the writer felt every confidence that the young gentleman would do honour to his father's memory, of whose death he had heard."

"Did the letter say when he would return?" asked Dobbins.

"No; but there was a postscript, in which it was said that the bearer was the returned prodigal."

"Singular enough," said Tweedle; "but I suppose you were too much of a lawyer to admit his identity without farther proof?"

"To tell the truth," said Mr. Menzies, "I felt the whole affair to be a very delicate one for me to appear in, and therefore washed my hands of it altogether. I recommended each of them to friends of my own in my profession, and never further interfered one way or the other. I, of course, watched the case rather anxiously, but had no idea of such an unhappy result to George."

"Nor I, Mr. Menzies, nor I; but it's an ill wind, you know, eh, Dobbins? It gave us our popularity, did it not, Dobbins, eh?"

"It had that effect, sir, as regards you; but as to me—"

"Ah, never mind, Dobbins—never mind; you're equally useful in your sphere as I am in mine, eh, Mr. Menzies?"

"Undoubtedly."

"Do you really mean it, though, gentlemen?" inquired Dobbins.

"Certainly, certainly, Dobbins," said his governor; "both mean it."

"Then, confound me, if I don't make an open breast, and let you know all."

"Is the man mad? Dobbins—the ladies and oaths, non-assimilants—won't do, Dobbins—teach manners, Dobbins—teach manners!"

"I humbly beg pardon of the ladies," said Dobbins; 'but it was quite inadvertently that I so far committed myself."

"I freely forgive you," said Grace, "and I have no doubt my niece will do the same. But what were you going so say, Mr. Dobbins, when the good doctor interrupted you?"

"I was going to make the remark,' said Dobbins, "that I have no doubt Mr. Witherington shot himself in consequence of his elder brother taking the property."

"That all?" said Tweedle. "What a discovery! Everybody knew it! Why, Dobbins, you're drunk, surely! Brandy too strong, Mr. Menzies—too strong—eh, eh?"

"Well known, certainly," said Ralph.— "Dobbins is a little behind his age."

"True, Mr. Menzies. Lecture him—get him home and trepan him—polish up his brains, and sharpen his wits. Eh, Dobbins —eh?"

"Thank you, sir, for your kind intentions, but I'll think upon it."

"Well, Mr. Menzies, I think I'll step up stairs, and see how the young gentleman's getting on, and be down again directly."

The chattering doctor was not long on his errand, for he found his patient in a complete slumber; and after giving very precise directions to Maud, as to the diet and other particulars appertaining to the wounded man, he made his congee to the company, and departed, followed by his assistant, the patient Dobbins, who, as he turned his back upon the mansion, muttered to himself, as he placed his hand upon his stomach—

"I wish that the governor had such an operation as this every day. I wouldn't mind how many strings I burst off my waistcoat— no, that I wouldn't!"

CHAPTER XI.

DISCOVERY OF THE REMOVAL.—THE WATCH. CUTTS'S DISMAY.—THE QUARREL.

WITH a perfect conviction that the stranger was safely disposed of, Cutts and his companions hurried from the spot, and made their way back to the Jew's Harp, where they arrived before the party had quite dispersed. Those who remained were very far advanced in drunkenness, and it required all the captain's exertions to restore and to maintain some kind of order among the reckless crew who acknowledged him for their commander.

"Noble captain," hiccoughed a squat, brawny, bronze-faced fellow, "we missed your honour all at once, and—and have been quite disconsolate at—at—your loss—what's up?"

"The liquor seems to have that pre-eminence," replied the captain.

"Ay, ay: very good—what's done, then, captain, what's done?"

The inquirer answered his own question by immediately sprawling under the table, being quite overpowered by the very liberal libations he had been making at the font of Bacchus.

Indeed, very few of the gang were in a much better condition, but those who were capable, the captain very judiciously employed in assisting the incapable to their respective dormitories. This difficult task, however, was at length accomplished, and the parlour of the Jew's Harp numbered only the captain and his companion in the late attack for its tenants.

"Now, Grumps," said the captain, "this affair is one that requires to be kept particularly quiet."

"True, sir,—yet still, for all that, I'd like to have had the watch."

"Confound the watch!" said Cutts — "Would you risk your neck for a bauble?"

"Risk! Why, ain't I always a risking my neck? it's our profession to risk our necks—and I'd as soon run the chance for a watch as for anything else."

"It's done," said the captain, "and there's an end of it."

"Not so, captain, if you regret not having it, I'll go back for it."

"Stir an inch, scoundrel, and the next step will be towards eternity."

"Rather not go the journey now," said Grumps; "so as you've made up your mind —why, as you say there's an end of it. Now what's to be done?"

"Nothing is to be done," replied Cutts.

"Very good, then nothing more's to be said."

"Yes—not a word of what has happend is to be breathed to any of your companions. We cannot be too cautious in these matters— it is a question of life or death to us—the fewer in the secret, the less chance of the latter."

"I feel quite secure," said Grumps; "there's a special providence, as I've heard the lieutenant say, in the fall of a sparrow— and I believe I'm watched over by that same mystery—by which I am protected from any harm, and have a sort of licence to do what I likes—that's my firm opinion; and, therefore, feeling as I do, I'd as soon go and take that 'ere watch as not, and sooner."

"Confound the watch and you to. You are an ass for your pains, with your special providence; why, what do you think there is in such a fellow as you for any extraordinary power to throw the shield of protection around you ?"

" Well, captain, you have your opinion, and let me have mine. I tell you I've played first fiddle in similar scenes, and without taking much care as to results, and here I am, you see, a favorite.   I'm sure I'm right, quite sure."

" Enjoy your own opinion, then, but understand that I am not one of the elect, and, therefore, I request you to use some circumspection for my sake."

" Well, well, captain, be it so ; our customer has been well cared for, and it'll be your own fault if anything comes on it, that's all."

" I'm glad to hear you say so ; and now listen to me : you see that I took every precaution to mislead those who stumble over the body—they will find that he had money —his watch——"

" I beg pardon, *your* watch, captain, *your* watch !"

" Well, well, it's all the same. Now, you see, there is *prima facie* evidence that the man had committed suicide, and the knife I took care to leave by his side will be confirmatory of the opinion ; so you see we are tolerably secure."

" Yes, captain, yes, I am cock sure."

" Ay, ay, I hope so. So I may depend upon your secrecy ?"

" Undoubtedly."

" Then, good night."

" Good night, captain ; I wish you hadn't left the watch."

" Good night, good night !"

" Well, Mr. Captain," said Grumps, as the captain retired, " with all your tact and shrewdness, you're not quite up to the mark ; howsomdever, you've placed some confidence in me, and I feel bound to do you a good turn. It isn't everybody as'll pick out a man for a special occasion like this, and I feel proud of the distinction. I'll have the watch yet ; if I don't may I be tied up under the gollows like a common gaol bird ! Yes, I'll have an hour's sleep, and then go back again for the watch, and no mistake. I shall be doing the captain a good turn ; and if that lieutenant's bite should turn out queer, and we're obliged to smother him, I stand a fairish chance to walk into his shoes—blow me !"

The calculating Grumps stretched himself upon the form with the determination, as soon as he awoke, of proceeding to the body, and recovering that great object of his anxiety —the watch.

The chances are that Grumps would have slept much beyond the time he had limited to himself, if he had not been aroused by a curious and rather alarming accident, which threatened not only to wake him, but to put an end to his project and himself at the same time.

It will be recollected that the lieutenant, into whose leg the unmusical dog had insinuated his teeth, had, according to the direc-

tions of Cutts, been accommodated with a bed in the house. The strength of the liquors with which he had been plying himself, overcame and drowned the pain at first felt by reason of the bite, and induced a drowsiness which he could by no means control, although he had every wish to do so, as he had determined, should a favourable opportunity occur, to steal down in the night and take vengeance on his assailant—the unhappy dog. Before the resolution, however, could be carried into effect, he was in the land of dreams ; and, as the savage intent had been uppermost in his thoughts, to the very moment of sleep overtaking him, so in his sleep his mind was wholly occupied by the same feelings. The man who had undertaken to keep watch with him had quietly taken up with him a small bottle of spirits, to keep him up, as he called it, but which in effect had a quite contrary consummation, and long before the catastrophe happened which we are going to record, he was stretched on the ground in as helpless a state of drunkenness as any one need wish to be ; and, therefore, all obstruction to the project of the lieutenant was removed, supposing that he had been in a condition to carry it out.

By the time that Grumps had reposed about half an hour longer than he had intended, the lieutenant's dream had worked so much upon his imagination that what he failed to do in his waking moments, he partially carried out in his sleeping ones. In a complete state of somnolency, he sprang out of bed, and cautiously stooping over the body of his careful and trustworthy attendant, he seized the candle, and at the same time armed himself with a long and sharp dagger-edged knife, and stealthily opening the door, skulked down the stairs, and made up to the door of the parlour, in which lay the unconscious Grumps.

In his attempts to open the door, he made so much noise that it awakened Grumps, who, still but half awake, was for a time perfectly bewildered, and at length much alarmed at the grim appearance of the lieutenant, as he marched into the room. The sickly rays of the candle added to the cadaverous appearance of his face ; his eyes were wide open, but were fixed on vacancy. In one hand he carried the candle, the other being temporarily at liberty, he having transferred the knife from it to his mouth to enable him to open the door.

Now Grumps was by no means a coward, but he had some share of superstition still clinging to him, the remnants of injudicious early training probably, and he could not help thinking that the lieutenant had departed this life, and had got permission for five minutes' absence from purgatory, for the sole purpose of letting him know it an hour or two before he could have become acquainted with it in the usual course of things. He accordingly, as is usual in all such cases, indulged in a most copious perspiration, and as far as his fears would permit him, narrowly watched the motions of his supposed ghost.

The lieutenant advanced to the table, and having placed the candlestick thereon, again went to the door and locked it, taking out the key and placing that also on the table. He now examined his knife, muttering to himself the while, and seeming satisfied with the result of his scrutiny, peered about the room as if in search of an object.

"It's no use," said he, "I'm satisfied you're here somewhere; so you may as well come out and let me stick you at once, and save me the trouble of looking after you."

Grumps now altered his opinion, as to the incorporeality of the appearance, and came to the conclusion that it was the lieutenant *in propria persona* in a state of madness, and with this conclusion became doubly alarmed for his own personal safety, and was rather alert to ward off the attack he felt confident the lieutenant had made up his mind to commence upon him. Several times the eyes of the lieutenant seemed, to his fancy, to rest upon him, and he was in momentary fear of having to enter into a struggle with the lieutenant, of the most awful character.

"There's no escape, my lads," said the lieutenant, "I've locked the door, and locked it shall remain until I've ripped open your bowels, and then anybody may come in who pleases. Do you hear? come out you brute. What, you're hiding there, are you, eh? Come out, I say, and save me the trouble of getting at you. You may as well come and take it quietly; you're sure to have it, you know. I never put up with an affront from any one, and much less from such a whelp as you. Come out, sir, come out—what, you won't? Well, then, we'll see what a little inducement will do."

The lieutenant immediately began to whistle, and coax, and coax and whistle, again and again, but all to no purpose, for the dog was out of his ken.

"Come—come," said he, "come, my boy, I only want to stick this knife into your heart, and I won't worry you any more. It's no use, you might as well have it at once—I am determined you shall have it—and as you won't take it by fair words, I must drag you out, that's all. You think I don't see you, I dare say, but you shall soon find out your mistake."

The lieutenant appeared to look in the direction in which the alarmed Grumps was reeling at full length on the form, and as the lieutenant put down the candle, and prepared himself for action, he thought it was high time to stand on his defence. He had not long to wait to be assured that the lieutenant meant mischief, and of course, concluded that he was to be the victim. He accordingly let himself down from the form, and creeping under the table, well observing where the lieutenant was standing, thrust his head up on the other side, and blew out the light. The lieutenant, just previous to this move-

ment of Grumps, had suddenly awakened from his sleep, and was endeavouring to collect his scattered senses, when he received such a severe pommelling in the face from the alarmed Grumps, that he was more bewildered and amazed than before, and, in the suddenness of the attack, knew not what to do. Grumps did not allow him much further opportunity for thinking; for continuing his heavy blows, which came rattling in the face of the unfortunate lieutenant like hailstones on a greenhouse, what little sense he had left was completely annihilated, and he fell heavily on the ground, and lay without sense or motion.

"I've done for you, my cove, I think," said Grumps, as he groped for the key. "That'll teach you manners. I suppose you were envious of the captain's favours; you have now got mine, and much good may they do you."

Grumps having found the key, let himself out, and, in pursuance of his original intention, made his way to the plantation, for the purpose of securing the watch which the captain had transferred from his own fob to that of the traveller's.

The morning was sufficiently advanced by the time he arrived at the spot to enable him, without any difficulty, to observe the objects around, and his surprise may be more easily imagined than described, on discovering that the object of his search had disappeared. It was much too early yet for any one to travel in that direction, either for business or for pleasure. That the stranger could have left the place by his own exertion was quite improbable, as the knife of Cutts generally told its tale with undoubted effect. How then, could the body have been removed, and by whom? Surely he had not mistaken the place; no, that could not well be, for he knew every inch of the road as intimately as a poacher is acquainted with the preserves, for it was his (Grumps's) manor that same neighbourhood.

Such were the thoughts that rapidly passed through the mind of Grumps, as he stood contemplating the place where he had expected to find his victim. All thoughts of recovering the watch, and by that means doing a good turn for the captain, in return for the particular honour conferred upon him, in singling him out from the rest of his companions to do such a notorious work, vanished from his mind at once, and he was upon the eve of retracing his footsteps to the Jew's Harp, crestfallen and dispirited, when his attention was arrested by observing some one in the distance apparently making towards the spot.

The very unusual occurrnce of any one passing in that direction, at so early an hour, excited the curiosity of Grumps, who imagined that possibly the party approaching might have had something to do with the mysterious removal, and which idea was more strongly impressed, as the approaching stranger, the nearer he advanced, seemed to do so with much caution, ever and anon suddenly standing still, and looking behind him. Grumps was satisfied that he himself had not been observed, and, determining to see the end of the adventure, glided behind a tree, and waited the coming of the early-visitor.

On came the stranger, and at length being arrived opposite to that part of the plantation where the dark deed had been done, he, without hesitation, darted among the trees, and made up to the spot where the body had been dragged.

Grumps had long before this discovered who it was, but still retained his position, unable to decide whether to advance, retreat, or remain where he was; but while cogitating on the subject, he observed the stranger stoop and pick up something from the ground, and hastily place it in his breast. This action decided his wavering thoughts, and at once starting into full sight, he, at the top of his voice, with considerable anxiety, roared out—

"Well captain, has you got it—has you got it?"

The suddenness of Grumps's appearance, and the startling effect of his voice in the still air of the early morning, came upon Cutts—for Cutts it was—like a thunderclap. He gave a decided start, and was some considerable time before he could find nerve enough to make any reply.

"Grumps," he at length uttered, "how is it you are here, and what have you done with the body?"

"Has you got it again?" asked Grumps, without heeding the questions of the captain.

"Answer me, Grumps, and without evasion—what have you done with the body?"

"That's what I'd like to come at," said Grumps. "I've never seed it since last night."

"Why are you here, sir?"

"Well, captain, if I were to ask you the same question, what answer would you give me?"

"I am in no humour for trifling," said the captain; "my motives are beyond the reach of your scrutiny—but not so with yours. I insist upon a straightforward and candid answer."

"Well, captain, I suppose you must have it. I came to get a mouthful of fresh air."

"Indeed—nothing more?"

"Why, no, nothing 'tickler."

"Is the air more refreshing in this particular locality than in any other?"

"Not as I am aware of."

"Then, Grumps, you are a liar, and you had some ulterior object. What was it?"

"Well, if you must have it, then, you must. I came for the watch."

"Confound the watch—still hankering after the watch. Well, Grumpus, and have you found it?"

"No, captain, but I hope you have. What was that you picked up?"

"Psha! the knife."

"Do you know what's become of the body, captain?"

"Nothing whatever. I expected to have found it here, and had intended to watch how matters went, but we're too late; and how and by what means it has gone, I am at a loss to know."

"Well, captain, I'm very sorry, but I'm afraid matters are worse with you than you thinks for, that's all."

"What do you mean, Grumps? Speak freely, and without reserve. What is it?"

"Why didn't you let me, as I particularly wanted, bring away the watch last night, and you would have been safe, and the body might have gone where it likes; but now all is doubt and mystery; ay, and danger too."

"Curse you, Grumps, for a long-winded jackass; why, in the devil's name, don't you say what you have to say in plain language, and at once, without all this preparation?"

"If you please," said Grumps, "it's all the same to me, you know, because I'm one of the elect, and I may cut anybody's throat without fear of punishment in this 'ere world or in the next, because, it was so arranged afore I was born; but, however, I know you don't believe in these matters, and therefore I'll say no more upon the subject; but if that 'ere watch don't scrag you, may I be blowed."

"Ah!"

"Yes, my noble captain; surely don't I know that on the brass plate of that watch, there's your very name in full length."

"Oh, Grumps, you're correct."

"Of course I am, and yet you wouldn't let me bring it away, not with all my persuasion."

"Idiot that I am, and you—you mealy-mouthed scoundrel, why did you not, recollecting the facts as you did, make me acquainted with it at once?"

"Because you are so precious irritable, and don't stand much upon the value of human life, when everything doesn't chime in with your views, and that's why. I saw you were determined that I shouldn't have it, and made up my mind that you had some particular object to carry out in leaving it; but I afterwards thought, when you left me for the night, that it must have slipped your memory about them 'ere beautiful Roman characters on the brass plate, and so thinks I, now if I goes early in the morning, and just eases the dead 'un of that watch which is of no manner of use to him, but may play the devil with the governor, and consequently with his gang, why, I shall be doing him a good turn, and mayhap myself too, for who knows if the lieutenant goes off the hooks, if he's taken with the hydrophiby and smothered, that the captain won't put me in his place; and there, captain, you have my motives, which you say you have a right to."

"No, not if I hadn't another in the troop fit for the post, not if I could save you from

TONY THONG MAKES A SLIGHT MISTAKE AS REGARDS THE WHISKY BOTTLE.

the gallows by the exertion of a word, would I do it, scoundrel."

"Hard words, captain, hard words. However, now I know your mind, I shall know how to act."

"What, do you threaten, villain?"

"Oh dear no, not by no manner of means —I only speak my mind; I say again that, knowing your feelings towards me, I shall know how to act, that's all."

"Betray me, I suppose?" ironically inquired the captain.

"That's as may be," coolly answered Grumps.

"Say you so?" said Cutts. "I'm glad you have spoken your mind; I like plain speaking at all times, and honour you for it. Here, Grumps, give me your hand, and forget and forgive."

The captain stepped forward with outstretched hand, in all the apparent frankness and cordiality of an old friend and boon companion, which, completely taking Grumps off his guard, his career would have been of very short duration in this world, notwithstanding his special providence, had he not, while his hand was in the grasp of that of the captain, caught a glimpse of the bright blade that his treacherous friend drew from his breast, and which he immediately upraised, with the deadly intent of plunging into the body of his follower.

"No, you don't captain, no, you don't," said Grumps, as he caught the wrist of the ruffian; "you wouldn't be so cruel, I'm sure you wouldn't—what! sheke hands and cut throats at the same time—quite a mistake."

"Stand back!" roared Cutts, "or I will smash your brains out against this knotted oak."

"That would be more picturesque than pleasant, captain," said Grumps; "and as I perceive that you really do mean mischief, why my life's as good as yours, and we'll see who's the victim."

A prolonged and desperate struggle now took place between the two worthies, first Cutts, then Grumps, getting the better of the other in turn, until at length Grumps, who was much the cooler man of the two, succeeded in throwing Cutts a tremendous fall on his back. It was the work of a moment for Grumps to secure the knife which had dropped from the grasp of his adversary in his fall, and to maintain the superiority of his position, by grasping the throat of Cutts, at the same time pinning him to the earth, with one knee on his chest.

"Now, you see, captain," said Grumps, "a practical illustration of the accidents of war; a minute ago and you were my master —I am yours now, and what's your captainship worth? Why, not a minute's purchase. This knife that was to make acquaintance with my internal arrangements has altogether cut the idea, and has almost settled the point with you."

"admit you have got the better of me,

Grumps, and as you know I am no flincher, and I can't help myself, be kind enough to cut the matter short and finish the business."

"Oh, you want to be despatched off-hand, do you?"

"I do."

"Then you just shan't now, mind that; I'll disappoint you there, captain. You did me a good turn, as I said before, in giving me the preference to assist in cutting this man's throat, for which I feel much honoured; but you have since tried to take my life, and I may say treacherously. Well, I'll say nothing about that, but this I will say something about—that, take you for all in all, I don't think we shall find a better captain. Take your life, and now we're quits. All I have done or intended to do was meant for the best; anything I've said which has been unpleasant to you I'm sorry for, and there's an end to it; so get up."

"Well, Grumps," said the captain, "I must admit that of the two, you show the noblest spirit, and I candidly ask your forgiveness for what you have such good reason to object to; we were both in the wrong, and, as you say, let the matter be dropped, and think or say nothing more about it."

"Agreed, captain, agreed. And now, sir, what's your opinion about the dead man's removal?"

"That," said the captain, "is a perfect mystery to me; it must be found out by some means—my only fear is that I didn't effectually kill him, and that he has sought refuge somewhere. If I were sure he were dead, I should take no thought on the matter. What is your opinion?"

"Why, this here, captain, that he's still alive."

"For what reason do you think so?"

"Observe, captain, that here is about the spot we hid him when we received him from the road; that's plainly seen from the quantity of blood in this one place."

"Well?"

"Why then, notice, captain, the trail of blood from here to the margin of the plantation. Now it's plain to me that if he had been discovered and removed from this spot, he would, most probably, have been lifted clean off the ground, and if any blood was dropped at all, it would be only here and there; but you see that here is one continuous smear, if I may so call it, which shows to me that the man must have dragged himself along the ground, without moving much the position of his body; and if you follow the track, as you observe, there is an accumulation of blood at every ten feet or so, as if he had taken rest every now and then; and you'll observe here, now that we are at the margin of the plantation, there's a still larger collection of blood, and there it stops, as if he had finally rested here, and then had been removed."

"You are quite right, Grumps; I'm afraid the explanation is more than plausible, and the only thing now remaining to be done is to find out whether he be dead or alive. If dead, it matters not—we are safe; but if otherwise, the case is very doubtful; you recollect, Grumps, he said he knew us."

"True, and that was why you knifed him."

"Just so; now, Grumps, we must trace him, and until that is done there is no security for us."

"Well, captain, how is it to be done? I haven't much inventive genius, and therefore I'll leave it to you, sir."

"Very good—I'll think on the matter, and in the meantime be silent."

"Depend upon me, captain; and if I may be allowed to give a little homely and well-meant advice, never have your blessed name engraved on your watch again; but if you do, never thrust it into the fob of a man whose wizen you've cut—it can't do no good, and you may depend upon it that it 'll get us into a devil of a mess, that watch. Ah, captain, captain! I wish you had let me have gone back for it as I wanted—I wish you had."

CHAPTER XII.

THE MEETING.—THE MYSTERY UNRAVELLED. THE SCHEME.

CUTTS and his man had hardly concluded their conversation, and were on the point of issuing from the plantation, when they were interrupted by the approach of some one, and they immediately retreated under cover again, till the intruder had passed on.

The person who now approached was no other than Tony Thong, who had been despatched by Mr. Menzies to London, to procure the attendance of his (Tony's) mother, whom he undertook should attend upon the sick man, in the character of supernumerary nurse, and, as he said, without opening her mouth from the time she entered the house till the time she should leave it, except, as he said, it was to convey away her wittals. He had executed his errand, and was on his return to Menzies' house, when he was discovered by Cutts.

Tony had not quite got over the alarm of his recent adventure, and as he approached nearer to the spot, he slackened his speed, looking very cautiously above and below and on each side of him, as if fearful of coming in for another such adventure; and when he reached the exact spot, which could not easily be mistaken, he made a dead stand, and his knees knocked together with an unmistakeable clapping, such as little dirty boys produce with bone castanets.

"I thought I had more pluck," said he, "than I find I have. Why, what have I got to be afraid on? It isn't every day that a man's murdered here—pho! come, Tony—Tony, courage, my man, courage. What! you won't go on?—come, come, steady, boys, steady—you've a pretty pair of pins, and

don't think to get up such a clatter as this about nothing—come, get on."

It was all very well for him to try to coax his legs into a quick trot—but somehow or another they only answered with a violent shaking, obstinately resisting all importunities to carry their master from the place.

"This is downright humbug," continued Tony, "and blow me if I stand it any longer; and to let you know that I'm not to be beaten by such a pair of vagabonds as you are, I'll take you bang into the wood, so there's an end of it."

As good as his word, Tony made a bold dash, and overcoming the resistance of his legs, marched in triumph into the wood; the farther he proceeded, the more courageous he got, and laughed at his own weakness in having hesitated on his journey.

"I thought I'd get the better of that anyhow," said he; "but what if I should be attacked in the same way—ah! I never thought of that. I'd better make a fresh start and get out again."

"What do you mean?" said Cutts, suddenly darting from behind a tree, and clapping his hand upon the shoulder of Tony.

"Ay, what do you mean?" said Grumps, taking the same familiarity with the remaing shoulder.

"Now, gentlemen," said Tony, who felt quite himself again, when there was real danger, "what do *you* mean, eh?"

"You were talking," said Cutts, "about being attacked in the same way; now we've heard this is a queer neighbourhood, and have been on the look-out for some days, and this morning we have discovered marks about here which lead us to think there has been foul play not long ago—do you know anything about it?"

"Yes, I should think I do, spooney."

"What do you know?"

"Are you officers, my tulips?"

"Why?" said Cutts.

"Because I mean to be very cautious how I gives my evidence, that's all."

"You seem a sharp lad, at all events; you may say what you know about this affair, and if you can give us any information that is likely to benefit us, I'll give you a crown."

"Are you officers, I ask again?"

"Of course we are."

"Well, that's satisfactory—you don't look like officers much somehow."

"Probably not, my lad; you wouldn't have officers who are upon the watch hang their insignia about their necks, would you?"

"No," said Tony, "nor would I have cut-throats and highwaymen walk about in the broad day without an attempt at disguising themselves."

"What do you mean by that, you young vagabond?" growled Grumps.

"Peace," said Cutts, "the youth's quite correct; he's a sharp lad, and I admire his caution."

" It may be all very well," said Grumps, " but for two respectable servants of the king to be insulted by a shrimp of a stable-boy like this is too bad—a good deal too bad."

" Ha, ha, ha," laughed Cutts, " come, come, Smith, the lad didn't mean to say that you were a cut-throat or a highwayman ; he was only talking in the abstract—only in the abstract."

" He may talk in the abstract or the extract," said Grumps, " but he should have a little more respect to his elders. Now, my young horse marine, are you going to give us any information about this 'ere man ?"

" What man ?" said Tony.

" Didn't you say something about a man ?" asked Grumps, who detected the slip he had made.

" I should rather imagine not," said Tony.

" You certainly said something of the sort," said Cutts, endeavouring to help Grumps out of the scrape.

" Oh, did I ? Very well, my coveys, I suppose I did then, for it wouldn't be very polite to contradict two such respectable-looking gentlemen as you are—would it ?"

" Not precisely," said Cutts ; " but however, my man, we are pressed for time, and if you can give us any information about this matter, the evidence, which is pretty plain, that is, that some outrageous piece of business has taken place here, we shall be much obliged."

" Is that all ?" asked Tony.

" Not quite," said Cutts, " we should then have some clue to the perpetrators probably, and be doing a service to the public by pouncing upon them, and bringing them to justice."

" Well," said Tony, " there's something in that, and as I can't be doing any harm, I don't mind telling you all I know."

Tony now entered into a recital of his morning's adventure, and had proceeded in his narrative as far as the removal of the body, when Cutts interrupted him by inquiring whether the stranger was dead or alive.

" Alive, of course," said Tony.

" And is at Mr. Menzies, eh ?"

" I believe you, my boys."

" Did he say anything about—about——?"

" About the men who attacked him ?" said Cutts, interrupting Grumps, who was again just upon the point of committing himself.

" He has not spoken yet," said Tony ; " so he hasn't, of course."

" And what does the doctor say of him ?" asked Cutts.

" That he will get him round again."

" What part of the house is he in ?" asked Grumps.

" Why ?" said Tony.

" Ah, why—well, I don't well know why ; I suppose he was robbed of everything he had."

" No," said Tony, " I don't think he could have lost anything."

" What did you find on him ?"

" Oh, there was a purse with money in it, a pen-knife, a pencil case, and one or two other little things."

" Was there nothing else ?" asked Cutts.

" No, I think not "

" No watch with——"

" Confound you, Smith, I wish you wouldn't interrupt one when I'm collecting evidence ; one at the time's quite enough—we shall only confuse the witness."

" Oh, no ! not by no means—not at all—very far from it, my young 'uns. I'm quite cool and collected, as the cucumber said when it was cut up and huddled into a plate —quite—go on."

" Well, so then there was nothing else found upon him but those trifles you have mentioned ?"

" Yes, as your friend observed, there was the watch."

" The man cut his own throat, probably, as he wasn't robbed."

" That I can swear he did not," said Tony.

" Ah ! how ?"

" Because his throat wasn't cut, that's all."

" Shot himself, I suppose ?" said Cutts.

" Wrong again," said Tony ; " he was stabbed all over the chest, and the doctor said that he couldn't have done it himself."

" Indeed, and what made the doctor come to that conclusion ?"

" Because he said that the position and direction of the wounds luded the idea—I think that was the term he used."

" Well, my boy, I thank you for the information, and I have no doubt it will be of service to me. We must make inquiries into the matter."

" Don't you think, Brown," said Grumps, " that we'd better wait upon Mr. Menzies in our official capacity, and endeavour to get a clue to the robbers ?"

" We'd better communicate with a magistrate first, and get his instructions before we do anything," said Cutts.

" Yes," chimed in Tony, " I think that would be the better way—perhaps you'd better bring a magistrate with you when you come, and one or two more police officers ; it 'ud look more imposing, wouldn't it, eh ?"

" You may go now, my lad," said Cutts.

" Thank you, Mr. Brown—then you've nothing else to tell me—nor you Mr. Smith ?"

" Nothing more—good morning."

" Ah, good morning, my tulip—and I say, Brown, if you were to take a little of the hair off your face, I think you'd be a good-looking fellow; blowed if I don't—and then, you know, the thieves wouldn't know you."

Tony made a polite bow, and went on his way.

" Curse that boy," said Cutts, " I think he smells a rat. If I were sure——"

" I suppose you'd make cock sure that he should not smell any more rats ?"

" True, Grumps; you see the matter wears a most sinister expression, and as you say, I'm terribly afraid that watch will wind us up; however, we must think of something, and that quickly too. Grumps, meet me at the Harp, at four, and we'll devise some plan to prevent it."

" Very good, captain—I'll be there. In the meantime, I've something to do on my own account—and so farewell."

" Farewell—be punctual."

" Ay, ay, captain—punctuality's the soul of business."

The captain and his man now separated—the first taking the direction of the Jew's Harp, the latter towards the country.

" No," said Grumps to himself; " I have a scheme in my head which, if I carry out, will get us out of all trouble, and make me stand high in the gang. I'll get that watch, if I don't may I be crucified; and who knows but that I may be able to complete the captain's intentions by giving the patient another dig in the ribs—ay, who knows? There won't be much harm in that; in fact, it would be quite a mercy to put the poor wretch out of his pain—and dead men tell no tales—a good idea. I'm not used to this sneaking sort of business—housebreaking; but if I can't get in to do the job in the ordinary way, why I must get in the extraordinary way—that's all. I know I shall be successful, because I never failed yet in any enterprise I undertook, when I alone was concerned; because, as I told the captain, there's a special providence that looks after me, and what I do is always done with a good motive, and as the old parson that my blessed sainted mother used to attend, said, ' Never mind the means, so that the intent is good.' Now, my motive is good, as why? Because I mean to save the captain's throat from the hempen cord, and that's a good motive. Well, how can I do this good? Why, by removing that which would tie the knot. I'm quite clear upon that head; and if I can punch out from this young vagabond the whereabouts of the watch and the patient, it 'll save me a good deal of trouble, so here goes."

By the time Grumps had given utterance to his thoughts he had overtaken Tony, who was rather surprised at seeing him so soon again.

" Hilloa, my tulip!" said Tony; " what's the matter now?"

" Oh, nothing very particular, my lad."

" Very good. What's become of Brown?"

" Why, he's taken your advice, I believe, and gone to have some of his hair taken off."

" That shows his sense," observed Tony. " We shall make a man of him now. How long has he served his majesty, Smith, eh?"

" Oh, ever so long. But I want to talk to you about this sick man at your establishment."

" Talk away, Smith; talk away, my man. What's up, now?"

" Where is that said watch you were speaking about?"

" In the sick man's chamber, of course," said Tony. " We haven't moved anything."

" He sleeps on the ground floor, I suppose?" said Grumps.

" Oh, does he? Well, I wasn't aware of it."

" Do you think I could see him?"

" I've not the slightest doubt about it."

" When?"

" Oh, when you meet him, of course."

" Yes, yes—I am aware of that; but I mean, can I be introduced to him? I may be able to get some information out of him that may lead to the detection of the villains who made the attack on him."

" Yes, you may; but he can't be seen or spoken with by any one at present; so, Mr. Smith, you must wait, I'm afraid."

" Well, if I must, I must, that's all. I hope the poor man will recover. I suppose you have taken care to put him in a well-aired room?"

" You seem to be very curious about that, Mr. Smith, and, as I don't see any objection to your knowing all about it, why, I don't mind easing your mind upon that 'ere pint, if it's only for the pleasure of getting rid of your company, for, you know, it don't do anybody any credit to be seen walking with a blessed Bow-street runner."

" True, my lad, but that's a wulgar prejudice; however, you may as well let me know."

" You know Menzies' house, of course?"

" Oh, yes, all over outside."

" Well, then, the gentleman sleeps, being at the top of the house, in the front room immediately opposite to the head of the staircase. Now, I hope you're satisfied?"

" Perfectly; and, as a further favour, will you oblige me with your name?"

" By all manner of means. My name is Tony Thong, at your service."

" Many thanks, Tony Thong; and allow me to say, Tony Thong, that you're a little more green than you think you are; so, once more, a very good morning, Tony Thong;" saying which, Grumps turned on his heels, and retraced his steps.

" Ha, ha, ha!" laughed Tony. " Mr. Smith, you'll find I'm wide awake enough for you."

CHAPTER XIII.

THE BREAK IN, AND ITS UNEXPECTED RESULT.

THE sick man, as Doctor Tweedle had prognosticated, after a night of uninterrupted quiet, awoke in the morning with all his senses about him, though, of course, considerably weakened by the immense loss of blood he had sustained. When he first opened his eyes, he was for some time at a loss to account for the position he found himself in, until the scene that had so recently happened, and in which he was the principal actor, flitted across his memory. He at once concluded that he had been rescued from his perilous situation by some good Samaritan, who had provided the comfortable quarters in which he found himself located; he once or twice attempted to raise himself up in his bed, for the purpose of making a closer inspection of his room, and of ascertaining if there were any one present, in attendance upon him: but the effort on each occasion was abandoned, and he felt as though he were actually fastened down, so incapable was he of making the slightest movement, by reason of his extreme weakness. The pain from his wounds was severe, but he had sufficient nerve to bear that with fortitude; his only anxiety being to know to whom he was indebted for the kindness he was receiving, and to hear the means by which he had been saved.

Maud, according to the directions of the worthy doctor, had paid the most untiring attention to her patient, although her exertions were not, as yet, called into active operation: she had, from the first moment she entered upon her duties, hardly stirred out of the apartment; and at the time when the stranger awoke, she was sitting at the side of the bed next to the door, the furniture screening her from his observation; she caught a momentary glimpse of the sufferer as he opened his eyes, but which glimpse was quite sufficient for her to come to the conclusion that he was conscious, and she immediately retired to communicate the intelligence to her uncle, preferring that he should have the first interview with his visitor, considering him to be a better person to give what explanation might be required, and also to impress upon him the necessity of following out the doctor's regulations with regard to his recovery.

Ralph Menzies accordingly repaired to the apartment, and introducing himself to the stranger's attention, entered into a short explanation of how matters stood; at the same time requesting that all further communication might be postponed until the doctor had reported in his favour, and had given permission for a full and free liberty of speech.

The sick man made Ralph understand by signs that he understood what was said to him, and also the importance of the revelation, had he had the will to answer by word of mouth, he had not the power; for he was even too weak to make the necessary exertions.

Ralph Menzies perceived the ineffectual attempt, and wishing his visitor a speedy recovery, and promising to send him a careful nurse, left him, highly delighted that he had recovered his senses.

By the time Ralph had descended to the parlour, Tony Thong had returned from his errand, and was awaiting to communicate the result.

"Well," said he, "what news, Tony?"

"If you please, sir, the old woman will be here, I expect, almost directly."

"The old woman?"

"Yes, sir, my blessed old mother, rest her soul!"

"Why, my lad, I must take an exception to the freedom, if you speak in connexion with your parent. Don't you think, Tony, it would be more respectful to call her your mother, and drop the old woman?"

"Lord love you," said Tony, "she's used to that sort of thing! I always call her so, and she'd hardly know who was spoken to, if I called her mother."

"Well, everybody to their taste, certainly," said Mr. Menzies; "but for your own credit sake, I should be a little more choice in the language I used. Should you like to change your master, Tony?"

"I shouldn't mind having one, sir," said Tony, "for I'm out of collar, and no mistake!"

"Out of collar—oh, I suppose you mean out of place, eh?"

"You've just hit it, sir—my governor's going, if not already gone, on to the Contranent—that's somewhere abroad, I believe, and didn't he give me turnips, eh? I believe you, he did!"

"What did he give you turnips for, Tony? Did he pay you in kind, eh? The truck system?"

"I don't know what you mean by the truck system, or paying in kind, but he shook the bag at me; and here I am, quite an orphan, and at liberty to be any one's servant."

"Am I to understand that you are discharged, then?"

"Why, bless you, sir, didn't I just say so?"

"Have you anything else in view?"

"Yes, I have something in view, I can tell you—a devilish good joke it 'll turn out, if the ball comes home safe; and somebody will suffer for it, I guess."

"You're quite beyond my comprehension, Tony; and, therefore, I'll give up the attempt to understand you. Now, Tony, you have done me good service in causing me to rescue that unfortunate gentleman from a certain and untimely death, for which I owe you a return. You are out of a situation, you say—if you like to enter into my service, say so, and the matter is settled. I've no particular occupation for you, but I dare say you will be able to make yourself handy. What say you, sir?"

"Nothing I should like better," said Tony. "I'm something like a gentleman's son—always on the look out for a place where there's nothing to do except write a receipt for the quarter's salary. Why, sir, I shall be better off than a government elk. I shan't have the trouble of being obliged to read the newspaper, even, to get rid of the two or three hours they are obliged to kick their heels in some room, to justify, in some sort, the receipt of the money."

"That'll do, Tony—that'll do. Go into the kitchen, and make yourself acquainted with Susan, and see if you can do anything for her."

" Do you mean that, sir ?"

" Certainly—you've no objection ?"

" Not none in the least. It's the very thing of all others I should most like. I'm very fond of that Susan—very."

Tony made a leg, as he called it, and darted into the kitchen at once, where he communicated to that fair creature—whose late misbehaviour had been forgiven—the welcome intelligence of his being placed upon the establishment, and who was as much delighted as he was at his good fortune.

*　　*　　*　　*

We will now return to that scheming gentleman, Mr. Grumps, who, it will be recollected, parted from Tony, evidently rejoicing in the discovery which he thought he had made, at the expense of the sagacity of that individual, and at the probability he now thought there was of carrying into execution his so much cherished plan of getting back the watch, if not of putting an end to all possibility of the stranger furnishing a link in the evidence—supposing things should arrive at such a climax—by putting a finishing stroke to what his captain had so nobly commenced.

The appointment with Cutts, of course, he felt bound to keep ; but at the same time he resolved that, whatever might be thought of, he would most religiously promise to fall in with it, only with this difference—that he would follow out his own, only supposing the time did not clash ; and he thought that, by so doing, he should have an extra claim for the admiration and reward of Cutts, which he was quite satisfied would be the case, because he was so certain of a happy result to his enterprise.

He accordingly met Captain Cutts at the rendezvous ; but as the plan which Cutts had in the meantime concocted was not adopted by Grumps, it would be useless to enter into any particulars concerning it ; and, therefore, we will follow Grumps and his fortunes, and trace the success of his operations.

Although the profession of Grumps, to which he had regularly served his articles, and in which he was a proficient, was considered by all the collateral branches to be of the highest and most respectable class ; and Grumps himself being also of that opinion, yet upon an emergency he could turn his attention from those high notions, and step a spoke or two lower down on the trade ladder. He had done so on more than one occasion, of course, under the rose ; and, therefore, was something more proficient in the science of housebreaking than might have been expected for one in his peculiar line of business. Besides, Grumps had something more in view than the recovery of the watch, and keeping back the other evidence. Why couldn't he do a little business on his own account while his hand was in, eh ? Why not ?"

These considerations, therefore, him thereunto moving, as the gentlemen of the legal profession say, as soon as he could disengage himself from the company of Cutts and his comrades, he did so, and went about his pre-

parations with all the business and tact of an old professional.

Long before the early hours of the following morning—nay, before the darkness of night had reached its climax, Grumps was anxiously prowling about the locality of Menzie's house, cautiously watching every movement that he could detect, both in and out of it. It was not until twelve o'clock that night that he saw the last of the lights disappear, and he determined to wait yet another hour, to give every one of the inmates a better chance of being in profound repose, ere he commenced operations.

The window of the room in which he fancied, from Tony's information, the wounded man to be, was no small object of his attention, and he more than once felt very uneasy misgivings as to the truth of that information, in consequence of not being able to see any appearance of a light there, as undoubtedly, in his opinion, there should have been ; but having come to the conclusion that probably a curtain interposed itself between the candle and his perception, he at length felt more confidence, and hesitated no longer to begin the attack.

There were many more assailable points of attack than the principal door ; but as the matter was pressing, the principal object to be attained being of much more importance to the parties concerned than the amount of swag he should be enabled to transfer to his own account, he could not afford the usual time generally employed by professed housebreakers of pumping from the servants and others the different localities occupied by the various tenants, so as to avoid collision, which in his case would have been extremely perilous, he being single-handed ; and therefore he determined to avoid making his entrance through any easier means of ingress, in case he should have the misfortune to stumble upon any of the domestics, and by that means frustrate his grand object.

The first thing he did was to introduce a pick into the key-hole, but here he was disappointed, for whoever had fastened up the house, had taken the very necessary precaution of leaving the key within the lock, and turning it, so that it could not be pushed out of its wards from the outside.

" Done there," said Grumps. " Come, he's an artful dodger the same cove who fastened this 'ere door—why there's not one blessed flunkey in a thousand up to the move. Well, let's see if the door's plated behind ; this is the little gentleman that'll do the business, if it isn't. Come out, you little vagabond, will you ? Don't yer know I loves yer ?"

This little endearing apostrophe was made to a small pocket centre-bit, which Grumps quickly adjusted, and tried upon one of the panels.

" That'll do," said he, " that'll do—no impediment—ha ! ha ! in ten minutes I shall be on the other side of you, my heart of oak. Into him again, my boy—show him no quarter; and if you're a good boy, I'll give you a little more fat—ah! what, you begin to squeak a bit, do you, at the very mention of grease? Well, well, I s'pose you must have a bit as I promised—blow me, you've had hot work, my little dear, and don't sweat over it either."

The little instrument did its work in first-rate style, and when it showed symptoms of uneasiness, Grumps gave it a little fat, as he promised, to keep it quiet; and in about ten minutes, the panel was perforated with numberless holes all around its margin, so close together, that it only required the introduction of a long, thin, and sharp cutting instrument, something in the shape of a delicate saw, to entirely remove the panel, which was accordingly done without the least noise.

All obstructions being thus removed, Grumps pocketed his tools, and creeping through the door, found himself in the hall, about the middle of which he soon perceived the grand staircase which Tony had alluded to. Having taken off his shoes, and adjusted his dark lantern, so as to allow him just sufficient light to direct his steps, and no more, he cautiously ascended the stairs, neither turning to the right nor to the left, but steadily maintaining his principal object, that of reaching the door exactly opposite to the head of the stairs. The staircase was of stone, and built in a spiral direction, or what is commonly called a well staircase; at every landing-place of which were corridors, leading to the various chambers of the mansion. At length, Grumps ascended as high as he could, a door preventing any further progress in the upward direction.

"All right," thought Grumps; "here's the door Tony Thong was so good-natured as to point out to me. I'll just listen if anybody's stirring; no, all is quiet. A rum sort of bed-room for a sick man this, if there's as much wind inside as comes through the key-hole into my ear. I don't understand this. By gad, this is no room after all, but some door dividing the top landing; I wonder what's the meaning of this—it must be so, because I can see beyond it by looking over the banisters."

Grumps was quite right in his calculations; it was merely a door separating the next landing from the top of the stairs whereon he stood It happened that the upper staircase being of wood, in many places was in rather a decayed state, and Mr. Menzies having no use for the upper part of the mansion, had had the door put there to prevent any use being made of that part of the mansion. The door had been kept locked for many years: and the key duly labelled in lawyer-like fashion, was with others hung up in its proper recepticle, a little mahogany key-box, which was kept in Mr. Menzies' study.

All this was perfectly well known to Tony, the use he made of which knowledge will be seen presently.

If we had been giving a description of the internal arrangements of the mansion, we certainly should not have omitted one of the principal and most essential ornaments of the hall, and that was an immense lamp upwards of six feet in depth, and of proportional circumference. The chased frame was of the most elaborate description, terminating in a *fleur-de-lis*, through the neck of which was a contrivance for fastening the chain by which the lamp was suspended. The chain itself was a massive bronze one, being fixed into a beam in the roof, the whole being of a ponderous wieght; but the elegance of the design, and the large proportions of the staircase, down the centre of which it came, and the colossal dimensions of the hall, gave the lamp and its appendages comparatively a light appearance.

Grumps having satisfied himself that he must remove this obstruction to his further progress, began to collect his implements, and on applying a pick to the key-hole, the door opened without its assistance, it being unlocked.

'Ah," said he, "that puts me in mind of the old adage, 'Look before you leap;' however, I'm all right now, and I guess I shan't be long before I get that which I've come for, and which I fancy I well deserve."

Grumps thus mounted the first stairs, but notwithstanding that he took every precaution to guard against making the slightest noise, a loud creak followed his step, which was considerably added to by the echo which accompanied it. This rather alarmed the burglar, and he paused some time to listen if anybody had been disturbed by the noise, and hearing no movements, he determined to proceed; but first well surveying the height and number of the stairs, he had to ascend before he could reach the top landing, in order that he might arrive there with safety in the dark, he closed the shade of his lamp and walking as near to the banisters as possible to prevent as much as he could a similar noise happening, he once more began his ascent, in the confident assurance that he should ultimately succeed in his project.

But alas! human calculations are often based upon an unsound foundation; that young gentleman, who was so much in love with himself, and with his white buckskins, Tony, had been there before him, fully expecting from the tenour of the questions put to him by Cutts and Grumps, but more particularly the latter, that such a domiciliary visit was intended; nor had he been there for nothing—oh dear no; on the contrary, quite the reverse, as he would have said. He had busied himself in taking up one of the first boards of that flight of stairs, and very ingeniously replacing it again, but in such a manner, that any one treading on it, must inevitably have lost his balance, and have slid under the hand-rail, as the stair descended with his weight, into the hall below and that any one must have done so, there

THE DEATH OF UGLY DICK IN THE JEW'S HARP.

can be no manner of doubt, Tony having also removed two of the rails, allowing sufficient room for any one to go quietly through, with the unpleasantness of abrading his sides.

Grumps had proceeded as high as the fifth stair with, comparatively, no noise, but the sixth put an end to the idea of its continuance; for no sooner had he fairly got one foot on it, and had raised the other for the next step, so that the whole weight of his body was upon it, than the resistance was overcome, and, as Tony had anticipated, the board declined to an angle of about forty-five degrees, and Grumps slipped through with all the ease in life.

Who shall tell, or what pen can express, the thoughts that rapidly passed through the mind of Grumps at that awful moment? He knew that nothing could save him. A loud shriek rent the air as Grumps toppled over and over down that fearful well-staircase—another moment and his head came in contact with the *fleur-de-lis* of the hall-lamp, piercing and splitting it in divers awful and terrific fractures, and penetrating clean through the brain. It was an awful moment, but it must have been but a short one to him. The impetus with which he came, accelerated by the fearful height of the fall, snapped the chain and down came the massive lamp on to the stone hall, shivered into a thousand fragments, and with a noise that would have awakened the Seven Sleepers.

All in the house were awakened by the dreadful crash, and, except the sick man, huddled on some articles of apparel, and made to their respective rooms, each anxiously waiting to hear some one do the initiative.

At length, Mr. Menzies, having adjusted his small-clothes to his satisfaction, issued forth, candle in hand, and repeated two or three times in succession, "Hilloa, hilloa, there!"

"Oh, Ralph, what in the name of God can be the matter?" said Grace rushing out of her room, and clinging fast round the neck of her brother. "Oh, he's committed suicide! I'm sure he's committed suicide! Didn't you hear the noise?"

"Hear the noise!" said Ralph; "why, who could help hearing it?"

"Dear uncle," said Maud, also making her appearance, "what has happened—what has happened?"

"Really, my dear, I am as much at a loss to know as you. We must see; here, Tony, Susan, some of you. Where are you, and what are you about?"

"Oh, lauk, master," said Susan, who was looking over the banisters above the landing on which the group were standing; "it's a ghost, it's a ghost; I am sure it's a ghost! Oh, gracious Heavens! what shall I do? Here's a pretty thing!" and off Susan retreated into her room, as though, indeed, she had seen a ghost. The fact was that in her excessive alarm, instead of putting on her clothes, she had taken off

her bedgown, and only discovered her mistake after she had been addressing her master in the language we have just recorded; but, unfortunately, not before Ralph and the ladies had perceived her unfortunate plight; and, notwithstanding the uncomfortable state of mind which Ralph was in, he could not forbear breaking into a hearty laugh at poor Susan's misfortune.

By this time all had collected together, and Tony was the first to perceive, as might be expected, the catastrophe which had caused all the alarm.

"Well, I'm blow'd," said the governor, "if the blessed chain hasn't broken, and let the lamp fall!"

"It is even so," said Ralph. "Thank God it is no worse. Fortunate, indeed, that it happened in the night time, otherwise some of us might have been crushed to death. I should have thought that chain would have lasted for ever."

"Well, now, I should not," said Grace "Everything must have an end, and why shouldn't the chain have it now, as well as by-and-by?"

"Very well, sister, as you please; but, in my opinion, it's a very curious circumstance, and a very providential one. Tony, take a light, and see what damage is done."

"Very good, sir," said Tony; and taking the candle out of his master's hand, he descended into the hall. He was prepared to see something more there than the lamp, and, accordingly, through the obscurity he traced a dim outline of some black mass, which convinced him that the plan had taken effect.

"By gum," he said to himself, "here's Mounseer Smith again, and no mistake. Yer vagabond, I told you I was wide awake enough for you;" and then hastening back again to his master, he whispered into his ear his suspicions.

"A man, do you say, Tony?"

"I'm positive of it, sir."

"Grace, Maud, retire to your own rooms. This is more serious than I at first thought," said Ralph. "I will descend with Tony, and see the state of the mischief. Pray retire, and I will inform you of the particulars in the morning. Ask no questions at present; but pray go – pray go."

The ladies retired as Ralph had requested them, and he and Tony descended into the hall, and making their way to the fallen lamp, much to Ralph's horror and to Tony's dismay—for he had not calculated upon the serious results of his scheme—there lay the body of the burglar. The skull was crushed in and split—to compare great things with small—like the top of an egg that has been battered with a spoon. The brain had spirted out as the sharp ornaments had entered the head, and lay in thick clots, matting the surrounding hair together in clammy flakes; the blood was oozing from the mouth and ears, and, in addition to all this, the spine was completely broken in half, as was evident at the first glance, from the way in which he was doubled up, the back of the neck and the heels being nearly together.

"How dreadful!" exclaimed Ralph.

"Dreadful indeed," said Tony, aloud; but, *sotto voce*, he added, "if people will volunteer to come and light other people's lamps when they're inexperienced, and an accident happens, why I say it serves 'em right."

CHAPTER XIV.

THE INQUEST.

DEATH, when it comes in the ordinary way, is an exceedingly disagreeable object, even with one of the members of a man's own household; but when in the form of a stranger who has intruded into the family, and whose means of exit are accompanied with such dreadful circumstances, it is beyond all description terribly annoying, to say the least of it. Mr. Menzies thought so at all events, and took immediate steps to get the body removed from the house, by losing no time in giving immediate notice to the necessary persons to have the disagreeable forms of an inquest got through with all possible celerity. The wretched man was, by Mr. Menzies' directions, suffered to remain in the same position precisely that he was found in; in fact after ascertaining that there was no hope of life in him, the communication between the back and front part of the house was for the present stopped, and the family made use of the back entrance until the body should be removed; for none of them liked to pass too close to the mangled corpse, not through any superstitious feeling, but from a natural and inherent feeling of sense possessed by all the civilised race, excluding, of course, doctors and undertakers.

In due course the worthy coroner, Mr. Scruton, arrived at the mansion where the jury had previously assembled, and under the care of the beadle, were waiting his arrival; and in consequence of a paragraph having been the round of the papers, shortly stating the singular circumstances as far as was known of the extraordinary death, a few stragglers had collected, and, by the permission of Mr. Menzies, were allowed admission, and were also anxiously waiting to witness the examination.

The jury having been duly sworn, accompanied the coroner to examine the body, as did also Mr. Menzies and Tony; and on their return the coroner proceeded in his investigation, Mr. Menzies being the first witness called.

"Mr. Menzies," observed the coroner, "this is really a very shocking occurrence, and I feel much sympathy for you; but you know accidents will happen to the best regulated families, and I suppose this was one that could not be avoided. Do you know anything of the unfortunate man?"

"Nothing whatever."

"Indeed! very surprising."

"Not at all, sir, with all due submission to you."

"Excuse me, Mr. Menzies. I was going to say that it is very surprising that the man should be found in that extraordinary fix, and you didn't know him."

"I won't presume, sir, to question your reasoning, but to me it is not at all surprising. The man evidently broke into my house for an unlawful purpose."

"Broke into your house, sir? When—how—where? I've no evidence of that."

"You will have directly, if you wait long enough, Mr. Crowner," said Tony.

"Who is that impertinent fellow?" asked the coroner, throwing into his countenance a most intense expression of insulted dignity.

"I beg you will excuse him, for he's a servant of mine, who, I am sorry to say, has a very poor acquaintance with the amenities of life Tony, I request that you will not interrupt or speak until you are requested."

"Very good, sir—oh, very good. Ah!—oh yes—certainly!"

"And," said the coroner, "if you interrupt the solemnity of these proceedings again, Mr. Thorny——"

"Tony, sir, at your service."

"Stony, then—if that's your name—I say, if you interrupt these proceedings again, I shall commit you."

"Very good, sir. If you're going to commit me, why I won't commit myself—it 'ud be unwise: so you may go on."

"Silence, sir! Now, Mr. Menzies, you were saying that the man broke into your house. How do you know he did, eh?"

"The evidence, I think, is conclusive. One of the panels of the door has been removed."

"Have you any evidence that the dead man removed it?"

"I have no direct evidence, certainly," said Mr. Menzies; "but, *prima facie*, I think that, in ordinary cases, that would be sufficient. The house was locked up as usual on the night of the accident—in the middle of the night we hear a great noise—we hasten to see what has caused it—we find this man in the condition you have just seen him in, with a dark lantern in his hand—and, to wind up the facts, we find that the house has been broken into. What more need be required?"

"Well, sir, that evidence may do for you, it won't for me, that's all. Did you find any housebreaking tools upon him?"

"No, I did not."

"Why not?"

"Upon my word, Mr. Coroner, you are asking most extraordinary questions, and, in my opinion, quite irrelevant to the matter in hand. I didn't search him."

"Then you should have done so. Here, you beadle—Grubstick, do you hear; just go into the hall, and search the fellow's pockets—who are you staring at?"

"I, sir?" inquired Grubstick, with his

eyes expanded much beyond their usual size, 'I, sir?"

"Ay, sir; why not, sir; eh, sir?'

"What all alone by myself? Why, sir, you wouldn't have the only beadle of the parish go and expose himself in that sort of a way, I'm sure. What would the vestry do without their Grubstick, if anything should happen to him? I'm one of the most *deficient* officers in the blessed parish, and we should have all the boys in the place go stark staring mad, if anything was to happen to me. I can't think of such a thing, sir."

"Oh, very well, sir, I shall report you to the proper authorities."

"Will anybody go with me?" anxiously asked the beadle, looking round imploringly. "Will anybody go under my protection?"

"I'll go with you, old cock," said Tony, "if you're afeard."

"Will you though — do you mean it? Come along then, but I'm not afeard. Oh, no! me afeard—Whenever was a beadle afeard?"

"Very much like it," said Tony, as he walked out of the room with the beadle.

"Gentlemen," said the coroner, "that appears to me to be a very curious case—a very curious case, and requires to be looked into with great caution and sagacity. Now, gentlemen, Mr. Menzies has made a broad assertion that this unfortunate man, whose death we are to inquire into, was nothing less than a burglar; that's an assertion, gentlemen, quite unjustifiable, inasmuch as no man should speak ill of the dead, he? Do you understand me, Mr. Foreman, eh?"

"Why, sir," said the foreman, who was an intelligent tradesman in the neighbourhood, "I think it would puzzle the devil himself to understand what you're driving at."

"Eh?" said the coroner, with a stare of astonishment.

"It appears to me," continued the speaker, "that the only inquiry we have to make is, how the man met with his death; and, as things are going on, you and I appear to differ in opinion."

"Very likely," said the coroner. "I have a peculiar way of doing business; and if God hasn't given you brains to perceive the drift, I can't give them to you. But I can tell you your duty, Mr.—what's your name?"

"Isaacs," answered the man.

"Isaacs? Why you're a Jew! You've no business on a jury. Who the devil summoned you for a juryman?"

"I am not a Jew," said the man.

"I insist upon it that you are."

"Oh, well if you are positive, there's an end of the matter," said the man.

"Permit me to say," observed Mr. Menzies, "that I have known Mr. Isaacs for the last fifty years, and the last forty of which I have met him regularly once a week at the parish church."

"Well, sir, I'll take your word for it, and admit, on this occasion, that he is a Christian, though I believe him to be otherwise; and, as I was saying, Mr. Moses, I can tell you your duty, and that is, to wait patiently till the inquiry is over, and give your verdict."

"I understand so," said Isaacs.

"Then don't interrupt, or volunteer any more opinions, Mr. Isaacs. Now, Mr. Menzies, we'll resume the examination. Oh, Mr. Grubstick, you're back, are you? Well, what have you found?"

"I found this here toothpick, this here carving-knife, and this here twist-'em-turn-'em thing."

"Oh, you did, eh? Ah, let's look. Can any gentleman tell me what these instruments are?" inquired the coroner.

"Certainly," said one of the jurymen. "The first is——"

"Don't interrupt," said the coroner. "Mr. Menzies, what do you say—what are they?"

"Why, sir," said that gentleman, "I'm not very conversant with housebreaking implements, but——"

"Oh, that'll do, that'll do—you know nothing about 'em, I see. Can anybody give me the information—you can speak, sir, now," said he, addressing the juryman who had volunteered to explain, but who did not come under the coroner's first invitation, not being, in his opinion, a gentleman.

"Why, sir, the first lot is a bunch of skeleton keys, or picklocks; the second is a knife for the purpose of completing the performance of the third, which is called a centre-bit."

"You seem to be well informed upon the subject—are you in the line?"

"Sir!"

"Ah, I see, I see. Well, Mr. Menzies, I begin to be of your opinion that the man came here for a bad purpose. By-the-by, funds are very high, Mr. Menzies, just now. Did you read the king's proclamation yesterday?—a most decisive document—they talk about opening the ports, so that there may be no impediment to a full and free exportation of import—but the thing that I required to be satisfied, is by what means he met with his death "

"The man must be mad or a fool," muttered Mr. Menzies; and addressing the coroner, he suggested that an examination should at once take place, as to the probable route the man had taken, when he first entered the house. "It's quite plain," he said, "that he must have gone up stairs, and ascended higher than the lamp, and by some means must have gone over the banisters.'

"How do you make that out, sir, eh?"

"For this reason—the lamp itself is evidence that he must have fallen upon it, some of the hair and brains still adhering to the *fleur-de-lis* at the top of it; and I should say that there can be little doubt that that was the case, and that his weight brought down the lamp."

"Ah, well, there's something in that. Gentlemen, we'll see, if you please, if there are any traces of his descent; at the same time, I can't perceive what could be his motive for clambering over the banisters for the mere purpose of falling on to the lamp. I must say that I have my suspicions that your verdict will be anything but accidental death. It looks like design, gentlemen, very like design—he must have been thrown over. We shall have to bring it in murder, Mr. Menzies, I'm afraid."

" I hope not, sir," said that gentleman; " but we had better proceed in our examination."

The coroner and the rest of the gentlemen present ascended the stone staircase as determined upon, narrowly examining the handrail, to endeavour to discover any trace of the point where the burglar made his extraordinary summersault, and began to despair when they had reached the door, beyond which the solution was palpable enough, and found nothing that would account for the accident.

" This door," said Mr. Menzies, " has been closed for years, and as there is nothing beyond it, but empty rooms, I should think we have come to the end of the search."

" You should think, eh? Well, I believe it's my business to think in these matters, Mr. Menzies. Now, I think we should examine further."

" Ah, that's right, old cock," said Tony. " Go a-head; who knows but something may turn up trumps."

Fortunately for Tony the worthy coroner didn't quite catch the tenour of his words, otherwise it might have gone hard with him.

" Here, Grubstick," said the coroner, " lead the way, and open that door."

" Oh, certainly, yes, sir—to be sure—keep close to me, gentlemen, in case of accidents. Cling to me as your protector and you're safe—come a little closer, gentlemen, a little closer."

The valiant beadle thus backed summed up courage to thrust open the door with a violent push of his foot, and as it flew forwards, he retreated a step or two backwards with such excessive haste, at the same time lifting up his arm as if to protect his face from some apparently well-directed blow, that the impetus with which he came against Mr. Menzies, who was immediately behind him, caused that gentleman also to fall backwards against the coroner, who, in his turn, made a most unexpected back leap into a group of the jurymen, who were a few steps lower down; the consequence of which was that he and two of them who had caught him round the neck, not knowing what to think or do in the excitement of the moment, comfortably rolled down to the next landing together in a most fraternal embrace.

" My dear sir," said Mr. Menzies, who had saved himself from falling by catching a firm hold of the banister, ' I really hope there's no mischief done."

" What's the matter—what's the matter?"

said that worthy gentleman, struggling to free himself from the embraces of the two jurymen. " Hands off! what ho, there! Thieves, assassins, murderers, pickpockets, and petty larceners. In the name of the king I call upon all honest men to release me from the hands of these cut-throats."

The two unfortunate men who were fellow sufferers with the coroner, were in fact as much alarmed as himself, and were fighting and struggling with wonderful vehemence with and at each other and the coroner, who didn't forget to do his duty in the affray. The fact was that each thought the other was a burglar, who had hid himself behind the door and had sallied out on its being opened, for the purpose of making a determined rush to escape, and all were fully determined to frustrate the fancied design.

" Good God, gentlemen," said Mr. Menzies, coming down the stairs, " what are you about? You will be the death of one another : come, leave off for God's sake."

" Let 'em fight, governor," said Tony, " it will do 'em good. Shall I go up and give that blessed beadle a licking ?"

" Assist me in parting these belligerents," replied Mr. Menzies, " or they will commit some serious injury upon each other."

" If I had my will," observed Tony, " so they should ; but as you've said part 'em, why o' course you're the governor, and it's all right ; so here goes."

Tony made up to the group, followed by Mr. Menzies and two or three others, and what with bawling in their ears, and giving them some various sly pokes and pinches, particularly the coroner, with whom he had a bone to pick, he and the rest at length succeeded in parting the combatants, who, when they had thoroughly shaken their feathers, stared at each other in amazement, heartily ashamed at the ridiculous figure they cut.

" Mr. Menzies," said the coroner, staunching the blood that came from his nose with his handkerchief, " this is the first inquest I have held in your town, and rest assured it will be the last. I have been thwarted in every way, and beaten in the execution of my duty. I must have redress, and will report the circumstances in the proper quarter. It's not to be borne that a gentleman who is a coroner, who has the power of life and death in his hands, pays his taxes, goes to church, and honours the king, has made his will, settled his daughter, and effected an insurance on his life, should be attacked by a couple of plebeian scum like these."

" Oh, thank you for nothing, Mr. Goldsworthy Scruton," said one of the unfortunate jurymen, who had been a principal actor in the scuffle. " Don't go so fast. Don't I recollect when your mother kept a coal-shed in Little Britain, eh? I believe you, I does; so you needn't make such a cock-a-doodle-doo about nothing ; and as for your daughter, pho! she settled herself, without your interference, on Sam Buggins, the blacksmith's apprentice, who was exportated, at the expense of the government, for thrusting his nose into his master's iron safe one fine night, just to keep his poor wife from starving. Settled, indeed! pho! you're a spooney, every inch of you."

"Gentlemen, hold," said Mr. Menzies, " I have a few words to say, Mr. Scruton, and shall expect attention. I have permitted very ungentlemanly and outrageous scenes to be perpetrated in my house, merely from a delicacy of feeling as regards yourselves; but things may be carried too far. You have a simple duty to perform; it is to inquire how this man, who has been found dead in my house, met his death; and your mode of procedure is to arrive at the best conclusion you can from the evidence you elicit, and in accordance with that the jury will give their verdict. Hitherto the inquiry has been conducted without decorum —you must excuse me for saying so - and in anything but a business-like way. Now, sir, it is with every respect for your feelings that I insist upon this inquiry being concluded with all due regard to the amenities of society, and as is usual in similiar cases, otherwise I shall feel compelled to intrude upon the time of the Secretary for the Home Department. You understand, Mr, Scruton, I hope?"

"Eh, eh? I beg your pardon—did you speak to me? I really have to apologise, I haven't paid any attention to your words; I was thinking about the best way of disposing of this matter. Gentlemen, I think we had better go on with our examination."

The party once more proceeded to the door which had caused so much consternation, and at once perceived the cause of the accident—the uprights in front of the loosened stair, and that at the end both appeared to have fallen inward, and consequently the foot-board at that part nearest the handrail was very considerably lower than that part inserted into the wall. No part of the stair was removed, but remained precisely in the same condition as Grumps had left them when he succeeded in so cleverly gliding through the aperture made for him by breaking away the necessary rails.

"I am quite satisfied," said the coroner, "and I suppose, gentlemen, you are also aware how the accident happened; you see the staircase is not in the best of conditions, and the weight of the man has caused that stair to give way; and, falling against the banisters, he fell where we have seen him. You agree with me, I suppose, gentlemen?"

The answer of course was in the affirmative, for however pig-headed the jury as a whole may have been, as juries generally are, not excluding even special juries, the cause of the catastrophe was beyond all cavil or dispute.

Being satisfied, then, as to the cause, the coroner once more retired to his throne of justice—the arm-chair in Mr. Menzies' parlour—and resumed the inquiry.

"Gentlemen," said he, " we have arrived at the fact that the man died by his own act; it now becomes necessaay to ascertain who was the guilty—I beg pardon –what was his name? Is there anybody here who can give any information on the subject?"

"I can, sir," said Tony Thong, stepping forward.

"Oh, you can, eh? Do you know him?"

"No, I don't—I did, though."

"Is he a friend of yours?"

"No, nor was he."

"What do you know of him? Come, answer the question without equivocation."

"I don't know what you mean by kivication," said Tony, "but I'll answer your question—what is it?"

"How did you become acquainted with him?"

"Ah, come," said Tony, "now that's putting a straightfor'ard question, and, in course, I'm bound to answer it in the same manner," and he then entered into the full particulars of his meeting with Cutts and Grumps, and all that passed between them thereupon, as detailed in a previous part of this work.

"And you are satisfied that this is one of the men?"

"Quite certain, sure."

"Permit me to put a question, Mr. Coroner," said Mr. Menzies. "How was it, Tony, that you didn't tell me of this last night?"

"Because, sir, I wasn't cock sure of it, till I seed him in broad day-light, and now I'm positive of it."

"And so he said he was a Bow-street officer, did he?" asked the coroner.

"He did."

"And do you believe him to be one?"

"Not now, certainly, if ever he was one. I have know him afore now, the vagabond. Why, I've seen him prowling about the Jew's Harp, with a lot more of the like kidney; and we pretty well know what sort of chaps them there is."

"And do you think you should know the man who was with him, who called himself Brown, if you were to see him again?"

"Oh, most confoundedly."

"And Smith, you say, was very anxious about a watch that the wounded man had about him?"

"Oh, very, most maliciously anxious, a watch with ins."

"A watch with ins! what do you think he meant by that, eh?"

"I'm danged if I know," said Tony.

"I think I can clear up that point," said Mr. Menzies; " the stranger has a watch with initials upon it : the initials are M. J. in a wreath of laurel leaves—I suppose the initials of the gentleman to whom it belongs ; he has not yet been able to speak, and therefore we are at present without the knowledge of his name, but I have no doubt it will turn out so."

"Very likely, very likely," said the coroner; "and so, witness, you think that you should know the dead man's companion, were you to see him again? Brown, I think you said he called himself?"

"Yes, your memory is extraordinary, for that's the name; but he's here to answer for himself."

"Here—where?" said the coroner, looking anxiously around him, as did all the rest of the company except one who stood near to the door muffled up in a horseman's cloak, and who was standing with folded arms, his cloak hiding the greater part of his face.

"Just look about you, gentlemen, and see who out of the lot looks most like a gentleman, a Bow-street officer, or a thief; and the one who looks the least like a gentleman is Brown. What think you of the gentleman by the door, with his face muffled up? Come, Brown, come out of that, and give us an account of yourself—come, let us see whether you have got your hair cut, as I recommended."

"Are you positive, witness, that that is the man?"

"Ay, as sure as I am that you are a first-rate crowner."

"Then I call upon you, gentlemen, in the king's name to arrest him. Forward, Gru stick, you are a constable by virtue of your office—forward, and arrest him."

"But he seems, sir, as if he wouldn't let me. Look! my eyes, he's outting with his pistol. I'm a married man, and have got a large family, and another or two coming; and I must decline to risk danger. It won't do, sir, the blessed infants would be collared into the workus, and I can't stand the idea of that."

The careful beadle, while he was delivering himself of these sentiments, softly approached towards the coroner's chair, behind which he got, and immediately made himself exceedingly scarce, by creeping under the table.

"Surrender!" said the coroner.

"What! to such a noodle as you? Ha! ha! What, do you take me for a fool?"

"Noodle? Damnation, sir! If no one has courage to arrest a ruffian like you, I will;" and suiting the action to the word, Mr. Goldsworthy Scruton, with a most astounding show of bravery, advanced a step or two towards Cutts—for he it certainly was.

"Hold!" said he. "Advance one more step, and you're a dead man;" and he held a pistol pointed to the head of the worthy coroner. "Consider," continued he, "what an immense loss such a clever fellow as you would be to the county, the electors of which did themselves the honour to make you a coroner; so much intelligence and acuteness are seldom to be met with in these days. No, no, most worshipful Mr. Scruton, remain a coroner; and, by-the-by, what do you think of the last proclamation?—it was a famous

thing, was it not—and likely to be a good thing for the exportation of imports, eh? Well, well, good-by, Mr. Coroner and gentlemen, of course including the jury and beadle; and I trust that by the time you have got sober, Mr. Goldsworthy Scruton, you will come to a verdict. In the meantime, I shall take the liberty of locking you in, so that your deliberations may be without interruption. Good-by."

Cutts, as good as his word, made his exit, and very coolly locked the door upon the party, much to their consternation, and deliberately walked down the avenue, and away from the place as though nothing were the matter.

"Well," said Mr. Menzies, "that's excessively cool, at all events. He'll be far enough off before we can get out of here; and, therefore, it is useless to attempt it. We had, probably, better finish the inquiry at once; and, at all events, as Brown says, we shall not be intruded upon."

"I agree with you," said Scruton. "Very little remains for me to do, gentlemen. You have heard the evidence, and I dare say are as well able as I to come to the proper conclusion. It would be a waste of time, therefore, to sum up; so, if you please, you will consider of your verdict while I take a nap."

The jury accordingly consulted for a few minutes, and the foreman, addressing the coroner, commenced by saying that he did not agree with the rest of his fellow jurymen, but he had no objection to fall in with their views, as he considered it was of very little consequence.

"Very little consequence, sir?—do I understand you aright, sir? Why, bless my heart—why, it's one of the greatest blessings of our free country that a man should have the privilege of being sat upon, and the manner of his death put upon record. Pray let's hear the verdict."

"This is what they wish to be the verdict, sir:—We find that the deceased man, who called himself Smith, was a burglar; and, in an attempt to commit a burglary, he fell over the banisters to a depth of fifty feet, on to a lamp, which entered into his brain; and, therefore, that he died by the 'visitation of God,' and that it serves him right."

"Oh, then, gentlemen, you have come to the conclusion that it was a judgment of God upon him?"

"Yes, yes," said several.

"May I ask," said the coroner, "whether you have had any special revelation to that effect, or is it a mere presumption on your parts?"

"Oh," said one, "it's quite plain—he was doing something wrong, and the judgment of God came upon him in consequence."

"If that be the case, then, sir, it appears that you differ from the generally-received notion on those subjects. It is stated by our parsons that the judgment comes after death, and not before it. May I ask if you ever did anything wrong?"

" I don't think," said the man, " you have any right to ask me that question."

" Well, gentlemen, I can't receive such a verdict. I only require the matter of fact, and no metaphysical reasoning upon it. Did the man die by his own gilful act, was he murdered, or did he meet with his death accidentally?"

The jury again consulted together, and amended the verdict by leaving out from the word " that," as they say in parliamentary phraseology, to the word " God," and inserting in the place thereof the words, " his death was accidental."

" Well, gentlemen, that's better; but I must have your opinion as to the man's deservings expunged."

" Very good—very good," said the foreman : " take it out, and cut the matter short, pray."

" None of your imperence, Mr. Juryman," blustered out the beadle, who had come from his hiding-place now the danger was over. " How dare you, sir, use such confiscating language to a coroner?—eh, sir—eh?"

" He's coming back, Grubstick," roared Tony, in the beadle's ear. " Look out!"

" Oh, spare my life—spare my life, good Mr. Brown!" supplicated the parish functionary; and down he flopped on his obese extremity, much to the amusement of Tony and the company.

" Why, what a courageous brick you are!" said Tony. " Had your parents many more like yer?"

" I tell you what it is, Mr. Stony," said the beadle, who fully appreciated the ludicrous situation he was in, " if so be you tries your gammon upon the sacred person of a beadle, by gum, when I catches you among the tombstones trying to spell out the name of your father, I means him as was hanged, blessed if I don't give you the crown and cushion of my baton on your——"

" Silence, beadle. Gentlemen, the inquiry is over; you may depart," said Mr. Goldsworthy Scruton.

" Perhaps, Mr. Goldlace, you'll open the door, and let out the respectable coroner," said Tony.

The beadle, and then the foreman and two or three others, made several ineffectual attempts upon the doors, separately and conjointly, till at length Tony, advancing to one of the windows which opened upon the lawn, and putting one of his feet out on to the green sward, turned round, and with a decided expression upon his face of extreme contempt for the imaginative faculties of the gentlemen in the room, he exclaimed—

" Well, if I ever seed such a set of spooneys in all my blessed life, may I be shot; and I've seen a good many, too. Come, come along—come along, spoonies. Grubstick, he's a coming—he's a coming—look out—look out!"

CHAPTER XV.

THE RECOVERY.—THE INTIMACY.

UNDER the very able Mr. Tweedle and the very attentive Maud, and her silent assistant, Tony's mother, the stranger progressed rapidly towards convalescence; indeed, a fortnight had hardly expired since his admission to the hospitable mansion ere he had recovered sufficient strength to be removed for an hour or two into an easy chair.

George Selby—for that was the name of the invalid—was one of those wild, rackety, reckless men about town whose career is more pleasurable to themselves than profitable to others—a sort of devil-may-care individual, who acted upon impulse, never calculating upon results, and when any unlucky termination did happen to a mad trick of his, he would get out of it the best way he could; and if he couldn't, why, he must take the consequences, and put up with them, and then he was ready again. He had good luck in respect to pecuniary matters from his cradle, for, by virtue of the settlement made on his mother's marriage, he was amply provided for before he was born. In addition to this, he survived his father, who one fine night, getting a little excited at some mad pranks of his promising son, most imprudently put his blood into such a state of alarm, and so suddenly departed this life with, " I'm going," for his last words, that George immediately walked into the old gentleman's shoes, property, and all, and merely because the old fellow took too long a time to deliberate about his will. His more tender parent had deserted the family some long time before, and had more assuredly entered into Paradise, as Obadiah Wheazletop, the dissenting parson, most confidently communicated to the poor bereaved husband when he came to solicit the continuance of a sort of annuity the dear lady had been allowing to the chapel in general, but he, the said Obadiah Wheazletop, in particular, for the last many years.

Now, it may be easily supposed that a young man, who, up to the decease of his last surviving parent, has had something like a check-rein to keep him a little within the bounds of good behaviour, would, as it is now elegantly called, ' flare up' a bit, and spend his ' tin' like ' a regular brick,' as, in fact, he did; for no sooner were the old gentleman's easy slippers put aside for once and aye, than the young gentleman doffed his college cap, and pretty well addled the brains of the learned Doctor Creatorium, D.C.L., &c., in his attempts to place it on the pericranium of that most learned man, and to keep it on by a most severe bonneting there and then given.

It was very unfortunate, that same death, for George in one respect, and that was, that it prevented him from getting a degree, for he was within an ace of it, and in those times a degree was a great feather in a young man's

THE ATTEMPED ASSASSINATION AND ROBBERY OF GEORGE SELSBY.

cap—almost a peacock's feather—but in these times when all young men are very—very clever, or their examiners very stupid, the degrees don't at all come by degrees, but are distributed with a most liberal indiscrimination, and, therefore, the merit to the wearer is as nothing—very little more than a sparrow's feather in a student's cap, and, *ergo*, a degree now is thought nothing of. However, George lost the degree, if a man can be said to have lost that which was never in his possession, and coming to London, entered into a course of study, by which he attained degrees of a different nature and quality with most surprising rapidity. In fact, in two years' time he was fully qualified to take a professor's chair in the university of London life, had there been such an one on the foundation, and unoccupied.

That part of the property which was not settled, but which George came into as heir-at-law of the 'old Griffin,' as he called his father, familiarly, suffered most fearful inroads, and the constant traffic upon such a road of dross, where there were no turnpikes to keep it in repair, was plainly perceptible, even to the faculties of George; still, after a few years' wear, the ruts were not so deep but that they might have been filled up with a little care, and have furnished a secure and safe road for many a traveller for a long time to come. And of this fact George was perfectly aware, and exerting a little of the reasoning power of which he had as large a share as anybody else, although not so often calling it into play, he came to the conclusion that he could just as easily enjoy the same amusements with less money as not, and therefore resolved to try the experiment.

The experiment he did try, and it succeeded—his amusements were fewer, but those of his friends who were more needy were much more circumscribed, as they no longer had the pull upon the lavish George's purse-strings. It was an easy lesson, and soon learned.

It was a short time after he had formed and carried out this resolution, that he was attacked, as we have seen; he was then on his way to see a maiden whose charms had smitten him, as they had many before him, and the accident not only put a stop to the interview that was expected on that evening by both, but altogether broke off the connection, much to the fair lady's pecuniary loss and chagrin.

It often happens that a man, when he fancies death has lifted up the knocker of his house, begins to be very repentant for the sins of a past life, and makes the most reasonable promises, supported by the most satisfactory arguments in their favour, that if the knocker doesn't come down with a thump, he'll lead a widely different life for the future. And so it was with George Selby. He most thoroughly believed that his time had come, and that it was time he began to count his beads, and turn up his eyes until

nothing but the whites were to be seen; but as he acquired strength day by day, so day by day more of the pupil and less of the white gradually appeared, until at length the white and the pupil appeared in their due proportions. It is the way of the world, and it may be put down as an axiom, that when a sick man or woman shows no more than the ordinary proportion of the white, that they're in a fair way of recovery, and are ready to start again on the old world. When they think they are booked for the long stage, all white, with a heavy groan occasionally, it looks pious; but when the coach is full and no place to be had, quite the reverse. It would look so stupid, except the party were in the saintly profession, and then of course it's a matter of business and quite professional.

In a month's time young Selby was quite recovered, although certainly not so strong as was his wont; if he had then proposed to a new insurance company, or association rather, who made it a boast that they were without capital, and undertook to perform all their engagements, upon the strength of their annual premiums merely, including a reduction of forty-five per cent. in every five years, in reduction of the premium to the assured, leaving out of their calculations the chance of an epidemic when a most alarming call might be made upon the funds, or the double of a second Rowlandson, stepping forth and walking off with fifteen thousand or so of the trust money—he would most certainly have been rejected.

It will not be a matter of surprise to the reader, that George Selby should have taken a liking to the lively and amiable Maud, who had been so kind, so attentive, to him in his illness, who would to dissipate his *ennui*, sit for hours by his bed reading some carefully selected book from her uncle's library; not Coke upon Littleton, on the statues at large, but some entertaining moral book, or a lively novel, or an outrageous romance by the way of change, where all gentlemen are knights, with such pretty names as Sir Orlando, Sir Ronaldo, Sir Ormond de Lacy, and hosts of others equally captivating, and taking and euphonious sounds, not forgetting Schedoni the Monk, Bruno the Bravo, Lady Abbesses, pimping nuns, dark caverns, prisons, secret panels, blood, thunder, deaths' heads, crosslines, mystification upon mystifications, enough to turn the heads of boarding-school young ladies all manner of ways except the right way.

Now, kindness such as that displayed by Maud towards a perfect stranger, combined with such personal charms and sterling qualities of mind as were hers, went very far towards turning the current of George Selby's erroneous idea into an entirely new channel; and he had almost made up his mind to forsake his old companions, his old vices, and everything else that was not within the pale of the moral code, as laid down by those who consider themselves the scrutineers of human actions, and who hold themselves up as the mirrors that reflect back upon the lookers in their deformities; but, as he felt his strength rapidly returning, he also felt his new idea slowly receding, and he began to consider whether he might not combine the pleasures of a virtuous connexion and those of a vicious one without the two coming into collision. He did not like altogether to give up those amusements which ought only to be allowed in the single and unfettered state, and which to him were second nature. The pleasures of old chumship, the theatres, billiards, night-houses, and all the various fun of London, were to him a great sacrifice to give in exchange for the—to his notions—humdrum of a married life, where regularity and domestic habits, in the opinion of the initiated, are absolutely essential qualifications for the full enjoyment of that blessed state—that elysium of hope—married life. It was a subject that clung to him like the phantasms to the imagination of a diseased brain: it was continually before his mind's eye. Waking or sleeping, the thought was ever uppermost, as to the practicability of combining the two antagonistic principles, with reference to the harmony and easy sailing of the unnatural conjunction.

Perseverance will accomplish almost anything; and at length he arrived at a conclusion satisfactory to himself that the thing might be done, and kept from the knowledge of those who might have the right to inquire into the rectitude of his conduct

Having, then, arrived at this conclusion, he next considered whether he migt be agreeable to his sweet attendant and her friends—a matter which he was by no means despairing of, as he had observed what he considered to be a few sympathetic symptoms in his favour appearing in Maud Menzies; and having no mean opinion of himself, he naturally enough concluded, that if her heart's affections were untouched, his chances of carrying that citadel were as favourable as might be.

He had quite made up his mind that he would not live without Maud. He was unhappy out of her presence, she had so completely wound round his heart by the sweetness of her disposition and the amiability of her manners. He had never before experienced such a delightful feeling of pure happiness as when she was in the act of ministering to his wants, like some guardian spirit waiting on and watching a sacred charge committed to its care. She was the perfection of his idea of the gentle sex—the goal of his ambition: and yet, to give up all for her!—ah, that was a sacrifice—a great sacrifice! He, frolic's favourite—the pet—Ah, a great sacrifice!

As Mr. Selby gradually recovered from his desperate wound, he obtained Doctor Tweedle's permission to leave the confinement of his chamber, and accordingly associated with the family in the common room. His society was much appreciated by Mr. Menzies, and he almost regretted the haste with which he was recovering, inasmuch as

he would then lose the pleasure of his companionship, which somehow had become essential to his happiness; and various were the schemes he proposed to himself to wheedle his accidental visitor into a longer stay. Even his sister Grace was charmed with the conversation of the young gentleman, and made it a rule never to contradict or oppose him in any way. Whether she had any designs against his liberty is a question we have no means of ascertaining; but Ralph observed that the acerbity of her temper was much qualified since the stranger's introduction to the domestic board; and he had his thoughts upon the subject, which often produced a quiet smile upon his countenance, much to the curiosity of the persons assembled as to the probable reason thereof.

The thought of how he should be able to throw out a hint of his inclination in regard to George Selby prolonging his visit at the mansion, was ever uppermost in Ralph's mind; and one day after the cloth had been removed, along with the ladies, and the wine was on the table, he determined to take advantage of the first opportunity to introduce the subject through some crevice or another that might be open to him during the conversation.

If he had had the faculty of seeing into another's thoughts, as the physician has, by means of the stethescope, of becoming acquainted with the actions of the inward organs, he would not have given himself so much trouble upon the subject; for he would have discovered that George Selby had the strongest wish in the world to fall in with his ideas, and was also scheming as hard as any mortal could scheme, by what means he should be able to remain there longer than was absolutely necessary for the recovery of his health. His anxiety upon the subject was so strong, that on one or two occasions he had almost determined to dispose of the doctor's physic in a very different way to what that worthy Esculapius had given directions for its disposal, for the mere purpose of making his recovery more lingering; but upon second thoughts he considered, perhaps wisely, that by so doing he should only hasten his cure, and consequently defeat his wish.

"And so, Mr. Selby, you maintain that our laws are in an unhealthy state and require revision?' said Mr. Menzies.

"I do most certainly."

"Will you favour me with your reason for so thinking?"

"In the first place," said George Selby, "I consider that the law should be so simple and easily understood by the many, that there would not be the smallest possible chance of their breaking them; whereas now a man may break I don't know how many of them without knowing anything of the matter, until he finds to his cost that somebody else has a better knowledge of the subject, and calls him to a severe account. In the next place, I would have cheap law—

and every man should have it at his own
door."

"I differ from you in both cases," said Ralph.
"Everybody knows the broad principles of
right and wrong, and therefore by steering
clear of the left road when he knows that the
one on the right side is the one he should
follow, he will escape collision with the law.
Again, how is it possible that the laws necessary for the well-being of a society so
populous as ours can be contained within the
embrace of a pocket book ; the laws relating
to merchants—navigation—the clergy, and
various other laws peculiar to the occasion
for which they were made ? Why, sir, it
has taken me my whole life to master them
all—even if I have done so yet. Again,
certain laws are required by the changes in
society to be repealed and others framed in
their places, and this is continually going on.
And would you have people who work at the
bench neglect their business to read up the
new laws for the gratification of personally
settling their disputes without the aid of those
better informed, which seems to be your idea
of few laws and cheap process ? No, sir, depend upon it, that the people are better
without understanding the law. The only
cheap law that I would give them would be
the usual notice stuck up against the dead
walls of gentlemen's houses—or, in their
parks and preserves, 'Beware, &c." Even
as the law stands now, the lawyers find
plenty to do, through the litigiousness of
the people, and God knows if it were any
cheaper, they would be so ravenous after it,
that we shouldn't have a bit left. It's my
opinion also that to see a learned judge trol-
ling a wheelbarrow of law about to the door
of everybody who wished it, and dispensing
it the same as a cat's-meat purveyor vends
his commodity, would be extremely ludicrous,
and tend most decidedly to bring the law
and its makers into contempt, besides en-
couraging litigation."

"You have very curious ideas upon the
subject, I must say," said Selby, "and I
suppose I have not sufficiently studied the
matter, and therefore perhaps I ought not to
have attempted an opinion."

"Then you suffer judgment by default,
eh ?" said Ralph.

"Admitted ; but I bar execution. Now,
pray, why should not the legal phraseology
be reformed so that a man of plain—ay, I
may say refined and cultivated, intellect may
understand it, without having recourse to a
law dictionary to translate into plain under-
standable language anything in a legal shape
that may be laid before him, such as a settlement, for instance, which he is making upon
the marriage of his daughter, and which of
course he is anxious should contain everything he can wish ; what does he understand,
for instance, by this 'first tenant in tail,' 'in
possession with cross limitation over in
favour of the right heirs of A. B. &c.'
'tenants in *capite*,' '*cestui que trust*,' '*cestui
que use*,' and various other legal cant terms

which you lawyers would as soon think of
omitting in a legal document as you would
of the settlement itself being engrossed in
the Chinese character."

"Well, but, my dear sir, the heads of a
settlement are generally laid before the
parties interested, which contain the intention written in what you call intelligible
language ; and the mature deed is drawn up
from that document, and contains all which
is in that, but amplified only ; and therefore it is merely a form after all, to send the
draft of the deed to the parties ; for I agree
with you that not one-half of them understand it, except in its broad scope, and
which is quite enough for them to do in my
opinion ; for were it otherwise, they would
go blundering on, on their own responsibility, and getting the thing into a devil of
a mess, making finally a rare job for the
lawyers to get them out of it ; whereas now
they can't move without asking advice, and
consequently always keep in shallow water ;
I dare say you may recollect the old saw,
Mr. Selby, which is as old as the days of our
second Edward, that 'every man who is his
own lawyer has a fool for his client ;' 'and
it's as true as that mulberries are not in the
habit of growing upon hazel bushes.'"

"I agree with you there," said George ;
"every man to his business."

"Ay, to be sure ; why, Mr. Selby, you've
no idea what a deal of business is done by
the gentlemen in my profession, through the
stupidity of people attempting to make their
own wills ; I might just as well set down
and attempt to make a pair of boots. I
should fail, of course, and the man who was
brought up to it would get the job, and I
should be laughed at, and very justly too ;
you can have no notion what lamentable
mistakes arise by this stupid practice, and
how very different things turn out to the
testator's intention, in consequence of not
complying with the usual formularies. Leaving out of the question the want of a clear
adaptation of words to the intention, the most
serious results often occur; and, if you
notice, the generality of these wills drawn
by an amateur pen are a chaotic mass of un-
intelligible intentions, which may be inter-
preted according to the tastes of the parties
who fancy themselves interested under them.
I can assure you that it is a source of considerable profit to us, a regular annuity in
fact, and I have long been of opinion that
every man who draws up his own will is an
ass.'

"And it appears to me," observed George,
"that he is particularly anxious to wish himself an ass without the possibility of one
forming a sceptical notion upon the assertion ; for I have observed that these amateur draftsmen, as you call them, conclude
their testamentary documents with a most
impressive ' Written with my own hand.'"

"True ; but how, Mr. Selby, is it that you
have such a knowledge of the legal cant, as
you express it ?"

" It was my peculiar study at the university. I was intended for a doctor of laws, but I doctored the intention as soon as I could, of course."

" You didn't like it, eh ?"

" Yes, tolerably ; but I liked, I suppose, pleasure more. I could return to it with much satisfaction, particularly as I have had enough of what is called seeing life."

" Indeed ! Come, what say you to reading up, and following the law as a profession ?"

" Nothing would please me better. Not that I require to follow anything where emolument is essential to its practice, for if I were to take it up, it would be for the honour of the thing merely ; but, to tell you the truth, I should not care to go through the necessary formalities requisite to put on the gown ; it would be irksome to me. Now, if I could find a friend who would give me the benefit of his experience, without the drudgery of wading through the——"

" I beg pardon, Mr. Selby ; I understand your meaning ; you don't like the usual practice, eh ? What say you to put yourself under my wing ? I'm an old bird, you know, and have brought up some broods in my time."

" I should be delighted," replied Selby.

" Then that feeeling is mutual, my dear sir. From what you have indulged me with, relating to your habits, relatives, and pursuits, I conclude you have no particular locality, which is more a favourite with you than another ?"

" No."

" Then what say you to making this your place of habitation ?"

" My dear sir——"

" Nay," interrupted Mr. Menzies, " no excuses ; I see what you would be at. You've no objection, I see. I insist upon it. Come, I may consider you my visitor till I give you three months' notice."

" I cannot allow myself to take advantage of your liberality, my dear sir—I really cannot."

" Pooh, pooh," said Mr. Menzies, " you've scruples, I suppose, about the currency question, eh ? I tell you what, my friend, we'll compromise the question. I have a servant who is useless to me, Tony—you know, Tony—now, you shall take him off my hands, you know—it will be doing me a favour. He'll be of use to you, I dare say."

" Well, sir, since you're so pressing, I must needs comply ; and so I at once enter as your pupil in the knotty science of the law."

" Bravo, well said," observed Mr. Menzies, rubbing his hands together, and then giving his visitor a thwack of no light quality on his back. " We shall get on together amazingly—I see it, I see it ; and I'll venture to predict that the pupil will leave the master in the lurch very soon."

" Sooner than you expect, probably," thought George.

CHAPTER XVI.

THE PLACARD.—THE INTRIGUING JUDAS

GEORGE SELBY was not the man to tamely put up with such an attack as had been made upon him ; not only for the sake of punishing the villains on his own account, but for the protection of the public, he was determined to leave no means untried to bring the men to justice ; and under the advice of Mr. Menzies, he caused advertisements to be inserted in all the London papers, and the metropolis to be posted with placards, offering a reward of five hundred pounds to the person by whose assistance the guilty parties should be brought to justice.

The advertisement was very precise as to the date, place, and time of attack ; but was deficient in personal description, as Mr. Selby had very little means of making any accurate survey of the features of the assassins. The only thing at all likely to lead to a discovery of the parties was a most minute and particular description of the watch which had been the subject of so much disquietude to, and finally been the quietus of, Grumps. This part of the advertisement ran in the following terms—

" And whereas the gentleman who was attacked had at the time, in his fob, a gold watch, maker's name, King, Bloomsbury Square, No. 5060, and to it were attached a gold curb chain, a small topaz key, and a seal of the same, bearing the crest of a greyhound on a mount, collared and chained, but for which was substituted a silver hunting-watch, maker's name—Twist, John Street, Clerkenwell, No. 260 ; in addition to which, on the same plate, are the initials M. J., in a wreath of laurel leaves, supposed to be the initials of the owner of the said watch."

In addition to these means, the celebrated officer of those days, George Smith, who, before he was an officer, was one of the cleverest thieves of the day, and who after he had retired with independent means, 'and a fair name from his public duties from a real passion he had for the art, returned to the thieving profession again, and was, at length, guillotined at Paris, where he had committed his last and most astounding robbery, received instructions from Mr. Selby to use his best exertions in obtaining all the information in his power, and the promise of an extra reward in case he should be successful.

Now, Cutts, whose eyes were always about him, was among the first who perceived this very unpleasant placard placed on the signpost of the general meeting house, the Jew's Harp ; and the drunken lieutenant, whose somnambulism had been so summarily put to flight by Grumps, and who was now again on his legs, was about as soon as his captain, a greedy devourer of the most enticing, to a party not concerned, announcement.

To think well and to act at once were the characteristics of Cutts ; and though he felt that he was perfectly safe from any of the gang, the rascal Grumps being dead, who was his only companion in the attack, and who was alone privy to it, yet he though that the watch might be the means of tracing the robbery to him; and, therefore, discretion being the better part of valour, it would be most advisable for him at once to make his retreat, until the affair should blow over; but, before carrying this resolution into effect, he considered that in honour he was bound to make some arrangement with, or communication to, his gang relative to their future proceedings, without actually informing them of more than was barely necessary, and that was merely, that he was about to leave them.

Captain Cutts was much mistaken when he thought that the defunct Grumps was the only party intimately acquainted with the particulars of the watch. The lieutenant had also seen it by mere accident, and it had made a strong impression upon him at the time, the initials not being those of his captain—not that it was a strange thing by any means that a robber should possess a watch with initials on it not his own—but it produced an impression that it was part of some plunder of which he had no knowledge, and which he considered he ought to have had.

The lieutenant was by no means slow in coming to the conclusion that Cutts was the man who was sought for, and five hundred pounds was a most tempting offer, a very large sum for the sale of a friend—more than he should gain by his profession, for some time—and accordingly, brooding over the thing, and making it quite a matter of calculation, he determined to bid for the reward, let what might come of it.

He had hardly come to this conclusion when Cutts himself, who had been watching for some of the men, came upon him.

"Grey," said he, "get your men together to-night, I have something to to say to them. Let it be before the usual time of meeting; say at dusk, at the old place."

"Anything very special?" asked the lieutenant.

"You will hear in good time, and until then, farewell."

"Oh, farewell, captain, if you're going; you may depend upon my exertions——by-the-by, have you noticed the placard offering a reward for the apprehension of the murderers?"

"Ay, a goodly shot, Grey, and I should say would bring down the bird. I hope they'll get him."

"Eh? Hope they'll get him?" said Grey, taken a little aback at the captain's coolness.

"Ay, he's a lame duck—not one of our sort, Grey, or he wouldn't have made such a barbarous exchange of watches."

"No, truly, captain—it was a stupid affair. I should like to lay hold of the reward."

"Use a little discretion," said Cutts, "and it's yours. Ferret it out like a man of law would. Go to Mr. Twist, and from him

trace it to it's late owner. Persevere, and you'll be sure to get the reward."

"Do you think so, captain?" asked Grey, who was evidently staggering in his belief.

"Do I think so? Here, Grey," said he, familiarly leaning on the shoulder of the lieutenant, and speaking in a confidential tone of voice into his ear, "listen to me."

"All attention, captain," said Grey.

"Do you recollect the time when you were a little child?"

"Perfectly:—when I wore a little skeleton suit of corduroy, with sugar-loaf buttons."

"Do you recollect your blessed parents?"

"Without doubt."

"Good. Then, I dare say, you may recollect them, when you have been ambitious of catching a little bird, and were eager in the pursuit, seriously recommending you to put a little salt upon its tail, eh?"

"Ay, many a time."

"Then you may take my word for it, my worthy lieutenant, that you'll be just as likely to meet with the same result with respect to the five hundred pounds, if you follow the advice I have just given to you—Farewell:" and Cutts turned on his heels, and departed, with something like a sinister smile upon his countenance.

"Well," said the lieutenant, "he takes it cool; but, for all that, I am still of opinion that he is the man, and, hit or miss, I'll try."

Determined upon mischief, the business now uppermost in his mind was by what plan he could secure his object. Many schemes were formed and abandoned, until at length he was satisfied that the best plan would be to inform the men of their captain's wish to meet them that night before the usual hour, and afterwards make the necessary arrangements for his capture at the meeting.

Acting upon this decision, then, he informed the gang—whose several haunts he was well acquainted with—of the place and time of meeting, and then wended his way to Menzies' house; and having made the usual summons for admission, Tony presented himself at the door.

"We don't want any," said Tony.

"Want any what?" asked the lieutenant, with a stare of amazement.

"Oh, haven't you got anything to sell?"

"Sell? No—I want to see your master."

"Very good: I beg pardon. We have so many beggars and thieves in this part of the neighbourhood, that if anybody presents himself here what hasn't got quite the appearance of a gentleman, I puts him down at once as one or the other."

"In many cases a distinction without a difference, my friend, I have no doubt; but is Mr. Menzies or Mr. Selby within?"

"Both—what is it you want with 'em?"

"Tell them I want to see them on private and particular business."

"Oh, gammon! Come, none of your tricks, my covey: we have too many of you gentlemen who come here on private and particular business. I've been bit once or twice; and whenever anybody comes here now on that 'ere speck, I just doesn't let 'em see the governor, that's all."

" Well, but——"

" Well, but—we want no buts. These private and particular gentlemen, as soon as they get the presence, out with a begging petition, with a whole list of superstitious names 'tached to it. No, no – no go, Mr. Tickler—you don't hang up your hat here :" and so saying, Tony was about to close the door without further ceremony, but was prevented by Grey interposing his foot between that and the jamb.

" Not so fast, my young gentleman," said he. " If your curiosity must be satisfied, why then I want to see them relative to the robbery."

" Oh, you do, do you ? That's a very different hand o' cards, that is. Walk in, pray, and let me lock the door, and take the key with me, before I announce you. Them 'ere cloaks and hats are waluable, hanging up there ; and you know it's best to be cautious. Birds of a feather flock together."

" Yes; and as the saying is, some people are in the habit of measuring other people's corn by their own bushel."

" True ; and, therefore, I say, there's nothing like caution."

The lieutenant was not long kept waiting; for Tony having announced his presence, he was immediately ushered into the presence of Ralph Menzies and George Selby.

" I understand," said Ralph, " that you have some information to communicate with respect to the subject of our adventure—is it so?"

" Under certain conditions," said Grey.

" Certainly—what are they ?"

" You offer £500 to the person who shall be the cause of the offenders being convicted."

" True."

" If one be dead ?"

" Then for the survivor."

" Good—then consider him in your power. I shall want some security for the payment of the reward."

" What do you suggest?" asked Mr. Menzies.

" I am not used to matters of this sort," replied the lieutenant ; " the time for its preparation is short, for I shall have him to-night. Can you think of anything ?"

Mr. Menzies considered for a few moments, and then said—

" I have thought of a plan which, under the circumstances, I think will be sufficient to satisfy your requirements. I will draw a cheque on my bankers in your favour only— that is, payable to you alone ; you shall meet me at his house of business this morning, and in your presence I will instruct him to honour it when you shall produce to him personally a newspaper-report of the conviction of the offender."

" Good. I shall see Smith, the officer, and arrange with him. When shall I meet you ? Two o'clock will suit me."

" Be it so—Coutts is my banker in the Strand. Now let us hear a little of the particulars."

" Excuse me, I will perform my contract and nothing more—good morning."

" Oh, good morning, sir ; I hoped that you would have been a little more communicative."

" It doesn't pay ! good morning."

" I should like to go halves, my tulip," said Tony, as he opened the door for him ; " and if you don't tip me something, I'll split."

" Split ? Split and be damned !" said the lieutenant, as he coolly walked away.

" Well, there's nothing like trying it on," observed Tony, as he closed the door.

———

CHAPTER XVII.

THE LAST MEETING.—THE ATTACK, AND THE ESCAPE OF CUTTS.

As the dusk of evening approached, the gang, one by one, slunk into the little road-side inn, and waited, in the room appropriated for their especial service, the coming of the captain.

Many were the surmises and consultations formed and entered into by the troop, as to the extraordinary summons of the captain— a thing that had never happened before ; what could it be for ?

" I tell you what it is," said a fellow with long, yellow hair hanging over his shoulders, bearing much the appearance of a shelter especially got up for the sole purpose of accommodating a race of little travellers, more persevering than pleasant,—" I tell you what it is, my friends, you may make up your minds that it's a desperate case to-night ; we shall have some tough work. I shouldn't wonder but what we shall have to attack the king, God bless him."

" Lauks, you dosen't say so, Trap," said another, " sure-ly ?"

" I do though, and our captain's just the sort of man as dosen't stand upon trifles ; he'd as soon fly at such high game as that of meaner breed."

" With all my heart," said another. " He's a trump of a fellow, and I'll stick to him like a brick."

" You ?—what you ? Pooh ! Stick to him like a brick ! Yes, if you want to draw any blunt out of him, I grant you you will," said the yellow-haired laddie.

" What do you mean by that insinuation, you vermin-breeder, eh ? Your lantern jaws and the back of this hand will be more intimately acquainted if you don't keep that ass's tongue of yours a little more within its refuge.'

" Ha, ha, ha !" roared Trap. " Did ever anybody hear the like unto that ? All I can say is, Mr. Robin Clark, that if your actions were as big as your words, you'd be an invaluable treasure to our corps "

" Oh, take a fit and burst !" replied Robin.

"You're always precious liberal of your sentiments, when they doesn't add much to a fellow's reputation; but, howsumdever, without overlauding my own abilities, I'm as good a man as you are any day in the week."

"Ah, say you so?" said Trap. "Suppose we have a round or two, just by way of amusement, till the captain comes, eh? And whichever smashes the conk or gouges out the eye of the other first, let him stand a gallon of flip. What say you, comrades?"

"Ay, ay—a ring, a ring!" cried several: "a ring. Come, Rob, off with your cover, and let's see the colour of your shirt. Come, gentlemen, gentlemen—strip—that's it. We shall have some rare sport here," was the general observations among the lookers-on; for, in fact, the two worthies who were in opposition to each other at that moment had the reputation of being the rankest cowards and poltroons in the whole troop, which fact must have been known to each of them—and thus the apparent eagerness each showed for the coming contest.

A ring was speedily formed, and the men stripped, each supported by a second. The word was given, and the mortal struggle commenced—and we use the word "mortal" only in this sense, that it was a mortal waste of time; for the men stood sufficiently far apart from each other to prevent the slightest chance of any other part of their persons than their fists coming into collision. Such a stepping backwards and forwards, and dodging and feigning, were never before seen; and for a whole quarter of an hour not a single blow had been struck, nor probably would there have been if they had stood up till doomsday, so extremely cautious were the combatants. But the prospect of their standing up so long was put an end to by the entrance of the captain; and then, but not till then, was the first stroke made—a blow which certainly would have been accounted anything but a fair one by the fancy, inasmuch as while Trap's attention was directed to the captain, Robin struck behind him, and gave him a smart blow under the belt—or, in other words, on the most obese part of his person.

"That was a cowardly blow, my man," said the captain, walking into the middle of the ring.

"I thought it was well schemed," said Robin, "and planted in a most scientific manner. However, it seems to have had all the effect I intended it; for, you see, comrades, he's had enough of it."

"Ay," said the captain, "and as enough is as good as a feast, why, let the matter drop. Now, my men, I have called you together for a most important business. Where's the lieutenant?"

"All right, captain," said that individual, who entered the room at that moment, and closed the door behind him. "What is it?"

"Oh, I'm glad you're come; I was about to say, my men, that business of a very important nature which requires my immediate and undivided attention, will call me away from your councils for an indefinite period. It will, therefore, be necessary, my movements being so uncertain, that some provision should be made either for keeping you together till I shall be amongst you again, or that our society should be altogether broken up. Now my opinion is, that it will be more advantageous as a body, to keep together, and therefore I should suggest that, in my absence, you cannot have a better substitute than our worthy lieutenant. What say you, comrades?"

The men held a short consultation among themselves, and then one of them stepping forward, as if deputed by the rest, said—

"Why, captain, if so be as you are in real downright earnest, and not poking fun at us, we think that we shall be better collected than separated; and, therefore, if, as I said afore, you ain't trying us merely, which we hope is the case, it will be necessary to have somebody as'll act in your place, though, without meaning anything disrespectful to our lieutenant, I thinks we shall be a long time afore we gets another like you. We must have some spring to move us; and if the one you propose to substitute isn't such a finished piece of mechanism as our present one is, why it can't be helped."

"Very good. What says my lieutenant, eh? Will you, sir, undertake the duty the men are anxious should devolve upon you, or shall we proceed to an election?"

"Why," said the lieutenant, "if circumstances were not considerably altered with me since the morning, I might have been glad at the selection; but you remember your advice, captain, as to the £500 reward?"

"What of it?"

"It is within my grasp," said the lieutenant; and laying hold of Cutts's collar, he gave a shrill whistle, which was answered from without, and immediately the door was burst open, and half-a-dozen officers rushed in.

"Comrades," shouted the captain, "protect yourselves—out with the lights—that's it! Now, every man for himself, and God for us all!"

It was but the work of a moment for Cutts to take from his breast a pistol; and feeling about for the head of the lieutenant, who still retained his grasp, he introduced the muzzle into his ear, and fired. The fingers of the lieutenant relapsed their hold, and he fell at Cutts's feet a dead man!

The flash from the pistol disclosed to the officers the form of Cutts for a moment, and it also showed Cutts the position of the officers, and which way he could best avoid them. Not a moment was lost by the officers in hurrying to the spot where Cutts had stood; but he equally quick had made his way up to the window, which he opened, and passed out unobserved.

Unfortunately, one of the officers, more active than the rest, got the start, and arriving first at the spot, was most spiritedly attacked by those who followed, under the

THE MISUNDERSTANDING BETWEEN MAUDE AND GEORGE AT RUSSELL SQUARE.

impression that he must be Cutts himself, and before he could make himself heard to explain the mistake, he was nearly throttled by the rough hands of his brother officers; and as under such process he naturally struggled hard, giving the appearance of a most determined resistance to a capture, had not the landlord suddenly entered with a light, most undoubtedly the poor fellow's wind would have been shortened for life.

"Well, I'll be hanged if we ain't got into a pretty considerable mess here, comrades," said the man who had exercised the unjust treatment the poor fellow of an officer had experienced. "We've pretty well done for old Donny. Come, old fellow, tip us your flipper, and say no more about it; all's well as ends well, and as you ain't absolutely strangled, thank Providence it isn't worser than it is. You'll have some idea now, and much clearer one, what sort of a sensation a poor gallows convict feels when the hemp is put across his wisen, and it'll be an excellent practical lesson for you through life to steer clear of it. Come, cheer up, my hearty, and don't look so precious sour, as if you'd been boiled in vinegar for a month."

"You seem to have all the jaw, my boy, which is worse to me than the throttling system; here's my hand, however; I never bears malice, and him as can't put up with such a trifle as this, ay, or worse, is not fit to be a Bow-street officer. Why, this here informer here, Mr. What's-his-name, has more reason to blubber than we, for, you see, instead of the five hundred pounds for which the scamp sold himself, his expectations are settled by a bullet in his brains. Now, it strikes me, my lads, that we have a chance of coming in for the swag now this pitiful wretch is out of the way, and the sooner we starts on the trail the better; and I think we'd better agree amongst ourselves that whoever should be the fortunate captor, shall divide the tin between us. It'll be a fair way of doing business."

"I doubt that," said Smith. "In the first place there are six of us, and there are five hundred pounds, according to your scheme, to be divided equally amongst us; now that will create fractional parts. In the second place, if all share alike, every man having to receive the same amount, catch him or not, will be more likely to trust to the exertions of the others—that's objectionable; therefore, I propose that he who actually catches Captain Cutts shall have two hundred pounds, and the other five sixty pounds each. This will be an inducement to each of us to use his best exertions to obtain the larger portion, and as none of us, can say who will be the lucky man to win, it's as fair for one as the other."

All readily entered into the views of Smith, in hope of being the gainers of the larger portion, and after having had a drain to keep the "night dew from their insides," as they expressed themselves, they left the house in search of the escaped Cutts.

CHAPTER XVIII.

THE ELOPEMENT.

THINGS went on very smoothly at the mansion of Mr. Menzies, and the worthy owner was much pleased with the speedy progress his pupil was making in the difficult science of the law. As time wore on, the gentle and amiable Maud felt a more than friendship-feeling towards Mr. Selby, and they lost no opportunity of enjoying each other's society. While they were one day taking a walk in the sequestered neighbourhood, George, by a species of argument which was so familiar to him, urged Maud to be united to him without the knowledge or consent of her friends; assigning as a reason for doing so, that he was serving a friend that was in London, in difficulties, and that in order to serve him effectually his presence would be required two or three days a week; and that if they knew he was married to her, they might expect an explanation of his absence from his wife for that time, which he could not give, as the business was of a purely private nature. Maud told him that she would consider the subject, and they parted for the time.

The venerable and kind-hearted Ralph Menzies had now been the victim of deception for some months, for he was entirely ignorant that his niece and young friend, George Selby, were man and wife—but so they were; for as George had concluded that, when Maud had made up her mind to consider of it, the matter was as good as settled in his favour, he was right, and shortly afterwards they were married in London by banns, and immediately after the ceremony returned to Menzies' House, and all went on apparently as before. The old gentleman and George still continued the study of the law together, as was their wont, with the exception that George was very frequently absent from the house days and nights in succession, much to the surprise of the good old man, though he never made any observation on the matter, it being a business, as he considered, in no way concerning him, as George was not at all responsible to him for his actions.

Time at length revealed that to Maud Selby, which certainly must have revealed itself to others, and consequently the secret of their marriage would be a secret no longer, if some means were not taken to elude the observation of Ralph, and the vigilance of Grace.

A variety of suggestions occurred to Maud, but all were overruled by her husband, who still most strongly objected to the step he had taken becoming known.

However much Maud felt aggrieved at continuing so unkind a deception, yet her love for George, and her high sense of the duty she was bound to observe to her husband's requirements, effectually prevented a word of expostulation, when he suggested that they should retire, for a time, from the mansion clandestinely, and that he would take means of pacifying her uncle, and explain to him the real state of the case.

you know all about it, and if you are well as I am well, well and gud.

"I shud have write to you long before, behind in these matters i always am, for i so Seldom take up a pen that I hardly know which end to dip into the ink; so you see if you look at the top of this pissel you'll see i am quite a French forrener already. I regret I didend take a few lessings in sum foren language to make me what master says ficient; if i stay here much longer, I shall shortly be down to their lingo, tho i find it's preshus hard to speak thro' the mouth and nose at the same time: hoping to astonish you when you hear me making luv to you in such a comical langwage gives me the pluck to persevere, if you had told me i should have the pashuns to snuffle thro' so many hard words, I shu'dent have believed you, tho' what you say is gospel to me.

"Master's very civil to me—have little to do, but eat like a fish. Frogs, they say, these people liv upon here; but I haven't seen any yet, nor rounds of English beef. Turnips and mutton legs isn't a favourite dish among these 'ere French yankee-doodles, and i hope God will forgive 'em for it, in which I'm sure you'll join me, won't you Susan dere? i went to one of their chapels last night, where I didn't stop, and the celebrated Fransay Thong, I think they call him—my namesake—plaid the part of Othello, in dryden's farce written by Ben jonson, at the Theater de Roy, where i dropped in afterwards. i didn't much like him, for he dident paint his face so black as I've seen some of the London chaps do it, tho' i believe there rong, for I've seen mores anything but black, a sort of brown, but I dare say this more is meant to be a blacky more, and that accounts for it. When I went for the doctor and the nurse, I couldent make myself understood, and missus might have died if I hadn't suddenly thought of delivering the note which my master gave me to deliver; with great nerve he bore it; when it was over, he jumped up as if he was mad, which showed he luved her. The old nurse he grasped in his arms, and gave her such a smack on the lips, that quite startled the little skin and-grief shrivelled up doctor. I would rather he than me, for her breath is not so swete as Susy's, nor her lips so rosy, nor her teeth so white and purly, but every one to their taste, as the stink-pole said to the countryman, who mistook him for a rabbit. Baked sugar and lollypops are quite common in these parts, and I know you won't believe me when I say that men go about here with little kegs of sugar-water, at a farthing a glass full, and portable water-closets, and every lamp post is a convenience where they have one; but there aint many of them, here and there one, and they save every thing for manure.

"I was going to close this decoction, but I thought you'd like to hear a little more about missus, she's got a nice little boy, and is doing well, and I mean to hint to master that

i should like to be godfather: I'd bring him up to a move or two, and there's no noing what he may come to, and if, supposing he should turn out to be a valley de shamber, it wud be useful to him to know how to dubble his salary, wouldn't it? i've seen Smith here—you recollect Smith—the man wot locked us all in at the Quest; i'm sure it's him, because of his knows and hair, and he seed me and slunk away as if he owed me something—but he doesn't—more tother.

"I think i havn't not no more to say just now till I cum back; before closing this sheet give my best respects to old master and old missus, and tell them that we all hope soon to cum back grateful for all past favours, which I am much obliged to him for, though he spoilt my fancy breeks which you was so fond on—though there wasn't much in 'em, after all, to tract much attention. Before I seal this up for good, I shall kiss your dere name at the head, and you can kiss mine at the tail, and that'll be an exchange.

"So hoping that I have made myself understood, which of course I have, I remain,
"Yours till death,
"TONY THONG."

THE RETURN.

As Tony had written to his true love, the beautiful Maud had given birth to a fine boy; and taking into consideration all the circumstances, and the depression of her spirits, caused by the neglect of her uncle to send to her that forgiveness which she so urgently prayed for, she rapidly recovered her usual health.

The duties of a young mother quickly absorbed the whole of her attention, and if she ever thought at all of Menzies House, it was by mere chance, and the desponding feeling suddenly created by the thought would as rapidly dissipate as she looked upon the face of her child. Not so with George; he had long, in fact, given up the idea of being again received into the friendship of Mr. Menzies, and the feeling of regret that he once had, that he was the cause of interrupting this intimacy, was changed into one of a more bitter character, and he began to think that he was the injured party whose forgiveness was to be sought.

As soon as the necessary arrangements could be made, George and his wife and child returned to London, and until he could find a house to suit him, and furnish it, he put up at one of the hotels at the West-end.

At length a house having been selected in the neighbourhood of Russell Square, and all the necessary arrangements completed for its habitation by Selby and his family, thither they removed. "And now," thought Maud, "I shall have much more of my dear George's society, this annoying business being disposed of."

But, alas! she was doomed to be disappointed. It was not to be expected that Maud, who had a large share of the finer feelings, could calmly and tamely submit to such unreasonable conduct on the part of her husband, and accordingly she determined on the first opportunity occurring of speaking to him upon the subject, and if possible, of obtaining some explanation.

For this opportunity she had not long to wait, for after an absence of three days, very shortly after she had resolved that things should be explained, her husband made his appearance about breakfast-time, certainly a little elevated with wine, though as much exhausted by an apparent night's debauch.

There could be no possible mistake about his having over indulged in wine, for when he stalked into the breakfast-room he rang the bell and ordered his slippers to be brought to him, together with his chamber candle.

"My dear George," observed Maud, "what can you mean?"

"Mean, my dear? I hope you haven't been sitting up for me. I confess I am a little late; but then you've plenty of servants, you know, to wait upon me without your troubling yourself."

"Surely, George, you have been indulging a little too much; this is morning, and we have only just commenced the day."

"No, Maud, you must have been indulging a little. I can assure you I am perfectly *compos mentis*, and I say it is time to retire to rest."

"I will not deny that you may require rest; you appear to me, on the contrary, to very much require it—nevertheless it is morning."

"Well, be it so, Maud, you are always obstinate, and, I suppose, as usual I must let you have your way. What's o'clock?"

"Where have you been, George, the last three days?"

"Eh?"

"I am sorry to trouble you with a repetition of the question, but I shall be obliged if you will inform me what business you have been engaged in for these last three days?"

"Ah—ah, I understand—oh, business of the first importance—you know—my friend—you understand."

"No, George—I do not understand."

"Well, my dear, if your intellect is so obtuse, as not to understand a plain answer to a plain question, I am very sorry, that's all I can say."

"I didn't expect," said Maud, "so much unkind treatment from you, George; and without the slightest intention of hurting your feelings, I must say that I do hesitate to believe that it is business that takes you away so much from home. No married man would so greatly neglect his family for the dearest friend in the world. I am inclined to think that pleasure is the greatest component part of your business."

"You are quite right, my angel; it gives me extreme pleasure to do a good action, particularly for a friend of so long standing as he whom I assist."

"A mere quibble, George, and unworthy of you."

"Never mind, Maud; I do not wish to quarrel with you."

"Nor do I wish you, George; but I think, in justice to myself and your child, I should be informed of the reason of your repeated absence, I may say, desertion, of your home; and, as in these cases, I think it better to speak freely, openly, and candidly——"

"Undoubtedly, my dear—pray proceed."

"I must request," continued Maud, "that you will at once give me an explanation of your conduct."

"Anything more, pray?"

"Yes, and follow the explanation by a reformation."

"Very good, my dear. Now hear me, and I say it without the slightest intention of hurting your feelings, that I at once flatly decline to give you or any one else any further or better explanation than that which I have already given."

"Very good, my dear. I shall not sit down and weep as other women would do, and ask forgiveness for having attempted to intrude upon your motives of action, to commence the process again, and conclude it in a similar manner; but now, from your refusing to honestly open your mind to me, I am convinced that my conjectures were right and I shall act accordingly."

"You're quite at liberty, my dear angel, to do whatever you please, except to interfere in affairs appertaining to me—that I forbid. I also shall act as I please; but at the same time, understand me, that if any unexpected result happen in consequence of what has just passed, do not blame me. It is your own seeking. Everything surrounds you that should make you happy and contented."

"Except yourself, George," interrupted Maud. "Oh, if you were now what once you were to me, indeed I should be happy. On my knees, George, let me entreat of you to alter your course—look upon the innocent face of the babe as he smiles upon you. Surely that should be sufficient to reclaim you if I have lost your affections."

"Ha, ha, ha!" laughed Selby. "I thought you were to be a tragedy heroine—no tears for you; oh no—you would act—ah, Maud, Maud, after all you are like the rest of womankind—feigning, eh?"

"As God is my maker,' exclaimed Maud, rising from her supplicating position, "He knows that I am so; but not only to be refused, but to be ridiculed, and laughed to scorn, is not to be endured. I retract my submissiveness, and fall back upon my original intention—I will act."

"That shows spirit," coolly remarked George; "and as you are now going to act, we shall both be playing our parts, and there is ample room upon the stage of life for us both to do so without jostling. For the present, farewell."

"Are you going so soon, Selby?"

THE REMORSE OF SELBY FOR THE SUPPOSED LOSS OF MAUDE.

No. 14.

" I am—a little business calls me from home."

" For how long shall you remain away ?"

" That is as matters turn out."

" And without a parting kiss to your innocent child ?"

" Certainly not ; it gives me real happiness to see the dear boy ; in fact, if you raise no objection, I 'll take him with me. Ha! ha! it would look strange, too, Maud, would it not, to attend to business with a child slung round my neck ? Farewell, Maud, and the next time I see you, I hope you will have attained that philosophy which makes all things subservient to pleasure—that is, I mean that you will make yourself comfortable under all circumstances—by, by."

Maud had indeed been acting a part, and immediately after the unfeeling George had left the apartment, she threw herself into a chair, and burst into a passionate flood of tears.

CHAPTER XXI.

THE FATAL LETTER.

MAUD having failed in her attempt to produce a change in the behaviour of her husband by the means already stated, she adopted the plan of taking him for her model, and acting in a similar manner, or rather in apparently doing so ; for although she was seldom from home, yet, whenever George found it convenient to make his own house his residence for a short time, he seldom met her there ; and to his repeated questions to the domestics, the short answer was sure to be that she was not at home, nor had she been home all night. This having happened several times immediately after the conversation recorded in the previous chapter, had the effect of inducing him to stay at home longer at a time than was his wont, and with more lengthened intervals of absence, not that he had any other motive in so doing than to find out, if possible, the actions of his wife, for he now really believed that his amiable Maud was acting up to the spirit of her expressed intentions, and was alarmed lest she should have really taken a leaf out of his book.

Maud, who was all the time quietly located in a part of the house to which her husband had no occasion to go, was delighted to hear and to see, for, of course, she came occasionally into his presence, that there was something approaching a successful termination likely to result from her scheme ; but until she should be perfectly satisfied that such was the case, she decided upon continuing her present plan.

Matters went on in this uncomfortable way for some time, when George also determined to adopt some plan whereby he would be able to tax his wife with what he had reason to believe to be so serious a change for the worse ; and one evening, when they were together, he told her that he should be away for a week, with the design, however, of returning the following day. Now, had he ever before condescended to communicate to Maud, she would have been taken off her guard probably, but this being a singular instance of his communication, she immediately concluded that there was something more in it than was meant to meet the understanding, and she acted accordingly.

Having communicated her suspicions to the confidential domestic, who assisted her in her little plans, she caused her to report that she had occasion to make a particular visit, and would not return until that day week, the day limited by her husband for his absence.

The scheme took, and George returning on the following morning, and not finding Maud in her usual haunts, became anxious on the subject, and summoned Tony to his presence, and when that individual made his appearance, he said—

" Tony, where's your mistress ?"

" That's more than I can say," said Tony ; "you ought to know best."

" This is no time for foolery," said George ; " am I to understand that you don't know ?"

" Upon the honour of a gentleman," said Tony, " I do not."

" Did she say when she would return ?"

" I believe she did."

" And when is that to be ?"

" Yesterday week."

" I suppose you mean, Tony, in a week from yesterday ?"

" It's all the same, sir ; that's it."

" There, Tony, here's a trifle for you ; now attend to me. Immediately your mistress comes back, let me know ; but first tell her that I wish to speak to her upon most important and urgent business, that brooks of no delay. Do you understand ?"

" Do you think I'm a fool ?" said Tony.

" I think very little upon the subject," said his master ; " and if you think that she is not coming direct to me, then come to me yourself immediately. I shall be at home the remainder of the week."

" Very good," said Tony ; " I 'll do my best, you may depend, and thank ye for me."

Tony left the room, much wondering what all this mystery was about, and meeting Mary, the favourite and confidential domestic of his mistress, he stopped her, saying—

" There's a pretty kettle of fish somewhere, I think, Polly."

" What's the idiot mean now ?" said Mary.

" Why, I think, mistress will nap it above a bit when she does come home, that's all."

" What is it all about, Tony ? Tell me, there's a duck."

" Oh, you can deary now, can you, when you think there's something to be got by it ; but I doesn't do it. Oh dear no ; I should think not above a bit, my little domestic Venus."

" Do Tony—pray do—what is it ?"

"Upon the usual conditions," said Tony, "I don't mind if I do."

"Any conditions you please, Tony," said Mary; "but name them at once, for I don't like to be kept on the tenterhooks, you know."

"Very good, then," said Tony, kissing the lips of Mary about fifty times within the space of as many seconds; "those are my conditions; and now for what I've got to say :—It appears master didn't know his wife was going out to stop for a week, so he's in a bit of a sweat about it."

"What did he say?"

"That he should stop in all the week; and directly I saw missus, I was to send her to him, on urgent and particular business, which admitted of no brook."

"No brook? What did he mean by that, Tony?"

"I'm sure I don't know, except he meant Brook, the cheesemonger, round the corner."

"Very likely; and was that all—did he seem in a passion?"

"And if she wouldn't go to him, I was to take her by main force. He was very sulky, but he didn't seem in a passion, not by no manner of means; for a man in a passion don't often give away five-pound notes."

"Oh, then, he's been bribing you to play the spy, has he?"

"Not so, Polly. I was only to watch very earnestly for missus's return, and deliver to her in proper form the message delivered to me."

"Thank ye, Tony; and mind you do keep good watch: I'm glad master has discovered her goings on. I had always a mind to tell him, but I was afraid it might breed words between them, and therefore left the matter to take its chance."

"Is there anything wrong?" said Tony.

"Mind your own business, ducky, and keep a good look out," said Mary, as she departed on her business, which was to her mistress's apartments, to communicate what she had just heard from Tony.

"My plan works well, you see," said Maud; "he has much improved since I have adopted it, and I dare say begins to see the unreasonableness of his behaviour. I have no doubt that in a short time he will be entirely weaned from his vices; and when I am certain that he is, I will make my scheme known to him, and then we shall be happy as we once were. I do long for the expiration of the week, to know what is his urgent business. By-the-by, Mary, how am I to elude the vigilance of Tony, whom he has set to watch me, so that he do not detect how matters really are?"

"Leave him to me, ma'am. When the time comes, I will keep him in conversation until you have left the house; and then, when you knock at the door, he will be at liberty to open it."

"Be it so," said Maud. "It would be a pity that my grand plan should fail, for want of a little necessary precaution. I may depend, Mary, upon your tact in assisting me out of this difficulty?"

"Most certainly, madam; I think you may place some confidence in me, after keeping the servants in ignorance all this time that you are really at home."

"So far, Mary, you are a good girl, and I will not forget your kindness. Leave me for the present, Mary, and, should you hear anything further of your master's movements concerning me, forget not to tell me."

Mary promised to communicate the slightest thing that she thought likely to assist her mistress, and retired.

Now, although Mary had the best intentions in making the observation to Tony that she was glad his master had made the discovery, it had a very different effect, for Tony, naturally suspicious, imagined his mistress guilty of all manner of *laches ;* and having, also, ever an eye to his own advantage, determined to communicate his suspicions to his master, hoping to be liberally rewarded for his pains; in other words, being paid for making his master more miserable than he was.

Acting on this impulse, therefore, as soon as he got rid of Mary, and had occupied a little time for consideration, he stepped to his master's door, tapped thereat, and being summoned to enter, he did so on tiptoe, with his finger up to his lips, as though both their lives depended upon secrecy and silence.

"What antics are these, sir?" said George.

"I have something to say," said Tony, "that walls mustn't hear."

"Then you had better not tell them," said his master; "but what is all this to me?"

"Everything to you, sir," said Tony; "it concerns you, and I should not wish any one else to hear it."

"What is it?" said George.

"Missus," said Tony.

"Has she come home?"

"Oh, no, but I've seen her maid; and, oh, crikey! don't I think there's something in the wind above a bit? Ah, I believe you, I do, my boy. I beg pardon, sir—no offence, I hope."

"Well, go on."

"Well, sir, it's my opinion that missus has got somebody else what she likes better than you."

"You're a very good, honest, and trustworthy servant," said George, "and have my interest much at heart, I see; let me see whether I've a ten-pound note—yes, I have. I gave you five pounds this morning, I believe, Tony?"

"You did, sir."

"Be kind enough to hand it over to me," said George, holding the ten-pound note in one hand, while he held out the other for the money, which Tony was fumbling for in his fob.

"It is so seldom I see so much money," said Tony, as he presented the note at last to his master, at the same time holding out his hand to receive the other in exchange, "that I put it out of sight, to keep me from going stone blind."

"That will do," said George; "you will not be stone blind at looking at any more gifts from me, sir. Now this will be a lesson to you never to interfere in matters that don't concern you. If I lower myself by condescending to employ you in certain matters, you must not forget your station and take the initiative, but wait till your knowledge is required. You see, instead of gaining by your voluntary communications, you lose what you had already gained."

"Then do you mean to say that you mean to keep that 'ere note from me?"

"Yes."

"What after having once given it to me? Well I'm blowed if I don't think that's stretching a pint of law."

"I don't choose to argue with you," observed Mr. Selby. "I am doing this for your good; but as I had really given the money to you, you shall have it again on the completion of the business for which I retained your services."

"Oh, then I shall have it again, and no mistake?"

"Provided you never volunteer your confidence again."

"Well, sir, it's all the same to me. Of course you'll allow interest?"

"And will pay you in advance," said Selby; and walking towards Tony, he caught him by the ear, and opening the door, very politely, and in the most gentlemanly manner, kicked him down stairs.

"God tempers the wind to the shorn lamb," said Tony as he shook his feathers.

George, although before Tony he had kept himself, to outward appearance, tolerably cool, immediately when left to himself, paced the apartment in a state of great excitement He would have been glad to have heard more, but he could not bear the idea of a communication of an hour or two, as he expected it was, to come from the lips of a servant. He felt ashamed and terrified at the bare thought of a breath of suspicion being entertained of his wife's honour.

"Is it possible that she can have deceived me?" he exclaimed. "Bad as I am, I do not think she could punish me so heavily; and yet where can she go to? I know of no friends that she can call upon except the Menzies, and that she does not go there I have satisfied myself. It is a terrible thought, but I will abandon it; she never can be so bad; but why not? Other women, apparently as good as she, have done the same beyond all dispute. Pshaw! Why should I harbour such a suspicion?—why add to my misery by harping upon such a fallacy? Oh, nonsense! That rascal Tony evidently had some object in view in his communication; and yet it seemed genuine, too; he is too much a fool to act a part. Well, I will be easy till my wife thinks fit to return, and then I will have an explanation of her conduct, and force the truth.

Stay, why wait so long? Surely she is not more cunning than others of her sex; they seldom destroy the means of their detection. I will search; who knows but that I may make some discovery amongst her correspondence? That's mean, too—very mean; but I think, in such a case as this, I should be justified. I will do it—there should be no secrets between man and wife, except, perhaps, on the man's part; and it sometimes would be inconvenient to let the wife into every little thing that happens. Yes, I will do it—I will do it—ay, and at once too, and put myself out of my misery."

George took from his pocket a bunch of keys; and, after trying several, he carefully introduced into the lock one that he thought would open Maud's writing-desk, and was about to turn it, when he was startled by the handle of the door suddenly turning. As if guilty of some heinous crime, and conscious of the meanness of the action he was engaged in, he dropped his keys, and a paleness overspread his features, enough to proclaim to all observers that something was wrong; and turning towards the door, he saw Mary standing with her hand on the lock.

"I beg pardon, sir," said she, "for coming in without knocking, but——"

"What do you want?" said George.

"To know at what time you will dine, sir."

"Begone!" said George, "and attend to the work of your mistress. Send Tony to me in an hour's time, and I will inform him. I want no women to attend to me; and ask your mistress to teach you manners."

"May I ask in what respect?"

"To knock for admittance before you enter."

"I was going to explain, sir, but you——"

"Enough, enough—leave the room!"

Mary left the room accordingly, and George, again taking up the dropped keys, succeeded at length in opening the desk in which, unfortunately, was the letter from Rowland Symes, and which, it will be recollected, Maud had determined to reserve.

As all letters of every description were rapidly scanned by George, of course this unlucky letter presented itself in turn, and the contents of it were devoured with the most intense anxiety. The cold drops of perspiration rolled down the forehead of Selby as he perused the document, and when he had finished it, he sank into a chair completely paralyzed.

"Base woman!" said he. "So I have married a strumpet! Damnation!—that I—I should be so deceived! Rowland Symes—oh! and the plausible old villain, her uncle, to remain so quiet, when it appears by that unmistakable document that all the family knew it. Much reason, indeed, had he to flout me for ridding him of such an obnoxious devil. Rather should he have thanked me. Oh, woman—woman! your words are honied, but your deceit is deep as the depths of hell. Rowland Symes! Who is he? By Heaven! if we come across each other, it will be the first and the last meeting. There can be no mistake here. The letter speaks out on the subject with perfect candour and honesty; and, from what I can make out, he had the intention of redeeming her from her shame, but she refused. Unaccountable! Noble and amiable-minded creature that I once thought her—pshaw! how loathsome has she become! The graceful—the beautiful maid. The damned devil incarnate! Oh! does she not hug the thought that I am ignorant of the matter—glories in her wickedness, and takes credit to herself for her consummate tact. But she will find that she has stung a tiger—ay, one whose appetite for a deep and horrible revenge will never be appeased. Ha, ha! She will act, were her words. The hypocrite! She meant she would continue to act: and Rowland Symes—the stalwart Rowland Symes—is her friend in need. He it is with whom she takes shelter in her late absences. What a fool I have been to give her the necessary opportunities. I see now through the artfulness of her design in reproaching me for an occasional absence. Yes, yes—to disarm all suspicion, that she might have the greater opportunity to meet this Rowland Symes—this cursed Rowland Symes. Ha, ha, ha! Well, no matter—I can survive this crash. But she is very beautiful; and, if not guilty—pshaw! too beautiful to be good—too beautiful. Let a man marry a pock-marked, freckle-faced virago, if he wish to preserve his honour intact; but eschew beauty, but more especially if to it be added an apparent nobleness and amiability of deportment. They are nothing more or less than highly ornamented repositories for the blackest of venom. All hypocrites—all hypocrites! Rowland Symes! I don't recollect the name. I never could have heard it, surely. I will inquire. Stay—may not that impudent varlet, Tony, know something of the matter? I'll try—I'll try."

Tony was immediately summoned into Selby's presence, who, looking him sternly in the face, said—

"How long were you in the service of Mr. Menzies before I went to the house, Tony?"

"No time at all," said Tony; "I was there after you."

"Did Mr. Menzies hire you for my service?"

"Not that I know on. I believe he hired me, not because he wanted me, but because I had done him a good service, as he said, in taking you to that 'ere place."

"Is that the only reason?"

"That's one on 'em; the other is, that I was out of collar: my late master having gone over abroad to the foreign continent."

"And had you lived in that neighbourhood for any period—that is, sufficiently long for you to become acquainted intimately with the affairs of the different families living there?"

"Oh, yes—most decidedly—certainly; but I never took advantage of the opportunity, acos, as you know, I'm not of a curious disposition."

"Then I'm afraid you will be of no service," replied George.

"What is it you wish to know, sir?" said Tony.

"Did you ever hear of one called Rowland—Rowland S—s—s——"

"No, I never did——"

"Symes," continued George, who took no notice of Tony's interruption.

"Come, come—none of that, mister; you're poking fun at me," said Tony, putting his finger up to his nose.

"Confound your insolence," said his master; "how dare you presume to use such vulgar familiarity with me?"

"Begs pardon, sir," said Tony; "but Rowland Symes was my late master."

"Your late master?"

"Yes, sir, all up his back."

"Good—was he acquainted with the Menzies?"

"Ah, I believe you he was, above a bit, sir."

"Above a bit! was he particularly intimate with any one there?"

"I don't know that he was particularly intimate," said Tony, 'but I used to carry letters to missus often enough, and no mistake."

"Curse you!" said George, as he shook his fist in Tony's face, "and then——"

"Why, then I walked back again."

"With letters in answer?"

"No."

"Hum! Did they visit at each other's houses?"

"Yes; and walked out together often, until missus took offence at summat, and cut him."

"Were there any observations made by the servants of Mr. Menzies upon the subject?"

"Lor, no, sir! o' course there warn't, acos as how everything was done with the strictest propriety—there warn't nothing wrong, I can assure you."

"Have you taken leave of your senses, dolt? What do I know, or what do I care what was done, or what was not done, among the servants, sirrah? You may go."

"Thank you, sir. I hope I have given you satisfaction—there was nothing improper, on the honour of a gentleman."

"Scoundrel! go," said George, as he made an attempt to catch Tony, but whose activity foiled the intention; and who, when he was without harm's reach, coolly inquired whether he was still to watch for his mistress's return.

"I am now quite confirmed in my suspicions; there cannot be the shadow of a doubt that I have been entrapped into the meshes of a net, which they think it is an impossibility to get out of; but they will be deceived; most woefully; and if that perjured, perfidious woman, who has robbed me of my honour, be not the first to feel the intensity of my wrath, may the name of Selby ever after stick in the nostrils of society. Deep and bitter will be the revenge, entailing a long period of affliction, which shall be worse than death. No sudden and fatal punishment for me, where the victim has no time to *think*. No, time, long and lingering, whereby the iron may eat into the soul, shall be hers; and she shall pray earnestly that she may be released from the sweating agony of a guilty conscience by death—ay, by the most fearful death in the black catalogue; but she shall not succeed—no, no. I will take especial care that body and soul shall cling together, unless One who is higher than myself interferes—she shall ever curse the day that Rowland Symes first spoke to her. Ha, ha, ha! it will be glorious revenge—and the child—ah! the child—she loves her babe—she shall never see it more—not even know its fate; that will be a splendid additional punishment. Ha, ha, ha! Maud, Maud, I think I'll match you now. Curse you, I hate you."

*   *   *   *   *

Poor Maud, unconscious of what was passing with her husband, was, as usual, in her apartment, and congratulating herself that in a little time things would wear a better aspect; but, alas! very different was the result as regarded her fortunes.

In such thoughts as these, Maud indulged until the day on which George Selby had told her he should return, and in the early part of that eventful day numerous and anxious consultations were held between her and her maid, Mary, as to the disposition of the servants, more especially Tony, at the particular time when she was to leave the house but for a moment.

However, her maid undertook to manage all the preliminaries, and to so dispose of the servants, so that it should be impossible for any of them to witness her mistress leaving the house. She excited their curiosity by proposing to relate some family secret to them, of great importance, and she congregated them together, and amused them sufficiently long enough for her mistress to leave the house and return with a double rat-tat-tat.

As Tony had been previously ordered, he immediately informed his mistress of his masters wish to see her immediately.

They proceeded to the drawing-room, the door of which Tony having opened, Maud walked in. Selby was sitting by the fire, absorbed in the pleasures of a book; but, hastily turning round, he fixed his keen eye upon his wife, and with a most stern, cool look, said—

"Be seated, madam."

"George!"

"Be seated, I repeat. What I have to communicate will admit of no idle ceremonies; and to what questions I have to put to you I shall expect answers, uttered with deliberation, that there may be no plea hereafter in excuse for equivocation now. Will you answer me fairly and honestly?"

"Say on," said Maud.

"I find," said Selby, "that you take advantage of my absence, and absent yourself also. Why is this?"

"Because," replied Maud, "I act up to my word. You will recollect that I promised to *act*. I have done so—that is all."

"Good. Where do you go, and to whom do you go?"

"To an intimate friend. The residence I decline to state."

"For what purpose do you go?"

"On private and particular business.'

"What business?"

"The affairs of my friend require secrecy, and I cannot conscientiously disclose the nature of them—not even to my husband."

"Indeed! I can see at once through this. It is a mere retort upon me. But I require most distinctly to be informed of the real truth."

"Then, indeed, I cannot tell you."

"That answer amounts to this—that you will not tell me."

"If it please you, be it so."

"Good. Are you sure that you do not go on the private business of, and to see, Rowland Symes?"

"Ah! Rowland Symes?"

"Yes, madam: I said Rowland Symes. Why that start?"

"What can you mean?" said Maud.

"You have said enough, madam—quite enough—to convince me that I am right in my suspicions that your meetings are with that gentleman."

"Indeed, dear George, they are not—indeed, they are not. Do you know Rowland Symes?"

"Deuce take it!" said Selby: "are you playing with me? I do not know him. It is enough for me that you know him, and have known him too well."

"It is false, George—entirely false; and if any one has dared to whisper aught to my prejudice in respect of that man, he or she is a base calumniator."

"It is too true, base woman! I have it in his own words."

"It is false as hell!" said Maud. "Have you seen him?"

"I have not; but he has spoken to me."

"You speak in riddles," exclaimed Maud.

"There is the solution," said Selby, who threw down the fatal letter: "there it is, stamped upon your forehead."

"Cruel—cruel!" said Maud, bursting into tears. "I can explain this letter to you. Send for Rowland Symes, and ask him."

"Silence, strumpet! Am I a fool, that I should expect a man who had injured me to confess it?—Pshaw!"

"Oh! as the Almighty is my judge, this, Selby, was a villanous letter sent to me for the purpose of injuring me; and it has performed its commission to the letter. Inquire of my uncle. He can testify to my innocence."

"Ha, ha, ha! Weak evidence—weak evidence! No—no: the proof is too evident—

too evident—to admit of a doubt. Out of my sight, woman!—out of my sight!"

"Have patience, dear George, and hear me explain."

"I will hear nothing. You are guilty beyond the power of redemption—body and soul entirely guilty. Peace—peace, I say! I will hear nothing! We part from this moment—part for ever!"

"Dear George, hear me—my child——"

"Shall be looked after; but never again shall you press it to your heart! Never again shall you see its soft laughing eye! No —no: the child must not be contaminated—it must be kept pure, and all knowledge of his mother's sin must be for ever kept from its mind. It shall be looked well after."

"You will, I am sure, on consideration, alter this cruel resolution, George. You must, you must! Oh, God, I am innocent, entirely innocent, in word, thought, and deed! Indeed, I am—indeed I am!"

"I will hear no more, base and deceitful woman! From your great mother Eve to the remotest link in the chain, you are all alike—bad, bad, bad!"

"Oh! say not so, George; it is wicked, and the Almighty will not hear so much blasphemy from mortal lips."

"Tush, tush, argue not with me: I have done with you for ever!"

"Then if it be so—but for Heaven's sake think again—if it be so, I will go back to my uncle."

"Nay, not so, madam; I will not be a party to giving you fresh opportunities for a fond dalliance with the handsome Rowland Symes. No, although we separate, I still shall retain the control over your actions; and now business calls me away for a time, but for a time only; and till my return, you must remain here in this room; and to insure your compliance, madam, you must excuse me for turning the key in the door; I have already taken the precaution of having the windows secured. You see, therefore, that any attempt to escape will be futile. I will ring for your maid; it will be prudent, perhaps, to allow you her company; she shall be your keeper, madam, for the present, till I provide the means of procuring better attendance."

So saying, he coolly left the room, after requesting Mary to go in and attend to her mistress; and locking the door, put the key in his pocket.

CHAPTER XXII.

SELBY'S SCHEME PROGRESSES.

WE will now leave the unhappy Maud, and follow her husband in the pursuit of his scheme for the safety of his wife.

It happened that in a conversation at which he was present, the subject of lunatic asylums was introduced, and one establishment was particularly dwelt on in reference to its keeper, who had become celebrated by being concerned in the forcible detention of an inmate, who was certainly anything but entitled to the name of a lunatic, as was decidedly proved by the individual himself before the Lord Chancellor, whom by some means he had contrived to let know the circumstances of his case.

The name of this man, and the locality of the house, Selby retained in his memory, and after the interview with his wife, he determined upon at once proceeding there to make the necessary arrangements for her reception as an inmate. From the man's character, he was convinced that he would not stand at trifles; and, therefore, he was just the man that would suit him. He accordingly made his way to the asylum, and having inquired if Mr. Ironsides was within, sent up his card.

He had not long to wait for that gentleman, who being extremely anxious for business, was always on the alert to see his customers.

"In what way can I serve you?"

"In a most essential manner by taking care of a friend of mine till she recovers her reason," replied Selby.

"Good. I suppose you have the necessary documents?"

"No, I have not; but I believe you are in the habit of dispensing with these on certain occasions."

"The risk is great," observed Ironsides.

"True, but the reward is great."

"That alters the case," said Ironsides. "I am not very squeamish in these matters, as you observe; but still it is necessary to be cautious. Now I'm doing a good business here, and if anything should happen that is likely to call my house into question, you see I shall be a considerable loser; now understand me, I never take anything on my own responsibility—I must have everything done in the usual form—so that I am blameless. In the late affair before the Chancellor, I came off not only free from suspicion but with praises actually; this would not have been so, had I not thrown all the responsibility on the other side. You understand?"

"I think I can perceive your drift; but as we both understand each other, I believe you may as well honestly communicate what it is you require of me."

"As a *sine qua non*, I must have the necessary medical certificates."

"How can I procure these? It is quite impossible."

"Pho! can you write?"

"I see—I see; well, you shall have them."

"Very good; the next thing I require is security for the payment of my annual charge—you don't object to that?"

"It's troublesome, certainly," said Selby, "very troublesome; what say you to the first annual payment being made in advance?"

"That'll do for me, and a fig for the security. When will you be ready?"

"What is the time now?" said Selby.

"Twelve," replied Ironsides, as he drew out his watch.

"You're wrong," said the other; "my time is different; let us compare;" and Selby also referred to his watch, which he held close to the face of Ironsides; "you see?"

Ironsides started at the sight of that watch, and the colour forsook his cheeks entirely.

"Nay," said Selby, "be not alarmed, Cutts, at seeing an old friend of yours."

"I—I—I don't——"

"That will do, Cutts. I am glad to see you have changed your line of life. You see I have saved five hundred pounds by finding you myself."

"Do you come here," exclaimed Ironsides, who was really no other than the redoubtable Cutts, the highwayman, "upon that score? It is no use contending against facts; but understand me, you or I will not leave this house alive. Without there—Andrew! what ho! Andrew Stumps!"

"Not so," interrupted Selby. "I have no such intention. Countermand your call. I want no witnesses to what passes between us. I forgive you what has happened, but shall require something in return."

"Name it," said Ironsides.

"Your best exertions in keeping in close confinement the woman I shall entrust to you."

"Is that all?"

"No more, I assure you; but recollect, on this condition only, that if at any time she should elude your vigilance, and escape, the bargain between us is at an end."

"Easy terms—easy terms. I have a snug retreat for her, where even the light of day shall not visit her. Who is she—your mistress?"

"My wife."

"Indeed! Well, I will take special care of her. When shall I have her?"

"When will you be ready?"

"At any time—at all times. Shall I come for her?"

"Well thought of," said Selby; "I may have a difficulty in persuading her to accompany me. We must adopt some plan to cloud her preceptions. Stay, I have it. Do you think you can make your appearance in the character of a doctor of the civil law—a black coat, knee-breeches, silk stockings, buckles, white cravat—a little flour on the collar of your coat, eh? Do you think you can manage this?"

"Manage that? ay! I have managed more difficult matters in my time than that. What then?"

"I will prepare her for your reception by stating that I will have a separation drawn up in a legal way, but previous to doing so, have thought it better first to consult with a friend of mine, a doctor in the ecclesiastical courts, who I have requested to call upon me for that purpose—that, you see, will prepare her for your appearance; then we will argue the topic in her presence, as I mean to make that a chief point with her, that nothing shall be done without her having a voice in the matter. I will raise difficult points—you shall doubt and hesitate to decide, and at length propose that we shall all adjourn to the private residence of the celebrated Doctor Ironsides, at Hampstead, who, at present, is, in consequence of ill health, obliged to consult at home—this she will, I have no doubt, agree to, and consequently we drive to Doctor Ironsides, and when there, there I will leave her for the doctor to do with her what to him seemeth best. Will that do?"

"Famous! nothing would be better—there will be no unnecessary alarm; and she will fall into our scheme as easily as a fly into the web of a spider."

"True; and I hope she will find it as difficult to get out."

"Quite, you may depend upon it, quite—for those who enter here leave hope behind."

"You understand me," said Selby, "I do not wish any unnecessary cruelty to be pursued towards her."

"God bless you," said Ironsides, "this is the place where the mildest and meekest treatment is used. Cruelty! Well, this is the first time such a suspicion has been breathed in regard to my establishment. Why, sir, it's fit for a queen."

"At the same time," continued Selby, "I require that she be kept perfectly solitary."

"It's a plan I always adopt," said Ironsides.

"And no materials for communication to be within her reach?"

"It would be strange, indeed, if there were. What do mad people want with pens and ink? They talk foolery enough without putting it upon paper. You leave her to me, and you shall have no reason to complain."

"Well," said Selby, "I think I may do so, because your stake is heavy in the game; you know your life depends upon it."

"Say no more upon that subject, Mr. Selby; I admit it all; and now as matters stand between us, let us exchange watches again."

"Most decidedly not: I shall hold this over your head in terrorem. There's something so particularly attractive about the initials 'M.I.' to me, that I really have taken a most especial fancy to the article; the wreath, too, is pretty. It will speak volumes by-and-by, in case there should be occasion to refer to it."

"I see you distrust me," said Ironsides, "and as it is my interest to say and do nothing that will prejudice me in this matter, I suppose I must succumb."

"I suppose you must," replied Selby; "and now having arranged everything but the time, I propose that you should call upon me at my house about dark."

"Very good, I will attend; for the present then farewell, and make your mind quite easy that neither you nor nobody else will

ANDREW STUMPS ENDEAVOURS TO CAPTURE JACKY JINGLE.

hear anything more of Mrs. Selby when she is once under my roof."

"Farewell," said Selby, "and remember the watch."

"I shall not forget it," said Ironsides.

*   *   *   *   *

Poor George passed a miserable night, and after his interview with Ironsides, he returned to his house; and a short time before he expected a visit from the respectable Cutts, he entered the apartment in which he had left Maud, and her maid prisoner. He looked gloomy as he took a seat, without apparently noticing them. After preserving silence for a few minutes, he informed Maud that it was his unalterable determination to have a separation; and in spite of all her tears and entreaties, he would not listen to her supplications, nor believe in her protested innocence.

Ironsides performed the part selected for him with consummate skill; and as he had his carriage at the door, he urged the necessity of consulting a legal friend of his who was well-skilled in matters pertaining to the separation of man and wife, who lived in the neighbourhood of Hampstead, and that in the present instance he would exert his abilities with justice to each party.

Poor Maud's intellects were too much obscured by the weight of misery which had fallen upon her, to penetrate the design made upon her liberty, and passively yielded to his advice. Preparations in dress were speedily made, and in less than a quarter of an hour might have been seen a closed carriage progressing rapidly in the direction of Hampstead.

When they arrived, Stumps, the servant of Ironsides, accosted them with vulgar familiarity, and spoke of the room he had been preparing. For a few minutes Maud was left by herself in a dingy apartment, the walls of which looked to her more like the walls of a prison than anything else she could conceive; and if she had been left long to her conjectures, probably the truth would have flashed on her mind; but the door opened suddenly and Ironsides made his appearance, requesting Maud to accompany him to the presence of Mr. Todd's, which was the name of the fictitious legal friend, but as he was leading her through a subterranean portion of the house, the truth made itself evident, and she refused to proceed further. Resistance was vain, for Ironsides called Stumps to his aid, and they carried her forcibly to the cell destined for her, while Selby stood by the door witnessing her agonising shrieks for assistance.

Selby gave the lamp he carried in his hand to Stumps, and turned his back upon his captive wife; he beckoned to Ironsides, the door was locked upon her, and she was left in darkness.

"Buried alive! Buried alive!" faintly ejaculated Maud, and she sank upon the ground in a swoon in that cell in which we first introduced her to the reader.

About the time that these events happened, Vauxhall Gardens were in the meridian of their glory, and none but the elite of fashion resorted to them, or such whose curiosity led them there, the price of admission being such as would exclude the multitude. It was on the night that the unfortunate Maud threw herself into the river that a boat, containing a lady and gentleman, and rowed by a burley waterman, was making progress down the river. The night was intensely dark, and from the fears entertained by the lady and the replies from the gentleman, none who knew them could fail recognising the voices of Mr. Menzies and his sister, Grace. While the boatman was endeavouring to peer his way through the thick darkness, a piercing shriek smote their ears. The shock for the moment had nearly the effect of upsetting the frail wherry.

"There goes another unfortunate female," said the waterman; and before the echo of the words died away, they discovered a white mass floating on the surface of the water. The boat was carefully and swiftly rowed in the direction, and the inanimate form of a female was lifted into the boat. The promise of a five pound note by Mr. Menzies gave the waterman an extraordinary degree of energy, and she was soon in the Crown Hotel, near the Adelphi. No sooner did Grace see the face of the apparently lifeless form of the female, than she fainted. She had discovered their long lost, but beloved niece. Mr. Menzies was sensibly affected, but controlled his feelings so much as to give the necessary orders for an attempt at restoration. A surgeon was quickly in attendance, and Jacky Jingle at his heels, rendering most efficient service. A bath having been obtained, and other restoratives resorted to, poor Maud gave signs of returning life. All that medical skill could do had been done for her, and she only wanted undisturbed repose to restore her to consciousness. The doctor gave positive orders that no one was to enter till his return, which would be in a few hours; as he felt convinced that the means he had adopted, with the care he had enjoined, would have the desired effect.

*   *   *   *   *   *

Jacky Jingle informed Mr. Menzies of all that his memory served him, which was, that Maud and he had escaped from a mad-house, and that Maud had given him the letter he then held in his hand, which was addressed to George Selby.

No doubt many of our readers require some explanation of the sudden return to Jacky Jingle of his reason, and accordingly that individual shall himself satisfy those who have taken any interest in his welfare.

After the doctor had left, Mr. Menzies, Grace, and Jacky Jingle determined to remain till Maud could be left in some degree of safety. After making some scruples about communicating his history, he at length said—

" When I so suddenly and mysteriously recovered my senses, I had a perfect and distinct mental vision of what had occurred to me some years before, of a similar nature. I was then about twelve years of age, and was on a visit to the house of my father, during my school vacation, which happened at midsummer. I recollect that just previous to autumn, when I should have returned to my school, my father proposed to my mother, rest her soul, an excursion on the water, to which she consented, stipulating, however, that I should be one of the party, as I had so small a time left, previous to returning to the monotony of the school. To this my father raised many objections, which, however, she succeeded in overruling, and we accordingly went. I recollect it as well as if it were but yesterday; in fact, the intervening time that had elapsed, during which a superior Power thought fit for its own wise purposes to prostrate my senses, is a hiatus in my existence, and is as though it were not—and I have a difficulty in combating the idea that the events did actually take place only but yesterday – only that I see I have become a man since then. Well, sir, it was towards the close of a sultry afternoon, that we proceeded to Westminster Bridge, and from there my father hired a boat, and himself acted the part of the waterman, much to my mother's terror, for she plainly told him that she had little confidence in his skill."

" What, and did you really trust yourself without a boatman?" asked Grace.

" I had no voice in it, madam," replied Jingle, "or I would have opposed it. We proceeded as far as the bridge, I think they called it Battersea, and there we landed, and entering a public inn, my father called for refreshments, and stayed there until the shades of evening were thickening fast. I recollect my mother urging him to return before any danger should happen, by reason of the increasing darkness, and that her reasonings had little weight with him. At length," continued Jingle, " he thought fit to return, but not before the night had set in. We were alone upon the water, with the exception of a few barges that were leisurely proceeding down the stream, and when a considerable distance from the last which we passed, my father drew in his oars, and fumbling in the breast of his coat, I saw a bright gleam for a moment—I saw his hand uplifted—I saw it descend—I heard an awful heart-rending shriek from my poor mother, and recollect no more than that; when I recovered my consciousness, my father and I were alone, and I caught a last glimpse of her white garments through the obscurity: she sunk.

" I was absolutely paralysed and terrified to that degree that I could not speak, nay, scarce breathe—but, trembling, I threw myself at the feet of my father, and hid my face between his knees.

" ' Not a word, boy, not a word of this on your life—silence or death—the same death for you,' said he. ' Mark me; if you ever breathe but her name, you die.'

" ' Why,' said I, 'oh! why is this?'

" ' It is for a good purpose, boy ; and when a man does a thing, let it be ever so bad apparently, with a good motive, he does a praiseworthy and justifiable thing. I have gospel for it.'

" ' Oh, it must be a bad gospel that teaches such things,' replied I.

" ' Hush! hush! boy ; you are too young to understand these things yet—one day I will explain the matter to you—in the meantime remain silent.'

" ' Never,' said I.

" ' Nay, then,' replied my father, 'if that be so—but I will not kill you : no, no, you may be useful to me yet, and I will find a way to keep you silent—no, boy, you shall live ; yes, you shall live.'

" I said no more, but determined on the first opportunity occurring of revealing the terrible tragedy that had been enacted—but fate ordained that it should not be till now. That cruel man shot in his boat to a retired and secluded part of the shore, and taking violent means to prevent the possibility of my uttering a word, or raising the slightest symptom of alarm, hurried me on to a lone house in the outskirts of London, kept by a man of the name of Stumps, Andrew Stumps ; and there, after a short consultation with the man, he himself thrust me into a cold, dark, slimy cellar—a refuge for all kinds of disgusting reptiles, and I heard him lock the door, and walk away. In this miserable place I was confined beyond remembrance, for I can but recollect that for some time afterwards my father daily came and supplied me with food, and then all certain memory leaves me. It was during this time that I became an idiot, induced by the solitariness of my situation, and the dreadful remembrance of the scene of which I had been so fearful a spectator."

" Poor fellow, poor fellow," said Ralph, "and this, you say, took place when you were twelve ?"

" It did."

" And how old are you now?"

" I do not know."

" I beg pardon, I beg pardon," said Ralph ; "I had forgotten. Do you recollect any particulars that could identify your mother—any ornament—any article of jewellery?"

" Nothing but a ring which she wore at the time, and which was undoubtedly unique."

" Had it an exceedingly small and beautifully executed portrait of the murdered monarch?"

" Charles the First," exclaimed Jingle, with evident surprise.

" The same—the same !" said Ralph ; " God, how wonderful and inscrutable are thy ways !"

" What means this," asked Jingle, "tell me—does she live? Does my dear mother live?"

"Alas! no—alas! no. She was found, and it must have been some days afterwards, for her features were undistinguishable, close by the Temple-stairs. I was one of the jury on the occasion of the inquest, and I grieve to say she was not identified, notwithstanding the publicity of the affair—but, thank God, there is some chance now of bringing the murderer to justice."

"And was it not as I stated?" asked Jingle, "had she not a dreadful wound in the neck?"

"Not only so, my poor friend, but the knife was still remaining in the wound—it had penetrated the clavicle to the very hilt, and with much difficulty could it be withdrawn. But we must now see what is to be done. In the first place, you must furnish me with the means of identification of the unfortunate woman; and also of her murderer—what name shall I give?"

"Ironsides," replied he, whom we have hitherto only known as Jacky Jingle. "Gregory Ironsides—my father's name was Maurice."

"Good! and what has become of him?"

"Indeed," replied the other, "I have no direct recollection of having seen him, since he left me with Stumps, and his subsequent visits to me when there; though I have a sort of half dreamy idea floating through my brain, that his features were continually before my eyes, though this may be a mere vision of the brain, not founded upon reality."

"I am not so sure about that," said Ralph; "but we will for the present leave the matter in abeyance—as it has remained so long quiet, there can be no immediate occasion to devote our sole attention to the necessary inquiries to be made to bring this mysterious subject to light, to the exclusion of other matters, which are recent, of as much importance, and equally necessary to be arranged; and, therefore, as you seem to take so much interest in the fate of my unfortunate niece here, I propose that she shall be the first object of our attentions; and in return for the assistance which I have promised to render to you, and which I will most scrupulously perform, I shall claim, and hope that you will render to me all the assistance in your power in carrying out a sheme I have thought of for arranging affairs amicably between her and her husband. What do you say?"

"I shall most readily and heartily join with you in carrying out any object, the result of which is at all likely to be of service to that much injured lady."

"Thank you—thank you," said Ralph. "Grace, why don't you thank Mr. Ironsides?"

It was early in the morning when Gregory Ironsides started to find the residence of George Selby; but as he was unacquainted with the different localities through which he had to pass, the hour of eight struck just as he reached the house. The servants were peremptory in refusing to communicate any intelligence at that time in the morning, especially as he had not retired more than an hour; but young Ironsides was inflexible in his demand to see Mr. Selby, and would not be refused. At length he obtained permission to go to Selby's bed-room.

Soon as Selby heard his wife was dead, and that her messenger had a letter for him, his whole frame shook for a moment; and then he requested that the bearer should open it and read it to him. The letter ran as follows—

"MY DEAREST GEORGE,—Before you will receive this letter I shall be no more in this world. I have not strength of mind to bear the harshness of your treatment towards me. Oh, may Heaven forgive me the rash step! But I fear that it is my fate, and I cannot resist it.

"I now entreat of you to read this, my explanation of that passage of my life which has resulted in so disastrous a manner to both your happiness and mine."

"Now for the confession," interrupted Selby. "I am glad she has made a clean breast before her death: she stands a better chance."

"You would not allow me," continued Ironsides, resuming the letter, "to give the explanation in person, and by word of mouth, or things might have turned out satisfactorily; and what I am about to write, coming from one whose hours—nay, whose minutes, are numbered, should be received, and I pray that it may be received, as the truth. You must know so much of me as will, I am satisfied, convince you that I will speak nothing but the truth at such an awful moment as this, whatever your opinion of me may be in ordinary circumstances, and the fact also that I have no motive in writing that which is untrue will be another, and perhaps a stronger inducement to you to believe in my last words.

"That I knew Rowland Symes—that base and designing man—I cannot deny: that I was on friendly terms with his family, and his family with mine, I admit: that I was on peculiar terms of intimacy with him I most distinctly and emphatically deny, for I never had the least feeling of sympathy for him. On the contrary, I always felt a repugnance to his society—for no particular reason, that I am aware of; but these feelings, as you must be well aware, are not uncommon, though unaccountable. But with regard to him, I do not deny that he, much to my aversion, persecuted me with his addresses: indeed, so much so, that I was induced to forego the pleasure I had previously experienced in visiting his relations—some of whom were my most intimate and particular friends—rather than run the hazard of encountering him. My absence from his family circle did not escape his observation, and the reason for it, undoubtedly, he was not long in discovering; and then he took a new course of persecution by waylaying me in my walks, which were always confined within a very narrow circle of my uncle's residence. Indeed, so far did he renew his persecution, that on the last occasion he forcibly detained me, and had it not been for the timely arrival of my dear uncle—who was on his return from the inn—

the consequences might have been to me serious; but, thank God! my uncle was a sufficient protection to me, and I escaped. Since that time I have never seen Rowland Symes, for I took especial care to confine myself entirely to the house. Not satisfied with the checks he had thus received, a new course of annoyance presented itself to him, and several letters were clandestinely received into the house—the last one, and which has produced so much mischief, being the one you have now in your possession, and which I most foolishly determined to keep, the motive for which I am at a loss to explain. I had refused to read any letters he might send previously to this fatal one, and had ordered the servants to reject all letters addressed to me; and, by some means, the wretched man discovered this, and with a cunning and malignity worthy of a fiend, addressed the envelope in which it was enclosed not to myself, but, I believe, to my dear uncle—thus endeavouring to blast my reputation in his eyes. But he was well acquainted with the character of the man, and the attempt utterly and entirely failed.

" For a confirmation of the truth of what I have stated, I need only refer you to my uncle and his sister, to whom I have not written or communicated since our unhappy marriage; and, therefore, they cannot be influenced by any *ex parte* statement from me.

" That I did not inform you, before or after our marriage, of these circumstances, perhaps I am to blame; but I considered it—if I thought at all upon the subject—of so little moment, that I did not mention it.

" I have nothing further to say, dear George, but that God, I hope, will remove the film from your eyes, if it be only for the sake of our dear little innocent. And oh! pray, dear George, treat him tenderly—as tenderly as his mother would have done, had she been permitted. And that Heaven may forgive you as freely as I do, is the earnest and last prayer of your unfortunate and innocent wife,   " MAUD SELBY."

As Gregory Ironsides concluded the reading of this document, he folded it up, and laid it on the bed. Selby was silent for a few moments. A convulsive shudder seized him, and a cold perspiration broke out upon his face.

" God, if this be true!" he said : " if this be true!"

" Why not ?" said Ironsides.

" I will see Mr. Menzies, her uncle. I will throw myself at his feet for forgiveness and advice. Yes: I will see the good old man whom I have so much injured—whose niece I stole, and, at length, barbarously murdered. My good sir, let me see you again—let me know all that you know concerning my poor innocent Maud. But not now—not know. I am not myself."

" Shall I call to-morrow ?" asked Ironsides.

" Thanks — thanks. Let it be in the evening."

" Depend upon me," said Ironsides. " I will be here. In the meantime, farewell."

" Farewell," said Selby. " Farewell."

CHAPTER XXIII.

SELBY'S INTERVIEW WITH MR. MENZIES.

GREGORY IRONSIDES, as soon as he had left Selby, returned to the inn where he had left Ralph; and communicating to him the full particulars of this interview, the latter determined immediately to return to Menzies' house, in case Selby should follow up his expressed resolution of seeing him. Having, therefore, arranged that Grace should stay with his niece, together with Gregory Ironsides, until they should hear from him, he departed for his home, and fortunately arrived there just before Selby himself was announced.

There was a marked difference in the appearance of Selby now to what there once was. The healthful glow that once sat upon his cheek was now usurped by a deadly pale; the once bright eye was now lustreless; the bold, upright, manly bearing, was turned now into one of conscious guilt; and the eye that before could stand the most scrutinising gaze, now quailed before it, and dared hardly lift its vision from the ground.

As the servant opened the door of the apartment in which was Mr. Menzies, George crept in with an hesitating, stealthy kind of shuffle, as if he were about to receive judgment for some crime, and for which he was perfectly aware that he deserved no sympathy.

" Good God, Mr. Selby," exclaimed Ralph, affecting surprise, " is it yourself?—why, man, alive, I'm truly glad to see you—but how altered you are; have you seen a ghost ?"

" Behold in me," said Selby, " a very different man to what I was when you knew me better—I am a murderer !"

" A murderer ?—nonsense, man, you're dreaming surely—or are mad."

" Neither. Alas, it is true, too true. I am an unmitigated scoundrel, and deserving of the severest censure that it is in the power of man to heap upon me," said Selby.

" Explain yourself, George, explain—some horrible fancy has taken possession of you—the remains of some hideous dream."

" Oh, would to God that it were but so," said George; " oh, would to God that it were. But no, the facts are too startling—too real, too real. I have sent a pure, an innocent soul to the Almighty before its time—I am a murderer! a murderer !"

" Come, come, George, allow yourself to be calm, and then explain what is the meaning of this strange revelation."

" There is no need; I shall never more be calm, never again; the mark of the assassin is upon my brow, in my heart, my whole soul is engrossed with the one great overwhelming knowledge of the fact — I have murdered your niece.'

"My niece ?"

"Oh, God—'tis true—'tis true."

"Are you mad that you come here to me, her uncle, to communicate the sad intelligence ?—man, man, what shall I say to you ?"

"Make me glory in the deed, or plunge me into the very vortex of despair. Tell me, sir, tell me, did you know one Rowland Symes ?"

"Perfectly well, and his father for fifty years before him, and a very vicious young scamp he was."

"What do you know of him in connection with Maud ?'

"This much—that he endeavoured to foist himself upon her affections, and was repulsed with the contempt and scorn that he deserved; and the scamp, I suppose, to traduce my dear child in my estimation, took the base and dastardly means of writing to me and to her most wicked letters, insinuating that which I will not defile my lips by uttering."

"And was there no truth in the statement ?"

"I will lay my life upon it none—no, no. Maud has from time to time communicated to me everything that had occurred between them; his persecutions of her, her thorough detestation of him, and at length her resolve to exclude herself from all society in which he was likely to form a part. His letters fell harmless—quite harmless. I knew her, and I knew him, and the intended poison failed—totally failed."

"Merciful Father !" exclaimed Selby; "if what you say were true—oh, if what you say were true—but no, no—they did not fail—they did not fail, Mr. Menzies; here is one that had the intended effect ; the poison penetrated into my soul—deep—deep; and the innocent Maud has gone to her great account. I murdered her."

"I cannot believe so much from you, George, I will not believe it. How did it happen? Tell me."

"I traduced her character—reviled her—called her by the most opprobrious epithets—sent her away from my house—nay more, I caused her to be imprisoned in a lunatic asylum as mad."

"Horrible ! horrible !" exclaimed Ralph. "There is no excuse for that; that, indeed, was the maximum of cruelty. Bad—bad. Methinks there you might have stopped."

"There I did stop," continued Selby; "there she, the poor murdered Maud, commenced. She escaped, and calling at my house when I was in the heyday of pleasure, demanded to see me—I spurned her from the door—taunted her—persuaded her to kill herself, and she took my advice. Oh, God ! and innocent too ! oh, what would I not give if all were but a dream. Sir, I shall go mad myself—I feel I must do that or die."

"Nay, nay," urged Ralph, "you must endeavour to make your peace with a higher power, and then you'll feel easier in your mind; a true repentance is a passport to happiness you know. Who knows but that your wife is still alive ?"

"Alive ! Alive ! Oh, God, I wish she were; but why raise such hopes that they may be crushed again, and leave me tenfold more wretched ?"

"My dear George," said Ralph, "I don't see any reason not to entertain such a hope ; it is possible that some kind hand might have rescued her from such a lamentable fate, very possible."

"Oh, no, no no !" exclaimed Selby; "she was too good, too pure, for this world, and she is snatched away to a better, rescued from the hands of a cruel, relentless husband, who was unworthy of such a treasure. No, no, she is no more, she is no more."

"Well, I, at all events, am more sanguine," said Ralph, "and I will make it my business to personally arrive at the truth; and I hope it may so turn out, as I feel confident, from an unaccountable feeling that has taken possession of me, that she is still alive, and lives for you."

* * * * *

During the absence of her uncle, Maud had made a rapid progress to a state of health; and as soon as she heard that he was in the house, she was unceasing in her requests to see him, notwithstanding the medical man's order were to the contrary. Ralph started as his eye fell upon the features of his niece, always beautiful, but now, oh, what a changed beauty was there ! After she had asked for his forgiveness, her next questions were of her husband and child. Mr. Menzies satisfied her that they were well, and that he had a plot in hand which would have the effect of reconciling them to each other. But as he was fearful of the consequences of a protracted conversation, he left her, after persuading her to compose her feelings, and endeavour to sleep.

* * * * *

When Mr. Menzies left Maud, he took Gregory Ironsides with him to the house of a magistrate, who was a friend of his, and denounced the madhouse keeper for the murder of his wife. The worthy magistrate entered into the particulars with minuteness, and expressed as great a desire for the capture of the murderer as they had, recollecting also the circumstance of the woman being found with the knife in her throat. Early the following morning, Mr. Menzies, Gregory, and two active officers, by the use of a little strategy, effected his capture, without injury to any one.

By the time that Mr. Menzies reached the police-court, the last case of drunkenness was being disposed of; and as soon as the unhappy delinquent had forked out, as the turnkey called it, his five bob, the case of Maurice Ironsides was called on.

Sufficient evidence was gone into on that occasion to satisfy the mind of the magistrate that he was fully justified into coming to the conclusion to commit the prisoner; and after the usual question to him as to whether he had anything to say, but that he was not bound to say anything that might criminate himself, for that it would be brought against him at another place, had been put, and answered in the negative, he was fully committed to Newgate to take his trial for the wilful murder of Laura Ironsides, his wife; and the witnesses were bound over to appear in the usual way.

As Mr. Menzies returned from the police-court, he called on Selby, whom he found in his study. He had, as he promised, made great alterations in his household, and had dismissed all those that were not necessary to the establishment of a single gentleman. By degrees he led him on to think it possible that Maud was alive. But the idea of ever seeing her again took no hold of his imagination. He soliloquised—

"Poor Maud! Poor injured Maud! I am, indeed, your murderer. For our boy, and for him alone, will I live, and lead a life of repentance."

Selby threw himself into a seat, and for a few moments continued silent, with his eyes vacantly fixed upon the fire, then suddenly exclaimed—

"Where is she?—where is she? I must see her before the grave conceals her from my sight!"

"That at present," said Ralph, 'I must decline to accede to; when I am satisfied that you are sufficiently calm to undergo the ordeal, I will conduct you to her."

"I tell you I am quite calm and in a condition at once to bear anything."

"Then you must excuse me for saying that you must bear delay," said Ralph; "in three days I will take you to her."

"Why not at once?" asked Selby.

"I have other business to attend to," said Ralph, "which will not admit of the necessary time that it would occupy to attend with you for the purpose."

"Tell me the place where she is, and I can go alone."

"No, though she be dead," replied Ralph, "she is once more in my custody, and I will keep a strict eye upon her, till I am forced to let her go. I have been deceived once, and will not run the chance of being deceived again; you must wait till I find time to accompany you, so it is of no avail to urge me further; and now, if you will give me five minutes of your attention, I will relate all that has taken place between me and your friend, Captain Cutts, *alias* Ironsides, and so on, since I last saw you."

Selby nodded acquiescence, and Ralph related to him all the particulars of the story of young Ironsides, and of the capture and committal of his father, much to the surprise of Selby.

"Now you see," said Ralph, "as the sessions are just about to commence, I shall have much to do to get up the case, and as

your matter will wait, and this will not, you see the necessity of acquiescing in my determination. Are you quite sure that this individual—this Ironsides—is really the same identical man that robbed and well nigh murdered you?"

"Quite positive—you recollect the circumstance of the watch with the initials 'I. M.,' which I found in my possession evidently exchanged for my own?"

"Perfectly."

"Well, on the late occasion, when I gave him the custody of—of——"

"Yes, yes," interrupted Ralph.

"I produced the watch to him, and called the affair to his recollection, and held out the threat of proceeding against him if he failed in keeping a strict watch on—on——"

"I understand," cried Ralph, "and am much obliged for the information. If I get my matters forward earlier than I expect, you shall see Maud earlier than I promised; and then, when that business is over, which it shall be, before the trial of that horrible wretch, you will, perhaps, like to attend with me at his trial—it will be a change, you know."

"A change—a change," ejaculated Selby, as if unconscious of what he was saying. "A change, indeed, from the height of ecstatic delight and happiness to the very bottom of the deepest and blackest despair—a change, ay—it is, indeed, a change."

"Keep up your courage, man, till I again call upon you; and I live in hopes that your face will wear a more cheerful aspect. Now, mind you, be in the way if I should want you. Farewell."

"Farewell," said Selby; "I shall always be in the way."

Ralph was glad of the information he received from Selby, as to the particulars of the identity of Ironsides with Cutts, for a purpose which we will not frustrate by relating it at present, but allow it to be postponed till the proper time.

On his arrival at the tavern, he found his sister and Gregory waiting very impatiently for him, and as soon as he stepped into the parlour, Grace communicated to him that since he had left home Maud had expressed herself very strongly against protracting the intended visit of her husband.

"And," said Grace, "I really will not be bound to be security for the safe custody of her, brother. I cannot always be with her: and I am sure that soon she will elude all the vigilance I am able to exercise; and, therefore, I think it but reasonable that she should at once see her husband, particularly as she has sufficient strength now to undergo the ceremony."

"Well, sister," said Ralph, "I don't know that I have any particular reason to prevent the meeting taking place earlier than I intended. I must confess it was more from a little pique for being so unceremoniously treated on the late occasion, and also that the happiness in store for Selby should not fall upon him all at once, as I considered that he did not deserve so uncommon a share of felicity without some suspense; however, if Maud is so strongly inclined, I suppose it will be better to humour her, and therefore the sooner we make the arrangements the better. Let us proceed to her chamber."

"To be sure," said Grace; "poor thing, she'll be delighted—come, brother, come."

Ralph and Grace proceeded accordingly to Maud's apartment, and communicated to her the result of the conversation between them; and it is needless to say that she was grateful for the favour of a day or two being struck out of the interval which was to pass before she was to be rendered totally happy.

"Why not to-day?" said Maud. "Why not to-day?"

"Nay, nay; now you see," said Ralph, "I have indulged your whim to a great extent, and you take advantage of my good nature. No, it cannot be before to-morrow, at the least."

"If it must be so, dear uncle," said Maud, "let it be early to-morrow—very early."

"Early enough—early enough, niece," said Ralph; "now I wish you to carry out my scheme with regard to Selby. I will bring him here under the belief that you are really dead, and to keep up the fiction, we will allow as little light to enter the apartment, as will be just sufficient to support the delusion, and you will then have an opportunity of satisfying yourself, by the expression of his feelings, whether he is really penitent; and I shall also be better satisfied that he is fit to be entrusted with your care for the future. I have a dread of another confinement in the lunatic asylum—an absolute horror of it. No, no—I must be satisfied—I must be satisfied."

"Well, well, uncle, perhaps it is better that it should be so; but I feel I shall have a difficulty in keeping up the delusion."

"If you spoil my plan, Maud, I shall be very angry. I will not keep you long in suspense; and when I have uttered your name for the third time, then I give you permission to put an end to the farce."

"Agreed, uncle. Now let it be early to-morrow—pray let it be early."

"As soon as I can, Maud; and in the meantime I will be getting up the case against Ironsides, about which, Maud, I will tell you by-and-by."

After Ralph had made good progress in the business that was pressing on his hands, he hastened on the following day to Selby, and communicated to him that he had altered his intention of postponing the period of the visit to the departed Maud, and inquired whether he could attend at once.

"This is sudden," said Selby, "very sudden. My God! how shall I dare to enter into the presence of that sinless, injured woman? Oh, Maud, Maud, had you reposed a little more confidence in me, this would not have happened, and I should not have the sin of murder to add to the catalogue of my crimes. I tremble at the thought of approaching to the death-bed of that spotless innocent; I cannot—I cannot."

"Well, well—be it so," said Ralph; "I must pay the last attentions to her—those attentions that are of right appertaining to the husband, that's all—that's all. She lived despised, and died unregretted, and may close the sad history with the same finale that would attach to the life of a brute—be buried without the slightest show of decency or regard on the part of her self-justified husband; be it so—be it so. But what the husband neglects to do, I will perform."

"Stay, stay," said Selby. "Heaven knows that I am anxious to make every compensation in my power for my want of kindness in her life-time; but, oh God! how can I meet her face to face—how can I look upon the marble, icy countenance of that dear creature—how can I look upon the ruin that I have made and live? Oh, Heaven! assist me in my extremity."

"Will you meet me in the Temple," said Ralph, "to-day at three o'clock? and we will talk further of it. You must get rid of that feeling of your having committed so enormous a crime as murder, and endeavour to reason like a man. Although your behaviour led to the unfortunate result which you so much deplore, yet it was her own act and deed; and in the sight of both God and man, in my belief, you stand exonerated from so fearful a charge."

"Think you so," said Selby, "honestly, think you so?"

"I do, and therefore let me implore you, before the lifeless body is hid for ever from your sight, take a last look of the too-confiding girl."

"I will meet you," said Selby, "at three, and will make up my mind to undergo the ordeal. And do you not think I should take the little one also, to let him have a last sight of his poor mother, whom I have so suddenly snatched from his love? It will take a load off my mind to do so."

"By all means," said Ralph, "by all means."

*   *   *   *   *

The time that intervened between that interview and the period fixed upon for Selby to meet Ralph in the Temple, was passed by the former individual in feverish anxiety, and it was with much difficulty he could summon resolution enough to prepare for the dreadful scene that he imagined he had to encounter. Eventually he summoned sufficient self-possession to give directions to the nurse who had charge of the little one to be in attendance with it, and to follow him to the Temple; and as the hour of three was approaching, he left his house, following the nurse with her infant charge, and was in the Temple by the time fixed upon for their meeting.

Ralph, as punctual as a time-piece of the

THE DEATH OF MAURICE IRONSIDES.

first order, entered the precincts of that ancient place precisely as the hands of the clock pointed to the proper figure on the dial, and not before ; for he used to remark that to be before the time was as bad as being after the time, and that there was no more excuse for it than there was for a cashier, on balancing his book, to find himself a shilling in pocket instead of a shilling out of pocket.

"I am glad to see that you are a man of punctuality, at all events," said Ralph. "It speaks well for you : it's the first qualification for business, and the first step in the ladder of success. I always find it so, and I cannot charge my memory with having, in a single instance, failed to keep an appointment. Are you ready to proceed?"

"Quite," observed Selby.

"Let us go, then," said Ralph.

They accordingly proceeded towards the tavern, and little conversation took place between them on the journey. Ralph was too much taken up with his little plot, and Selby's mind was too fully occupied with the consideration of the eventful scene that he imagined awaited him, to allow either of them to indulge in any desultory conversation.

When they arrived at their destination, Ralph sent up Grace under the pretence to see if it were convenient for Selby to be admitted, but, in fact, in order to inform Maud of his arrival, and to prepare the chamber as agreed upon, the better to prevent a discovery of the truth till the time should arrive ; and on her return, announcing that Selby might proceed, he and Ralph at once proceeded to the dismal-looking apartment.

As Selby entered the room, which had all the character of a chamber of death—so dark, so lone, and so dreary and desolate had they made it appear—that his resolution had nearly forsaken him, and he hesitated to proceed above a foot from the threshold, until Ralph, seizing him by the arm, hurried him by force into the room.

"Shall I draw the curtains?" asked Ralph.

"Not yet—not yet! Oh, no—not yet!" said Selby. "Heavens, how shall I dare to look upon that accusing face!"

"Come—come," urged Ralph : "remember, it is a duty you ought to perform."

"Stay — stay," said Selby. "Let me pause—let me recover strength again before I undergo the dreadful ordeal. I am utterly prostrated in mind and body, and cannot endure the trial as yet. No—no : not yet—not yet."

"Well—well," said Ralph—"take your time ; but it must be done, and it may as well be done at first as at last."

"True—true. I am ready. Stay!"

"Nay, man—shall I draw now? But first, Selby, promise me that you will not touch the body ; for I am one of those old-fashioned believers that fancy if a person who is the cause of the death of another touches the body, the blood of the murdered will spontaneously flow. Anywhere but in this room, such an averment as this might create a smile ;

but, nevertheless, it is a prejudice of mine, and therefore, if you have any inclination that way, I pray postpone it till I have left the apartment, which I will do shortly. Do you promise?"

"Ay, anything, anything."

"Then behold," said Ralph, as he let in a stream of light which centred upon the face of Maud, "behold all that is left of one that was once the delight of her friends—behold the empty tenement of the brightest and purest spirit that is now flitting before the majesty of God—behold the wreck of the most beautiful creation of nature—and ask yourself, Selby, ask yourself, who is her destroyer, and why she was destroyed?"

"For Heaven's sake," shrieked Selby, "say no more, say no more!" and he then threw himself at the foot of the bed, and covering his face with his hands, he shed an abundance of tears, and the very room shook again with the deep and stifling pulsations of his heart, and through the loud sobs that at intervals escaped him might be heard a fervid and passionate prayer that he might be forgiven the deadly sin of having brought a human being to such an untimely end, and that, too, without the slightest justification.

He continued kneeling for some considerable time, pouring forth the most passionate ejaculations, and it was with the extremest difficulty that Maud could prevent herself from putting an end to the deception, by throwing herself at once into his arms, and probably she would have done so, had not Ralph entertained a similar opinion, and therefore to prevent this, if possible, he determined to give the first signal.

"Selby," said he, "your penitence seems to be sincere, and let us hope Maud has heard you, and interceded with the Ruler of all things for your forgiveness."

"Oh, never," said Selby, "can I hope to be forgiven! My crime is too great—too great."

"In the eleventh hour, if you are sincere, we are taught there is forgiveness still," said Ralph. "Shall we let the little one kiss its mother's cheek before she's laid in the cold earth?"

"Let him come—let him come," said Selby.

Ralph called for the nurse to bring up the child, and receiving it from her hands, he again entered the apartment saying—

"There's the little prattler ; poor child, how he looks upon the face of his departed mother. The first time he has seen death, probably. How dear Maud would have rejoiced had she been permitted to live to have cherished this dear little fellow."

The poor child looked earnestly in the face of Maud, and then at Selby, and with a smile, pointing to Maud, uttered the word "Mammy," and clapped his little dimpled hands together in quite a joyous manner.

This was too much for Selby ; he threw himself upon the ground in the very frenzy of despair, and deep short sobs came from him in such rapid succession, that Ralph became alarmed lest he should have carried the joke a little too far.

Placing the child, therefore, upon the ground, in order to render what assistance he could to the wretched Selby, he raised him from the ground, and said—

" Selby, do you believe in miracles ? What would you say were she again to rise from the dead ?"

" Oh, talk not to me of impossibilities," said Selby ; " urge me not on to utter madness."

" Nay, nay, I am not talking idly—I believe it is in my power to make you happy yet."

" Happy," said Selby, " nay, never again, never again."

" Do you think, if such a miracle were to happen, you could sustain the shock ?"

" For Heaven's sake do not mock me."

" I repeat the question, and in all soberness and truth answer me candidly—could you sustain the shock ?"

" I could."

" Then behold your *Maud* restored to you."

As Ralph repeated the name of Maud for the third time, according to the signal, she opened her eyes, and raising herself on her elbow, she fixed them upon her husband ; and smiling upon him with such a smile as none but those who loved as she did, could pourtray, she said—

" Husband—dear George—dear husband —come to me."

Selby for a few moments stood transfixed, as if he had been suddenly petrified, and making an exertion to throw himself into the outstretched arms of his amiable wife, before he could perform his object, the excitement overpowered him, and he fell on to the bed in a swoon.

This was something more than Ralph had anticipated, and without a moment's delay, he procured medical aid, and in a short time Selby was restored to the full consciousness of the unexpected happiness surrounding him.

It is useless to state the intense joy expressed by Selby at finding himself so happily deceived—the numerous inquiries made by him—the good humoured explanation by Ralph of his plot—the affectionate endearments between the re-united couple—the asseverated promises for the future—the regrets for the past—and, in fact, the whirl and confusion of the next two or three hours. Suffice it to say, that where sorrow and bitter feeling before existed, now reigned gladness amongst the whole party, and intense gratefulness on the part of Selby, for such a wonderful and glorious application of the old axiom, that " there is many a slip between the cup and the lip."

CHAPTER XXIV.

THE TRIAL.

THE session following close upon the committal by the magistrate on the charge of murder, the time necessary to get up the evidence sufficiently satisfactory to secure the conviction by a jury in the opinion of Mr. Menzies, not being ample enough for the purpose, he thought it advisable, under the circumstances, to prefer another bill against Ironsides, in relation to the highway robbery on Selby, hoping, before that trial was concluded, to be in readiness for the grand one—provided the verdict should be such as to render it necessary to proceed further at all—and this proceeding was much to the surprise of Ironsides, who most devoutly hoped that the first charge could not be sustained, and was, therefore, abandoned, and that rather than he should escape altogether, this fresh charge had been determined on.

An anxious time was passed by Maurice Ironsides during the interval, and the trial which was to decide his fate. Not that he felt that the facts were so strong as to leave not doubt of the result of the examination, but his knowledge and experience of the waywardness and ignorance of a British common jury raised an alarm in his mind that he found it difficult, nay impossible, to control ; he would quite as soon that the foreman, instead of deliberating with his brethren, should form their conclusion by the turning up of heads or tails of a tossed-up halfpenny—heads, he's guilty— tails, he's innocent—not guilty, my lord !

However, Ironsides did not despair of a favourable result, and so far as the regulations of the prison allowed him, exerted all his means in getting up any evidence that he thought would tend to mystify the jury ; and various strange-looking men, at times, sought and gained admission to the prisoner, and many close and whispered consultations were had between him and his visitors.

At length the day of trial came, and notwithstanding the precaution used by all parties to keep the collateral circumstances from the public, by some means a pretty correct outline of the story in all its minutiæ had reached their ears, and the result was a more than ordinary crowded court.

A universal buzz and suppressed coughing and blowing of noses, such as is constantly the case in the churches and chapels of this country, when any pause intervenes in the service, now took place as Ironsides was ushered between a file of officers to the dock. With a firm step and a lofty and erect mien he ascended the box, and respectfully bowing to the judge and to the jury, he folded his arms across his chest, and calmly and apparently unmoved awaited the opening of the proceedings.

As soon as the clerk had read the indictment, and Ironsides had pleaded not guilty, the counsel for the prosecution opened the case, and in a plain and straightforward manner laid the particulars of the robbery before the court, concluding with, as far as could be ascertained, the history of the prisoner, and then proceeded to call witnesses.

The first witness was Mr. Selby, who stated in precise terms the particulars of the attack upon him, and positively identified Ironsides as one of the parties connected with it, and the one who had inflicted the wound upon him.

To the usual question whether he had any questions to ask of the witness, Ironsides replied,—

"I have. Pray, sir, did you ever see me on any occasion previous to the attack you say was made upon you, and in which you allege that I was one of the parties?"

"I never did."

"That is some time since, is it not?"

"Not so long since but I have a perfect recollection of the parties."

"Consider that I have repeated the question sir, and be good enough to answer me."

"It is."

"And have you never seen in the course of your existence any one resembling another so much that having only seen each of them once, you might hesitate before you concluded as to their identity?"

"I certainly have."

"Have you ever seen any one resembling me in outward appearance?"

"Most certainly not."

"Why speak so positively?"

"Because there is that positive peculiarity of feature attaching to you that I believe no other man in the world ever had—I cannot be mistaken."

"I am quite sure that you are mistaken, and I hope to convince the court and jury that you are so. Do you recollect the occasion of what I call your first visit to me, but which, according to your evidence, would be the second time of our meeting?"

"I do."

"Did you recognise me then in the first instance?"

"I had my doubts."

"My lord and gentlemen of the jury," interrupted Ironsides, "you hear the witness —he had his doubts."

"I was," continued Selby, "about to add——"

"I do not want to know what you were about to add—my question is answered. You say that on the occasion of the robbery, your watch was exchanged for one with certain initials on the plate?"

"It was."

"Are you in a situation to prove that the watch you found in my possession was ever yours?"

"I am, by most undoubted evidence."

"And that the one left with you in exchange was mine?"

"The presumption is that it was."

"Was it?"

"I believe so."

"Was it?"

"I don't know."

"You don't know?—good. Did you yourself find it in your fob?"

"I did not."

"When and where did you first see it?"

"I saw it at Menzies House on the dressing-table by the side of my bed, and the time, directly after I recovered to a state of consciousness."

"Then you don't, of your own knowledge, know that it was actually placed in your fob?"

"I do not."

"And any one might, having access to the house, have placed it where you found it?"

"They might."

"I have nothing further to ask of this witness, my lord."

Ironsides continued to question the different witnesses in a severe but masterly manner; and by bringing forward persons who had been previously instructed to swear that he was in France at the time of the robbery, and to bear other corroboratory testimonies, as well as also bringing forward a supposititious pawnbroker from among his former confederates, who stated that the watch had been pledged with him by a late Bow-street officer, the judge would not permit the case to proceed further.

Ironsides bowed to the court respectfully, and was about to retire, when one of the officers touched his arm, and reminded him that there was yet another charge, and that of a graver nature, the murder of his wife, Laura Ironsides.

"Ay—ay," remarked Ironsides, "I had quite forgotten that. quite. It is only another Brown business, I dare say—a curious man that Brown must have been—a very great scoundrel too."

"I tell you what, Mr. Ironsides," replied the officer, "between you, me, and the post, I rather think that if he was a curious fellow, you're a precious lucky one, that's all."

"That is one of my peculiarities, my man. I have always been amazingly lucky. But silence, let me hear the indictment."

The clerk proceeded to read the indictment which contained various counts, ringing the changes as usual, and containing as many lies, or as they are technically called, legal fictions, as were they uttered by any one in sober earnestness, would most assuredly have sent his soul, if, as the Scotch metaphysician said, he had any, to the lowest pit of the warmest place that ever was imagined, if, quoting the canny Scotchman, there be any such pit.

The clerk, when he had finished reading the indictment, requested the prisoner to plead guilty or not guilty.

"Before I plead one way or the other," said Ironsides, "I must request permission—"

"Prisoner," remarked the judge, "you will have an opportunity of speaking by-and-by; you will now plead guilty or not guilty."

"My lord, understand me. I have not the remotest wish to throw any obstruction in the way of justice, or to cause your lordship the slightest annoyance; in fact, why I have stepped out of the usual way is, that I may be the means of relieving you from a lengthy and painful stretch of attention in listening to the evidence which I dare say the prosecutor is prepared to bring forward. My lord, the indictment charges me with the wilful murder of my wife, Laura Ironsides, and this is repeated throughout the various counts, although the ground in other respects is very cleverly shifted. Now, my lord, I apprehend that I must first be proved to have been married.",

"You can make your objections afterwards," interrupted the judge.

"This is merely a preliminary objection, my lord," continued Ironsides, "and may save much time and trouble. I say that it must be proved that Laura Ironsides was my wife, or the indictment falls to the ground. Now, my lord, not only did I never know that unfortunate woman, or ever hear her name mentioned, but I never have been married. I take it, my lord, that the prosecutor, if he wishes to sustain his case, will necessarily have to prove that—and that he cannot do so, I am as sure of as that it is a very unfortunate thing for me that Brown should have so much resembled me. Perhaps the counsel for the prosecution will say at once whether he is prepared to prove his allegation—the *onus* is upon him."

This preliminary objection of Ironsides caused some consternation to Mr. Menzies and the other parties interested.

A long and anxious whispering now took place between the counsel for the prosecution and Mr. Menzies; and Ironsides, addressing the court, said—

"My lord, while the gentlemen are consulting as to what course they shall pursue, I will save a little time by pleading not guilty."

"Let the plea be received," said the judge, and addressing the counsel for the prosecution, he continued,—"Well, Brother Bedwell, what do you say to the prisoner's objection? Are you prepared with the necessary evidence?"

"Why, my lord," said Brother Bedwell, "I must confess that we are taken a little by surprise, and therefore must request that the trial be postponed awhile."

"This is the last day of the sessions, and I cannot postpone it above an hour at the outside. Will you be ready in an hour?"

"My lord, that time, I am afraid, is too short."

"I canot help it."

"My lord," said Ironsides, "they have admitted that they cannot sustain the charge. I have pleaded to the indictment, and everything that the law requires on my part has been performed. I can demand my acquittal as of right."

"It must be so, Brother Bedwell."

"Ha, ha!" laughed Ironsides, "I thought as much. I told them at first that it was rash and thoughtless to accuse a gentleman of so heinous an offence. My lord, I presume I am at liberty to retire?"

"Not so fast—not so fast," exclaimed a rough, burly voice from amidst the dense audience; "not so fast."

"Who is that interrupting the business of the court?" inquired the judge, in an angry voice.

"Silence!" roared the usher.

"Not so fast," continued the voice; "stay till I make my way up to the box, and then, I believe you, my boys, you'll see what you will see."

"Silence, silence!" repeated the usher.

"Silence!" once more repeated the judge, addressing the unfortunate usher; "if I have to request silence again, sir, it will be of your successor."

The abashed usher now made more noise than the individual he was attempting to curb in the attempt, and after a considerable commotion caused amonst the crowd by the strenuous exertions of the individual who had created the interruption, he made his way up to, and into the witness box, before the grave functionary of the law had adjusted his eyebrows to their natural and peaceful disposition.

As the man stepped into the box, the sharp eye of Ironsides rested on his face, and all that firmness of bearing which he had displayed throughout the whole of the proceedings entirely evaporated, and an ashy paleness overspread his features, and dropping his arms, which had been folded on his breast, he exclaimed unconsciously and audibly, the name—

"Stumps!"

"Yes, Governor Ironsides, alias Captain Cutts, it is Stumps! old Andrew Stumps. I am glad you've acknowledged me; it'll save me a deal of trouble."

"Who are you?" asked the judge.

"My name is Andrew Stumps, your honour; and finding that the gentlemen below were at a loss for a witness, why I have graciously stepped forth to help a lame dog over a stile."

"My lord," observed the counsel, "I am totally unprepared to examine this witness, not having a previous knowledge of what he can depose to; and now I trust the trial will be postponed till I have ascertained what he is prepared to say."

"Not the slightest occasion in the world," said Stumps; "I have no wish to be examined; what I've got to say I can say without prompting. Am I to give my evidence, or am I not?"

"Swear him," said the judge.

This ceremony having been peformed, the witness proceeded as follows:—

"My lord, I have been present during the whole of these proceedings, and I was a little staggered when I heard the evidence produced by Captain Cutts—Ironsides, there—

the whole of which was a fabrication; and I should have interposed afore, for the purpose of forrading the ends of justice, only I met a individval in court, who insisted on drinking my very good health, and when I came back, I found that he had gained the day. Why, my lord, all of them witnesses was his own comrades, when he was the captain of a gang of highway robbers. I knew them all well, and I also knew the facts of the robbery, which were all truly set forth in the evidence for the prosecution; but, however, that business is all over, so it's neither here nor there, and being neither here nor there, it's nowhere; so, as I said before, there's an end on it. Now, to come to the points, as the parson said, when he asked for his fee, seeing that my noble governor there, Cutts, was likely to defeat the ends of justice a second time, and I having a particular respect to the due administration of our blessed laws, which I consider have been made by all the talents of the people, that is by the people's heredy legislators, considering this, I say, I stepped in, and stepping in, here I am, and being here, why here am I, and so there's no more to be said upon that subject. I hope your lordship understands me?"

"Why," said the judge, good humouredly, "I have as much regard for the ends of justice as you express to have, and therefore, although I have not heard much to the purpose at present, I hope to be able to collect enough to form a conclusion— pray, go on."

"I'm glad to hear it," continued Stumps; "you're an upright judge, and understands your business. Well, as I was saying, Ironsides says he was never married—now I denies the implication, and I expect, as I have said before, that he is, or was not only married, but that I was a witness in the ceremony."

"Where did it take place?" asked the counsel.

"Over the way at St. Bartholomew's, o'course," said Stumps; "he fully expected that one of these fine days he should be hung, and consequently lived hereabouts, and he wished the two great *epocks* of his life to take place in the same locality. If you cuts over, and searches the registry about twenty years ago, you'll find the blessed entry, and my name as a witness. This is the second time I've assisted Cutts in the same way. Do you mark that, Mr. Ironsides, eh? You see I have put that down in my diary, as you were in the habit of recommending me."

No time was lost in procuring the attendance of the clergyman, who happened to be by some chance in the way with the register books, and the entry, as Stumps had stated, was sure enough found, and handed to the judge for his inspection.

"That is perfectly clear," exclaimed the judge. "Witness, are you sure the prisoner is the same person as mentioned in the certificate?"

"Can ducks swim?" was the question in reply.

"He means," interposed the counsel, "that he is positive, my lord."

"Then I wish he would say so."

"It would be better, my lord. I think now we may proceed with the evidence."

"Hold," said Ironsides; "there is no occasion; I retract my plea, and plead guilty. I am sickened, sickened to the death at this farce. But I still defy you, ay, all of you, from the judge to the veriest reptile that threads the mazy cobwebs of the law. Yes, I am guilty! I did put away my wife— she was an adultress, and I took the law into my own hands. You may call it murder, but I had the authority of the Scriptures for it, and I did it. But ha, ha! there is one little secret that shall go out with me—one little secret that, if divulged, would make glorious sunshine in a family where now all is clouded. Ha, ha! Gregory Ironsides— Gregory Ironsides—my son—no, no—I never had a son—will you give me my life if I say whose son he is?—oh, what glorious news for his old father—what a grand thing to have a son and heir to be the recipient of all his wealth—to hand down his name to posterity—ha, ha!—rich, rich—Gregory Ironsides—well, well, remain Gregory Ironsides, and enjoy your adopted father's honours—ha, ha! I defy you all—ha, ha!"

During this rambling speech, which all the exertions of the usher and judge could not prevent, Ironsides had been burying his fingers in his bushy whisker, and suddenly withdrawing them, a glittering light was seen for a moment, between his fingers and thumb, and the next instant uttering a loud, wild shriek of demoniacal laughter, he fell a corpse.

* * * * *

Mr. Menzies had prophesied correctly. Selby had become really contrite, and he and his beautiful wife made this good old gentleman and his sister Grace happy by residing with them at Menzies House, until time had performed his unerring task with regard to them.

Tony, notwithstanding a fierce opposition from Susan's fellow servants, who had on the occasion of Tony's ejection from the mansion, used a little more violence than was absolutely necessary, out of spite, as Tony observed, for Susan's partiality for him, succeeded in securing that charming waiting maid; and it was quite pleasant to see with what pleasing regularity they produced their kind, very much to the annoyance, however, of the retired inhabitants of that then equally retired suburb, Hampstead.

Jingle or Ironsides, as we must call him for want of a better name, was taken under the protection of Selby and his wife, and all that could be done to calm his mind as to the mystery of his birth was done—no exertion was spared to solve it, and no other result was arrived at than that it was most satisfactorily proved that Cutts, otherwise Ironsides, had really spoken the truth when he disowned him, and from that time to the present moment the matter remains a mystery.